Anthony Capella is a food enthusiast and enjoyed researching Italian feasting. He has a wife and three children and lives in London and Oxford. This is his first novel. For more information please visit www.thefoodoflove.com.

'Food, love and Italy are all irresistible ingredients in this charming story . . . Italophiles, foodies and romantics will all adore this delicious tale' *The Australian Women's Weekly*

'[*The Food of Love*] joyfully captures the romantic essence of Italy – the food, the language, Rome and the Italian countryside' *Marie Claire* Australia

'Misunderstandings and laughter abound in a delicious mix of romance, charm and yummy recipes!' *Woman's Day* Australia

'*The Food of Love* is a splendid, linen suit, panama hat, distant lawn-mower kind of a book; guaranteed to whisk you far from this drizzly island, soothe you, warm you and return you home again without losing any of your luggage' Hugh Laurie

'A fantastic novel that makes you feel like you're there in Italy, in the story, smelling and tasting all the food' Jamie Oliver

'A delicious book – funny, foodie and romantic. The definitive Roman romantic comedy' Richard Curtis

'I read it while travelling in Italy and really enjoyed the whole concept of chefs, love, Italy, food and sex' Rose Gray, owner of The River Café

'Spicy, not only with food and passion, but with razor-sharp, if crude, wit, *The Food of Love* is a delectable treat' *Irish Examiner*

'Romance and food make the perfect partnership . . . Capella's love-lorn recipe includes all the necessary ingredients' *Glamour*

'A hot feast with all the right ingredients' *Scottish Daily Record*

'A deliciously romantic culinary comedy' *Heat*

'Hilarious' *OK!*

THE FOOD OF LOVE

Anthony Capella

TIME WARNER
BOOKS

TIME WARNER BOOKS

First published in Great Britain in 2004 by Time Warner Books
This edition published by Time Warner Books in June 2005

Grateful thanks to Macmillan, London, UK for permission
to quote from *The Essentials of Classic Italian Cooking*
by Marcella Hazan.

A CIP catalogue record for this book
is available from the British Library.

ISBN 0 7515 3706 3

Typeset in Galliard by M Rules
Printed and bound in Great Britain
by Clays Ltd, St Ives plc

Time Warner Books
An imprint of
Time Warner Book Group UK
Brettenham House
Lancaster Place
London WC2E 7EN

www.twbg.co.uk
www.thefoodoflove.com

Antipasto

'An Italian meal is a lively sequence of sensations in which the crisp alternates with the soft and yielding, the pungent with the bland, the variable with the staple, the elaborate with the simple . . .'

MARCELLA HAZAN, *The Essentials of Classic Italian Cooking*

One

In a little side street off the Viale Glorioso, in Rome's Trastevere, there is a bar known to those who frequent it simply as Gennaro's. It is, to look at, not much of a bar, being the approximate size and shape of a small one-car garage, but the passing tourist would note that there is room outside for two small tables and an assortment of non-identical plastic chairs that catch the sun in the morning, while the passing coffee lover would note that there is room inside on the stained zinc counter for a vast, gleaming Gaggia 6000, the Harley-Davidson of espresso machines. There is also room, just, behind the stained zinc counter for Gennaro, widely regarded by his friends as the best *barista* in all Rome and a very sound fellow to boot.

Which was why, one fine spring morning, twenty-eight-year-old Tommaso Massi and his friends Vincent and Sisto were standing at the bar, drinking *ristretti*, arguing about love, waiting for the *cornetti* to arrive from the bakery, and generally passing the time with Gennaro before jumping on their Vespas to go off to the various restaurants around the city that employed them. A *ristretto* is made with the same amount of ground coffee as an ordinary

3

espresso but half the amount of water, and since Gennaro's espressos were themselves not ordinary at all but pure liquid adrenaline, and since the three young men were in any case all of an excitable temperament, the conversation was an animated one. More than once Gennaro had to remind them not to all argue at once – or, as the Roman vernacular has it, *parlare 'nu strunzo 'a vota*; to only speak one piece of shit at a time.

The unusual strength of Gennaro's *ristretti* was the result of his honing the Gaggia's twin grinding burrs to razor sharpness, packing the basket with the resulting powder until it was as hard as cement, then building up a head of pressure in the huge machine and waiting until the dial showed eighty pounds per square inch before finally allowing the water to blast into the packed coffee. What came from the spout after that was barely a liquid at all, a red-brown ooze with a hanging quality like honey dripping off the end of a butter knife, with a chestnut-coloured *crema* and a sweet oily tang that required no sugar, only a gulp of *acqua minerale* and a bite of a sugar-dusted *cornetto*, if only the bakery had delivered them. Gennaro loved that machine like a soldier loves his gun, and he spent even more time stripping it down and cleaning it than he did making coffee. His goal was to get it up to a hundred PSI, way off the gauge, and make a *ristretto* so thick you could spread it like jam. Tommaso was privately convinced that even to attempt this feat was to run the risk of the Gaggia exploding and taking them all with it, but he respected his friend's commitment and ambition and said nothing. It was, after all, self-evident that you couldn't be a great *barista* without taking risks.

The conversation that morning was about love, but it was also about football. Vincent, who had recently become engaged, was being scolded by Sisto, to whom the idea of restricting yourself to just one woman seemed crazy.

'You might think today that you have found the best woman in the world, but tomorrow –' Sisto flicked his fingers under his chin – 'who knows?'

'Look,' Vincent explained patiently, or as patiently as he was capable of, 'how long have you been a Lazio supporter?'

'All my life, idiot.'

'But Roma are . . .' Vincent hesitated. He wanted to say 'a better team', but there was no point in turning a friendly discussion about women into a deadly fight. 'Doing better,' he said diplomatically.

'This season. So far. What of it?'

'Yet you don't start supporting Roma.'

'*E un altro paio di maniche, cazzo.** That's another thing altogether, you dick. You can't switch teams.'

'Exactly. And why not? Because you have made your choice, and you are loyal to it.'

Sisto was silent for a moment, during which Vincent turned to Gennaro triumphantly and ordered another *ristretto*. Then Sisto said craftily, 'But being a *Laziale* isn't like being faithful to one woman. It's like having dozens of women, because the team is made up of different people every year. So you're talking shit, as usual.'

Tommaso, who until now had taken no part in the argument, murmured, 'The real reason Vincent and Lucia got engaged is that she said she'd stop sleeping with him if they didn't.'

His friends' reactions to this piece of intelligence were interestingly different. Vincent, who had after all told Tommaso this in strict confidence, looked angry, then shamefaced, and then – when he realised that Sisto was looking distinctly envious – pleased with himself.

'It's true,' he shrugged. 'Lucia wants to be a virgin when we marry, just like her mother. So we had to stop sleeping together until we got engaged.'

Vincent's statement, apparently illogical, drew no comment

*Literally: 'That's another pair of sleeves'.

5

from his friends. In a country where literal, fervent Catholicism was only a generation away, everyone knew there were as many grades of virginity in girls as there were in olive oil – which, of course, is divided into extra-virgin (first cold pressing), extra-virgin (second pressing), superfine virgin, extrafine virgin, and so on, down through a dozen or more layers of virginity and near-virginity, before finally reaching a level of promiscuity so unthinkable that it is labelled merely as 'pure', and is thus fit only for export and lighting fires.

'But at least I'm getting it now,' he added. 'I'm sleeping with the most beautiful girl in Rome, who adores me, and we're going to be married and have our own place. What could be better than that?'

'Tommaso gets it too,' Sisto pointed out. 'And he isn't getting married.'

'Tommaso sleeps with tourists.'

Tommaso shrugged modestly. 'Hey, can I help it if beautiful foreign girls throw themselves at me?'

This amiable conversation was interrupted by the arrival of the *cornetti*, a tray of tiny sugared croissants, which in turn called for a final *caffè* before work. While Gennaro flushed the pipes of his beloved Gaggia in readiness, Tommaso received a sharp nudge in the ribs from Sisto, who nodded significantly towards the window.

Coming down the street was a girl. Her sunglasses were tucked up on the top of her head amid a bohemian swirl of blonde hair which, together with her calf-length jeans, single-strap backpack and simple T-shirt, marked her out immediately as a foreigner even before one took in the guidebook entitled *Forty Significant Frescoes of the High Renaissance* that she was holding open in one hand.

'A tourist?' Sisto said hopefully.

Tommaso shook his head. 'A student.'

'And how do you know that, maestro?'

'Her backpack is full of books.'

6

'Psst! *Biondina! Bona!*' Sisto called. 'Hey! Blondie! Gorgeous!'

Tommaso cuffed him. 'That isn't the way, idiot. Just act friendly.'

It seemed puzzling to Sisto that any girl fortunate enough to be blonde and attractive would not be impressed by having the fact pointed out to her, but he allowed himself to be guided by his more experienced friend and closed his mouth.

'She's coming over,' Vincent noted.

The girl crossed the street and paused next to the bar, apparently oblivious to the admiring stares of the three young men. Then she pulled out a chair, put her backpack on the table and sat down, arranging her slim legs over the next chair along.

'Definitely a foreigner,' Vincent said sadly. Because every Italian knows that to sit down to drink coffee is bad for the digestion and will therefore be penalised by a surcharge costing three times as much as you'd pay at the bar. 'You wait. She'll ask for a cappuccino.'

Gennaro, watching the pressure gauge of the Gaggia intently, snorted dismissively. No proper *barista* would dream of serving cappuccino after ten a.m, any more than a chef would offer cornflakes for lunch.

'*Buongiorno*,' the girl called through the open door. She had a nice voice, Tommaso thought. He smiled at her encouragingly. Beside him, Vincent and Sisto were doing exactly the same. Only Gennaro, behind the zinc counter, maintained a suspicious frown.

''*giorno*,' he muttered darkly.

'*Latte macchiato, per favore, lungo e ben caldo.*'

There was a pause while the *barista* thought about this. Although the young woman had spoken in Italian, she had revealed her origins as much by what she had ordered as by her accent. *Latte macchiato* – milk with just a splash of coffee, but served in a *lungo* or large cup, and *ben caldo*, hot, so that it could be drunk slowly instead of being thrown down the throat in a couple of quick gulps in the proper manner. She was indisputably

7

American. However, nothing she had ordered actually offended propriety – she had not asked for espresso with cream, or de-caf, or hazelnut syrup, or skimmed milk – so he shrugged and reached for the twin baskets of the Gaggia, while the three young men tried to look as handsome as possible.

The girl ignored them. She pulled a map out and compared it, with a somewhat perplexed expression, to a page in her guide-book. A *telefonino* rang in her backpack: she took that out, too, and proceeded to have a conversation which those inside could not overhear. When Gennaro finally judged his *macchiato* worthy of being served, there was a scuffle to be the one to deliver it to the girl's table, which Tommaso won easily. He took one of Gennaro's little *cornetti* as well, placing it on the saucer and pre-senting it to the girl with a smile and a muttered, 'On the house'. But the girl was engrossed in her call, and her smile of thanks was all too brief. He had time to notice her eyes, though – grey eyes, clear and untroubled, the colour of a sea bass's scales.

In fact, Laura Patterson was deeply troubled, or as troubled as it is possible for a twenty-two-year-old American girl to be in Rome on a fine spring morning, which was why she was glad to discover that it was her Italian friend Carlotta who was calling. Carlotta worked for a magazine called *Stozzi* in Milan. She was also part of the reason that Laura had come to Italy, having been a very good college friend back home.

'*Pronto.*' In Italy it is customary to answer the phone by snap-ping 'Ready!', for reasons which are now obscure.

'Laura. It's me. What are you up to?'

'Oh – hi, Carlotta. Well, I was looking for Santa Cecilia, as it happens. She's in possession of some rather fine frescoes by Cavallini. But it seems Santa Cecilia doesn't want to be found, so I'm having coffee instead.'

Carlotta ignored this nonsense and cut straight to the reason for her call. 'And last night? How was your date?'

'Ah. Well, it was fine,' Laura said in a voice that made clear that it hadn't really been fine at all. She had to tread a little carefully, because the date in question had been a friend of a friend of Carlotta's own brother. 'He, Paolo, was perfectly nice, and he knew a lot about architecture –' at the other end of the phone, Carlotta snorted derisively – 'and he took me to a really interesting restaurant near the Villa Borghese.'

'What were you wearing?'

'Um – the red top and the black trousers.'

'Jacket?'

'No jacket. It's warm down here.'

There was an audible sigh at the other end. Carlotta, like all Italian women, thought that anyone who committed offences against fashion had only themselves to blame for whatever calamities subsequently befell them. 'Did you wear sneakers?' she demanded suspiciously.

'Of course I didn't wear sneakers. Carlotta, you're missing the point. Anyway, as I was saying, the meal was good. I had squid pasta and a really nice lamb thing.'

'And?'

'Nothing else. Just coffee.'

'And afterwards?' Carlotta said impatiently. 'What happened afterwards?'

'Ah. Afterwards, we went for a walk around the Giardino di Lago, and that's when he jumped me. Literally, because unfortunately there was a slight discrepancy in our respective heights, which meant he had to actually propel himself off the ground in order to stick his tongue where he wanted to. Then after that, of course, he was trying to get me into bed – well, not bed exactly, since he still lives with his parents, so an actual bed was not part of the offer, but he was certainly trying to get me into the bushes. And before you say anything, I really don't think wearing a jacket would have made much difference.'

Another sigh. 'Are you going to see him again?'

9

'No. Honestly, Carlotta, thanks for the introduction and every-thing, but I think I've had it with Italian men. They're all so ridiculously over-sexed and, well, just *clumsy*. That's my fourth disaster in a row. I think I'm going to have to go back to dating Americans for a while.'

Carlotta was horrified. '*Cara*, coming to Rome and dating Americans would be like going to the Piazza di Spagna and eating at McDonald's.'

'Actually, a few of us did that the other day,' Laura admitted. 'It was kind of fun.'

There was an exasperated tut at the other end. 'Imagine what a waste your year in Italy will have been if the only men you've dated are people you could have met back home.'

'Imagine what a waste it'll have been if the only people I've dated are frustrated Italian rapists who still live with their moth-ers,' Laura retorted.

'You're just meeting the wrong people. Look at *my* last boyfriend. Filippo was a sensational lover. Considerate, inventive, slow, passionate—'

'And currently, I think you said, working in a restaurant in a ski resort, precise whereabouts unknown.'

'True, but it was great while it lasted. That's the thing about chefs. They know how to use their hands. It's all that chopping and slicing they do. It makes them dextrous.'

'Hmm,' Laura said, a little wistfully, 'I have to admit, dextrous would be a nice change.'

'Then, *cara*, you simply have to make sure your dates can cook before you agree to go out with them,' Carlotta said decisively. She lowered her voice. 'I'll tell you something else about Filippo. He liked to taste everything as he cooked it, if you know what I mean.'

Laura laughed. She had a remarkably dirty laugh, and the sound permeated into the interior of Gennaro's bar, causing the young men inside to glance up appreciatively from their *cornetti*.

'And I suppose, being a chef, he had a great sense of timing?'

'Exactly. And he never rushed. You know how we Italians like to eat – at least a dozen courses.'

'But all of them very small ones,' Laura teased.

'Yes, but believe me, by the end you can't eat another thing.'

Even as Laura continued to joke, a part of her couldn't help admitting her friend might have a point. Someone creative, who understood taste, and texture, who knew how to combine ingredients for the purpose of sensual pleasure . . . if only she'd met someone like that during her time in Italy.

'Well, there you are then,' Carlotta was saying. 'It shouldn't be hard. Rome's full of restaurants. It stands to reason it must be full of chefs as well.'

'Maybe,' Laura said.

'Listen, I'll tell you something else Filippo did . . .'

By the time Laura rang off she had half-jokingly, half-seriously promised her friend that from now on she was definitely only going to date men who knew their Béarnaise from their Béchamel.

Tommaso had made up his mind he was going to speak to the American girl. Who could resist a laugh like that? As Vincent had said, he had an excellent track record with female tourists, who seemed to melt when they saw his big-featured, handsome head with its shock of corkscrew ringlets. Not that Roman girls didn't melt as well, but Roman girls had a tendency to want him to meet their parents afterwards. Foreigners were altogether less complicated.

He waited for the right moment. The American girl stayed on the phone, occasionally sipping slowly at her *macchiato* – no wonder she'd wanted it hot – until Tommaso realised with a sigh that he was going to have to go. He would already be late getting to the restaurant. He slapped a few coins on the counter and waved a farewell to Gennaro. His *motorino* was parked outside, next to the girl's table, and he lingered for a last moment as he crouched down to unlock it, savouring one more glance at the slim honey-brown calves stretched over the chair opposite.

'No more Italians, then. Not unless they can cook,' she was saying. 'From now on, I don't date anyone who isn't in the *Good Food Guide*.'

Tommaso's ears pricked up.

She reached into her cup for the final frothy globs of latte, scooping them out and licking them off her finger. 'My God, this coffee is fantastic. Hold on. Yes?'

Unable to stop himself, Tommaso had tapped her on her shoulder.

'I'm sorry to interrupt your call,' he began in his best English. 'I just wanted to tell you that your beauty has broken my heart.'

She smiled appreciatively, if a little warily. Nevertheless, she tried to sound polite as she replied, '*Vatte a fa' 'u giro, a fessa 'e mammata*,' using the words that her first Italian date had told her to employ whenever she was paid a compliment. Tommaso's face fell. 'OK, OK,' he said, backing off and throwing his leg across the scooter.

Laura watched him go, then turned her attention back to Carlotta. 'Who was that?' her friend wanted to know.

'Just some guy.'

'Laura,' her friend said carefully, 'what do you think you said to him?'

Which was how Laura discovered that she had actually been telling the young men of Rome in perfect idiomatic Italian to piss off back up the orifices of their mothers from which they were delivered.

'Oh,' Laura said. 'Oh dear. That's a shame. He was quite cute, too. But it doesn't really matter, does it? Because from now on I'm holding out for someone who can cook.'

Primo

'Once the general and commonsense principles of menu-planning become clear, the choices remaining before us are an infinite number of agreeable and workable combinations . . .'

MARCELLA HAZAN, *The Essentials of Classic Italian Cooking*

Two

It was a week before Tommaso saw the girl again. He had gone to Gigliemi, the great food shop near the Piazza Venezia, to pick up some supplies for the restaurant. Earlier there had been a phone call to say that a hunter, one of dozens in the Castelli Romani who supplied Gigliemi with specialities, had driven in from the countryside that very morning, with his Fiat full of tender young *lepre*; baby hares, the first of the season. Tommaso had been instructed to be quick, so he walked straight through to the back, shouldered the box which Adriano gave him with only the briefest of pauses to discuss Adriano's family, his uncle's marriage, his second cousin's business and his brother's new girlfriend, and was hurrying out again when a movement in the corner of his eye caught his attention. It was a girl. She was reaching up to the top shelf for a packet of pasta, exposing a band of taut stomach. Tommaso caught a glimpse of a tiny whorl of belly button, as intricate and perfect as the knot of a balloon. A keen aficionado of female beauty, he muttered, '*Fosse 'a Madonna!*' under his breath. Quickly he swung the box down again. '*Momento*,' he called to her; wait up. He reached up, got the packet for her, and handed it

15

to her with a smile. '*Prego.*' Then he realised he'd seen her some-where before.

She smiled. '*Grazie, faccia di culo.*' Thank you, assface.

Of course – he remembered now. The girl from Gennaro's. He also remembered her saying that she was only going to sleep with – well, date, but it was famously the same thing with American girls – someone who could cook, and if she was buying her own pasta, the chances were that she hadn't yet found that someone. Which was remarkable because Rome was absolutely full of cooks, while blonde American girls were somewhat scarcer.

It was his opportunity, and he took it.

'*Spaghetti,*' he said, glancing at the packet in her hand. 'How nice.' Even to him, this sounded a little flat.

'Well, I hope so.'

'And what are you cooking it with? What sauce?'

'Well – I thought perhaps Bolognese.'

His look of bewilderment was not feigned. 'But you can't,' he objected.

'Why not?'

'First, because you're not in Bologna,' he pointed out reason-ably. 'And secondly, because what you have in your hand is *spaghetti.*'

'Yes. Spaghetti Bolognese.' She saw his expression. 'That's not a good idea, is it?'

'It's just impossible,' he explained. '*Ragù Bolognese* is a sauce for *tagliatelle* or *gnocchi*, or possibly *tortellini.*' He pointed to Gigliemi's glass-fronted display case. 'These are *tortellini.*' He snapped his fingers at the assistant, who handed him one of the soft, doughy parcels on a piece of tissue paper. He held it out to Laura to show her. 'The shape is based on the shape of a woman's – what do you call it?'

She peered anxiously at the *tortellini.* 'I'm not sure.'

He pointed to his own stomach. 'Tummy popper?'

'Button. Of course,' she said, relieved.

16

He remembered that glimpse of midriff and the tiny little whorl of her navel. It had not, in fact, looked very like the thing he was holding in his hand at all, which resembled nothing so much as a big fat oyster of ricotta cheese, or possibly a woman's *fica*. 'Anyway,' he said dismissively, 'we are in Rome, and Roman sauces are better. Well, strictly speaking we are in Lazio, but it's the same thing. We eat spaghetti *all'amatriciana*, with a sauce of *guanciale*, which is the pig's –' he ran his finger down her cheek, briefly, a touch so fleeting she was hardly aware it had happened – 'this part of the pig's face. We fry it in olive oil with a little chilli, some tomatoes and of course some grated *pecorino romano*, hard cheese. Or if you don't want *spaghetti* you could have *bucatoni*, or *calscioni*, or *fettuccinie*, or *pappardelle*, or *tagliolini*, or *rigatoni*, or *linguine*, or *garganelli*, or *tonnarelli*, or *fusilli*, or *conchiglie*, or *vermicelli*, or *maccheroni*, but,' he held up a warning finger, 'each of them demands a different kind of sauce. For example, an oily sauce goes with dried pasta, but a butter sauce goes better with fresh. Take *fusilli*.' He held up a packet to show her. 'People say this pasta was designed by Leonardo da Vinci himself. The spiral fins carry the biggest amount of sauce relative to the surface area, you see? But it only works with a thick, heavy sauce that can cling to the grooves. *Conchiglie*, on the other hand, is like a shell, so it holds a thin, liquid sauce inside it perfectly.'

'Are you a cook?' she asked, understanding dawning in her eyes.

'I am a chef, yes, at one of Rome's best restaurants,' Tommaso said proudly.

She hesitated. 'Can I ask you – what would *you* make if you were me? I don't do a lot of cooking, but my father's flown in for a few days and I stupidly said I'd make something for him. I'd love to cook him something Roman.'

'If I were you . . .' Tommaso thought hard. Then his eyes fell on the box of baby hares. 'I would cook *pasta con sugo di lepre*; pappardelle with hare sauce,' he said triumphantly. 'The hares are never better than when they're young and tender.'

'Is it easy?'

'It's fantastically simple. You cook the hare in onion and garlic for a little while, then you add some red wine, some cloves, some cinnamon, and that's it.'

'And I can buy the meat here?' she asked, looking around her doubtfully.

'No,' he said. 'They only supply delicacies like hare to those they know well. But for you –' He went over to his box, took out a hare and presented it to her proudly on the flat of his hand. 'It's a gift. So that you will never make Bolognese sauce again.'

She seemed to recoil a little. 'Don't they sell them skinned?'

'Ah, skinning it is easy,' he said happily. 'It will take you two minutes.' He called to the assistant for a paper bag.

'And is it – gutted?' she asked doubtfully.

'Of course not,' he said, sounding a little offended. 'Gigliemi wouldn't sell a hare with the best bits removed.' He dropped it in the bag and swung it round to close it. 'Here,' he said, pressing it into her hand. 'And – here.' He took out a pencil with a flourish and wrote his mobile phone number on the bag. 'If you need any help with the recipe, any help at all, just call me. My name is Tommaso Massi and I will be delighted to assist you.' He swept the box of hares up on to his shoulder before she could ask him about the recipe in any more detail.

'You mean that? I can really call you if I have a problem?'

He almost laughed out loud. The American girl was actually asking if *she* could phone *him*! 'But of course. You can call me any time.'

'Well, thank you. I'll do that. If I need help, that is.'

'*Ciao*, then.'

'*Ciao*. For now.'

Ciao for now! He liked that, it had a good sound. And the way she was looking at him – he had definitely made an impression.

◎◎

18

He had, indeed, made an impression.

He's nice, Laura thought. *Like a character from a Michelangelo drawing, with his big extravagant features and his hands waving in the air all the time like that. And, ah, undeniably easy on the eye. But he didn't hit on me, which is refreshing. Refreshing, and a little bit annoying. Because if he doesn't hit on me, how am I supposed to say no? Or, as the case may be, yes? Which it isn't, of course. The case is definitely no. Because you don't just bump into people like that, do you? Not people you're going to go out with.*

Mind you. A chef. How weird is that? Carlotta and I had that joke about me going out with a chef, and then here one is. A good one too, he says. A beautiful one, says I.

Serendipity?

It was only much later, when this internal reverie had finally played itself out, that she realised she was walking along the Via Aracceli with a smile on her face and a paper bag in her hand containing a dead baby hare.

Tommaso strapped the box of hares on to the back of his Piaggio and sped off through the traffic. *Uanema*, he was late. He had been told to be quick, and here he was wasting time yet again with girls. He wondered if anyone would notice that one of the animals was missing.

He took the Via Aurelia past the Vatican, his little scooter chugging up the hill towards Montespaccato, weaving expertly through the endless traffic jams and hold-ups. Finally he came to a part of the city that was higher, cooler, and calmer, where the buildings were larger, and where even the cars drove past each other in unnatural silence, with barely an insult or a gesticulation to smooth their interaction.

He parked the Piaggio around the back of a large white building, making sure that it was precisely in line with all the other scooters, then carried the box of hares shoulder-high through a pair of double doors into a vast room full of steam and heat.

There was no sign outside the big white building to announce it, but this was the kitchen of Templi, one of the most famous gourmet restaurants in the world.

Tommaso took the box of hares over to the head chef, Karl, who wordlessly picked up one of the dead animals to inspect it, sniffing its mouth and anus for decay before pronouncing himself satisfied with a nod. Only then did he say, 'You're late.'

'Traffic. An overturned lorry on the Ponte Garibaldi.'

'And one of the hares is missing. I ordered a dozen.'

'That's right. There was one that wasn't quite dead. Suddenly it jumped out and ran back to its mother. Through the traffic. Do you know the extraordinary thing? It was just as we were going past the Vatican. And they say the Holy Father is in residence. Perhaps it was a miracle. Yes, a miracle, that's it.' He was just warming to his theme when Karl, with a faint sigh, said, 'Go and help with the glasses, Tommaso.' He nodded towards the sink, where the bottle-washer, Amelie, was working her way through a mountain of glass.

Tommaso reached for a pair of polishing gloves. The glassware at Templi was all lead crystal, and there was never a single speck of lint or dust on it, let alone a smear of dirt or detergent. Every single one was polished by hand.

There are three kinds of restaurant in Rome. There are the local *trattorie* and *osterie*, most of which serve only *cucina Romana*, Roman cooking. It is a tradition firmly rooted in the ingredients available from the markets and slaughterhouses, with no part of the animal wasted. From the ears to the tail, there is a proper and correct recipe for everything, handed down from generation to generation. Then there is *cucina creativa*, the cuisine which takes that tradition and experiments with it. Many ordinary Romans remain deeply suspicious of experimentation, not to mention the increased prices that go with it, believing firmly that *più se spenne, peggio se mangia* – the more you spend, the worse you eat.

20

And thirdly there is *cucina gourmet* – the awkward collision of French and Italian indicating that this is a concept that doesn't quite fit comfortably in this region. The ordinary Roman loves his food with a passion but, however wealthy he is, he will probably pass his entire life without ever setting foot inside one of the handful of Michelin-starred establishments dotted around the Eternal City. The presence of major American and European corporations, however, many of whom have their local headquarters nearby, not to mention the stream of wealthy gastro-tourists doing the modern equivalent of the Grand Tour, means there is a small but steady demand for an international style of cooking the equal of that found anywhere else in the world.

Standing at the very apex of these restaurants is Templi, the three-star establishment of Alain Dufrais, the great Swiss chef and internationally acknowledged master of nouvelle cuisine.

Polishing glasses is boring work, particularly when you are in love. Tommaso relieved the tedium by whistling to get the attention of his friend Bruno, who was making *zabaione* nearby.

'*Ueh*, Bruno. *Psst*. I'm in love.'

'That's good,' Bruno said. He was concentrating on his zabaglione, which he was making in a traditional, round-bottomed copper pot, directly over a flame. 'But nothing new. You were in love yesterday as well.'

'This is someone else. An American girl. Blonde and very cute.'

Bruno grunted.

'*Ueh*, Bruno. How do you make *sugo di lepre*?'

This question, being about food rather than about women, did make Bruno glance up briefly. He was not good-looking like his friend Tommaso, being thick-set, heavy, and slightly awkward. His eyes, which tended to shy away from direct contact with others, only really settled when he was visualising something to do with cooking, as he did now. 'Well, you fry the hare with some *pancetta*,' he began.

21

'*Pancetta*!' Tommaso clasped his forehead. 'I knew I'd forgotten something.'

'Then you remove the hare and *pancetta* and you soften some onions and garlic, very gently. Add a bottle of red Sangiovese, some cinnamon, cloves, rosemary and plenty of thyme—'

'Thyme! Damn!'

'—and then you put the hare back and simmer it for at least two hours, until the hare starts to collapse into the sauce, which becomes so sticky it coats the pasta like glue.'

'Two hours!' Tommaso couldn't remember if he'd actually told the girl to cook it for that long.

'And, of course, just before serving you remove all the bones.'

'Shit!'

'Why do you ask?'

'Damn!'

'Tell me what happened,' Bruno said gently. He spooned the zabaglione into ramekins and slid them into the fridge. They were to form part of a complex assemblage of warm and cold, consisting of a fresh peach *gelato*, just starting to thaw; then zabaglione made with Barolo wine, slightly chilled; then a warm froth of more zabaglione, a thicker one this time, made with the yolks of goose eggs and rich, sherry-like Marsala; and finally a topping of crisp, fried mint leaves and freshly roasted espresso beans, arranged like the petals and seeds of a flower on top of the other ingredients.

When Tommaso had finished explaining, Bruno said neutrally, 'So you gave her a hare.'

'Yes. One of Gigliemi's finest.'

'That was romantic of you.'

'It was, wasn't it?'

'Other men give flowers. But you, Tommaso, give dead animals. Dead *baby* animals. To an American.'

A thoughtful expression passed across Tommaso's face.

22

'Still,' Bruno continued, 'at least she wasn't a vegetarian. Many of them are.'

'You think the hare might have been a mistake?'

Bruno shrugged.

'She did ask me how to gut it,' Tommaso said, remembering. 'I thought that was strange. I mean, most women know how to gut game, don't they?'

'Maybe not Americans.'

Tommaso smacked his fist into his palm. 'Don't their mothers teach them anything? What do they learn at school, for Christ's sake?'

'How to give great blow-jobs, apparently,' Bruno said dryly. 'I wouldn't know.'

'Shit! Shit! Shit! The hare *was* a mistake. I should have given her some *tortellini*. Even an idiot can cook *tortellini*. Even *I* can cook *tortellini*. If only I'd been picking up something different, this would never have happened.'

'*Si nonnema teneva 'o cazzo, 'a chiammavamo nonno**,' Bruno agreed calmly. 'Too many ifs. Why don't you call her and give her the right recipe?'

'I don't have her number. I gave her mine and told her to ring me if she had any problems.'

'Well, if she does call you, at least it'll prove she isn't in the mortuary with a hare bone stuck in her throat.'

A faint pinging sound came from beyond the swing doors that led to the restaurant. Someone had just struck a glass, softly, with a knife.

'You'd better go,' Bruno said gently.

'Shit!'

Tommaso raced to get into his uniform. Black trousers, white

---

*Literally: 'If my grandmother had a dick, we would have called her grandpa.'

shirt, black tie, black jacket. Franciscus, the maître d', didn't like to be kept waiting.

When Tommaso told Laura he was a chef, he wasn't exactly telling the truth, or indeed anything close to it. Tommaso wasn't a chef, or a *sous chef*, or even a *commis chef*. Tommaso was a waiter, a very junior waiter – a waiter so lowly that even Amelie the bottle-washer was allowed to give him orders.

The ritual about to take place in the restaurant was the same one that took place on the first day of every month. It was time to fill Templi's *libro prenotazioni*, the reservations book.

While the waiting staff stood round in a semi-circle, three or four vast bags of post were emptied on to a round table. One by one each letter was opened and handed to Franciscus, who perused the contents, gave a curt nod or shake of his head, and passed it to one of the two waiters to his left. One of these put the rejections into a rubbish sack while the other carefully wrote the names of those accepted into the reservations book, a leather-bound volume as weighty as a church ledger. Tommaso's job was to take the full sacks and replace them with empty ones, thus ensuring that the ritual, like everything else at Templi, proceeded with the smooth, uninterrupted solemnity of a state occasion.

It is not enough, of course, to telephone Templi and simply ask for a reservation. Even if you could find the number, which is ex-directory, the waiter who answers the phone would explain to you very politely that, due to excessive demand, reservations are only accepted in writing, on the first day of each month, for the period three months in advance. Even so, there are more applicants than places, and thus a great deal of care has to be taken when writing your letter to make sure you are one of the lucky ones.

It is rumoured, for example, that it helps to give some indication when you write that you are the sort of person by whom the legendary cooking of Alain Dufrais will be truly appreciated; a sort of brief résumé, detailing other restaurants you have eaten at – though you will want to acknowledge that they cannot be as good as Templi – or perhaps your appreciation of the philosophy outlined in one of Monsieur Dufrais's many books. Do not be tempted to go on at length, however, because this may indicate that you are a chatterbox – and if there is one thing Alain Dufrais does not appreciate, it is a chatterbox. Talking is not actually forbidden at Templi, but excessive conversation is certainly discouraged, it being assumed that you are there to concentrate on the flavours in your mouth, not to adulterate them with unnecessary verbiage. Mobile phones, cigarettes and children *are* forbidden – the latter not in so many words, but you will have been sent a discreet note well in advance of your meal which clearly states that Monsieur Dufrais cooks only for well-developed, sensitive palates.

It is also important not to let yourself down with your choice of paper or writing implement. To write in ballpoint, for example, rather than with a fountain pen, suggests that you are not really treating your application seriously. To use machine-cut paper might be all right – Monsieur Dufrais is not averse to simplicity – but the paper you choose had better be expensive as well as simple. On the subject of money, however, do not under any circumstances fall into the trap of enclosing a hundred-euro note with your letter. Many people do so, and to see the icy contempt which flickers across the maître d's face when the notes flutter from the envelopes is a chilling sight. The bills are handed to another waiter, to be added to the tips pool, but the letter always goes straight into the rubbish bag without another glance. Alain Dufrais is famously unconcerned with money, an attitude that permeates his whole establishment, which is why the menus have no prices and dinner for two will set you back anywhere between five hundred and a thousand euros.

◎◎

By the time the reservations had been sorted it was nearly noon, and the front-of-house staff took their places around the dining room to await the first guests and make final checks of glassware, silverware and placement. It was Alain's proud boast that the waiters at Templi always outnumbered the customers by at least two to one. To reach for a bottle at Templi was to find it floating as if by magic towards your glass; if you dropped a fork, it would be caught before it reached the ground, and just as swiftly replaced with a clean one.

At twelve-fifteen precisely Alain Dufrais himself made his daily tour of the dining room. You would never have guessed that he had been in his kitchen for nearly six hours: his whites were immaculate, untouched by a single drop of food. A tall, thin man of few words, he made a circuit of the empty tables like a senior commander inspecting his troops. Occasionally he picked up a glass and held it to the light, or pushed a fork a few millimetres to the left. On these occasions he said nothing, but Franciscus instantly pounced on the offending object, handing it to a waiter to be replaced. Then Alain returned to his inner sanctum, the kitchen. The double doors swung shut; the noise and hubbub of the morning subsided. There were no last-minute preparations, for the simple reason that everything was prepared and ready. Like an army that knows it has manned a perfect defensive position, the staff of Templi waited in silence for the first customer to show himself at their door.

Three

By half-past two the kitchen was humming like a well-oiled machine, pushing out intricate assemblies of *haute cuisine* in great gusts of fire and steam. The cooks worked like demons, their fingers dancing gracefully over the ingredients in a blur of dicing and stripping and mixing. Despite the extreme pressure they were under, and the urgency with which they worked, there was no yelling or swearing, and with the exception of the head chef, who called out the orders as the waiters brought them in, they rarely spoke. Alain's goal was consistent perfection, time after time, and no hint of chaos or temper was allowed to disturb the concentration of the dozens of craftsmen who toiled to realise his vision. Only once, when a *commis* dropped a saucepan, did the great man pause, turn to his head chef, and murmur something in his ear. No one heard what was said, but they all knew that the *commis* would be gone by the end of service. To work at Templi was a privilege. Staff came from as far afield as Australia, France and America for the opportunity to learn from the master. It was not an honour that could be squandered on incompetents.

Alain Dufrais ran his kitchen the traditional way, with a brigade made up of five distinct levels. At its apex was himself, the *chef de cuisine*, with a head chef, Karl, as his deputy. Karl ran the service, which was to say that he called out individual orders to the next levels in the hierarchy – the *sous chefs* and the *chefs de partie*. While the *sous chefs* worked the pass, putting the food on to plates, saucing, garnishing and checking it, the *chefs de partie* were each responsible for a different part of the kitchen. The *saucier* was responsible for meat, the *entre metier* for vegetables, the *garde manger* for cold dishes, and the *patissier* for desserts. Underneath these were a number of specialist assistants or *demi chefs*. Then, finally, there were the lowest of the low – the *commis,* who did whatever they were told to do by whoever told them to do it. It was a hierarchy as rigid and as immutable as a medieval society, in which everyone knew their place and knew, too, that their continued existence in that place depended entirely on the patronage of the person directly above them.

Bruno had recently been promoted to *patissier*. His corner of the kitchen was away from the rest – to protect the delicate threads of sugar and confections of raw egg from heat and bustle – but two or three times during service Alain Dufrais would come over to check that here, too, all was proceeding exactly as it should. Occasionally he dipped his finger into one of Bruno's saucepans to taste what was in it – he had never been known to show pain, even when the liquid was boiling – and on several occasions over the past week this had been followed by a curt nod of approval. These accolades had been noted by the other *chefs de partie*, and there was not one of them who did not wish that it had been themselves the nods were directed at.

Bruno himself had no time to consider whether he was doing well or not. By three, when the other chefs were winding down, he was still in a flurry of movement – caramelising, whipping, folding, creating airy extravagances of sugar and cream and ice that delighted the palate but magically seemed to have no sub-stance at all as soon as they entered the stomach. His powers of concentration were intense, and it was some time before he realised that something unusual was going on.

Throughout the service, a greater than normal amount of noise had been filtering through from the dining room. Occasionally, as the waiters pushed through the swing doors, a gust of raucous laughter or a bellow of conversation came too, which Bruno only noticed because it gradually affected the mood of the chef – something to which the kitchen brigade were as finely attuned as primates are said to be attuned to the emotions of their dominant silverback.

To begin with, Alain Dufrais raised his head, puzzled, and listened intently before going back to his work without comment. A few minutes later, however, a ragged cheer could be heard. Alain did not appear to react, but it was noticed that a little later he swept the delicate assembly of pigs' trotters and truffles he was working on into the rubbish bin and started again. The *chef de cuisine*, despite his almost impossibly high standards, very rarely had to start over.

By now almost the entire brigade had one eye on their chef and only one eye on their work. Mistakes, small errors of judgement and timing, were being made. Karl rejected more than one dish as it was passed to him for approval, putting yet more pressure on the sweating cooks as a backlog of sauces and garnishes instantly built up. The huge machine faltered, and Alain Dufrais, his nerves jangling, sensed it.

A waiter came in, bringing with him another cheer from the dining room. Dufrais stopped what he was doing and walked over to the waiter. 'What is that?' he said quietly.

The waiter did not need to ask what Alain was referring to. 'Table two. A birthday party.'

'How many people?'

'Twelve.'

Alain started to walk away. Then, as another waiter entered, followed by another bellow of raucous conversation, he abruptly changed his mind.

Straightening his hat, he marched out into the restaurant.

In the dining room, the birthday party had fallen silent – not because they were aware of the approaching storm, but because one of their number had just tapped on the table with his knife. As the hubbub subsided, he wiped his mouth with his napkin and got to his feet, grinning from ear to ear. A burst of applause greeted this manoeuvre. Umberto, the father of Federica, whose twenty-first birthday celebration this was, intended to make a speech.

'My friends,' he began.

The Swiss chef stalked towards him, his towering height magnified still more by his immaculate chef's hat, tall as a guardsman's bearskin. Umberto, not at all put out, turned to greet him. 'Hello,' he cried happily. 'This is fantastic, really fantastic. Isn't it, everybody?'

Alain took in the table with a single glance. He saw the unfinished food in front of Umberto, the row of corks that testified to too many bottles of good red wine consumed. A hush fell across the room as the other diners waited to see what he would do.

'You are leaving,' he said curtly. 'Now. All of you. Get out.' He turned on his heel and walked back to the kitchen.

Someone laughed, thinking it was a joke, but the laughter died on his lips when he realised that the chef was serious. A platoon of waiters, mobilised by Franciscus, was advancing courteously but with unmistakable determination towards the offending table. Umberto opened his mouth to protest but his daughter pulled at his sleeve, her face pink with embarrassment.

Slowly, silently, the group rose from their places and departed, each one escorted outside by a waiter, like prisoners with their own personal jailers. Tommaso found himself next to the birthday girl, who was by now in floods of tears.

'I'm so sorry,' he muttered to her. 'Chef is highly strung.' He patted her arm. 'And a bit of a prick as well,' he added truthfully.

The initial stunned surprise had worn off and the party guests were starting to get angry. Fingers were being poked at the waiters'

30

chests and fists waved in their faces. Only when a crack detachment of porters was despatched from the restaurant as reinforcements did the would-be customers finally get into their cars and leave.

The disruption meant that the lunchtime service rolled straight over into the evening one. All afternoon the chefs sliced and chopped and stirred and seasoned without a break, desperately trying to restore the kitchen – and the mood of their chef – to its normal equilibrium. By eight o'clock, calm once again reigned at Templi. The first diners of the evening were eating their *amuse-gueules* and sipping *mur royale* as they perused the menu in an atmosphere of studious rapture, trying to choose between *rôti* of quail stuffed with wild mushrooms, potato strings *au jus* with truffles, or rib-eye of lamb *en persillade* with a *cassoulet* of pole beans and thyme-infused olive oil.

It did not help, therefore, when a mobile phone somewhere began to play the 1970s Deep Purple anthem 'Smoke on the Water'.

The moment he heard it, Tommaso knew that it was his. Even in Italy there are not so many Deep Purple fans that a 'Smoke on the Water' ringtone could belong to two people in the same restaurant. In addition, he now remembered that he had been so busy thinking about the American girl that he had not, in fact, turned off his *telefonino* upon entering the premises, in accordance with the standing instruction to all staff. Failure to comply with this rule was cause for instant dismissal.

The ringing was coming from the staff coat cupboard. Tommaso had to act quickly. Hurling himself into its depths, he pulled his phone from the jacket where he had left it and pressed 'Answer'. 'One moment,' he whispered into it. Simultaneously, he patted the coat pockets until he located another *telefonino*, one that *had* been switched off. Slipping his own phone into his pocket, he emerged from the cupboard with the second phone held triumphantly aloft.

'This is the one,' he said to Franciscus. As the maître d' took the phone, placed it on the floor and calmly ground it under his heel, Tommaso slipped away into the garden.

'*Si?*' he said as soon as he was alone.

'Hello,' a girl's voice said hesitantly on the other end. Tommaso's heart leaped. It was the American. 'It's Laura Patterson – we met earlier? In the delicatessen.'

'Of course. How are you, Laura?'

'Well, I'm fine, but I'm not so certain about the hare sauce. I'm not sure I quite understood what you told me.'

In fact, Laura was at that very moment staring at a mound of steaming yellow *pappardelle*, perched on top of which was a whole, almost raw, baby hare. She had managed to skin and gut it, which had not been easy for either her or the hare, although it had to be said that of the two of them the hare seemed to have come off worst in the encounter.

'I guess I'm having a bad hare day,' she joked nervously.

'What?'

'Um – never mind. Terrible joke. Is there anything I can do?'

'Did you remember the *pancetta*?' Tommaso said sternly.

'*Pancetta*? Oh. I don't think so.'

'And how long did you cook it for?'

'Um – about twenty minutes.'

Tommaso scratched his head. Passing on a recipe was one thing, but rescuing a recipe gone wrong was way beyond his limited culinary skills. He began to walk rapidly towards the kitchen. Bruno would know what to do.

He would have handed the phone over to his friend but for the sudden recollection that his chances of seducing Laura depended on maintaining the pretence that he could cook. Tugging Bruno's sleeve, he pulled him into the most hidden recesses of the *patissier*'s corner and pointed to the mobile phone tucked against his own ear.

'So you have the hare, which you have cooked for twenty

minutes, and the *pappardelle*, which you have cooked for – what?' he said into the phone.

'Fifteen,' Laura said. Through the door of the kitchen she could see her father and Cassie, his odiously young personal-assistant-cum-girlfriend, glancing at their watches.

'Fifteen,' Tommaso repeated, looking at Bruno significantly.

Bruno winced. 'Fresh pasta,' he murmured.

'You'll need to cook another lot of *pappardelle*,' Tommaso said to Laura.

'But not yet,' Bruno added hastily. 'First we need to deal with this hare.'

'But first, we need to deal with the hare.'

'Does she have a frying pan?' Bruno wanted to know.

'Is there a frying pan?' Tommaso asked.

Laura, at the other end, said, 'Yes.'

'Yes,' Tommaso relayed to his friend. Laura looked at her phone, a little puzzled. Either there was an echo, or Tommaso was repeating everything she said to him.

Bruno nodded. 'Good. Now let's take a look at what's in her fridge. We won't be able to do proper *sugo di lepre*, not if she wants to eat before midnight, but we may be able to do something a little bit similar.' He picked up a lemon and began to dice the zest into tiny pieces with a paring knife as he talked Tommaso, and by extension Laura, through the preparation of a simple meat sauce. He had always been able to do two things at once if they were associated with food. It was only when it was nothing to do with cooking that he became all fingers and thumbs again.

It was midnight before the two young men left Templi. They had a nightcap at a small bar before walking home through the warm, quiet streets to the tiny apartment they shared in Trastevere.

Tommaso had stored Laura's number in his phone when she called. As they walked he dialled it.

'Hey, Laura, it's Tommaso. How was your meal?'

'Oh, hi, Tommaso. It was wonderful. I can't thank you enough.'

'Where are you? I can hear a kind of reverberation.'

'Oh, I'm in the bath, soaking. I was just going to bed.'

'She's in the bath,' Tommaso whispered to Bruno. 'It's a good sign.'

'That thing with the hare and the tomatoes was just inspired.' Laura said. There was the sound of splashing. 'Though I guess my sauce wasn't as good as *you'd* do it,' she continued. 'I mean, if I hadn't messed it up in the first place . . .'

Tommaso grinned at Bruno. 'You know, I'd like to cook something for you, Laura. Properly, I mean.'

'Really?'

'What are you doing tomorrow night?'

Laura paused. She didn't want to appear too keen, but that hare really had been delicious.

'Nothing much,' she said.

Tommaso ended the call and let out a whoop that echoed down the narrow street. 'She wants me to cook for her!'

'Fantastic,' Bruno said dryly. 'I will be interested to see what you decide to serve.'

'Ah. Well, I thought you might give me some advice there, my old friend.'

'*Hai voluto la bicicletta* . . .*' Bruno shrugged.

'Aw, come on. You know I'd do the same for you.'

'You could hardly do the same for me,' Bruno pointed out, 'seeing as how you can't cook for shit.'

'You know what I mean.'

They walked on for a few moments. Bruno said carefully, 'Just so I'm clear, what are you asking me for?'

'Just to come up with some ideas. Something so fantastic, so

---

*From 'Hai voluto la bicicletta? E pedala!' A saying meaning, literally: 'You wanted the bicycle, so pedal it.'

sumptuous and sexy that it will make Laura, the beautiful Laura, swoon with love and fall into bed with me.'

Bruno thought about this. 'But which?' he said at last. 'Because, you know, to make someone horny and to make someone fall in love are two very different things.'

'How so, philosopher?'

'If you want to make someone cry,' Bruno said slowly, 'you give them an onion to chop. But if you want them to feel sad, you cook them the dish their mother used to cook for them when they were small. You see the difference?'

Tommaso shrugged.

'And to make someone horny,' Bruno continued, 'well, that's harder than crying, but certainly not impossible. Seafood, of course, has aphrodisiac qualities. Molluscs, too – like *lanarche ajo e ojo*, snails in oil and garlic. Perhaps some *carciofioni* – baby artichokes cooked with mint, pulled apart with the fingers and dipped in soft, melted butter. Wine, obviously. And then, to finish, a burst of sugar, something light but artificial, so that you feel full of energy and happiness . . . but that's only one side of the story. If you wanted someone to fall in love with you, you would cook them something very different, something perfectly simple but intense. Something that shows you understand their very soul.'

'Such as?'

'Well, that's the difficulty. It will vary from individual to individual. You'd have to really know the person concerned: their history; their background; whether they are raw or refined, dry or oily. You would have to have tasted them, to know whether their own flesh is sweet or savoury, salty or bland. In short, you would have to love them, and even then you might not truly know them well enough to cook a dish that would capture their heart.'

'*Parla come t'ha fatto mammeta**,' Tommaso laughed. 'This is

*'Speak as your mother showed you', i.e. cut the bullshit.

too much thinking for me. Just get her into my bed and your cooking will have done all that I ask of it.'

'*My* cooking? I thought I was just providing a few ideas.'

'Ah.' Tommaso looked a bit shamefaced. 'It's just that – think how terrible it would be if I ruined your wonderful menu. You'd be unhappy, and then I'd be unhappy, and then I wouldn't be able to make Laura happy, and that would be a terrible thing to have on your conscience, wouldn't it? Besides,' he added craftily, 'how often do you get the chance to try out your dishes on a real live American? Your own dishes, I mean?'

'That's true,' Bruno said sombrely. 'I'm just a factory worker up there at Templi. A very high-quality worker in a gilded factory, but it's a production line all the same. Every day I make Alain's pastries, Alain's *dolci*, Alain's famous *crème caramel* with the baked vanilla pod in the centre – even when I could do something better, he doesn't want it. And as for Roman ideas . . .' He mimicked the chef's Swiss accent, '"We don't want any of those peasant recipes here, thank you." It's *Michelin, Michelin, Michelin*. Foie gras, white truffles, champagne sauce. Why? When a simple Roman *coda alla vaccinara** is more satisfying than any of them? And—'

'So you'll do it?' Tommaso said quickly, having heard his friend make this particular speech many times before. 'You'll cook something fantastic I can pretend to Laura I prepared myself?'

Bruno laughed and punched his friend lightly on the arm. 'Of course. I'll get you your *bicicletta*. Just make sure you know how to pedal it, OK?'

---

*Braised oxtail. *Vaccinara* is the old Roman word for butchers, whose favourite dish this was said to be.

Four

Laura phoned Carlotta the next morning and told her the news.

'I've found a chef. And, *cara*, he's so good-looking. Like a Michelangelo. He gave me a pasta recipe already and talked me through how to cook it. And I'm going round tonight for him to cook for me—'

'*Lentamente*, Laura. Slow down. You're going to his apartment? On the first date?'

'Well, yes. Where else would he cook for me?'

'Are you going to sleep with him?'

'Of course not. I've only met him once.'

'If you go to his apartment, he'll think you're going to sleep with him,' Carlotta said flatly.

'He didn't seem like that.'

'*Siamo in Italia*, Laura. We're in Italy. Trust me, he thinks you're going to sleep with him.'

Laura sighed. 'You're the one who's always telling me to follow my heart.'

'Sure. Just as long as you're clear where it is you're following it to. Do me a favour – take some *goldoni**, will you? That's something else Italian men aren't always good at.'

'Well, I've had plenty of practice at fending off unwanted attentions,' Laura said, a little huffily. 'Besides, I told you, he's nice. And he does have an apartment, so at least we're not talking about a grope in the bushes.'

'Aha. You *are* going to sleep with him.'

'Maybe,' Laura admitted. 'I haven't made up my mind. But a wild fling is certainly on the cards.'

'Then you should *definitely* take condoms. And remember – whatever you do, no sneakers.'

It was Bruno's morning off, and he spent most of it at the Mercato di San Cosimato, Trastevere's main food market, looking for ingredients for Tommaso's great meal of seduction. He had no menu at this stage, and no plan. He simply walked around, seeing what was available, listening to the competing shouts of the stall-holders and letting an idea of the seasonal delicacies sink into his mind. The *carciofini* were good at the moment, particularly the *romagnolo*, a variety of artichoke exclusive to the region, so sweet and tender it could even be eaten raw. *Puntarelle*, a local bitter chicory, would make a heavenly salad. In the *Vini e Olio* he found a rare Torre Ercolana, a wine that combined Merlot with the local Cesanese grape. The latter had been paired with the flavours of Roman cuisine for over a thousand years: they went together like an old married couple. There was spring lamb in abundance, and he was able to track down some good *abbacchio* – suckling lamb that had been slaughtered even before it had tasted grass.

From opportunities like these, he began to fashion a menu, letting the theme develop in his mind. A Roman meal, yes; but more than that. A springtime feast, in which every morsel spoke of

*Condoms.

38

resurgence and renewal, old flavours restated with tenderness and delicacy, just as they had been every spring since time began. He bought a bottle of oil that came from a tiny estate he knew of, a fresh pressing whose green, youthful flavours tasted like a bowl of olives just off the tree. He hesitated before a stall full of fat white asparagus from Bassano del Grappa, on the banks of the fast-flowing river Brenta. It was outrageously expensive, but worth it for such quality, he decided, as the stallholder wrapped a dozen of the pale fronds in damp paper and handed it to Bruno with a flourish like a bouquet of the finest flowers.

His theme clarified itself the more he thought about it. It was to be a celebration of youth – youth cut short, youth triumphant, youth that must be seized and celebrated. He wouldn't tell Tommaso that, of course. His friend got a nosebleed whenever Bruno tried to explain the deeper patterns he saw in cooking. The point was that it *would* work, at some subconscious level.

At the end of his tour of the market he came across an old man sitting in a dilapidated deckchair, snoozing. At his feet was a creased old carrier bag. Bruno crouched down and opened the bag carefully. Inside, like eggs in a nest of straw, were half a dozen *ricotte*. The old man opened his eyes.

'All from my own animals,' he said proudly. 'And made by my own wife.'

Bruno eased one of the cheeses to the surface and inhaled. Instantly he was transported to the tiny pastures of the Castelli Romani, the hilly countryside around Rome. There was a touch of silage in the scent of the cheese, from winter feed, but there was fresh grass, too, and sunlight, and the faintest tang of thyme where it grew wild in the meadows and had been eaten by the sheep along with the grass. He didn't really need any more food, but the ricotta was so perfect that he knew he would find a place for it somewhere in his meal, perhaps served as a dessert with a dusting of cinnamon and a dab of sweet honey.

◎

He was on his way to the pasta shop across the square when he saw the girl again. Bruno stopped, his heart in his mouth. He had no idea who she was, but he had seen her half a dozen times over the last few weeks, wandering round Trastevere; particularly here in the market, where she seemed to stare longingly at the stalls piled high with dozens of different vegetables: *radicchio, cime di rapa*, cardoons, *bruscandoli* – the little green hop shoots that appeared in the market for just a few weeks in springtime; *borragine, barba di frate*, even *lampascione*, hyacinth bulbs, and of course the baskets filled with *tenerume*, the first tiny courgettes, each one tipped with a veined, sunset-coloured flower. He had never seen her buy anything, though. Once he had been close enough to see that she had in her hand a plastic carrier bag containing a jar of Skippy peanut butter, from a food shop on the other side of the market that sold imported stuff. From this he deduced that she was American or Australian, and that she was homesick sometimes for the tastes of her own country. But the way she looked so hungrily at the piles of unfamiliar vegetables made him long to cook them for her, to show her what she was missing. Once he had got as far as walking up to her and saying, '*Buongiorno*,' but the moment she turned to him, those wonderful grey eyes lighting up with interest as she waited to see what he would say, he lost his nerve and pretended he simply needed to reach past her for some tomatoes. '*Scusi*,' he had mumbled, and she'd stood back to let him pass.

Today she was wearing a white halter top. He stood and drank in the way her shoulders were dotted with orange-red freckles beneath the swirl of blonde hair, like a scattering of chilli flakes. For a moment, with the clarity of hallucination, he could almost taste her in his mind, imagining on his palate the salty smoothness of her honey-coloured skin. *I will* talk to her, he thought. *I'll give her the asparagus. I can always buy some more.*

His mind made up, he started towards her; but he was just a moment too late. The girl had turned and walked away.

Bruno watched her go. On the other side of the market there was a row of tiny shops, each barely larger than a doorway – a minuscule hardware shop, a pharmacy, a shop selling nothing but olive oil and another selling lingerie, all packed into about ten yards of street. The girl stood in front of the display of lingerie for a moment, then pulled open the door and walked inside.

Bruno stopped short. *What are you doing, you fool?* he cursed himself. *She already has a boyfriend. A lover, in fact. Why else would she be buying lingerie? And what on earth made you imagine that a girl like that would be single in the first place?* He turned, heartsick, and went back to his shopping.

Laura loved to walk around Trastevere, the district where she was staying. According to the guidebooks it was a slightly seedy place, a working-class enclave in the heart of the Eternal City, but she loved the down-at-heel vibrancy of the cobbled lanes, barely wide enough to accommodate the Romans' miniaturised cars. The Mystic Dread Rock Steady Reggae shop stood shoulder-to-shoulder with a shop selling power tools, while the grandly named Institute of Sympathetic Shiatsu was a door crammed between a pharmacy and a booth selling lottery tickets. Furniture workshops stood cheek-by-jowl with churches; orange trees competed with restaurant parasols for every square inch of sunlight; and the herby odour of cannabis mingled with the smells of fresh coffee and pizza. In the squares and open spaces battered cars were parked in random chaos, like frozen traffic snarl-ups from which the drivers had simply walked away, and bright red splashes of geranium trailed from every window ledge and doorway.

One day soon after her arrival she had found herself passing a little shop. The window display was barely larger than a closet, but it held more than a dozen sets of the most beautiful underwear Laura had ever seen. Thongs as fine as necklaces were arranged in cases like precious jewels. There were delicate floral camisoles edged with lace, as fine as that for any wedding dress; sassy low-slung

41

hipsters; black suspender belts; creamy silk basques. At the time she had dragged herself away from the shop without entering, but now, preparing for her date, she found herself standing outside it once again. Carlotta's words rang in her head: *Trust me, he thinks you're going to sleep with him.*

A little light-headed, she opened the door and stepped inside.

There were no shelves in the little shop, no racks of stock or displays of merchandise. Instead there was an impeccably dressed Italian in her thirties reading *Il Messaggero*, who put down the newspaper as the door opened and scrutinised Laura with a practised eye.

'*Momento*,' the woman said decisively, disappearing into a tiny recess. When she reappeared it was with four slim boxes, which she opened on the counter one at a time. Inside, nestled in layers of tissue paper, were garments even finer than those in the window. No price tags were attached, and Laura soon discovered why: when she eventually made her choice, a red lace basque with complicated ties that made her feel almost lasciviously decadent, the figure on the till was more than her entire living allowance for the week.

'I'm going to teach you how to chop,' Bruno told Tommaso. 'That way, when she arrives you'll look as if you're doing the cooking.'

'Sure,' Tommaso said confidently. Bruno took an apple and placed it on the work surface. Then he unrolled his canvas knife bag.

'If you damage my knives,' he said, 'you'll be dead.'

'I won't damage them.' Tommaso picked up the biggest, a steel Wüsthof. 'Christ Jesus, it's heavy.'

Bruno gently removed the cleaver from his friend's hand. 'Uh-uh. Too big for you. You should start with this one.' He passed him the smaller Global. 'It's Japanese. Made of vanadium steel.'

Bruno poured a little olive oil on to a carborundum stone. 'First, I'll show you how to sharpen it.'

After five minutes of sharpening, Tommaso was bored. 'It must be ready now.'

'Nearly.'

When he was satisfied, Bruno took out a diamond steel. 'And now we hone it.'

It was several more minutes before Bruno allowed his friend to start on the apple. 'You use the heel of the knife for thicker objects, the point for finer work,' he instructed. 'Work across the apple at an angle, like so. Don't wait for the first slice to fall before you move on to the next one. And keep your fingertips tucked in. This blade can slice through a pig's trotters, so your little digits won't be much of an obstacle.'

While Tommaso practised chopping, Bruno baked. Unlike many chefs, he did not despise baking. He loved meat and vegetables, too, but there was another, different kind of pleasure in spinning artificial, dazzling confections of sugar and flour, or baking a tray of simple biscuits.

The *dolce* itself, after so much rich food, was to be a straightforward one – the ricotta, with honey and a sprinkling of cinnamon, and a glass of *vin santo* – sweet white wine – into which would be dipped *tozzetti*, handmade hazelnut biscuits. Bruno was just putting the biscuits into the oven when his friend came over.

'Here,' Tommaso said, pulling a little packet out of his jeans, 'some extra herbs for the *tozzetti*.'

'You don't put herbs in *tozzetti*,' Bruno began. Then he saw that the little packet actually held about an eighth of an ounce of dope.

'Trust me,' Tommaso said, winking. 'It'll taste even better with this.'

'Uh-uh,' Bruno said firmly, pushing his friend's hand away. 'It'll ruin the taste of the hazelnuts; and besides, you won't need

43

any more stimulants after a meal like this. How are you going to do justice to this girl if she's in the bedroom and you're out on the balcony?'

Bruno had decided to serve the asparagus with a warm *zabaione* sauce; not the complex version he prepared in the restaurant but a simple, sensual froth of egg yolk and white wine. What he hadn't yet told Tommaso was that finishing the zabaglione would have to be done at the last moment, just before it was served. Learning to use a knife was the easy part. Before the end of the day, his friend was going to have to learn how to use a double boiler as well.

At the Residencia Magdalena, the apartment block where the American students were housed, Laura was starting to have second thoughts about the basque. It was undeniably beautiful, but there was something almost fetishistic, not to mention impractical, about the dozens of tiny hooks and ties with which it fastened.

'What do you think?' she asked her roommate, Judith. 'Too much? Too complicated?'

Judith surveyed her through narrowed eyes. 'Put it this way: you'd better hope he's good with his hands.'

'I have been led to believe that he's quite dextrous,' Laura said. She blushed.

'Well, if he can get that thing off you, he must be. I'd say you're in for a great night.'

Tommaso was struggling with the concept of a double boiler. Time after time he started to whip up the egg yolks, only for the froth to collapse into a sticky mess.

'You're being too brutal,' Bruno told him. 'Here. Move the elbow as well as the wrist. Like this.'

Tommaso tried again. This time he was too energetic and the mixture flew off the end of his whisk.

'Be patient,' Bruno said. 'Now, one more time.'

'It's hopeless,' Tommaso said, wearily putting down the whisk. 'I can't do this.'

'It's necessary. Now, one more time—'

'Ah, but it isn't necessary, is it? Not really,' Tommaso said craftily. 'After all, we'll be sitting at the table, so what's to stop me from pretending to come in here and whip the zabaglione, while really you do it?'

Bruno thought about it. 'But where would I be?'

'In here, of course. Laura needn't know. Then, when it's all plated, you could just creep out.'

'Well, OK then,' Bruno said reluctantly. It certainly had to be easier than teaching Tommaso how to cook.

At eight o'clock Laura found the address Tommaso had given her, a dingy door beside a scooter shop. She rang the bell. Tommaso's face appeared high above her head. 'Come up,' he shouted. 'It's open.'

She stepped into a dark courtyard and trudged up endless flights of stairs until she got to the top. Here, too, the door was open, and she stepped inside. The apartment was tiny and by no means smart, a nest of four little rooms festooned with old film posters and pictures of seventies rock stars. But the view took her breath away.

Red-tiled rooftop after red-tiled rooftop stretched away below her, a chaotic jumble of houses, apartments and churches all crammed together, tumbling down towards the Tiber. On her left, along the long ridge of the Janiculum Hill, lights twinkled in the distance. In front of her, beyond the river, the palaces and churches of old Rome were floodlit islands among the darkness of the surrounding buildings.

'Wow,' she said reverently.

The window gave on to a sloped roof, which had been adapted into a makeshift and rather lethal-looking balcony by the addition of two battered old armchairs and a few pots of herbs, scattered among a thicket of television aerials. Tommaso was getting out of one of the chairs to greet her, impossibly beautiful, his sculptured face crowned by an explosion of curly ringlets as thick as the twists in a telephone cord. 'Hi,' he said. 'How are you, Laura?'

'I'm great.' Even better than the view, however, was the smell emanating from the kitchen, which almost knocked her off her feet. 'My God,' she breathed. 'What is *that*?'

'Dinner,' he said simply.

'It smells –' she inhaled deeply '– *fantastic.*'

'It's pretty good,' he said modestly. 'Needs another twenty minutes.'

'Twenty minutes!' She wasn't sure she could wait that long. She wanted to taste it now, right now.

'Sure. Don't worry. It will be even better if we have to wait a little. The anticipation will be part of the pleasure.' He ran one hand down her back as he kissed her cheek in greeting.

Laura gave a tiny, secret shiver. Carlotta had been right.

After a glass of *prosecco*, Laura was completely relaxed. Tommaso was an excellent host, attentive and interested – at least he was once she had persuaded him to turn off the atrocious music he had playing in the background.

'You don't like the Ramones?' he said, surprised. 'But they're American.'

'So's Mariah Carey,' she pointed out. It seemed strange that someone whose taste in food was so highly developed could be completely deficient in any musical taste whatsoever.

With the Ramones ushered politely out of the apartment, they chatted happily as Tommaso sliced tiny spring vegetables for *pinzimonio*, a dip of olive oil, vinegar, salt and pepper. The kitchen was full of professional-looking chef's equipment and some of the most ferocious knives Laura had ever seen.

46

'When did you learn to do that?' she asked, watching Tommaso's knife dance over the chopping board.

'Oh, it's easy. And,' he added, more truthfully, 'I had a very good teacher.'

The wonderful smells from the oven were making Laura's mouth water. 'So what are we eating tonight?'

'Here.' He handed her a menu with a flourish and a bow, like a waiter.

She looked at the card and read: *Antipasto: verdure in pinzi-monio. Primo: spaghetti all'amatriciana. Secondo: abbacchio alla cacciatora. Contorni: carciofi alla romana, asparagi con zabaione. Dolci: ricotta dolce; vin santo, biscotti.* 'My God. We'll never eat all that.'

'*Quanto basta*. Just enough. They are very small amounts, just enough to waken the palate. Not like American steaks, which sit on the stomach and make you—' He mimed exhaustion.

There was the sound of a door closing. 'Who's that?' Laura asked.

'Just my roommate. Don't worry, he's going out.'

'Is he a chef as well?'

'Bruno? Not exactly. That is, he's a trainee. Just a bottle-washer, really. Now, shall we eat?'

Laura had never eaten food like this before. No: she had never eaten before. It was as if these flavours had always existed, had always been there in her imagination, but now she was tasting them properly for the very first time. Each course was more intense than the last. The spaghetti was coated in a thick sauce of meat and wine; rich, pungent and sticky. The lamb, by contrast, was pink and sweet, so tender it seemed to dissolve in her mouth. It was served without vegetables, but afterwards Tommaso brought the first of the *contorni* to the table: a whole artichoke, slathered in warm olive oil and lemon juice and sprinkled with chopped mint. Laura licked every drop of oil off her fingers, amazed by the intensity of the flavour. Her stomach kept telling her that it was full, stretched to bursting point, but her appetite kept telling her she could take a little more, just another mouthful, until she felt quite dizzy with the excessiveness of it all.

Tommaso left her while he went to finish the asparagus. After a few minutes, missing his company, Laura decided she'd go and help. She piled up the dirty plates and carried them towards the kitchen. 'Tommaso? I'll wash these while you're doing that.'

She pushed the door, which didn't open. 'Sorry,' Tommaso called from within. 'It's, uh, stuck. It does that sometimes.'

She rattled the door handle. 'Want me to push it from this side?'

'No, I'll sort it in a minute.'

For a confused moment Laura thought she heard voices murmuring behind the door, but it was only Tommaso breaking into song as he cooked.

At last the door opened and Tommaso came out, holding a platter from which emanated the most amazing aroma. 'Fixed it. Tell you what, why don't you take this to the table?'

A few minutes later they were eating the asparagus. It was breathtakingly good. The stalks, nestled in their foamy sauce of beaten egg yolk and wine, were so tender at the tip that she could almost suck the plump heads off, but got progressively firmer as she chewed down towards the crisp base.

'Tommaso,' she said rapturously, 'I have to tell you—'

'I know,' he said, smiling at her, and she felt her whole body bathed in a languorous, sensual glow.

In the kitchen, Bruno carried the pans over to the sink and carefully, so that they wouldn't make any sound, lowered them into the water.

'So what are you doing in Rome?' he heard Tommaso say.

'I wrote an essay on art history for a competition,' a girl

48

answered. 'The winner got to come to Rome for a whole year. It's sort of like a scholarship.' There was something about her voice that made Bruno think of *dolci*, of meringues and sweet *zabaione* and peaches bubbling as they poached in wine. Unable to help himself, he listened for just a moment longer.

'But you can have some fun as well?'

'Are you kidding? Art history *is* fun.' Bruno, imagining Tommaso's expression, smiled. 'No, really,' the girl was saying. 'I mean, I guess you're used to it. You can go and look at a Caravaggio every day if you want to, but for me it's the chance of a lifetime.'

'Caravaggio?'

'You don't know Caravaggio?' The girl sounded surprised.

Tomasso said quickly, '*Sì*. Of course. All Romans know Caravaggio. Which is your favourite?'

'Well, it's hard to choose one—'

'Of course.'

'—but if I absolutely had to, it would probably be *The Fortune Teller*, in the Musei Capitolini.'

Hands in the sink, Bruno nodded. It was his favourite, too. Tommaso's girl had taste.

'If I were a painter,' Tomasso said reverently, 'I would only paint you, Laura. Then all my pictures would be beautiful.'

Bruno's smile broadened. When it came to the art of seduction there was no one to match Tommaso. Drying his hands, he tiptoed to the door that led out of the apartment.

Eventually even the ricotta lay in crumbs on its plate. Tommaso carried the *biscotti* and *vin santo* to the battered old sofa.

'I've drunk so much already,' Laura murmured.

'In Rome we have a saying: "*Anni, amori e bicchieri di vino, nun se contano mai.*"'

'"Years, lovers and glasses of wine; these things must not be counted,"' she translated.

49

'Exactly.' He dipped one of the biscuits in the golden liquid and held it gently to her lips. She hesitated, then opened her mouth. The sweet, raisiny taste suffused her tastebuds. She closed her eyes ecstatically. 'My God, that's beautiful.'

'*Sei bellissima*,' he murmured. 'Like you, Laura.' Now he dipped two of his own fingers in the wine. Again, she hesitated for just a moment, then allowed him to slide them into her mouth. She licked the sticky, honeyed wine off him until every morsel of sweetness was gone. A few drops fell on her neck and he kissed them off greedily even while she was still sucking his fingers.

He unwrapped her slowly, peeling off her clothes as if he were pulling the leaves off an artichoke, kissing her between each layer. *This is exactly what I hoped for*, she thought. *Who would have believed it? Carlotta, of course. Carlotta was right all along.*

He was untying the red basque now, pulling at the little bows that fastened it. She felt it loosen and arched her back, waiting for him to finish. He was pulling at one particular tie with a frown of concentration. Then he tugged at it.

'Wait,' she murmured. 'You'll tighten it.'

'I'll get a knife,' he said impatiently.

'I'll do it,' she said quickly. As she undid the ties Tommaso fell to his knees in front of her, clasping his hands in prayer and muttering in Italian.

'What are you doing?' she asked.

'I'm saying grace,' he said wolfishly.

Secondo

'When there has been time to relish and consume the first course, to salute its passing with wine and to regroup the taste-buds, the second course comes to the table. If one is ordering in a restaurant – one that caters to Italians, not to tourists – the choice of a second course is made after the first course has been eaten. This doesn't mean that one has made no plans, but that one waits to confirm them, to make sure that original intentions and current inclinations coincide . . .'

MARCELLA HAZAN, *The Essentials of Classic Italian Cooking*

Five

The next morning, Vincent, Sisto and the other early customers at Gennaro's were greatly entertained to see Tommaso running across the road towards the bar, still wet from the shower and naked except for a towel around his waist.

'*Due cappuccini, Gennaro, presto per favore,*' he shouted. From Tommaso's broad grin it was clear that he had a good reason to be in a hurry, and his friends knew what it was likely to be. They greeted him with a round of applause.

Pausing only to grab a couple of *cornetti*, Tommaso bore the two cups of coffee back across the street, dodging traffic. A Fiat van hooted at him, but although he shouted a ritual Roman insult back – 'Go and hoot up your wife's legs, dickhead, there's more traffic up there!' – his mind was already on other things.

Laura came back into the bedroom from the shower, wrapped in a towel, her skin wet and glistening in the early morning sunlight and her hair plastered back across her head.

'You're beautiful,' Tommaso said sincerely. '*Sei bellissima, Laura.*' He picked up a little digital camera from a table. 'Smile?'

She smiled and he pressed the button. 'Now, come back to bed.' He patted the space beside him, where the tray of breakfast waited invitingly.

She got back into bed and put her arms around him. He took a little froth from his cappuccino and flicked it on to the end of her adorable nose. She laughed, so he took her cup from her and, placing it carefully on the floor, turned to kiss her. After a moment's hesitation she wriggled into his arms, kissing him urgently, pushing back at him along the length of her body.

Laura had to run to get to her first lecture, but she managed to find time to phone Carlotta on the way. The first question her friend asked, of course, was: 'So?'

'Uh – I probably went a little further than I'd intended,' Laura admitted.

Carlotta's second question: 'And? What did he cook?' She was, after all, an Italian, and while any two *chiavati* are pretty much the same, no two meals ever are.

As Laura described the menu, item by item, and tried to do justice to the taste and flavour of each, there was a series of gasps and hisses at the other end of the phone.

'White asparagus? From Brenta? With *zabaione*? My God, Laura, that's a fantastic dish. I've only had it once, and I still remember it.'

'That was the high point,' Laura admitted.

'*Cara*, I'm so jealous. Maybe I'll have to come down and visit. What's he cooking next time?'

'He didn't say. Anyway, I've got to go. I'm at my lecture and I'm late.'

The college campus was housed in a Renaissance villa set in a garden of pine trees and fountains on the Janiculum Hill. As Laura had guessed, the lecture she was meant to be at had already started, and she took a seat next to Judith in the seminar room as unobtrusively as possible.

'So,' Kim Fellowes, the lecturer, was saying, 'the High Renaissance. A period of just thirty years, between 1490 and the sack of Rome in 1520, during which the patronage of a Pope and the talents of just a few dozen artists created the greatest flowering of genius the world has ever seen. Good morning, Laura. You look as if you've come hotfoot from a Bramante chapel or a Bernini fountain, so you can be the first to tell us what you have seen of the High Renaissance so far.'

Laura thought quickly as she sorted out her books. 'Well,' she said, 'I've been to the Sistine chapel, obviously, and seen the Raphaels in the Vatican, and some of Michelangelo's architecture—'

'*Momento*. Who is this Michael Angelo, please?' Kim interrupted.

'Oh. Er, sorry.' In her haste she had pronounced it the American way. 'I meant *Michelangelo*.' This time she pronounced it as he did, in Italian. But her teacher was still not satisfied.

'In this room,' he announced, 'we won't speak of Michelangelo, or Titian, or Raphael, any more than we would call Shakespeare Will, or Beethoven Ludwig. We are not yet on first name terms with these great men, nor will we presume to be until we have studied their works for many years. We will call them, therefore, by their proper appellations: Michelangelo Buonarroti, Tiziano Vecellio and Raffaello Sanzio. Please,' he gestured at Laura, 'proceed.'

Kim Fellowes was an American, but he had lived in Rome for so long that he was, as he said, almost a native: the staff at the University referred to him simply as *il dottore*. It was to be regretted, he told the students, that his book on the Renaissance – the same book Laura had been consulting during her futile hunt for the church of Santa Cecilia – had had to be written in English rather than Italian, thanks to the dictates of a publisher eager for a commercial bestseller. And a bestseller it had inevitably become: he kept the reviews, carefully laminated to protect them from greasy fingerprints, on his desk for the students to examine. It had been acclaimed as that rare thing: a work that combined the erudition of a scholar with the sensitivity of a true artist. Everything about Kim proclaimed his perfect taste, from the gorgeous linen shirts he wore – Laura liked to play a kind of mental game which consisted of trying to find the right word to describe their colours: she usually resorted to words like cornflower, cranberry, or aquamarine – to his pale seersucker jacket, and the straw Panama that kept the fierce Italian sun off his finely featured face when outdoors. Some of her fellow students found him a hard taskmaster. Laura was overawed by his sensitivity and intelligence, and did everything she could to impress him.

'So you saw the Sistine Chapel?' he was saying. 'And what did you think of it?'

She hesitated. But she couldn't bear not to tell him what she had really thought. 'I thought it was a barn.'

The other students laughed. 'A barn?' Kim Fellowes repeated questioningly, knitting his fingers together and placing them on his knee.

'Yes. I mean, it's beautifully painted and everything, but the paintings are so high that you have to look upwards all the time, and the room is so big and rectangular . . .' She trailed off, certain she was about to be ridiculed. To her surprise, though, Kim was nodding approvingly.

'Laura is absolutely right. The Sistine Chapel,' he said, looking round at the students to make sure they all understood him, 'is considered by many experts, including myself, to be the embodiment of all the worst excesses of the Renaissance. The colours are gaudy, the design overpowering and the conception unharmonious. It was commissioned purely as a status symbol by a nouveau-riche philistine who destroyed some rather fine Peruginos in the process. Buonarroti himself didn't want to touch it, which is why we will be studying his drawings instead. Now then, who can tell me what *contraposto* is?'

◎◎

'That man is such an asshole,' grumbled one of Laura's fellow students as they packed up their books after the seminar.

'He knows what he's talking about,' Laura retorted. She was feeling a little guilty: for the first time she had found her attention wandering during Kim's seminar, remembering the feel of Tommaso's kisses, his body pressed up against hers as they'd shared the last of the *vin santo* on his battered sofa.

'As he keeps reminding us,' the other student said sourly. 'Anyone want pizza?'

'Where?' Judith asked.

'The mortuary?' This was their name for the marble-lined pizzeria down the road. 'One o'clock?'

'OK. See you there. Laura?'

'Uh – yes. I guess so.'

Laura had been surprised by her fellow students. For her, coming to Rome had been the chance of a lifetime, an adventure made even more attractive by her mother's insistence that it was (a) academically a waste of time and (b) perilously unhygienic, a consequence of the Italians' notorious inability to wash their hands after visiting the bathroom.

She had landed at Fiumicino airport just a few days before the first semester began. In her excitement she already felt a gulf between herself and all the package tourists getting off the plane: they were here to visit, but she was here to live. Accompanying her were a backpack crammed with art books and two small suitcases, all she had been allowed to bring. As the letter of acceptance from the Anglo-American University in Rome had breezily informed her, 'Closet space is cramped in even the grandest Roman apartments – and believe us, yours won't come into that category.'

Before she could get to her suitcases, though, there was the small matter of Passport Control. Like Passport Control halls the world over, the one at Fiumicino contained two separate areas: one for locals and one for everyone else. A series of zigzags painted on the floor, culminating in a yellow line in front of each little booth, indicated where you were meant to form an orderly queue before stepping up to present your papers. That was the theory, at any rate. In practice, only one booth in the entire place was open. Crammed into the tiny interior were three young men in elaborate uniforms, complete with military hats tilted at jaunty angles, while in front of them surged a great sea of travellers of different nationalities, all brandishing their passports in the air, gesticulating, and shouting angrily at the trio of officials, who paid them no attention whatsoever.

From her position at the side of the mob, Laura was able to see the cause of the delay. A young woman wearing tight cutoffs and a very brief top, which highlighted the small tattoo high up on one shoulder, and whose sleek blonde hair was threaded with the earphones of an expensive-looking MP3 player, was leaning up against the booth chewing gum while the three men flirted with her under the pretext of examining her passport. One of the officers even seemed to be writing out his phone number for her, an action that caused the hubbub from those waiting behind to double in volume. Eventually the young woman was allowed to pass, though it was not until her impressively pert behind was completely out of sight that the young men were able to drag their attention back to the job in hand.

When Laura finally had her own turn at the booth, she laid her passport on the ledge and tried her very first '*Buongiorno*'.

The official glanced at the photograph, then back at Laura.

'Good afternoon,' he said in perfect English. 'Where will you be staying in Rome?'

'At the Residencia Magdalena. It's in Trastevere.'

'*Bene*. I will come and meet you there on Saturday night. We will go out on a date.'

Laura's mouth dropped open. Then she laughed.

'No, why not?' he insisted, sounding a little hurt. 'It will be fun. We will have a good time.'

'*Scusi*.' This was one of the other officials, reaching over and picking up her passport. He was wearing a more extravagant uniform than his colleague so presumably he was the more senior. He examined her passport minutely, turning it this way and that.

'Is there is a problem?' Laura asked.

'*Si*. The problem,' he announced gravely, 'is that you are so much more beautiful than your photograph. I should like very much to take you out to dinner.'

The third man said something rapidly in Italian. The first official translated. 'Alessandro, he would like to take you out too. But I asked you first.'

A very short nun pushed her way to the front of the booth and started haranguing the men in a shrill voice. 'Enjoy your stay, Laura Patterson,' the first official said, unperturbed, as he stamped her passport. '*Prego*.' All three came smartly to attention and saluted her as she walked away. The nun they waved through without a second glance.

When Laura found the minibus that was to take her to where she was staying, the girl with the small tattoo was already sitting in it, surrounded by a vast pile of luggage. It soon became apparent that this was Laura's roommate, Judith. It also became clear that Judith's interest in Michelangelo and Raphael was rather less than her interest in Versace, Prada and Valentino. She was majoring in Fashion Psychology but had almost been thrown out after a term: her parents had insisted she go abroad in an effort to get her to concentrate on her work. 'They wanted to get me away from my boyfriend, mostly,' Judith confided as they were driven at breakneck speed through the suburbs. 'They seem to think I'll calm down if I'm not with him. He's a vampire.'

'What?'

'You know. We drink each other's blood.' Judith dug into her cleavage and retrieved a phial on a silver chain. 'This is Jeff's, and he's got mine. Great farewell gift, huh?'

'Right.' Laura's visions of discussing fifteenth-century painting techniques late into the night were evaporating rapidly.

After they had settled in – the letter had been right, by American standards the apartment was minuscule – they set off to explore Rome, armed only with bottles of water and identical copies of the Lonely Planet guidebook. It was hot, and both women wore shorts. The reaction was extraordinary. Cars sounded their horns like huntsmen sighting prey. Shopkeepers standing in their doorways hissed at them like geese. Young men on scooters – even those with girlfriends on the back, impossibly beautiful Italian girls with cascading black tresses and perfect burnt-umber skin – slowed down alongside them to call *'Ueh, biondine!'* appreciatively, muttering rapid-fire suggestions.

'Do you get the feeling we might be underdressed?' Laura said eventually.

They took to the subway, only to find themselves trapped in a carriage with three beggars, a mother and her two tiny gypsy daughters, who immediately surrounded them, clamouring for money. Judith pressed a note into the smallest child's hand. The money vanished and the child's pestering redoubled.

'No,' Judith said firmly. '*Finito*. No more. *Chiuso.*' The beggars ignored her, pawing her eagerly with their outstretched hands. At the next stop a uniformed guard got into the carriage. The girls heaved a sigh of relief, then watched open-mouthed as the mother reached into the folds of her clothing and pulled out a fistful of money, which she brazenly handed to the guard before resuming her harassment of the Americans unchecked. To cap it all, when they finally got to the object of their journey, the Museo Vaticano, a nun picked them out of the line and sent them away for showing bare legs.

The next day had been Orientation Day. The first to stand up to address the assembled students was Casey Novak, the president of the grandly titled Student Government. Casey smiled brightly as she gave the assembled newbies the benefit of her own six months' experience. The food here was nice, if a little oily, but be careful what you ate – many restaurants had really gross stuff on the menu, like wild songbirds or veal. Remember to tell your waiter you wanted clean cutlery for each course. Everything was shut between two-thirty and five for siesta, and on Mondays and Thursdays most shops were closed all day, which was a real pain but you got used to it. Girls should wear a wedding ring to deter unwelcome attention. The university could provide a trained counsellor if you got really homesick, though there were so many social activities on offer that you were unlikely to have time to get depressed.

'What else?' Casey had mused. 'Well, CNN is on channel sixteen. MTV is on twenty-three. There's a good American music radio station called Centro Suono. Italian music is truly awful, by the way, but not as bad as Italian TV. They use the same two voices to dub every American show – there's a guy with a butch voice, and a girl who's supposed to sound like a sex kitten, which is kind of weird when you're watching *Friends* – which, incidentally, is on every Thursday evening.'

By the time Casey sat down to a scattering of applause, Laura felt a bit like a moon-colonist – safe as long as she stayed inside her air-tight capsule with the other colonists, but surrounded by a deadly atmosphere outside.

The next person to stand up was the elegant figure of *il dottore*. '*Bienvenuti a Roma, la città eterna*,' he began. He spoke in fluent Italian for a minute or so, then switched to English. 'Welcome to the birthplace of Western civilisation. I promise that you are about to have the most extraordinary year of your life.'

This was more like it. Laura listened intently as Kim Fellowes told them which art galleries had ruined their treasures with restoration, and which were closed all day Monday. He told them which galleries had introduced half-hour time limits on viewing, which famous sights were ghastly, and which were exquisite. The former included almost anywhere frequented by tourists; the latter

61

included most small churches. He even told them which guide-books to buy: 'Whatever you do, don't get Fodor's or the Lonely Planet, unless you want to be taken for a tourist. Baedeker is prob-ably still the best one. And some of the Italian-language art guides are quite good, if a little insular.'

Laura had wondered if by the end of her year she, too, would be reading guidebooks in Italian and, even more impressively, finding them a little insular. She resolved to throw away her Lonely Planet guide just as soon as she got back to her room.

'But,' he concluded, 'if I could say just one thing to you about your year in Italy, it would be this. You are not only here to study the Renaissance, but to live it. This is the only city in the world where Renaissance masterpieces are *housed* in Renaissance master-pieces, where the drinking fountains, the bridges over the river, the churches, even the city walls, were designed by the likes of Buonarroti and Bernini. To walk the streets, to eat in a restaurant, to have a conversation with an ordinary taxi driver about his foot-ball team, or to buy some fruit at a market stall is to be part of a living work of Renaissance genius. Open yourself to Rome, and Rome will open herself to you.'

'Oh, I almost forgot,' Casey said, standing up as Kim Fellowes sat down. 'The main place we hang out is an Irish bar, the Druid's Den, particularly on Saturday nights. And there's a baseball team that plays every Sunday.' The cheer that greeted this remark seemed to indicate that the majority of Laura's fellow students found Irish bars and baseball a rather more enticing prospect than Bernini fountains.

Luckily, Laura got on well with her roommate – better than she had expected to, in fact. Her own reproduction Caravaggios and Judith's posters of death-metal rappers shared the apartment peacefully enough, as did their owners, even if Judith's vast hairdryer tripped the apartment power-breaker every time she plugged it in. The phial of blood, however, proved ineffective at warding off the temptations of distance. Every week or so Laura would bump into one or other of the male students from the course, half-naked, in the apartment's tiny bathroom. Maybe, she thought to herself, Judith's parents had known what they were doing by sending her to Rome after all.

Little by little, Laura's own days and nights fell into a kind of routine – lectures and seminars in the morning, followed by art galleries or language lessons in the afternoon, and CNN or pizza in the evenings. Friday nights saw her at the Fiddler's Elbow or the Druid's Den with the other students, drinking Bud and watching American or British sports on TV. Occasionally they might go to one of the little restaurants in Trastevere, and even more occasionally she might have a date with an Italian, each romantic disaster being subsequently relayed by phone to Carlotta in Milan. When homesickness crept up on her, as it did from time to time, either she or Judith would make the trip down to Castroni's and hand over huge bundles of euros for a tub of margarine, some sliced bread and a big jar of Skippy peanut butter. But then, quite by chance, she wandered into a little bar off the Viale Glorioso, and Rome – noisy, impetuous, colourful, chaotic – decided to reach out and haul her into the dance.

At the restaurant, Bruno, unable to understand why nothing was going right for him, shouted at the *commis* that the eggs must be stale. He had never had this problem before with his *zuppa inglese*, and the meringues he was making had refused to harden too.

The unfortunate lackey scurried off to find more eggs. Bruno felt bad. He knew it wasn't the eggs. It was something to do with himself. To make *dolci* you had to be able to conjure yourself into a mood that was as joyous and light as the dishes you were creating. But today he was distracted. He kept thinking about the girl in the market, the girl he'd barely spoken to, wishing that he could have cooked for her the meal that he had cooked for Tommaso's girl last night. He could imagine her expression as she slid the first

63

piece of lamb into her mouth, a mixture of rapture and astonishment, and then the gradual contentment settling over her face as her appetite was sated by another mouthful, and then another. . . He sighed, and tried to put the whole thing out of his mind.

The pizzas were cooked in the Roman fashion: thin slivers of dough, as crisp as poppadums, slathered with a sauce of fresh tomatoes, mozzarella and basil. Traditionally, a Roman pizza is cooked for the length of time that the cook can hold his breath, and these had been fired to perfection in the wood-burning oven at the front of the restaurant, making them hard underneath but leaving the sauce still liquid.

To her surprise, Laura found she was starving. Last night's meal, far from leaving her sated, seemed to have awakened her appetite, and she tucked in with gusto.

'This isn't a pizza, it's a pancake,' a student called Rick muttered, poking his food with a finger. 'Do the words "deep" and "pan" mean nothing to these people?' The boys had all ordered side salads. Laura almost told them that in Italy you had the salad afterwards, but thought better of it.

'Who's got the ketchup?' another student called. Rick produced from his backpack a bottle of Heinz Tomato Sauce, which was ceremoniously passed around the table.

A mobile phone rang. It took Laura a few moments to work out that it was hers, since for some reason it was now playing the Cream classic 'Sunshine of Your Love'. Then she realised Tommaso must have changed it while she'd been in the shower.

'*Pronto*?' she said cautiously.

It was Tommaso. 'Laura! Do you like your new ringtone?'

'Thank you. I love it.'

'I don't know why I called you. I just can't stop thinking about last night,' he said dreamily.

She lowered her voice. 'Me too.'

'I don't think I've ever had a night quite like that before.'

'Me neither.' She remembered the taste of that *zabaione*. 'It was fantastic.' She blushed a little.

'When can I see you again?'

'Well, I guess I'm free on Saturday.'

He sighed. 'Unfortunately Saturday is our busiest night. But I can get Sunday off.'

'OK. Would you like to go to a movie?'

'No, I'd like to cook for you,' Tommaso said. 'Something really special.'

Just the sound of his voice was enough to make her blush again. 'OK. I'll look forward to it. Ciao, Tommaso.'

'Ciao for now, Laura.'

'Seafood,' Tommaso hissed.

'What?' Bruno said. He was busy making a series of tiny meringues stuffed with soft chestnut paste and hard nuggets of chopped fresh pistachio.

'Next time, we'll give Laura *frutti di mare*.' Tommaso, who was in the middle of service, pushed a pile of dirty bowls into the sink and dashed back to the pass, where a neat line of plated dishes waited to be carried into the restaurant. 'First, it will make her horny, and second, once she's had a few oysters in her mouth she's hardly likely to object to playing trombone with my *belino* for dessert,' he called gleefully as he spun out of the kitchen doors into the restaurant, a tray held over his head in one hand like the swirl of a matador's cape.

Bruno opened his mouth. He wanted to point out that the art of culinary seduction required a little more subtlety than that, but his friend had already gone.

Although the centre of Rome is only twelve miles from the sea, the excitements of the city have always tended to distract its inhabitants from the pleasures of the coast. Eels from the Tiber are a traditional Roman delicacy – pan-cooked with soft onions, garlic, chilli, tomatoes and white wine – but a much more common dish is *baccalà*, preserved salt-cured cod, which is fried in thin strips, then simmered in a tomato sauce flavoured with anchovies, pine nuts and raisins. For really good, fresh fish you are better off heading either up or down the coast, towards Civitavecchia to the north or Gaeta to the south.

'I don't understand,' Tommaso said when Bruno explained all this to him the next day. 'Am I meant to go all the way to Civitavecchia just to bring back some fish?'

'I thought perhaps, instead of bringing the seafood to Laura, you could take Laura to the seafood,' Bruno suggested.

Tommaso's brow furrowed. 'No, I still don't get it. How will that work?'

'You could borrow Gennaro's van and drive her to the sea. You could even do some surfing, if you go far enough. Then you just build a charcoal grill on the beach.'

Tommaso looked a little shifty. 'But that will mean I have to cook.'

'Yes, but grilled fish?'

'My grilled fish,' Tommaso said sadly, 'won't be as good as *your* grilled fish. You have to come too.' He brightened. 'I know. I'll pretend to be giving you instructions, so it'll look as though you're preparing the fish under my guidance.' Tommaso nodded enthusiastically. He rather liked the idea of talking to Bruno like a chef. After all, he'd watched enough of them over the years, giving their underlings hell. 'And, ah, afterwards . . . well, you'll just have to go for a walk or something.'

'I'm not sure—' Bruno began.

'I like it,' Tommaso said. 'We'll have a romantic day at the seaside, just the three of us. Well, two of us. Well, three. You know what I mean.'

Bruno opened his mouth to protest. The thought of playing gooseberry for a whole day when he could be back in his kitchen, working on new recipes, didn't appeal at all.

'Oh, come on,' Tomasso said impatiently. 'What else are you doing this weekend? Nothing. Besides, Laura's got a roommate, another American. Apparently she's as hot as hell. I'll get her to come along too. It'll be a double date. You just have to remember to pretend that I'm the one who can cook. How big a deal is that?'

There were two very good reasons why Bruno agreed to go to the sea with Tommaso, and neither had anything to do with the chance of a double date.

Years ago, when he had first come to Rome, he had been forced to take the only restaurant job open to someone without any qualifications: a waiter. He had been terrible at it. Distracted by the food that was coming out of the kitchen, he had forgotten which table was which and even mixed up the bills. Only the quick-thinking of another young waiter, who saw what was going on and intervened to sort the problems out before anyone noticed, prevented him from being fired on his first day. That waiter was Tommaso. Taking Bruno under his wing, Tommaso taught him the rudiments of the job and covered for him when Bruno drifted off into one of his frequent culinary-inspired daydreams. He showed Bruno how to steal tips instead of sharing them with the maître d'; how to magic half-full bottles of wine and spirits away at the end of the shift; and how to pocket enough food from the kitchen to keep from being hungry on their rare days off. In return, Bruno had cooked the stolen food for them both. Tommaso only needed to take one mouthful to realise his new friend had talent. It was Tommaso who pushed Bruno into attending catering school to get the all-important qualifications, Tommaso who made sure he kept getting a share of the tips while he was studying, Tommaso who let him stay in his apartment and cook instead of paying rent. By the time Bruno had graduated – he easily came top of his year – Tommaso was still a junior waiter, happily wasting his time flirting with pretty foreign guests. But

Tommaso was as loyal to his friends as he was fickle to his women. He knew through his network of contacts where the best job openings were, and he always made sure that Bruno was working in the best place. Bruno owed Tommaso a great deal, and he found it very hard to refuse him anything.

The second reason was even simpler. He rarely got a chance to cook really good fish.

On the other side of the city, Umberto Erfolini, the Italian who had been forcibly ejected from Templi, paid a visit to an impressive house in a quiet suburb. He walked into the entrance hall and stopped so that the two large men who waited there could pat him down before they nodded him forward towards the study.

In the study, the man in the chair put down his cigar and stood up. Umberto, who was himself only five foot eight, towered over him. 'Umberto. My old friend,' the other man said, reaching up to kiss Umberto on both cheeks, 'how are you? And how is my beautiful goddaughter?'

'Federica's well, Teo. Well, but a little upset.'

'Upset?' Teodoro asked, an expression of concern flitting across his face. 'Why?'

'I took her to a restaurant to celebrate her twenty-first birthday, a fancy foreign place. I know,' he shrugged, 'what was I thinking of? But I thought it would be an interesting experience for us. It was a restaurant called Templi, up in Montespaccato.'

'And?' Teodoro prompted gently.

'Well, it *was* an experience. But a humiliating one.'

As Umberto explained, the expression on the other man's face darkened. 'Truly, Umberto, this does require our attention, and I want to thank you for bringing it to my notice. But be patient. *Si pigliano piu mosche in una gocciola di miele che in un barile d'aceto*.*'

---

*'You'll catch more flies in a drop of honey than in a barrel of vinegar.'

Six

They had agreed to meet at Gennaro's before setting off. This was partly because it was necessary to fortify themselves for the trip with several coffees and a croissant or two, but also because Gennaro had removed the fuel pump from the old van's engine to see if it would improve the performance of his Gaggia, and they had to wait while it was returned to the vehicle.

It was the football season, and all of Rome seemed to be wearing either the yellow and purple colours of Roma or the blue and white of Lazio. The fans, or *tifosi* – the name means, literally, those afflicted by typhus – had festooned their team's colours from every car window and balcony. In Gennaro's bar there was much hilarity because Sisto had lost a bet with Vincent and, as a penalty, had been forced to wear the colours of the hated *Romanisti* for a day.

'What he doesn't know is that I've got the Lazio strip on underneath,' Sisto confided to Bruno. 'As soon as we get near the ground I'm going to take these damn things off and burn them, bet or no bet.'

Bruno wasn't listening. He had just seen two girls walking down the street towards them. They were carrying backpacks and rolled-up towels, and each of them was holding a bottle of water. They were dressed, in fact, for a day at the beach. One of them was a typical Tommaso girl – pretty, curvaceous and tanned, with a mass of dyed blonde hair and a small tattoo. And the other – he simply couldn't believe it – was *the* girl, the girl with the freckled shoulders he had seen so many times around Trastevere. His whole body quivered like a plucked string.

'Ah,' said Tommaso. 'Excellent. Here are the girls.'

The two girls were pointing at the van, and then they were coming into the bar. Bruno wanted to kiss his friend. For once everything had worked out perfectly. He would be spending the whole day with her at the beach! That was even better than talking to her at the market.

His exultation was quickly followed by a spasm of terror. What if she didn't like him or, worse still, what if he was so tongue-tied that he never got the chance to impress her? But then he relaxed. He would be cooking, and that meant he wouldn't get nervous – he was never nervous when he cooked.

The two girls had come into the bar by now, in a flurry of *buongiorno*'s. Vincent and Sisto were staring open-mouthed at Tommaso's girl. Bruno, his heart pounding, waited to be introduced to her roommate.

Sisto quickly pulled off his Roma shirt, revealing the blue and white of Lazio underneath. 'There are limits,' he whispered to Bruno. 'My God but you're a lucky bastard.'

'I know,' Bruno said. He still couldn't believe it himself.

'I mean, Tommaso's girl is all right, but she's nothing compared to what you've landed yourself.'

'Bruno, this is Laura,' Tommaso said as he did the introductions. 'Laura, Bruno; Judith, Bruno.'

'Hello, Laura,' Bruno said. Then he turned towards his girl, holding out his hand with an awkward smile on his face. He wondered if she would remember him from the market. 'Hello, Judith,' he said softly.

The girl laughed. 'No. I'm Laura. *She*'s Judith.' She pointed at the girl with the tattoo.

'Hey, Bruno,' the other girl said. 'Nice to meet you.'

Bruno was still staring at the first girl. 'You can't be.'

'I can't?'

'I mean—' He desperately tried to salvage the situation. 'Right. So you're Laura. And she's Judith.'

'That's the general idea,' Judith agreed.

'Nice going, Romeo,' Sisto muttered under his breath. He stepped forward and shook Judith's hand himself. 'Hi. I'm Sisto.'

'And you're going out with Tommaso,' Bruno blundered on. 'Well, of course you are. You're Laura. For a second there, I was confused. You see, I've seen you before. In the market. Do you remember?'

'I'm afraid not,' Laura said, looking puzzled.

Bruno stopped, his face burning red. She didn't remember him. He was looking more of an idiot with every word that he said.

'What is *wrong* with you?' Tommaso hissed as they loaded up the van with borrowed surfboards and wetsuits.

Bruno shrugged. Now that the embarrassment had worn off, there was the awful realisation that he was actually helping Tommaso in his seduction of Laura. As they drove out towards the coast, Bruno found himself staring miserably at the floor of the van.

'Sorry,' Laura muttered in Judith's ear. 'He's not a bundle of laughs, I'm afraid, your Bruno.'

'Don't worry. Perhaps he'll perk up later.' The van swayed from side to side as Tommaso swerved exuberantly around a *motorino*. The girls yelled. Bruno, lost in thought, seemed not to notice.

⊚⊚

Judith was telling the story of their wedding rings.

'There was a girl in the class who said that if we wanted to avoid getting hassled we should buy ourselves some wedding rings,' she explained. 'So Laura and I found this little jewellery shop, just over the river, and tried to explain what we wanted. Only our Italian wasn't very good at that point, and we found ourselves asking for *circonvallazione*.'

'Which, of course, means ring roads, not wedding rings,' Laura said. 'Though we didn't know that at the time. I had a dictionary, and I found that *Buci di orecchini* means earring, so I told her to try *buci*—'

'*Due buci*,' Judith said. 'By this time I was sort of gesticulating with my fingers, miming putting on a wedding ring—'

'A gesture that turned out to be open to misinterpretation—'

'As we realised when we discovered that *buci* actually means hole or piercing—'

'But we were so relieved when he seemed to understand us that we followed him downstairs to this sort of cellar. And it was only when he told us to get undressed that we realised he thought we wanted piercings—'

'In an intimate part of our anatomies,' Judith finished. Tommaso roared with laughter, and even Bruno managed to smile.

'So Laura chickened out and I had to go ahead on my own,' Judith added. Tommaso's eyes widened thoughtfully.

Bruno and Judith ended up playing Bohnanza, the bean-trading game, on the table in the back of the van while Laura read a book on art history. Bruno suddenly realised that he was having too good a time to feel jealous of Tommaso. And when, during one of Tommaso's more spectacular swerves, Laura gasped and grabbed on to his arm for support, Bruno felt a great surge of happiness. *What does it matter if I can't have her?* he thought. *At least I can be with her. At least I can cook her a meal she'll never forget.*

☙❧

They parked on a long strand of beach just below the harbour at Santa Marinella, unloaded the boards and ran straight into the water. The others were still in the sea an hour or so later when Bruno came out to begin the preparations for supper. First he made a firepit on the beach, which he filled with charcoal and aromatic vine prunings from a sack he had brought with him in the van. Then he went in search of the menu.

On the harbour front there was a long, low wooden building, unprepossessing from the outside, its function given away only by the rows of fishing boats tied up next to it, their decks still littered with glittering nuggets of ice, discarded crab shells, rolled-up nets and other fishing paraphernalia. On the other side of the building the surface of the road was coated by an iridescent sheen of fish scales where each day's catch was loaded into vans. In the shade, an ancient fisherman sat and worked his way methodically through a pile of *totani* – red squid – beating each one with a wooden club to tenderise it.

Bruno's heart quickened as he stepped inside. *Now this is a fish market*, he thought to himself.

It took his eyes a moment to adjust from the brilliant maritime sunshine to the gloomy interior. Piles of fish rose on either side of him in the half-darkness and the pungent stink of fish guts assaulted his nostrils. On his left hung a whole tuna, its side notched to the spine to show the quality of the flesh. On his right, a pile of huge *pesce spada*, swordfish, lay tumbled together in a crate, their swords protruding lethally to catch the legs of unwary passers-by. And on a long marble slab in front of him, on a heap of crushed ice dotted here and there with bright yellow lemons, were the shellfish and smaller fry. There were *riccio di mare* – sea urchins – in abundance, and oysters too, but there were also more exotic delicacies – *polpi*, octopus; *arogosti*, clawless crayfish; *datteri di mare*, sea dates; and *granchi*, soft-shelled spider crabs, still alive and kept in a bucket to prevent them from making their escape. Bruno also recognised *tartufo di mare*, the so-called sea truffle,

73

and, right at the back, an even greater prize: a heap of gleaming *cicale*.

Cicale are a cross between a small lobster and a large prawn, with long front claws. Traditionally they are eaten on the harbour front, fresh from the boat. First their backs are split open. Then they are marinated for an hour or so in olive oil, breadcrumbs, salt and plenty of black pepper, before being grilled over very hot embers. When you have pulled them from the embers with your fingers, you must spread the charred butterfly-shaped shell open and suck in the meat *'col bacio'* – 'with a kiss' – leaving you with a glistening moustache of smoky olive oil, greasy fingers and a tingling tongue from licking the last peppery crevices of the shell.

Bruno asked politely if he could handle some of the produce. The old man in charge of the display waved him on. He would have expected nothing less. Bruno raised a *cicalea* to his nose and sniffed. It smelled of ozone, seaweed, saltwater and that indefinable reek of ocean coldness that flavours all the freshest seafood. He nodded. It was perfect.

Bruno bought a sea bass, as many *cicale* as he could afford, some oysters, a few *tartufi*, some clams, a double handful of spider crabs and one of the squid he had seen the fisherman beating outside. He watched as the old man slashed the squid with his knife, just once, then jerked the sac away from the tentacles. Another movement of the knife and the long shapeless head was gone. He plucked off the beak with a quick squeeze of his fingers, then rinsed everything under a cold tap, pulling the bone from the sac as he did so. '*Prego*,' he said, handing the various parts to Bruno. '*Buona forchetta*.' The whole procedure had taken him just a few seconds.

Bruno walked back into the sunshine, which was turning redder now that the sun was low in the sky, and wandered down the shoreline to where Gennaro's old van was parked. He had lit the fire before going to buy the fish; a plume of glassy smoke crackled from the firepit. The others were still in the sea. He stood for a moment, gazing at Laura, her sleek figure outlined in a wet-suit as she clambered over the waves with her board. As he watched he saw her put an arm around Tommaso and pull him towards her for a kiss. Bruno flinched, and turned his attention back to the meal.

This is for Laura, he told himself. *From me to her, even if she never knows it.*

He spread a tarpaulin, found a stone to use as a chopping board and set to work. He had brought garlic, courgettes, fennel and potatoes with him from Rome, and now he busied himself peeling and chopping. After a few moments his mind went blank and he drifted into the semi-automatic trance that cooking always seemed to induce in him, looking up only when the long shadows of the others fell across what he was doing.

'Ah, Tommaso, you're here. It's nearly ready for you to start cooking,' he said respectfully.

Laura squatted down next to Bruno to look at his haul. 'It's all so beautiful,' she breathed, picking up a clam shell in which red shaded through to orange, like a sunset.

Bruno glanced at her hair; wet, tangled from the sea and crusted with salt. Her face, too, was daubed with apache-streaks of dried salt under each eye, and the cold of the water had raised the skin of her neck into little bumps where it was exposed above her wetsuit, like the tiny nodules on a sea urchin. He closed his eyes and inhaled. Just for a moment, he could taste her – her skin rinsed with seawater, the salt in her hair . . .

'You haven't washed the squid properly, Bruno,' Tommaso said, tossing the shapeless polyp into his lap. 'You'd better take it down to the water and clean it again.'

The squid, of course, was fine. 'Sure,' Bruno said, getting up.

'What are you cooking us, Tommaso?' Judith asked.

'Sea bass stuffed with shellfish, and a mixed grill of marinated *frutti di mare*,' Tommaso said proudly. 'It's very simple, but I promise you, you'll never have eaten anything like this before. Pass me that knife, would you?'

Bruno had spent an hour or so back at the apartment teaching Tommaso how to open clams. By the time he returned from the sea with the squid Tommaso was in full flow, explaining how he had been preparing this recipe since he was a child, giving orders, tossing shells in all directions, and generally making an exhibition of himself while Bruno quietly got on with the real work.

'*Ueh*, Bruno, you need to put some more flavours in that fish. Chop some garlic, would you?'

'Certainly.' The garlic was for the potatoes, not the fish, which would be annihilated by its pungent flavour. Bruno made a show of smashing some garlic on a stone, then quietly put it to one side. His hands twitched helplessly as he watched Tommaso clumsily stuffing the shellfish into the sea bass. Even worse, he saw that Laura was watching Tommaso, apparently transfixed by what he was doing. He felt a brief, terrible stab of jealousy.

'Now we simply put the fish in the dish . . .' Tommaso was saying. Bruno quickly passed him the bottle of wine, a cold, white Orvieto.

'Thank you, my friend,' Tommaso said, taking a long swig.

'The fish,' Bruno muttered. 'It's for the fish.'

'And the fish needs a drink too,' Tommaso said smoothly, upending the bottle into the fish's jaws.

Several more times Bruno had to intercede surreptitiously as a flame got too high, or a piece of skin was left unoiled, but by and large – somewhat to his surprise – Tommaso talked a good game as a chef.

When at last it was time to eat, Bruno watched Laura intently as she pulled the shellfish apart, cramming them into her mouth with noisy expressions of delight, the buttery juices running down her chin, giving her skin a glossy sheen in the fading light. He loved the way she ate: without inhibition or guilt, sucking the oil off her fingers with gusto, revelling in every new taste and unfamiliar flavour. He had seen so many elegant women at Templi picking delicately at their food as if it was something dangerous, pushing it around their plates or fussily cutting it into dozens of pieces before leaving half of it untouched. Laura ate with genuine pleasure, and the pleasure she felt was echoed in his own heart.

'You eat like an Italian,' he said to her sincerely.

'Is that good?' she asked with her mouth full.

'*Si*. It's the only way to eat.'

'Actually, I eat like a pig. Always have done. My mother despairs of me.'

'What are the herbs in this, Tommaso?' Judith wanted to know.

'Er,' Tommaso said anxiously, looking at Bruno.

'I can taste fennel and oregano,' Laura said, screwing up her face. 'And something else. Ginger?'

Bruno nodded surreptitiously at Tommaso.

'Well done,' Tommaso declared. 'Fennel, oregano and ginger. Laura, you are exactly right.'

Bruno's heart swelled with pride. There had been only the faintest whisper of ginger in the sea bass. Even a professional chef would have been hard-placed to identify it. Laura's palate was untrained and untutored, but she had the tastebuds of a true aficionado.

When the last *cicala* had been pulled from the embers and devoured, and the discarded shells lay hissing in the fire, Tommaso passed round a joint. As the sun slipped beneath the sea and the sand started to get a little chilly, they pulled the surfboards up to the fire and sat on those. Soon the only light came from the glowing embers. For a long time nobody spoke. In the cab of the van, even Tommaso's Blue Oyster Cult compilation was finally, mercifully, reduced to tape-hiss and silence.

Laura leaned back against Tommaso. 'I'm stuffed,' she said dreamily.

'*Sono pieno come un uovo*,' Bruno murmured.

She smiled at him. For a moment his eyes smiled back, then his gaze slid away shyly. 'What does that mean?' she asked.

'It means "I'm as full as an egg."'

'Italian is such a beautiful language.'

'American sounds pretty good too.' He wanted to add, 'when *you* speak it', but he couldn't. Tommaso could say it – not just because she was his girlfriend: Tommaso could pay anyone a compliment and make it sound, if not sincere, then at least charming and funny. Only if he, Bruno, said it would it sound like a corny, desperate pick-up line.

'*Sono pieno come un uovo*,' Laura repeated.

'Hey, Laura,' Tommaso said. 'Tell Bruno what your first Italian date told you to say to anyone who got fresh with you.'

'Well,' she said, considering, 'there was "*Cacati in mano e prenditi a schiaffi*."'

Tommaso laughed uproariously. 'Take a shit on your hands and then smack your own face,' he translated. 'What else?'

'Uh – "*Lei e' un cafone stronzo, vada via in culo*."'

'Excellent. "You're a piece of shit, so get back up your own arse." We'll make a Roman of you yet. Any more?'

'"*Guardone ti sorella e allupato ti bagnasti*."'

'That's harder to translate,' Tommaso said, shaking his head. 'It's something like: "It turns you on to watch your sister and me." But there's no English word for *guardone*. It's like voyeur, but stronger. Someone who's afraid to fuck, so he watches other people.'

Bruno felt an awful moment of self-disgust. *That's me*, he thought. *A watcher*.

'I was sure I was being polite,' Laura said. 'It sounded so beautiful.'

'What do you mean? It *is* beautiful, and it is polite – for a Roman.' Tommaso put his arm around her shoulder. It was the signal Bruno had been waiting for.

78

'I'm going for a walk.' He got to his feet, his heart heavy.

'I'll come with you,' Judith said quickly. She reached out a hand to him. 'Pull me up?'

As Bruno pulled her upright, Judith came a little further into his arms than he had been expecting. He suddenly realised that, while he had been thinking about Laura, her roommate had evidently been considering the possibility of a romantic encounter with him. He glanced at Tommaso for support but his friend was already entwined with Laura, their lips glued together.

'OK, let's walk over there,' he said. He looked down at the lovers. 'I expect we'll be gone some time,' he added reluctantly.

This is perfect, Laura thought. *I'm on a deserted beach with my beautiful Roman lover, who has just cooked me the most amazing seafood I have ever tasted. What more could I want?* They were far enough away from the road not to be seen, and in any case they would only be two silhouettes against a fire, so she made no protest as Tommaso's lips worked their way down her body.

Soon after they had left the others, Judith put her arm through Bruno's. *She's waiting for me to kiss her*, he thought awkwardly. They reached the water's edge and she leaned into him meaningfully.

'Judith,' he began apologetically, 'there's something I should tell you.'

'What?'

'Well – there's someone else.'

'A girlfriend?'

'Not exactly.'

'A boyfriend?'

'No, no, not that.'

'What then?'

'The usual thing. Just a girl who isn't in love with me.'

Judith thought about this. 'Well, there's not much point in

being faithful to her if she isn't in love with you,' she pointed out.

'I know, but – I can't help thinking about her.'

'Suit yourself. But I need to cool down,' she said decisively. 'I'm going to swim. Want to come?'

'Why not?' As they plunged together into the creamy white spume, he called, 'Now surf!'

'But the boards are back at the van.'

'Who needs a board?' He waited for a wave, then threw himself into it, letting it carry him towards the beach.

The first half-dozen waves they tried took them head over heels and they went under, spluttering. But it was exhilarating, and as soon as they found their feet they waded out again for more.

At last, just when Laura couldn't bear for Tommaso to delay any longer, he slipped his tongue into her, spreading her like a *cicala*, sucking the sweet flesh into his mouth. 'Oh, Tommaso,' she whispered, 'that's fantastic.' He swivelled round, working his tongue deeper, and she felt the first small ripples of gathering pleasure. *It's like lying on a surfboard*, she thought dreamily; *waiting for the right wave to come along and lift you up*. She breathed more deeply, willing it to happen.

Eventually they all piled into the van for the long drive back. Unfortunately Tommaso's driving, while perfectly adapted to weaving a scooter in and out of endless Roman traffic, was hardly conducive to sleep. It was all right for the girls in the back: they couldn't see the other road users, though some of their insults and the blare of their horns must surely have permeated even the deepest dream. Bruno stared out at the darkness. In his imagination he was cooking meals for Laura, presenting her with dish after dish, simply for the pleasure of watching her eat.

He longed to educate her palate. She had so enjoyed the unfamiliar tastes of the seafood that he began to dream of all the other things he might introduce her to. No one knew better than he that to enjoy a new flavour was to be changed by it for ever. But what should he cook her?

As a particularly exuberant piece of road-skating threw them all from side to side, Laura stirred. Bruno couldn't help himself. He turned round to look at her. She lay curled up against her room-mate on the back seat, the two of them wrapped in Bruno's sleeping bag. His heart lurched as erratically as the van itself had just done.

For you, he thought, *I would cook such a wedding cake . . .*

He shook his head to clear the thought away. She was Tommaso's girl, not his. What was he thinking?

Bruno suddenly realised that Judith's eyes were open. She was watching him even as he watched Laura. He quickly looked away, wondering if it was now obvious that it was her friend he'd been talking about, and if so, whether she'd say anything.

At last they were back in Rome, making their way through Testaccio, the old meat-selling district. Many of the warehouses here had been turned into clubs and bars: this was the one part of the city that never slept, and more than once they had to slow down as groups of people spilled across the street, moving from one club to another.

'Look at that,' Tommaso said as they passed a new bar. 'We've got to try that place.'

Bruno grunted. Even quite recently, this area had been full of slaughterhouses and butchers. Now the meat men were being forced out.

As far as he was concerned it was Testaccio, not the Via del Corso or the Piazza del Campidoglio, that was the real heart of Rome. For centuries animals had been brought here to be butchered, with the good cuts going to the noblemen in their palazzos and the cardinals in the Vatican. The ordinary people had had to make do with what little was left – the so-called *quinto quarto*, the 'fifth quarter' of the animal: the organs, head, feet and tail. Little *osterie* had sprung up which specialised in cooking these rejects, and such was the culinary inventiveness of the Romans that soon even cardinals and noblemen were clamouring for dishes like *coda alla vaccinara*, oxtail braised in tomato sauce, or *caratella d'abbacchio* – a newborn lamb's heart, lungs and spleen skewered on a stick of rosemary and simmered with onions in white wine.

Every part of an animal's body had its traditional method of preparation. *Zampetti all' aggro* were calf's feet served with a green sauce made from anchovies, capers, sweet onions, pickled gherkins and garlic, finely chopped, then bound with potato and thinned with oil and vinegar. Brains were cooked with butter and lemon – *cervello al limone* – or poached with vegetables, allowed to cool, then thinly sliced and fried in an egg batter. Liver was wrapped in a caul, the soft membrane that envelops a pig's intestines, which naturally bastes the meat as it melts slowly in the frying pan. There was one recipe for the thymus, another for the ear, another for the intestines, and another for the tongue; each dish refined over centuries and enjoyed by everyone, from the infant in his high chair to the *nonnina* – the grandmother who would have been served exactly the same meal, prepared in the same way, when she herself was a child.

It was known that foreigners did not always share the Roman's love of the *quinto quarto*. Even a Neapolitan, for example, could become a little squeamish when faced with some particularly obscure byway of the gut or stomach, or a quickly seared kidney with its sharp aftertaste of *piscia*. Bruno thought that Laura, however, might be different. There was something about her that seemed ready for new things, for adventures. And if she did have any culinary inhibitions left, his dishes would smooth them away, luring her with smell and texture and taste on a journey of the senses, step by step; an adventure into the entrails of Rome itself.

For his first dinner he had cooked her the countryside. For his

82

second he had cooked her the sea. For his third, he decided, he would cook her the city – the rich, dark, intense, blood-soaked city, in all its pungent history. If he was right, it would awaken something in her. If he wasn't – well, at least he would have cooked her a real Roman meal.

Seven

As they walked to their first lecture of the day, Judith told Laura about Bruno's curious behaviour on the beach.

'So he basically said that he was too much in love with this mystery woman to fool around with me,' she explained.

'Ahh. That's so romantic.'

'Just my luck. I thought Italian men were supposed to be fickle, faithless horndogs, and I get one who doesn't want to play.'

'I didn't realise you liked him that much.'

'After a meal that good, I would have done it with the Pope,' Judith said, with some feeling.

Laura's dirty laugh caused a cat, sleeping on the seat of a nearby scooter in the sunlight, to raise its head, startled for a moment. Then, seeing that it was only two girls animatedly discussing a boy, it settled back to sleep.

Bruno was building a house of cards. Or so it felt. In fact he was cooking a fruit *millefeuille* – layers of delicate pastry leaves, crushed fruit and cream. This being Templi, however, the dish had been adapted by Alain so that it was a bravura display of technical virtuosity. First, the layers of pastry were cooked between heavy weights to make them flaky and crisp. Then they were sprinkled with icing sugar and caramelised with a blowtorch. Between each of the three layers was a filling of the lightest, most delicate fruit soufflé. Because it looked exactly like pastry cream, the diner would only realise it was a soufflé when he took a mouthful. But there were a frightening number of things that could go wrong with this concoction. Each soufflé had to rise with a smooth, hydraulic motion, lifting its delicate ceiling of caramelised pastry without tilting it, so that it could provide a level floor for the next layer up. The slightest sticking or swelling would mean that the whole assembly would lean sideways like the tower of Pisa. Again, each soufflé had to be just a little smaller than the one below, so that the weight of the top layers did not crush those underneath. And finally, the very top layer had to accept a spoonful of *coulis* without breaking or sagging.

There was always a certain amount of wastage, and Bruno habitually cooked more than had been ordered, just in case one didn't turn out right. Dishes like this couldn't be made in advance. Each soufflé spent just seven minutes in the oven, and had to be served within three or four minutes of being cooked, before the mixture started to sag. Coordinating this with the orders of a whole table of diners, some of whom might have ordered lengthy oven-baked dishes such as *tartes fines aux pommes*, was a logistical nightmare.

Bruno had taken an order for two *millefeuille* and as usual had cooked three, just in case. He had not been thinking about pastry, though. In some part of his mind he was thinking about offal – about dark, sticky sauces of braised calves' liver; about combinations of mushrooms and kidneys, sweetbreads and artichokes; turning over and over in his mind the various possibilities of his next meal for Laura. Back in the real world, his timing faltered. Two of the soufflés collapsed and he was obliged to halt the delivery of the dishes to the table while he started again from scratch.

To save time, he didn't make a spare. His arm went numb as he frantically folded the sieved fruit into the egg white, which meant that he couldn't tell from feel alone whether it was just stiff enough to produce the light, airy consistency Alain required. There was no time to wait and check. He eased the second batch of soufflés into the oven and turned immediately to make the *coulis*.

A few moments later there was a faint popping sound from the oven as an air bubble in one of his imperfectly folded soufflés exploded, sending shreds of half-cooked egg mixture in all directions.

'*Un ce pozzo credere,*' Bruno cursed. On the other side of the kitchen, Alain raised his head. Knowing he was now being watched made it even harder for Bruno. He also knew that there was no way Alain would allow the one soufflé that hadn't exploded to go out – it would be past its best by the time the other one was ready. He started again from the beginning on two more soufflés. Sweat was trickling down the small of his back as he whipped and folded and sieved. Eventually the replacements were ready, and this time he was lucky. They weren't the best *mille-feuille* he had ever made, but they were acceptable – or so he thought. When he finally carried them, with shaking hands, over to the pass, he had to suffer the humiliation of having the *sous-chef* inspect them, wordlessly, for several long moments, as if Bruno were a *commis* on his first job. To make matters worse, Alain himself came over to take a look. For another agonising moment both the *chef de cuisine* and the *sous* peered at his dessert like doctors examining an open wound. Then Alain glanced at the clock, and Bruno's cheeks flushed with shame. Alain was communicating to the whole kitchen, as clearly as if he had said it aloud, that he would have liked to redo the dishes completely but Bruno had taken up so much time that it was not possible. At last he nodded reluctantly, and the waiter quickly placed the substandard dishes on to a tray.

A subtle shift had taken place in the pecking order of the kitchen. Bruno could sense it. He hadn't thought he cared about being Alain's favourite, but he realised now that was only because he was so accustomed to it. He saw that, in fact, Alain's approval could come and go as quickly as the heat on a hob, and that most of the young chefs had to compete desperately for their share. There was only one person whose work Alain seemed consistently pleased with: Hugo Kass, the newly appointed *saucier*. A handsome young Frenchman with a sleek mane of floppy black hair, Hugo had worked under Ducasse in France and Beck in Italy before coming to Templi. He was only twenty-two years old and already people were talking about him as a future Michelin winner. Alain treated Hugo almost as an equal, and once that afternoon even asked his advice on a marinade, holding up a spoon for the younger man to taste. Bruno was too far away to hear what Hugo said, but he saw Alain nod vigorously as if he agreed with him.

Bruno also began to notice just how hard the young Frenchman worked at keeping Alain's favour. As a new *chef de partie*, for example, he had the perfect reason to quiz the *chef de cuisine* about the dishes he was cooking – but not, perhaps, to make quite so many flattering remarks in response as he seemed to be doing now.

'Hey, Bruno. How's it going?' That was Tommaso, finished now for the afternoon.

'Terrible,' Bruno muttered. Tommaso followed his gaze to where Hugo Kass was once again tasting one of the maestro's signature dishes appreciatively.

'He's so far up chef's *culo* I'm surprised he can taste anything except *cacca*,' Tommaso commented. Bruno laughed. However bad things were, he could always rely on his friend to come up with a suitably Roman response.

Laura, sitting in Dr Fellowes' seminar room, hums to herself as she writes notes about *torsione* and *contraposto*. On the whiteboard there is a large projection of a Michelangelo drawing, a male nude. His elegant buttocks flit across Dr Fellowes' equally elegant face as *il dottore* paces back and forth, explaining in clear, well-rounded sentences the nobility of the ideals that lie behind them.

On her notepad, Laura doodles buttocks. Her humming becomes audible, until her neighbour gives her a surreptitious nudge.

The hush of the restaurant was broken suddenly by a loud crash. In the kitchen, everyone jumped. There was the sound of shouting from the direction of the dining room. Then the doors to the kitchen slammed open and one of the waiters ran in shouting, 'Come quickly!'

The kitchen emptied as the staff went to see what was going on. It seemed that a delivery man had been carrying a box of fresh eels through the foyer when the bottom of the box had burst open. About half a dozen eels were now zig-zagging like silvery lightning across the deep-pile carpet of the restaurant in desperate search of freedom.

Franciscus clicked his fingers as he snapped out orders. 'Pieter, Stephanie: move the customers to the bar. The rest of you, deal with this.' But it was easier said than done. The eels were Roman mud-eels – small, agile and determined – and the staff were hampered by having to crouch down at carpet level to apprehend them. Again and again there was a yell of triumph, followed by a curse as the slippery *anguilli* wriggled through someone's fingers. The customers, ushered to the bar and initially distracted by glasses of free Dom Perignon, were soon crowding back into the restaurant with their glasses in their hands; offering advice, cheering a successful catch or groaning with disappointment as yet another eel slipped through its captor's grasp. It took five minutes before two eels were back in the box, and another five before the next one joined it. The staff, exhausted, paused for a rest.

Tommaso nudged Bruno. 'Where's the delivery man gone?' he muttered in an undertone.

Bruno looked around. It was true that whoever had caused the mayhem had disappeared.

'And how come he didn't bring them to the kitchen door?' Tommaso continued. 'Everyone who delivers to Templi knows to use the kitchen entrance. There's something strange about this.'

'You two,' Franciscus snapped. 'Talk later, when you've caught them all.'

Obediently, Tommaso went and prodded an eel from under the table where it had taken refuge, only for it to slither beneath a nearby chair before he could grab it.

As the free champagne did its work, the diners' sympathies began to side with the escapees. They started applauding ironically each time the eels managed to wriggle out of their captors' grasp. Alain stood watching from the side, his face like thunder.

It was Hugo who eventually broke the stalemate. He turned on his heel, went into the kitchen and returned a few moments later with two huge knives, one in each hand. They were steel Sabatiers as long as icicles, each ending in a lethally sharp point. He advanced on one of the eels and, rather than trying to catch it, simply stabbed it behind the head with the point of his knife, spearing it on the steel blade.

The watchers fell silent. Without pausing to remove the *anguilla* from his knife, where it thrashed around in a writhing treble-clef, Hugo moved on. Again the point of the knife stabbed down. Now there were two eels wriggling and twisting on the bloody blade. A third eel was making a break for freedom across the floor. Calmly, Hugo took three paces towards it and, crouching down in one fluid movement, speared it behind the gills with his second knife. He turned towards the next, and moments later the fourth and final eel joined the others on his knife. Without a word he went back into the kitchen. As the doors closed the sound of blade snicking on blade could clearly be heard, followed by the quiet thump of eel pieces falling to the floor.

'Back to your places, all of you,' Alain ordered. 'And thank God someone around here has some sense.'

When the kitchen brigade returned to their stations, the eels were gone and Hugo was calmly preparing sauces.

It was Tommaso, clearing away the broken box from which the eels had escaped, who found the words written on the side: 'Be careful who you throw out of your restaurant. They may have slippery friends.'

Finally it was Bruno's day off and he could go in search of ingredients for his next feast. The *mattatoio*, the old municipal slaughterhouse in Testaccio, was long closed, turned into stabling for the horses that pulled tourists around the city in little traps, but there were still several smaller places nearby which took delivery of carcasses and butchered them on site; as the saying went, throwing away nothing but the bleat. One of these was Elodi, a butcher's shop hollowed out of the base of Monte Testaccio – which was itself not a hill at all but an ancient rubbish mound some thirty-five metres high that dated back to Roman times, formed from an orderly heap of broken amphorae, the terracotta jars in which the ancient Romans transported olive oil. Around the base of this centuries-old bottle bank various motor repair shops, butchers and even restaurants had excavated long, windowless caverns with arched roofs. Elodi was gloomy, and the sawdust on the floor was spotted with dark pools of blood, but the quality of the meat was known to be second to none.

Bruno spent twenty minutes talking to the owner, Iaco. With offal, you were working on trust, and the consequences of being sold some dubious meat were far worse than with ordinary cuts. He let the other man know he was a chef, and discussed various recipes with him until the butcher was as excited as Bruno himself about the meal Bruno was preparing. Iaco went into the back and

90

returned with his bloody hands full of treasures – the intestines of a baby veal, the brain of a sheep, a pig's tongue, and a whole oxtail, still unskinned, like a rider's whip. From these they made their final selection. The old man impressed upon Bruno that he was not to make the dishes too fanciful. 'Stick to the simple recipes and you won't go wrong,' he insisted. 'Resist the temptation to make them your own. I know you young cooks, you always want to tinker.' With these words ringing in his ears, Bruno took his haul, carefully wrapped up in newspaper, back across the river to Trastevere.

In the event his menu largely reflected the old man's advice. His *antipasto* was the classic Roman *fritto misto* – tiny morsels of mixed offal, including slivers of poached brains and liver, along with snails, artichokes, apples, pears, and bread dipped in milk, all deep-fried in a crisp egg-and-breadcrumb batter. This was to be followed by a *primo* of *rigatoni alla pajata* – pasta served with the intestines of a baby calf so young they were still full of its mother's milk, simmered with onions, white wine, tomatoes, cloves and garlic. For the *secondo* they would be having *milza in umido* – a stewed lamb's spleen cooked with sage, anchovies, and pepper. A bitter salad of *puntarelle al' acciuga* – chicory sprouts with anchovy – would cleanse the palate, to be followed by a simple *dolce* of *fragole in aceto* – gorella strawberries in vinegar. To finish the meal off with a theatrical flourish, he had tracked down a tiny amount of *kopi luwak*, a rare coffee bean from Indonesia. Despite what the old man had said, however, he could not resist the occasional twist; substituting an ingredient here and there, or breaking down a sauce into its constituent flavours and deducting anything that wasn't completely essential.

In his heart happiness and sadness were now inextricably mixed together, like the yolk and white of an egg when they are whisked together in an omelette. The pain of not having Laura himself was exactly balanced by the pleasure that it gave him to cook for her, until he no longer knew where the sadness ended and the happiness began.

☙❧

Even before she got to Tommaso's apartment Laura could smell the rich, earthy miasma that wafted down the little street. She stopped, closed her eyes and inhaled deeply. The smell was as complex and pungent as old port, but unmistakably carnivorous. Just for a moment she shuddered. There was something dark about that smell, something almost rank – a musky, feral richness that belied the sweet, inviting top notes of clove and garlic. Her nostrils flared and her mouth watered. Pushing open the door into the courtyard, she hurried up the stairs.

The door to the apartment was opened by Tommaso's roommate. 'Hi,' she said. 'Is Tommaso here?' She smiled at Bruno, whom she liked.

'He's just putting the finishing touches to dinner,' Bruno said. 'Come on in.'

The door to the kitchen was closed and from behind it came the sound of various Romanesco oaths and curses. 'I wouldn't go in there if I were you,' Bruno advised shyly. 'He's a bit obsessive when he's cooking – you know how it is: he likes everything to be exactly perfect.' A crash, and the sound of shattering crockery, served to underline his words.

'I guess it's hard work, following a recipe.'

'Sometimes, yes, but there's much more to being a chef than just assembling ingredients.'

'Really? Like what?'

Bruno hesitated. 'It's like the difference between a pianist and a composer,' he said hesitantly. 'The pianist is creative, certainly, but he is only the mouthpiece of the person who dreamed the tunes into life. To be a cook, it's enough to be a pianist – a performer of other people's ideas. But to be a chef you have to be a composer as well. For example, the recipes you are going to eat tonight are all traditional dishes from old Rome – but if all we do is simply recreate the past, without trying to add to it, it stops being a living tradition and becomes history, something dead. Those dishes were refined over centuries, but only through people trying different things, different combinations, rejecting what didn't work and passing on what did. So we owe it to the chefs of the past to continue doing as they did and experiment, even when we are dealing with the most hallowed traditions.'

Laura nodded, fascinated, and he plunged on, 'Take one of the dishes you will be eating tonight: *fritto misto*. The old butcher who sold me the meat was most insistent that it should be cooked the old way – so brains, for example, are always poached in vegetables, then left to cool before being sliced and deep-fried in batter. But then you think, this batter is not so different to Japanese tempura, and tempura can be served with a sweet chilli and soy dipping sauce, so why not make an Italian version of that, perhaps with balsamic vinegar from Modena instead of soy, and see what happens—' He stopped, suddenly aware that he was getting carried away. Not only was he waving his arms around and becoming overexcited, but he had also completely forgotten that Tommaso was supposed to be the chef. He thought back rapidly. Had he said anything stupid?

But Laura had other concerns. 'Tommaso's cooking me *brains*?' She pulled a face.

'Among many other things that you won't have tasted before,' Bruno said gently. 'Brains, liver, intestine. You just have to trust –' he wanted to say *me*: with an effort he swallowed and went on – 'trust Tommaso. He knows what he's doing, and there is nothing that you won't think is delicious once you've tried it.'

'Like that old saying: "I've never tried it because I don't like it."'

'Exactly. I think you, Laura, may surprise yourself with what you like.'

'Maybe.' Laura felt a little uncomfortable. Bruno was looking at her in a weird way, and his conversation was full of awkward pauses and gaps during which he glanced at her and then shyly moved his gaze away again.

She noticed, though, that when he was talking about food he

wasn't shy at all. Then he looked her straight in the eye, his own eyes blazing with passion. To try to get him back on to the subject, she said, 'So it was you who bought the food, not Tommaso?'

'What?'

'You said an old man sold you the ingredients.'

'Did I?'

Laura gave up. After a minute Bruno mumbled something about going out. He got up and dashed for the door.

There was a triumphant yell from the kitchen. 'Eh, Bruno! Who says a cock can't learn to lay eggs!*' The door opened and Tommaso appeared, holding a salad bowl in both hands at shoulder height as if it were a race winner's cup. '*Puntarelle al' acciuga*, Tommaso-style.' He stopped dead. 'Oh, Laura. I didn't hear you arrive.'

'Bruno let me in.'

'Is he still here?'

'No, he's gone out.'

'Oh. OK.' Tommaso became aware that he was still cradling the salad bowl. 'It's a very difficult salad,' he explained. 'First you have to slice the chicory just so. And the anchovies – the anchovies need chopping too. Salt, pepper, oil . . . it's tricky to get it just right.'

'It doesn't sound all *that* hard. Not compared to some of the other things you've cooked me.'

Tommaso's face took on a serious expression. 'Ah, but in cooking, the simplest things are the hardest. It's a zen thing.'

'Now you sound like Bruno.'

'Bruno? Yes, I call him the philosopher of food. Not that he knows much about it, of course,' Tommaso added quickly. 'But he's picked up the odd bit of knowledge here and there. Crumbs from the master's table.'

---

*From the expression: '*A gallina fa l'ovo e 'o gallo c'abbrucia 'o culo*' – The hen makes the eggs, the cock just strains his asshole.

'Is the master going to give me a kiss?' Laura asked prettily.

Tommaso put the bowl down and kissed her upturned mouth, followed by her neck, her chin, her eyes and the rest of her face. 'Hey, forget supper,' he whispered urgently into her ear as he nuzzled and bit at her earlobe. 'Let's just go to bed instead, hmm?'

'You must be kidding,' Laura breathed. 'It smells fantastic.'

'We can have it later.'

'But I want to see what you've cooked me.'

'It'll keep.'

Tommaso's hands were expertly undoing buttons all over her body. She felt her trousers loosen as the button on her waist was popped. At almost the same time her bra was being undone. For a moment she was in two minds, then she pulled away. 'So will I. Please, Tommaso?'

He accepted the inevitable with a shrug. 'OK. Food first, then we'll go to bed.'

Laura felt a momentary flash of irritation. It wasn't that she didn't want to go to bed with him, just that she didn't want him to assume that she would, or that the meal was just courtship. She opened her mouth to explain, then closed it again. For all his charm, she didn't think Tommaso understood the complications and contradictions of the way her body worked. She wasn't altogether sure she understood them herself.

Once they had started to eat, though, she had to revise her opinion. Anyone who could cook *antipasto* like that – who could put what must have been hours of work into a few delectable mouthfuls of crisp, light batter, each one concealing a single morsel of tender meat or sharp crunchy fruit, each individual flavour as precise and decisive as the sound of different instruments in an orchestra – must surely have depths of complexity and feeling, even if he kept them very well hidden.

'It's like a lucky dip,' Laura sighed happily. 'I just have no idea what I'm putting in my mouth.'

'I'll tell you afterwards.'

She pouted. 'Bruno already told me it included brains.'

'Have you eaten brains before?'

'Once, in an Italian restaurant back home. They were horrible, not like this at all.' She speared another piece of the *fritto misto* with her fork. 'What about this? What is it?'

'That is a sweetbread. A piece of the thymus.'

'And what's a thymus?'

Tommaso had absolutely no idea. 'It's a part of the thyme, which is inside the animal, just here.' He pointed to his chest, somewhat vaguely, with both hands.

'Oh. Well, it's good, anyway. How about this?'

'That, I think, is a *testiculo d'abbacchio*. A lamb's – well, testicle.'

'A testicle? Let's try it.' She put it in her mouth. Tommaso could hear the noise her sharp front teeth made as she chewed it. 'Mmm. It's crunchier than I expected.'

'Yes,' Tommaso said faintly. 'I wasn't sure you'd like it, actually.'

'Oh, it's wonderful,' she assured him. 'Chewy and gloopy at the same time. Are there any more in there?' She stabbed the bowl of *fritto misto* with her fork.

Tommaso put his own fork down. Suddenly he wasn't feeling hungry. 'I'm sure there are. You help yourself while I get the pasta.'

Like most Romans, Tommaso had been brought up eating offal, but for that very reason he had never really stopped to think about it. It was just there, something that was put in front of you by your mother and which you ate appreciatively while talking very loudly across everyone else. He had never considered the origins of the various dishes he had been served. Now, under the glare of Laura's curiosity, he started to do so, with the result that he was soon feeling a little squeamish.

Laura ate everything he put in front of her. What was more, she wanted to know what each new thing was, which part of the animal it came from, what its function was in the body and how it had been prepared. 'It's so illogical,' she was saying. 'Why are people happy to eat a lamb chop, but not a testicle or a kidney? It hardly makes any difference to the lamb. In fact, as far as the lamb's concerned, it would much rather you did eat its testicles or kidneys – I mean, it could survive without one kidney, and without either testicle, but as soon as you decide to slice up its ribcage for chops, it's had it.' She forked another mouthful of *rigatoni alla pajata* on to her plate. 'Aren't you eating? These *pajate* are so creamy, it's like you're suckling the cow yourself.'

Tommaso consoled himself with the thought that Bruno had, at the very least, succeeded in pulverising any shred of inhibition Laura might have had. So long as he could get through dinner, what happened afterwards was going to be fantastic.

Eventually they got to the strawberries, the sweetness of the fruit colliding with the sharp tang of vinegar in an explosive conjunction of flavours. Laura exclaimed softly with pleasure each time she put one in her mouth. 'Oh – oh – *wow* – that's *so* good.'

Tommaso smiled modestly and shrugged. *She hasn't made those noises yet with me*, he thought a little jealously, *only with Bruno's cooking.* Then he stopped himself. It was he, Tommaso, who was going to go to bed with Laura. What did it matter if she liked to put Bruno's food in her mouth first?

'I'll make the coffee,' he said.

When he came back from the kitchen with the little octagonal espresso pot and two tiny cups, Laura had turned the lights down and was lying on the floor, leaning against the sofa. She had kicked off her shoes, and she smiled up at him invitingly. *This is more like it*, he thought. He poured two cups and sat down next to her. She sniffed appreciatively. 'Interesting. What kind of coffee is it?'

'*Kopi luwak*.' He tried to remember what Bruno had told him about it. 'From Indonesia.' He tried some. It had a slightly musty, smoky taste.

'*Kopi luwak* – wow.' Laura took an experimental sip. 'I've heard of this stuff but I never thought I'd actually drink it.'

'No? Why not?'

She looked at his face. 'You do know how it's produced, don't you?' When he didn't say anything, she explained, 'In the coffee plantation, there's a kind of rodent called a *luwak* which eats coffee berries – and because there are so many, it chooses only the very ripest, reddest berries it can find. The coffee bean, which is the seed in the centre of the fruit, passes right though the *luwak* and is excreted. It's considered a great delicacy, and the young men who work in the coffee fields give it to their sweethearts, so it's not usually exported. I love coffee, but I've never come across any of this stuff before.'

Unobtrusively, Tommaso put his cup down. He couldn't believe it. Bruno had given them coffee made from rat crap.

'How about a *distillato*?' he suggested. Anything to take away the taste of that coffee.

'You go ahead.'

He poured himself a *sambuca* and put his arm around her. That was better. She turned her head towards him and leaned in close, her eyes closing as her lips found his.

That damned coffee. He could taste it in her mouth, and behind that a faint ghost-taste of all the other dishes they had eaten that evening. The word 'thymus' popped back into his brain. As her tongue explored his mouth and her teeth nipped at his lower lip, Tommaso found himself wondering exactly where in the body the thymus was. For all he knew, it was the same as a prostate, and a prostate was . . . He closed his own eyes and tried to think of nice, simple things – pizza, meatballs, *spaghetti alla carbonara* . . .

He felt Laura's hand slide inside his trousers and drew in his breath. Now that was more like it. She was doing things with her long, delicate fingers that he certainly hadn't expected. There was no doubt about it, she was a dark horse. He slipped his own hand under her T-shirt and expertly unclipped her bra. She took his hand away for a moment, then pulled her T-shirt over her head for him before going back to what she had been doing.

He peeled her remaining clothes off her, kissing each area of exposed skin. Then she was doing the same to him. He had been right: the meal had shattered any inhibitions she had left. He took a strawberry from the bowl and stroked it down her breasts, before going in with his tongue to lick up the trail of vinegary sweetness it left behind.

A few minutes later Tommaso said, 'Oh.'

'Do you like that?'

'Um – I just didn't know heterosexuals did that.'

Laura laughed, a deep, throaty laugh. 'Then there's a lot of things you don't know yet.'

'Oh,' Tommaso said again. He yelped, and tensed. 'Careful with those, too,' he said anxiously.

She felt strange and wild. Her body was just a collection of organs. She was blood and plumbing, like any other creature, and there was nothing that was forbidden about any of it. She gnawed on Tommaso ravenously, like an animal plundering a carcass, and when she had had enough of that she swung her leg over him, like a rider swinging into a saddle, and galloped.

She was riding naked on a big horse, among a pack of hunting wolves, at night. The flanks of the horse were slippery with foam. She could sense something in the distance, some small animal which was desperately trying to escape the pack, but they were getting closer to it every second. The wolves could sense it, too, and increased their pace. She galloped faster, urging her mount on with little cries and squeezes of her thighs. Closer and closer they got to their quarry. Now there was a jump ahead, a vast wall rushing towards her, but it was too late to stop. She dug her nails in hard and held on for dear life. As she finally took off into the air, she arched her back and shouted. The animal was screaming, too, as the wolves finally caught it and tore it apart, ripping its soft *pajate* open with their sharp teeth, devouring the *coratella* and the bloody bright red heart—

'Are you OK?' Tommaso asked.

'Uh,' she panted.

'Could you perhaps . . . ?' He tapped one of her hands, which were still squeezing his pectorals.

Her fingers were stiff, and as she unclasped them she saw she had left deep claw marks in his skin. 'Oh Tommaso, I'm so sorry. I got carried away.' She climbed off him and, as she cuddled up against him, tried to tell him how amazing it had been, to explain the weird fantasies that had been flitting though her mind just before she came, that incredible sensation of flight. But Tommaso, exhausted, was already asleep.

Eight

Next morning, Bruno walked into the bathroom and stopped short. Laura was crouched by the bathtub, wrapped in a towel, washing her hair. She hadn't heard him come in. The suds had turned her hair into a soapy white meringue. For a moment he stared at her, transfixed. Then he backed away and shut the door, his heart pounding.

Later, when she had gone, he went into Tommaso's room. His friend was printing out some photographs of Laura from his computer.

'Hey, Bruno. The meal was a triumph!'

'That's good,' Bruno said. He looked over his friend's shoulder at the pictures. Something moved deep in his heart, like tectonic plates grinding against each other.

'She's a dark horse, all right,' Tommaso confided. 'Wild as hell once she's been warmed up.' He opened his cupboard door and pinned a photograph of Laura alongside the other pictures. He stood back to admire it. 'What do you think?'

'A worthy addition,' Bruno agreed. 'In fact, she's the prettiest girl in your cupboard.'

'She is, isn't she?' Tommaso agreed enthusiastically, looking at the dozens of photographs. He pointed at one. 'Except maybe for that one. Mädchen, her name was. German. But she was a model.' He sighed. 'You know something tragic, Bruno? There's only one Tommaso in the world, and so many women.'

Laura phoned Carlotta for a serious talk.

'Carlotta,' she began cautiously, 'do you ever have random thoughts pop into your head during sex?'

'Of course. Sometimes I think about shoes, sometimes I think about bracelets. It's generally always accessories though.'

'So you don't ever think about being naked on a big black horse and hunting down a small furry animal with the help of a pack of wolves?'

There was a short silence. 'Uh-uh.'

'Or tearing it apart with your bare teeth and devouring its intestines by moonlight?'

'I think I'd remember that one.'

'Just checking.'

'That must have been some meal he cooked you.'

'Oh, *cara*, it was just amazing.'

As Laura listed the menu, Carlotta clicked her tongue and murmured, '*Yay, yay, yay*,' appreciatively. When Laura had finished she said, 'All that and erotic fantasies as well? I am definitely coming down to Rome next weekend. And you can bet I'll be bringing Andrea with me. It's time he met my parents, anyway.'

Bruno was dismayed to find that Hugo Kass had been assigned to work alongside him on the *patissier*'s station. Even more worryingly, and against all normal etiquette of a three-star kitchen, it had been left vague as to which of them would be in charge. Ostensibly the move was because Alain had been developing some new *dolci*, but Bruno knew that it was really because the chef wanted to play a little mind game with Bruno, to punish him for his recent lack of performance.

It did not take him long to realise that Hugo was intent on seizing any opportunity to demonstrate his own superiority. As the orders came in and were called aloud, it was customary for the underling who was to cook each dish to respond with a crisp, '*Oui*, chef.' Bruno found that an order would barely be out of Karl's mouth before Hugo had claimed it as his own. Hugo even took on orders that required him to work on two dishes simultaneously, while Bruno was left fuming and twiddling his thumbs.

Tommaso, passing on his way to the sink with a tray of dirty dishes, saw what was happening. 'Why aren't you doing anything about this?' he hissed.

'There's nothing I can do,' Bruno hissed back, watching Hugo build an intricate terrine of fruits in layers of alcohol-soaked sponge.

'So? You're better than he is.'

'I'm not so sure,' Bruno said as Hugo's hands danced over the ingredients.

'Do you want to work here or not?'

'Yes, but—'

'Then you need to *levati questo camello dai coglioni**. Your problem, Bruno, is that you're a nice guy. Too nice. If you want something, you have to fight for it.'

'OK, OK. Point taken.'

The next time Karl called out an order, Bruno had rapped out a '*Oui*, chef' before Hugo had even opened his mouth. It was an order for *papillote de banane*. Even in the sophisticated version served at Templi – cooked in a parcel, with strips of vanilla pod and a passion fruit *coulis* – it was a dish Bruno could have cooked to perfection in his sleep. Hugo stood back, his face expressionless, as Bruno brushed some greaseproof paper with egg white.

'Table fourteen, one *tarte fine aux pommes*,' Karl called.

'*Oui*, chef,' Hugo said instantly, turning to his station.

'One *gratin de fruits*—'

*Literally: 'Lift this camel off your balls.'

103

'*Oui*, chef,' Bruno snapped. Even before Karl had finished speaking, he was reaching for the eggs.

A waiter handed another order to Karl, who scanned it quickly and added, 'Table eight, another *gratin*.'

Bruno was about to respond but this time Hugo beat him to it. '*Oui*, chef,' Hugo said quickly, reaching for some eggs himself.

So now they were effectively cooking the same dish, *gratin de fruits*, in parallel. It was a deceptively simple recipe: fresh fruit in a *sabayon* sauce, lightly caramelised. *Sabayon* is simply the sophisticated French cousin of the Italian *zabaione*. The difficulty of the dish came in the way it had to be cooked, which required absolutely precise timing. Fresh egg yolks were whisked in an electric mixer at the highest speed until they had tripled in volume. Meanwhile, rhubarb was cooked with sugar and lemon juice and strained through a sieve to make a syrup. Then the mixer was reduced to its lowest speed and the hot syrup poured drop by drop into the *sabayon*. It was this hot mixture that both cooked the egg yolks and stabilised them. If the syrup hit the cold sides of the bowl it would solidify into thick lumps. If it touched the spinning blades of the mixer it would spit drops of boiling syrup back at the face of the cook.

Like choreographed dancers, the two chefs reached in unison for lemons and halved them. Their knives, as they chopped the rhubarb, were as perfectly synchronised as a drummer's sticks. Each wore an expression of grim determination as they tried, unsuccessfully, to edge ahead of the other. They both squeezed the lemons with two deft twists of the wrist. They both hurled the husks of their juiced lemon into the bin, where the two fruits collided as they fell. They both turned to the big gas stoves at the same moment, and the two coronets of blue flame appeared on both their burners at exactly the same time.

The other chefs had realised by now that something was happening. They watched, surreptitiously at first and then with open-mouthed amazement, as the two young men battled it out.

As he whisked the egg yolks, Bruno plated the *bananes en papillote* with his left hand and slid them down the counter towards a *commis* to go to the pass. Hugo, though, had neglected his *tarte*. With an oath he had to break off from the *sabayon* and lower the heat before the apples burned.

Now Bruno was precious seconds ahead. Calmly he lowered the mixer speed and prepared to add the hot syrup, drop by drop.

'*Soufflé aux fruits de la passion,*' Karl called.

Neither chef responded. Neither wanted the burden of yet another dish to prepare until the battle of the *sabayon* was resolved. There was a long silence, broken only by the hum and descant of the two electric mixers.

'*Soufflé aux fruits,*' the head chef repeated.

Bruno was torn. On the one hand, he didn't want to do the order. On the other, this was his station. It was his responsibility to make sure the customer wasn't kept waiting.

'*Oui*, chef,' he muttered. Opposite him Hugo smiled wolfishly.

Bruno reached for another mixing bowl with his left hand. He poured in equal amounts of passion fruit purée and pastry cream for the soufflé and flicked the second mixer on. Luckily he had kept the egg whites left over from the *sabayon*. Still with his left hand, he started to whisk them in a bowl, at the same time adding a thin trickle of hot syrup to the *sabayon* with his right.

'*A faccia d'o cazzo!**' one of the other chefs breathed. 'A DJ couldn't work those decks better.'

Bruno placed the fruits on a plate, poured the *sabayon* on top and reached for his blowtorch. While his left hand still folded egg white into the soufflé mixture, with his right he began to glaze the surface of his *sabayon* with the naked flame.

His attention on the food, it was only the sudden intake of breath from the onlookers that alerted him. He leaped back just

---

*Literally: 'The face of the dick.' This expression translates roughly as, 'Amazing!'

as a foot-long flame lanced out of Hugo's blowtorch, missing him by inches.

'I beg your pardon, Bruno,' Hugo said calmly, adjusting the nozzle.

Bruno said nothing. The surface of his *sabayon* was webbed with caramel now, crisp and brown. It was finished. Wiping the sides of the plate carefully with the end of his cloth, he called a *commis* to take it to the pass. One or two of the other chefs broke into applause.

'Quiet,' Alain snapped. Bruno realised that he must have been watching silently from the other side of the kitchen. 'Get back to work, all of you.'

It was at least another minute before Hugo's dish was ready. Bruno quietly got on with preparing the soufflé. Out of the corner of his eye he saw Alain walk over to the pass and bend over the two *sabayons*, inspecting them minutely. Then he came over to where the two young men were working.

'If I ever see the pair of you doing anything like that again,' he said quietly, 'you will both be out of here. Do you understand?'

'Yes, chef,' they muttered.

'This isn't a racetrack. It's a kitchen.' He stalked off to inspect a plate of vegetables.

Bruno turned back to the oven, pulled out the soufflé and cursed. The top had burned. Then he saw why. He had set the oven to 190 degrees. Now it was at 210 degrees. Someone had changed the setting while he'd been distracted. He glanced at Hugo but the Frenchman's head was bent over his counter and it was impossible to tell what kind of expression he had on his face. Bruno chucked the soufflé in the bin and started again. He might have won this battle, but he was prepared to bet that the war had only just begun.

'We come now to the difficult notion of harmony,' Dr Fellowes is saying. 'Harmony was not just an aesthetic ideal for the great men

106

of the Renaissance but a spiritual one also. It is the point at which conception and creation mesh; the painter's skill reflecting and celebrating the greater harmony of the Divine.' He plucks a piece of fluff from his shirt, which today is of a colour best described as grape.

Laura smiles at him dreamily. She smiles at everyone today. He coughs and continues: 'The grace of the human figure, the delicacy of forms, the precise symbolism of colour and placement – these are all elements of harmony.'

As Laura bends her head over her notebook, Dr Fellowes admires the *quattrocentro* profile of her neck, both delicate and harmonious. For a moment he falters. He thinks how amazing it is that Italy can do this, can bring out the beauty in the most ordinary people.

Laura, meanwhile, is thinking thoughts so completely filthy that she is amazed they aren't making her blush. Quite the reverse, in fact. She glances coolly up at her teacher and pictures herself in bed with Tommaso. Ah yes – that goes *there*, and this goes *here*, and wouldn't it be a nice surprise if that went *there* as well—

'Harmony,' Kim repeats, favouring Laura with a smile.

'So we're cooking for Laura's best friend. And her best friend's boyfriend.'

'We are?'

They were at Gennaro's, savouring the first *ristretti* of the day. Bruno felt a little light-headed. He wasn't sure if it was because he was in love, or because Gennaro had now turbo-charged his Gaggia by fitting to it a vast pump from an industrial pressure-washer. This sent the pressure inside the machine right up to the maximum, into the red part of the dial, and the *caffè* was now so potent that even die-hard regulars sometimes found themselves staggering to a table and sitting down.

'Yes. Although I have to tell you that a slight complication has arisen.'

'It can hardly be any more complicated than it already is,' Bruno pointed out.

'Perhaps complication is the wrong word. A small change of plan. No, not even of plan. Of venue, that's all.'

'What do you mean?'

'This friend of Laura's has told her parents about me, you see. These parents live here, in Rome, and the result is that they want me to go and cook for all of them at the parents' house, where this Carlotta and her boyfriend will be staying. So of course I had to say that would be fine.'

Bruno stared at him. 'Are you crazy?'

'What's crazy?' Tommaso shrugged. 'I'll go and commandeer the kitchen, throw the mother out and then we'll just have to find a way to get you inside.'

'I take it I'm not actually invited?'

'Well, no.'

'So let me get this clear, Tommaso. You are expecting me to break into this house—'

'Apartment.'

'Apartment. Even better. I suppose it's on the sixteenth floor?'

'Uh – second, I believe.'

'To break into this apartment, which is on the second floor, conceal myself somehow in the kitchen, and then, without being spotted, cook a meal?'

'Exactly. Bruno, your grasp of the situation is masterly and shows that you are clearly the man to formulate a plan to carry us through.'

'Sooner or later, Tommaso, we're going to be found out. Have you thought of that?'

'Of course. And then we'll run like hell, before we have a good laugh about it all. *Meglio un giorno da leone che cento da pecora**, as my father used to say, God rest his soul.'

☙

*'Better to live one day as a lion than a hundred as a sheep.'

At the restaurant, Alain had positioned himself so that he could see everything taking place in the *patissier*'s corner. He was clearly looking for any excuse to elevate one of his two protégés at the expense of the other.

As Bruno pressed a mixture of pastry cream and mashed apricots through the sieve to make a syrup, he noticed that it was coming out lumpy. Surprised, he spooned it back into the sieve and tried again. Again, the puree had blobs of fruit and even seeds in it. He picked up the sieve and looked at it more closely.

Someone had pressed something sharp a dozen times into the metal surface, enlarging the holes.

He replaced the sieve without saying anything and inspected the rest of his station. A chef's work area is called his *mise-en-place*, and each chef surrounds himself with his own individual combination of tools, prepared ingredients, knives, seasonings and favourite gadgets. In the pressure of a service, you reached for whatever was needed automatically, barely looking at it. You assumed, for example, that your bowl of cream was the same bowl of cream you had taken out of the fridge and checked a few hours before, that your vinegar was the same brand you always used, that your sugar really was sugar . . .

Bruno dipped his finger into his sugar bowl and licked it. Along with sugar, there was another taste. Salt.

With a sudden lurch of dread he tasted his vinegar. Instead of vinegar, the bottle contained liquorice water.

He felt sick. How many dishes had he already sent out with the wrong ingredients? Thank God there had been no complaints, though it said something very strange about the customers at Templi that they hadn't dared to mention that their desserts were full of salt and their fruit slathered in aniseed.

Marching over to where Hugo Kass was holding court to a small group of acolytes, Bruno pushed him roughly on the shoulder, making him turn around.

'Did you mess around with my *mise*?' he demanded.

'Of course not,' Hugo said shortly.

One of the acolytes sniggered. It was the only excuse Bruno needed. All his frustrations suddenly boiled up into one moment of complete fury. Pulling back his fist, he punched the Frenchman right on the chin, sending Hugo crashing back against a pile of vegetable crates. It felt fantastic, even though Karl saw the whole thing from the other side of the kitchen and immediately marched Bruno off for a tongue-lashing from Alain Dufrais and an instant demotion. From now on Bruno would have to report to Hugo; and, Alain informed him icily, if Hugo wasn't happy with his work, Bruno would be out on his ear.

Laura, at the residencia, receives a call from the porter to say that there's a delivery for her. She comes downstairs and is surprised to be handed a curious-looking bouquet.

Only on closer inspection does it become apparent that this is, in fact, a bunch of candied flowers – pale orange blossoms, bright blue florets of borage, even tender young rosebuds, all encased in hard clear shells of sugar, like tiny toffee apples.

There's no note, but she knows that there's only one person in the world who could make her such a present. She goes to sleep with the sweetness of toffee on her lips, and dreams of her Roman lover with the crazy, passionate eyes.

Bruno, standing in his little kitchen, looks out at the sleeping city and touches a morsel of the crunchy caramel to his lips. As the sweetness floods his mouth he thinks: *this is what her mouth tastes like, right this moment, as she eats my gift.* His heart fills with joy as he imagines her now, experiencing the same taste at the same moment he does, like a kiss flying between them across the rooftops.

Nine

Bruno had decided that the only way Tommaso could possibly pass off a meal cooked in Carlotta's parents' apartment as his own was to assemble and cook everything beforehand. He would make something simple but impressive that could be smuggled into the other kitchen for Tommaso to heat up. And since there is nothing simpler or more impressive than really good fresh pasta, that was what he was busy making.

He had placed a large wooden board on top of his work surface. Handmade pasta is never prepared on marble; its coldness stiffens the dough and prevents the breakdown of glutens. A pile of Tipo 00, the finest grade of flour, stood to one side, light as ash, its top gently flattened to make a small crater. Into this he had poured some beaten eggs. Drawing flour over the egg mixture with the tines of a fork, he worked the two together a little at a time. Then he put the fork aside and started to use his fingers. Gradually, the sliminess of the eggs and the dryness of the flour became one smooth, muscular mass, worked and reworked until there was no trace of stickiness. After Bruno had washed and dried his hands, he was able to press his thumb into the mixture and pull it out again without the dough clinging to his skin at all.

Using the heel of his palm, he pushed the dough away from him, then folded it over. A quick half-turn and then he did the same again, slowly breaking down its inner resistance. Push, fold, turn. Push, fold, turn. Pasta-making is a ritual, both in the kneading and the stretching; the same hand motions performed over and over again, as automatic and precise as the movements of a master plasterer or a pianist. Bruno kept up his kneading for exactly eight minutes. It was hard, physical work and he was soon perspiring freely, but slowly the dough became elastic, its surface as smooth as Laura's skin.

Inevitably, as he worked he found his thoughts returning to her. The physical exertion was having a corresponding effect on his mind, filling his head with erotic daydreams. Push, fold, turn . . . His arms ached with the longing to hold her, and his body tensed with sexual frustration. Feverish images danced through his mind. Push, fold, turn. *I will make her a dessert that will set her blood on fire*, he decided. *I will let her feel what I am feeling now.* Although a part of him recognised that it was Tommaso, not him, who would reap the benefits, the need to express his feelings as food was overwhelming.

After their exertions, both dough and cook had to rest. Bruno prepared his *secondo*, which was to be *saltimbocca*, the classic Roman sandwich of veal beaten paper-thin and folded over a slice of *prosciutto* and a couple of sage leaves. Once prepared, the *saltimbocca* could be flash-fried in minutes, something even Tommaso couldn't mess up.

After about ten minutes Bruno returned to his dough, squashed it down a little and picked up his pasta-rolling pin. The pin was as long as a sword – thirty-two inches or eighty centimetres, to be precise – and thinner than a conventional rolling pin, so that it would spin faster between his hands as he pushed it over the pasta. The trick was not to use force. You were not so much squeezing the pasta flat as pushing it gently outwards, like spreading icing across the surface of a cake.

When the rolled dough was the size of a pizza base he changed the movements of his hands, letting them slide sideways along the pin as he worked it, distributing pressure evenly along its length. This was the hardest part. Bruno knew he was not as good at this as a housewife somewhere like Emilia–Romagna, who did it every day of her life, but there was no time to be cautious. If he went too slowly, the pasta would lose its moisture and crack before he was done. He felt his way into the dough, stretching it little by little until it became as thin and filmy as silk, fluttering a few centimetres off the table each time he rolled it. It was time to stop and cut the pasta into *tortellini*.

'Signora, do you have a colander?' Tommaso called through the kitchen door. Carlotta's mother bustled in to open a cupboard and show him where the implement was kept, passing a critical eye as she did so over the array of ingredients he had assembled on the work surface.

'You are making fresh pasta?' she said in surprise, looking at the pile of flour and the eggs which he had ostentatiously placed to the fore.

'Of course.'

'Do you want to borrow a rolling machine?'

Tommaso looked down his nose haughtily. 'I never use them. I prefer to do everything by hand.'

'But do you have a rolling pin?'

Tommaso waved his hand airily. 'I'll improvise.'

Carlotta's mother looked sceptical. 'How can you possibly improvise a rolling pin for pasta?'

Tommaso decided it was time to change the subject. 'I'll need a large jug, please, *signora*, ceramic not glass, and six egg cups of different sizes. Oh, and a bottle of good marsala, the best your husband has.' *That should keep them distracted*, he thought, watching her scurrying off to do as he had asked. He hoped Bruno wasn't going to be long. This was turning out to be harder than he'd expected.

'How's it going?' Carlotta asked her mother. The would-be diners had been banished to the dining room to await Tommaso's masterpiece, and everyone was getting impatient.

'He hasn't started the pasta yet, and he's been chopping the same stick of celery for twenty minutes. Now he wants egg cups. And a bottle of marsala.'

'I'll get it,' Dr Ferrara said quickly, getting to his feet. He still wasn't quite sure how it had come about that a stranger had commandeered his wife's kitchen, but after years of living with her he knew a potentially explosive situation when he encountered one. Costanza Ferrara's mouth was set in a thin line, and she had pulled her hair back so tightly that her scalp had gone white.

'I promise you it'll be worth it in the end,' Laura said loyally. From the kitchen the sound of pans crashing together could be heard, followed by a burst of song from Tommaso. Andrea, Carlotta's boyfriend, laughed and lit another cigarette.

The Piazza Agnelli was in the middle of a grid of identical streets, each containing dozens of identical white apartment blocks. After scouring the area on Tommaso's scooter for half an hour, Bruno finally located the right place and sounded his horn twice. Above him, on the second floor, a window flew open.

'*Pe' ventinove e trenta*,' Tommaso said urgently. '*Tengo certi cazzi che mi abballano per 'a capo*.* You're just in time: this is doing my head in.'

'Sorry. I got lost.'

---

* Pe' ventinove e trenta – literally: 'For twenty-nine and thirty.' *Tengo certi cazzi che mi abballano per 'a capo* – literally: 'There are so many dicks dancing in my head.'

Tommaso was already lowering a bucket on a string which contained a mess of flour and eggs hurriedly scraped off the work surface. When it reached the street below, Bruno carefully replaced it with a pan containing his parcels of pasta, which Tommaso rapidly hauled up again. 'These are the *tortellini*, *sì*?' he called.

'Yes. The sauce is in the jar.'

'Where are the *saltimbocche*?'

'Coming up next. Send down the ingredients.'

Tommaso sent down the raw veal and loose sage leaves, and Bruno sent up the meat he'd prepared earlier. 'You'll remember what to do?' he called anxiously.

Tommaso tapped his head. 'Of course. Years of remembering orders. It'll be fine.'

Bruno shrugged and got back on the scooter. He didn't have Tommaso's confidence that this would work, but it was out of his hands now.

Tommaso burst out of the kitchen with a dish of *tortellini* and set it down on the table with a flourish. 'Here, everybody. Time to eat.'

Carlotta's mother's face was a picture of surprise. 'It's ready?'

'Of course.' Tommaso served them all with a flourish. 'While you eat that, I'll get back to the kitchen and make the *secondo*.'

'It smells amazing,' Carlotta said.

'It tastes pretty good,' her boyfriend, who had already started eating, confirmed.

Costanza sniffed. Men might call themselves chefs, but that was a very different thing from being able to cook. She had rarely eaten in a restaurant that in her opinion served food as good as that which she herself prepared at home. She speared one of the *tortellini* on her fork and held it up.

'It's not a good shape,' she commented critically. She put it in her mouth. Everyone looked at her, waiting for her verdict.

'Hmm,' she said at last, spearing another. That was all she said until the end of the *primo*, but it was not lost on those around the table that she finished every single scrap of pasta on her plate. Even after that, there was a little dribble of sauce left on the side. She eyed it hungrily. The others were all taking pieces of bread and wiping their sauce up. Costanza resisted for several minutes, then her plump hand snaked out and grabbed a piece to do the same.

As the meal wore on, Laura, who was seated to Dr Ferrara's left, couldn't help noticing two things. First, he seemed remarkably eager to engage her in conversation; and second, during those conversations he seemed to be making eye-contact with her breasts rather than her face. By the time they had eaten the *saltim-bocche*, he had draped his left arm around the back of her chair as he told her breasts in some detail about the wonderful time he'd had in the 1960s living in a hippy commune in Tuscany. From time to time his fingers brushed against Laura's back as he emphasised a point.

On the other side of the table, Carlotta was making eyes at Andrea. She slipped her shoe off and worked her foot up his leg, laughing at the effect this had on his attempts to make conversation with her mother, who was sitting next to him.

Eventually Costanza lurched unsteadily to her feet and announced that she was going to see Tommaso in the kitchen. Bouncing off the doorframe, she advanced on the young man with outstretched arms and a cry of congratulation, folding him into her ample bosom. Caught in her embrace, Tommaso felt her hands pinching at him as if he were a piece of chicken she were testing for freshness at the butcher's.

'The *dolce*,' he gasped. 'We have another course still to come.' Reluctantly, Costanza released him.

'I'll bring it in just a minute,' he added.

The dessert was *tartufo*, a dark chocolate *gelato* dusted with cocoa.

Around eighty-five per cent of the world's chocolate is made from the common-or-garden Forastero cocoa bean. About ten per cent is made from the finer, more subtle Trinitario bean. And less than five per cent is made from the rare, aromatic Criollo bean, which is found only in the remotest regions of Colombia and Venezuela. These beans are so sought after that, kilo for kilo, they can command prices many times higher than the other local crop, cocaine. Having been fermented, shipped, lightly roasted and finely milled to a thickness of about fifteen microns, the beans are finally cooked into tablets, even a tiny crumb of which, placed on the tongue, explodes with flavour as it melts.

A *tartufo* is a chocolate *gelato* shaped to look like a truffle, but it is an appropriate name for other reasons too. Made from egg yolk, sugar, a little milk and plenty of the finest Criollo chocolate, with a buried kick of chilli, Bruno's *tartufo* was as richly sensual and overpowering as the *funghi* from which it took its name – and even more aphrodisiac.

The arrival of the *tartufo* at the table finally persuaded the diners to return their attentions to the food. For a few minutes there was a stunned silence as they spooned the rich ice cream into their mouths, each of them lost in a private reverie of sensation.

It was Costanza Ferrara who finally broke the silence. 'That was remarkable,' she said at last. Around the table, heads nodded vigorously, or as vigorously as they were able to. Tommaso himself smiled modestly. 'After such a meal,' she continued, 'we must certainly all have a siesta.' She rose majestically from her seat. 'Come, Aldo.'

Startled, Dr Ferrara disentangled himself from Laura's chair and hauled himself upright. His eyes had suddenly acquired the thousand-yard stare of a soldier walking out of the safety of his trench into No Man's Land.

'I'm rather tired too,' Andrea announced when they had gone, with a meaningful glance at Carlotta. 'Tommaso, a fantastic meal. I feel as if my trousers are suddenly much too tight.'

'Let's hope so,' Carlotta murmured. 'Laura, there's a spare room through there if you and Tommaso want to take a nap as well.'

Fifteen minutes later the apartment echoed to muffled grunts and gasps as the three couples succumbed in different ways to the passions engendered by their lunch. Dr Ferrara, who had not made love with his wife for many months, was gasping for breath as she bounced on top of him like an over-enthusiastic space hopper, making the legs of the bed splay alarmingly every time she did so. Carlotta and Andrea were enjoying a more relaxed coupling. And Tommaso and Laura were in the spare bedroom, their clothes strewn across the floor, when Laura broke away from Tommaso and whispered, 'I've got an idea.'

'So have I,' Tommaso said. 'My idea is that we screw like rabbits. What's your idea?'

'Ice cream.'

'Hmm. Tell you what, let's do my idea first and then we'll do your idea.'

But Laura was already tiptoeing away from the bed. 'Wait here.'

Pulling on a T-shirt in case she met anybody, she crept to the kitchen where the remains of the chocolate *tartufo* sat in the ice box of the refrigerator, and took it back with her to the bedroom.

'Now close your eyes,' she told Tommaso as she climbed back on to the bed. 'And lie very, very still.'

Obediently he closed his eyes. She took a spoonful of the cold ice cream and carefully placed it over his left nipple.

'Ow,' Tommaso said. 'It's cold.'

'It'll soon warm up.' She spooned a second mound on the other nipple. He gasped again.

'Good?'

'Um,' he said, shivering a little.

'And one *here*,' she said, putting a third on his belly, just below the navel. 'Now, which one shall I eat first?' She looked at him,

118

trying to choose. The *gelato* was already starting to melt. Rivulets of dark ice cream were running down his sculptured chest. She bent to the little mound of *tartufo* in his navel and slipped it into her mouth. She sighed ecstatically. *Oh* . . .

Bending back to his supine body, she followed one of the streams of melted chocolate up his chest with her tongue. *Oh* . . .

She felt dizzy, unable to tell where her taste buds ended and her nerve endings began. Switching the other way, she began to nibble down towards the crumbs of half-melted chocolate around his hips. He squirmed with relief as she licked the last morsels of icy chocolate off him with her warm tongue, like licking a cone. Then she could wait no longer. Straddling him, she pushed down on to him in one molten movement, arching her back as she felt him sliding up inside her, so hard and urgent it seemed almost as if he must be touching her spine from the inside.

Oh . . .

She hunkered down to get him even further in, and leaned forward to kiss him with a mouth that was itself cold and sweet from the ice cream.

Oh . . .

Tommaso gasped too. After the *gelato*, the warmth of her was almost burning him.

Oh . . .

Laura suddenly realised something was missing. Her mouth felt empty. The *gelato*. Grabbing the dish, she spooned some into her mouth. *Yes* . . . She closed her eyes in rapture. Another spoonful, and then another . . . faster and faster went the spoon, from dish to mouth.

The two sets of movements were becoming synchronised. Every time Tommaso pushed into her, a spoonful of *gelato* slid into her mouth. Every time he pulled back, the spoon left her mouth too and dipped into the dish for another scoop. She balanced the dish on Tommaso's chest, so that she could get at it more easily. Tommaso winced from the coldness of it but Laura was past caring. Dropping the spoon, she scooped a handful of ice cream out of the bowl with her fingers and crammed it into her mouth.

Bruno, meanwhile, was back at the apartment, desperately baking bread to try to take his mind off Laura. Every time he stopped, erotic images – painful images – seared into his brain. He seemed to glimpse Laura out of the corner of his eye, naked, smiling at him, only for the apparition to vanish as soon as he turned his fevered gaze directly towards it.

He regretted the *tartufo* now. It had been too much. He had eaten some himself, just a few minutes ago, and had been shocked by just how potent it was. That chilli, in particular. It was an idea he had borrowed from Mexican cuisine. Initially disguised by the coldness of the ice cream and the sweetness of the chocolate, it lingered as a tingle on the tongue and a gentle sting on the lips that seemed to grow in intensity the longer you left it.

Bruno stuffed pieces of dough into his mouth to try to calm himself. But it was no use. Far from cooling him, the ice cream had simply made things worse.

While Andrea snored gently beside her, Carlotta lay awake. An idea had occurred to her, one so irresistible that she simply couldn't get it out of her mind.

Carlotta was thinking that, even now, as her boyfriend slept, there was a dish in the refrigerator in her mother's kitchen containing the remains of that delectable *tartufo*. Earlier, the six of them had gorged themselves on it, but the *gelato* had been so rich, so dense, so explosively chocolatey that they had been unable to finish it all. Carlotta remembered quite clearly that there had been, at the end, a single portion left – a portion which was now calling to her. The call was all the louder because Andrea had, as usual, fallen asleep as soon as he was satisfied, leaving her tantalisingly unfulfilled. In some strange way, her lack of sexual fulfilment was

120

translating itself into a powerful yearning for just one more spoonful of that wonderful dessert of Tommaso's.

Throwing back the covers, Carlotta pulled on a robe and tiptoed to the door. The apartment was silent. She crept into the kitchen – and stopped.

Her mother, also wearing a robe, was just walking through the other door.

Mother and daughter looked at each other, both immediately guessing why the other was there. The fridge was exactly halfway between them. Casually, as if she were just going to the sink to get a glass of water, Carlotta sidled towards it.

On the other side of the room, her mother also moved nonchalantly in the direction of the fridge.

Carlotta moved a little faster. Across the room, her mother picked up momentum too. Throwing dignity to the wind, Carlotta broke into a run. But her mother could move surprisingly fast for such a small, stout person. As Carlotta reached the fridge and yanked on the handle of the ice box, she found her mother's thick arm blocking the way. They stopped, glaring at each other. Then, as if by unspoken agreement, they both pulled on the handle together.

The ice box was quite empty.

At that moment Laura walked into the kitchen bearing the empty *tartufo* dish, which she carefully carried over to the sink before greeting them with a smile.

While the three women did the dishes in silence, the cause of their discord was discovering a common bond with Carlotta's father, who had put on one of his old CDs.

'Ah, "Return to Fantasy",' Tommaso said, listening. 'One of the greatest album tracks ever.'

'I'm amazed you recognise it. I was still a young man when this came out.'

'Oh, I'm a big Uriah Heep fan.'

'See if you recognise this, then.'

He put a different CD on the player. Within moments Tommaso nodded. 'Hawkwind. "Warrior at the Edge of Time." A classic.'

'Shit, you're good. What about this?' Dr Ferrara changed the CD again.

'"Bad Company."'

'Fantastic,' Dr Ferrara breathed. He started to dance, a little creakily. 'You know,' he said over the music, 'you're a pretty good cook too.'

Tommaso shrugged modestly.

'Today I fucked my wife three times, and I still have a hard-on like a concrete cucumber.'

'*Prego*. You're welcome, really.'

'The thing is, I have some money to invest,' Dr Ferrara said. 'Costanza's mother died and left us a pile, the tight old skinflint. And I don't want to put it in the stockmarket; the government just takes whatever you make. I want to put it into a cash business, something small and local where I can take the profits straight out of the till when times are good and shout at the staff when they're not. Like a restaurant, for example. And it seems to me that people would pay good money to eat like I did today, particularly if they knew that it was going to make their date hotter than a ewe in September.' He tapped his head craftily. 'What's more, I have the perfect place. Old Cristophe has a little *osteria* right in the centre of Rome and I know for a fact he wants to sell up. What do you say?'

'Oh, I'm very happy where I am,' Tommaso assured him.

'I'd make you a partner, naturally. Well, not an equal partner, but you'd have a share of the profits.'

For a moment Tommaso was almost tempted. 'No, really,' he said. 'I love to cook, but I don't think I'm ready for my own restaurant.'

@

122

'He's amazing,' Carlotta said to Laura later. 'Your Tommaso is simply *amazing*. What an artist.'

'Isn't he?' Laura agreed.

'You know my father wants to back him in a restaurant of his own?'

'No, he didn't tell me that.' It occurred to Laura for the first time that Tommaso didn't actually tell her very much. In fact, when she thought about it, she could barely remember one proper conversation they had had. There was the food, of course, which was fantastic, and the sex, and the jokes, and there were the sweet Italian endearments he murmured when they were either about to eat or about to have sex, but she very rarely knew what was really going on in Tommaso's head.

But then, as Carlotta said, he was an artist; and food, not words, was the medium through which he expressed himself.

'Dr Ferrara wants me to open a restaurant with him,' Tommaso said. He laughed. 'Can you imagine? He even offered me a share of the profits. He was most insistent. If I hadn't known what your reaction would be, my friend, I might almost have said yes.'

They were in Gennaro's. Bruno drank his *caffè* with a thoughtful expression on his face, but said nothing.

'Of course,' Tommaso continued, 'I told him it was impossible. We have enough complications without trying to set up a restaurant as well.'

Bruno still didn't say anything. Erotic images of Laura kept erupting into his head. He was imagining what the different parts of her body might taste like. The sensation was so real that his mouth watered.

'I've been thinking,' he said as they left the bar. 'Next time, I'd like to cook Laura something a bit different. Some old country recipes, perhaps.'

'But why?' Tommaso said, puzzled.

'Well – I think she'd enjoy it.'

123

'No – I meant why does there need to be a next time?'

'Well,' Bruno struggled, 'for Laura, of course.'

'But your cooking has done all that I asked of it, and more. *I* can take over from here.'

'You can?' Bruno said doubtfully.

'Of course. I'm getting bored with all this rich food, in any case.'

'But what will you cook her?'

'Simple stuff. Simple, but wholesome.' Tommaso waved his hand dismissively. 'Pasta, for example. Salads. Risotto.'

'Risotto is harder than it looks.'

'Nonsense. My mother used to make it when I was a child. There's nothing to it. A little rice, a little wine, a little parmesan . . .'

'She's used to the best,' Bruno warned. He felt sick. Not even to be allowed to cook for her! It was as if his tongue had been ripped from his throat and he was to be left mute, unable to express his feelings. But Tommaso was adamant.

'She'll soon get used to it. When all's said and done, it's only food. You'll see.'

Ten

Bruno could only stand by and watch as Tommaso took over the kitchen and set about preparing his first solo dinner for Laura. Despite Bruno's warning, he had decided to cook a risotto.

'You have to make sure that you use *superfino* rice,' Bruno said, trying to be helpful. 'Carnaroli, for example, is the best, although Vialone Nano will soak up more liquid—'

'Enough!' Tommaso thundered, pushing him out of the kitchen. 'I will make it as my mother made it.'

Privately, Bruno thought that Tommaso's mother might not have been a very good cook, to judge from the ingredients he had seen assembled on the kitchen table, but Tommaso was determined and there was nothing he could do about it. 'I'll be at Gennaro's if you need me,' he said, accepting defeat.

Tommaso opened a bottle of wine and set to work. It was good wine, he thought as he poured himself a glass to try it; and with risotto, that was really all that mattered. He put the rice in a pan with some butter and started to chop an onion into chunks. What else did he need? Some oil, some garlic. And herbs. He couldn't

125

remember precisely which herbs his mother had used, so he cut a generous selection at random from Bruno's window boxes.

When he had finished adding the herbs his risotto still looked a little sparse. He opened the fridge and peered inside. Ah yes, some cream – cream always made things better. In a cupboard he also found some dried *porcini*. He dimly remembered his mother making risotto with *funghi* sometimes, so he chopped up the *porcini* and threw them into the mix as well.

A ring at the door heralded Laura's arrival. As usual, she came straight into the kitchen to see what was cooking.

'Uh-uh,' Tommaso said. 'Tonight it's a surprise.' He replaced the lid on the pot she'd been trying to smell and gently pushed her out of the kitchen.

'Then for the time being I'll just have to make do with the chef,' she said, slipping her hands inside his shirt and lifting her head up for a kiss.

Five minutes later she said breathlessly, 'How long until it's ready?'

'Don't worry. We've got ages,' Tommaso said, continuing with what he had been doing.

Five minutes after that they were entwined on the sofa, half-naked, when Tommaso suddenly smelled burning.

The risotto. He'd completely forgotten about the risotto. Dashing into the kitchen, he lifted the lid on the pan. Instead of a creamy liquid soup of wine and rice, what stared back at him was a stinking, sulphuric crater of blackened grains, like the remnants of a burnt-out volcano.

'Fuck,' he said with feeling.

'Is everything OK?' Laura called from the other room.

'It's fine. Everything's fine.' He thought rapidly. Bruno had said he'd be in Gennaro's. Perhaps his friend could still salvage this.

'I'm just popping out for more ingredients,' he called. 'I'll only be a moment.'

❧

Bruno listened to his friend's explanation and immediately guessed what must have happened. 'Did you remember to soak the *porcini* before you used them?' he asked.

'Soak them?'

'Never mind. Look, you won't be able to use any of that rice now, it will have tainted the whole dish. Let's go upstairs and we'll see what we can do.'

'But we have to stop Laura seeing you,' Tommaso said. 'I know – I'll go first and blindfold her.'

'*Blindfold* her?'

'Sure. She'll think it's a game. Girls love that kind of thing.'

'They do?' Bruno said doubtfully.

'Just leave it to me.'

Bruno waited outside the door of the apartment. After a few minutes Tommaso slipped out. 'Done it,' he whispered. 'She doesn't suspect a thing.'

'Well . . . if you're sure . . .'

'Don't worry. Now, what do you want me to do?'

'Run down to the store and get another bottle of red wine. As fast as you can.'

'OK.' A quick thumbs up and Tommaso was gone.

Bruno pushed open the door and crept cautiously into the apartment. It was silent. Then there was a dirty giggle from the direction of the sofa. Laura was lying on it, half-undressed. A thick woollen scarf was tied round her head, covering her eyes. 'Tommaso?' she said. Bruno froze.

'I know you're watching me because I can't hear you cooking.' She turned her head this way and that, trying to detect his whereabouts with her ears alone. 'And if we're going to play this game, I want a kiss,' she announced. 'A kiss for every five minutes you keep me waiting for my meal. So that's at least two you owe me already.'

Bruno stood stock still, not daring to move.

'Or else I take the blindfold off.'

Unsure what to do, he took a step towards her. He must have made some sound because she said 'Aha,' and lifted her head up, waiting.

He couldn't help it. He bent his head. He touched his lips to hers, briefly. The lightest of kisses, so brief and fleeting that it barely counted. And then a second . . . His stomach felt as though he were falling through space; and afterwards, his lips stung and his cheeks were as red as someone who has bitten a *diavolillo*.

'Hmm,' was all Laura said, and he thought in his guilt that she sounded a little puzzled.

He went into the kitchen and tried to pull himself together. A risotto would take at least twenty minutes, but he didn't have the ingredients for anything else. He put the rice on and started frying up the other ingredients. While they were cooking he quickly assembled some *antipasti* from the bits and pieces in the fridge: olives into which he stuffed some capers and sage; breadsticks wrapped in slices of *prosciutto*.

'Time's up,' Laura called from the other room.

He tiptoed out and, when she lifted her mouth for a kiss, carefully pushed one of the olives inside it.

'Mmmm,' she said, her mouth full. 'Very nice. But I want a kiss as well.'

Bruno hesitated, then quickly dipped his head and kissed her, briefly. The taste of the olive mingled with the sweeter taste of her own mouth. He gasped, and took a step backwards.

'More,' Laura murmured. 'Tommaso, stop teasing me.'

The sound of his friend's name shattered Bruno's reverie. *What on earth am I doing*? he thought, aghast. He went into the kitchen and leaned against the door, trembling.

At last Bruno heard Tommaso coming up the stairs. When he slipped into the apartment, holding his bottle of wine, Bruno pointed at the sitting room and quickly left his friend to take care of the rest of the evening.

☜☞

He wandered the tiny cobbled streets of Trastevere for hours, trying not to imagine what Laura and his friend were doing now. He had a *distillato* at a late-night bar to calm himself, shaking his head when the beautiful transsexuals who were its only other customers tried to proposition him.

He was still shaking as he contemplated how close he had been to disaster. If the blindfold had slipped . . . it didn't bear thinking about. He could imagine all too readily the horror and disgust in Laura's eyes. Not to mention, of course, Tommaso's red-blooded rage. What had he been thinking of?

But alongside that vision of horror, another version of events kept slipping unbidden into his mind. In that version, Laura looked at him not with disgust and horror but with love and longing, opening her mouth as she leaned towards him for another kiss . . .

Madness. It was all madness. *You have to get a grip on yourself*, Bruno told himself. *You've just got to exercise more self-control. She's Tommaso's girl, and that's an end of it.*

Bruno let himself into the apartment and listened. All was quiet. He went into the kitchen. There was only one remedy when he was feeling like this. Trying not to clatter the pans, which would wake the others, he poured some olive oil into a frying pan and added some slices of chilli and a crushed clove of garlic. In another pan he heated up some stock for *pasta in brodo*.

Lost in what he was doing, he didn't notice the face at the window, watching him, until he was taking the stock off the heat. Caught by surprise, his hand shook and some of the boiling liquid slopped on to his bare arm. He gasped in pain.

Laura, unable to sleep, had climbed out on to the roof to sit and look at the view – that incredible chaos of medieval rooftops tumbling down to the river, with the palaces and domed churches of Rome's centre immediately beyond. Hearing noises coming from the kitchen, she had assumed at first that it was Tommaso. Then she'd seen that it was Bruno, cooking. But what made no sense was that he was so good at it, even better than Tommaso. She had never seen anyone who could prepare food like that. Just the way he chopped the chilli was unbelievably deft, and yet he did it without even glancing down at his hands. Then he saw her watching him, and spilled the boiling liquid on himself.

'I'm sorry,' she said quickly, 'I didn't mean to frighten you.' Bruno had already thrust his arm under the cold tap. 'Wait, I'll come round.'

By the time she got to the kitchen he was trying to wrap a dressing round his arm one-handed, tightening it with his teeth.

'Here, let me.' A patch of skin on his forearm was starting to blister. 'Bruno, I am *so* sorry,' she said again as she took the bandage and wrapped it round his arm. 'I wasn't thinking.'

'It's OK,' Bruno said. 'It happens all the time in a kitchen.'

'When you're washing dishes?' she said, puzzled.

'Uh – sure. Sometimes the dirty pans are hot.' Luckily Laura was concentrating on the bandage, so she couldn't see that his face had turned almost as red as his burned arm. 'And I'm clumsy.'

'You didn't look clumsy to me.'

He looked down at her hair as she tied the bandage for him. Automatically he began to separate the various ingredients of her scent. Bergamot, citrus, cinnamon . . . and something else, too; a faint, sweet top note that was the smell of her own skin. He tried to capture it in his memory, to fix it precisely in his palate.

The wedding cake would have candied fruits . . . No, stop thinking like this, he told himself sternly.

'All done,' she said, stepping back to admire her handiwork.

'It's tight,' he said, trying to flex his arm.

'It needs to be.'

'But I need to finish the soup.'

'I can do it.' She put the saucepan back on the stove for him. 'Just tell me what to do.'

'There's a spoon on your right to stir it,' he said. 'And the chilli needs to go in now.'

130

'Like this?'

'Perfect.'

He watched her. 'It will be about ten minutes before it's ready,' he said. 'You don't have to wait.'

'No, I'd like to. Least I can do.'

There was a long silence. Laura said, 'When I was watching you through the window, do you know what you looked like?'

'No, what?'

'A wizard. Stirring your cauldron. Eye of newt and wing of bat.'

'Eye of newt?' He screwed up his face. 'That would taste of very little,' he said thoughtfully. 'Too small.'

She smiled. 'It's just an expression.'

'Oh. I see. Well, I suppose cooking *is* like magic, in a way. Spells are just recipes, after all.'

'Imagine if you could really cast a spell on someone just by cooking. That would be freaky, wouldn't it?'

'Yes,' he said, avoiding her eye. 'Imagine.'

'People turning into frogs all over the place.' She pointed at the soup. 'Should we taste this?'

'If you like.' He already knew exactly what it would taste like.

She took a spoon and tasted some of the broth. 'That's really good,' she said, surprised. 'I mean – really, really good.'

'It needs two pinches of salt and a little olive oil.'

'You haven't tasted it.'

He shrugged. 'That's still what it needs.'

'Okay, mister wizard. You're in charge.' She added the salt, then picked up the bottle of oil. 'How much?'

'Two glugs.'

'Could we possibly translate that into imperial measures?'

'Put your thumb over the top of the bottle and tip it up. When you let your thumb off, the olive oil will glug twice as it comes out. Then you've put in just the right amount.'

'Neat.' She put the bottle down and sucked the last drops of oil

131

off her thumb. Bruno felt his heart lurch. 'So how come you aren't a chef?' she said, not noticing. 'You've obviously got the talent.'

'Well – maybe one day.'

'Tommaso's teaching you, I suppose?'

'Something like that.'

'He's a very talented cook.'

'He's talented at lots of things,' Bruno said loyally.

'I guess he's always been a big hit with women,' she said casually.

'I suppose so.'

'Was there ever anyone – you know – special?'

'No,' he said truthfully.

'But there must have been other women he's cooked for?'

Bruno hesitated. How he longed to tell her the truth! But it was too late now. Too many lies had been told. If Laura ever found out what had really happened, she would be appalled.

'No,' he said. 'I can promise you: Tommaso has never cooked like this for any girl before.'

He saw the happiness flood into her eyes and had to turn away, full of self-disgust.

Eleven

In the kitchen at Templi, quiet reigned. The first diners were sending in their selections, Karl was calling each item, and all around the room chefs were quietly acknowledging their orders as they began to execute their allotted tasks. Surveying the scene, Alain Dufrais allowed himself a tiny nod of satisfaction.

Over in the *patissier*'s corner, Bruno was also feeling better. A shortage in the *garde manger* station meant that Hugo Kass had been temporarily removed from desserts, and Bruno was able to get on with his preparations undisturbed.

Suddenly he heard a '*Pssst*'. Looking around, he could not at first identify the source. Then he saw Tommaso crouching behind the stove.

'Hey, Tommaso. What's up?'

'We have to swap places. Carlotta's parents are here. You know – Dr Ferrara and his wife.'

'Why?' Bruno asked, puzzled.

'I don't know. Because they think I cook here, I suppose. He must want to get laid again.'

'I meant, why do we have to swap?'

'Because if they see me they'll know I'm only a waiter. And if I just go and hide, no one will serve them. So I need to hide in here, and you need to put on my uniform and look after their table.'

Bruno sighed. For a moment, he was tempted to tell Tommaso to forget it. But the memory of those stolen kisses was still on his conscience. 'All right. But I'll have to be back at my station before the first orders for *dolci* come in.'

At that very moment, a group of four men was sauntering through the front doors of the restaurant. Although they were expensively dressed, there was something about the rough-and-ready way they walked that suggested these were not the sort of customers Templi usually dealt with. Their leader was a tiny man, barely five foot tall, whose well-cut suits had clearly been specially tailored to fit his diminutive frame.

A waiter hurried forward. Before he could open his mouth, the small man said, 'We have a reservation. Four people, in the name of Norca.'

The waiter looked at the list. Sure enough, there was a reservation. He was not to know that the real Signor Norca, the businessman who had originally made the booking, had that very morning been persuaded to relinquish it in favour of some well-connected friends of friends. Initially he had resisted – he had, after all, waited three months to eat at Templi, and he was looking forward to it enormously – but a somewhat curt phone call from his chairman in Palermo, followed shortly afterwards by another from his most important client in Naples, had persuaded him that it would be altogether less stressful to spend his lunch hour in a small wine bar near his office, where he was even now taking a restorative *grappa* to steady his nerves.

'That seems to be in order,' the waiter said slowly.

'Good,' Teodoro said, patting the waiter's arm. 'In that case, you can lead us to our table.'

134

As they walked through the bar, one of the men casually helped himself to a bottle of whisky. The waiter pretended not to notice.

The news that there was a group of *mafiosi* in the restaurant went round the waiting staff like wildfire, and from them permeated into the kitchen. Alain Dufrais stiffened and reached for his hat. As he marched rigidly towards the doors into the dining room, however, the maître d' headed him off. Franciscus was an Italian and knew how these things worked. He whispered urgently in the chef's ear.

For a moment it looked as though Alain was going to ignore him. His face twitched. Then, with a mighty effort, he turned and went back to the pass.

It was a long time since Bruno had been a waiter. Moreover, each table at Templi bore a bewildering assembly of cutlery and utensils, and it was up to the waiter to pour the wine into the right glass and ensure that the correct implement was positioned next to each plate. Soon Bruno was horribly confused. Luckily Dr Ferrara and his wife were cooing over each other like a couple of teenagers and didn't seem to notice; at least until it came to ordering, when Dr Ferrara called him over.

'Am I right in thinking you have a chef called Tommaso Massi working here?'

'Yes, of course.'

'Can you tell me which dishes on the menu he would have prepared?'

'The *dolci*,' Bruno replied.

'In that case,' Dr Ferrara turned to his wife, 'we shall just have a *primo* and then one of Tommaso's desserts.'

Bruno slipped away before the maître d' could spot him. He was fortunate that there was such a vast crowd of waiting staff at Templi that one more went unnoticed.

❧

135

Franciscus himself served Teodoro's table. He started off by saying that the meal would of course be on the house. In addition, he murmured, the chef's signature dish, the *confit of lamb en persillade*, was particularly good at the moment.

'I'll have *pasta carbonara* and a steak,' the first man said firmly.

'I'll have the same,' his neighbour said.

'We don't actually . . .' Franciscus began, then stopped.

'Since it's Thursday, I'll have *gnocchi*,' the next man added.

'And I'll have *gnocchi* and a *piccata Milanese*, followed by *tiramisù*,' Teodoro said benevolently. He handed the menus, which none of them had opened, back to Franciscus. 'I'll leave the choice of wine up to you, since you're paying for it.'

'Of course,' Franciscus said with a slight bow, hoping that the Château Petrus was still in the cellar, and in good condition.

'Two *pasta carbonara*. Two *gnocchi*. Two steaks, well done. One *piccata Milanese*.' Karl called the order in an appalled whisper, as if by lowering his voice the words were less likely to sully the rarefied air of Monsieur Dufrais's kitchen. In equally hushed tones, various chefs acknowledged that they had heard.

There was a brief pause after Karl called the *tiramisù*. If there was something a little strange about the *patissier*'s voice when he eventually did respond, nobody noticed. They were too busy wondering how on earth they were going to cook the unfamiliar Roman dishes that had just been ordered.

Tommaso stared at the contents of the fridge. A *tiramisù*, he knew, was just *biscotti* soaked in espresso and brandy, topped with beaten egg and mascarpone. But in what proportions? What should he do first? If only he had a recipe book.

It is sometimes said of Romans that they are terrible at organisation but brilliant at improvisation. Desperately, Tommaso pulled some ingredients out of the fridge and prepared to improvise now.

◎◎

Franciscus, opening the Petrus, froze. He was convinced he had just seen one of the chefs, dressed in a waiter's uniform, pouring wine into a water glass. He passed the cork of the Petrus under his nose and the rich odour of long years of cellaring, magnificent and majestic, momentarily calmed him. He poured a little wine from one glass to another to check the quality, which was perfect, and then allowed himself a small restorative mouthful.

Bruno made it back to the *patissier*'s station just in time to stop Tommaso sending up to the pass a concoction so vile-looking that he, Bruno, wouldn't have served it to a dog. Fortunately, the head chef's attention was elsewhere.

'Is there no one who knows how to cook these peasant dishes?' he roared. 'For God's sake, one of you Italian barbarians must have some clue.'

'He's talking about *gnocchi*,' Tommaso whispered, pulling off his whites and grabbing his own jacket from Bruno. 'And *piccata Milanese*.'

'I do,' Bruno called. For a moment there was silence, then with a collective sigh of relief the whole kitchen turned towards the *patissier*.

Roman *gnocchi* are a completely different dish to the light, fluffy *gnocchi* that are found in the rest of Italy. For one thing, they are made not from potatoes but from semolina, the coarse-ground flour of the durum wheat. Essentially they are a kind of pancake.

'You mix the milk and the semolina in a saucepan,' Bruno was explaining as he cooked. 'Beat in an egg and leave it for a few minutes to cool. Then you just cut it into circles, sprinkle the cheese on top, and bake them in the oven.' While he talked he was also assembling another *tiramisù*. He had already explained to Karl how to make a *piccata Milanese*, and the head chef was busy chopping parsley and strips of parma ham.

137

'Add some pork rind to that, if you can find any,' Bruno called over.

Meanwhile, another chef was making the sauce for the pasta. Other orders were forgotten as the whole kitchen mobilised to cook the unfamiliar menu.

With the *secondi* sorted, Bruno turned his attention to vegetables. *Carciofini, zucchini,* cardoons and *treviso* were all found and prepped. Simultaneously he began to organise the orders of the other restaurant diners. He pulled all but a few sous chefs off the Italian food, and still found time to supervise the cooking of the meat.

'You know, we have a very similar dish to this in France,' Karl said as he cooked the *piccata*. 'But we would add black olives, and a little brandy.' He smiled nostalgically. 'I haven't tasted it since I left Provence, and this smell is bringing it all back for me.'

Bruno shrugged. 'Black olives would fight the parsley, but some brandy would be fine. Go ahead.'

To everyone's surprise, the *mafiosi* were reduced to silence by the unexpected excellence of the cooking, and the atmsophere at Templi slowly returned to normal.

'This is a very strange place,' Dr Ferrara commented as he looked around. 'That maître d' is quite drunk, you know.'

'They're just having a good time,' his wife said. 'How's your *primo*?'

'Fantastic. How's yours?'

Costanza didn't reply, but she squeezed her husband's thigh under the table.

After the meal, Teodoro and two of his companions sent a message via Franciscus, summoning the chef to their table.

Whatever Alain was, he was certainly no coward. He glanced at the clock and curtly told the maître d' to inform table four that

138

he would be out in a quarter of an hour, when service was finished.

Franciscus, who *was* a coward, was a little free with his translation of this message. 'Monsieur Dufrais has just popped out and will be with you as soon as he is back,' he told Teodoro.

When at last Alain did deign to visit the dining room, he made a point of touring all the tables in his customary clockwise direction, coming to the Italians' table last. But the *mafiosi*, soothed by large cigars and a hundred-year-old cognac, were too relaxed to care.

'Your restaurant is a little fancy for my tastes, my friend,' Teodoro told Alain, 'but your cooking is first-rate. Just make sure you're hospitable to any colleagues of mine and you'll do well.'

'And how will I know who your colleagues are?' Alain asked coldly.

Teodoro thought for a moment. 'You won't,' he said. 'Better be nice to all Romans, just to be on the safe side.' His companions laughed uproariously. Only Alain did not join in.

'Thank you for your compliments,' he said stiffly, moving on to the next table.

Dr Ferrara leaned across. 'You know, he doesn't really do the cooking,' he confided to Teodoro.

'He doesn't?'

'No. There's a young Italian in the kitchen. A genius with Roman food. His name's Tommaso Massi. I'm trying to persuade him to set up his own place, in the city.'

'Tommaso Massi,' Teodoro said thoughtfully. He nodded to one of his companions, who made a note of the name on his napkin.

'Get those plates out of my sight,' Alain ordered, marching back into the kitchen. 'Wipe the surfaces. And get rid of all that peasant food, too.' He swept the left-over pieces of *gnocchi* into the bin and glared at Bruno. 'Chef, your station is unmanned. And

139

what in God's name are *you* doing?' He was talking to Tommaso, who was hiding in the cupboard Alain had just pulled open.

'Finding a coat, chef.'

'Well, hurry up. And get yourself properly dressed.'

'Did they like their meal?' Bruno asked.

'Apparently.'

'You see, I was thinking. It might be nice, for local people, if some of those dishes were available on the menu.'

Alain stared at him. For a moment a vein throbbed on his forehead. 'Last time I looked, I was the *chef de cuisine* in this restaurant,' he said icily.

'Of course,' Bruno said quietly. 'Sorry, chef.'

'I want to do it.'

'Do what?'

'Open a restaurant with Dr Ferrara. I think it's a good idea.'

'Are you serious?'

'Why not?' Bruno shrugged. 'It's not so complicated, not compared to what we've been doing already. I'll do the cooking and you can help me.'

'Is this to do with all the trouble at Templi?' Tommaso said quietly.

His friend avoided his eyes. 'Perhaps.'

'You're really going to let those talentless bastards drive you out?'

'I don't know. Yes, perhaps. But it's more than that. These other dishes I've been cooking recently, for Laura – they're not Alain's, or Hugo's, or anyone else's. They're mine. And if I don't leave Templi and start cooking on my own somewhere, they'll just be lost. Don't you see, Tommaso? I have to give them the chance to exist. I can't explain it. It's like a woman wanting to have children, or something.'

'Except you want your children to be eaten.'

Bruno said helplessly, 'I told you I couldn't explain it.'

'Then there's the fact that we'd be trying to fool everybody. I mean *everybody*. Customers, critics, suppliers, staff – this is serious stuff, Bruno. It's not like a little joke to get a girl into bed. If we're caught – *when* we're caught – there'll be hell to pay. We'd never work in this industry again.'

'*Meglio un giorno da leone che cento da pecora,* as your father used to say, God rest his soul.'

'Ah, Bruno, did I ever tell you how my father died?' Tommaso asked.

'I don't think you did, no. And I didn't like to pry.'

'He ignored a stop sign and drove straight out in front of a truck. He assumed the truck would slow down for him. It didn't.'

'Ah.'

'Sometimes lions get killed. Particularly when they pull out in front of trucks.'

'It's a good thing we're only opening a restaurant, then, and not a transport company.'

Tommaso sighed. Something about this conversation told him that Bruno wasn't really listening. He knew from experience that his friend, normally the most easy-going of people, was also extraordinarily stubborn about anything to do with food. 'Wouldn't it bother you that Dr Ferrara would think it was me, not you, who was the head chef?' he asked.

'Not in the least. In fact, it could be a great partnership. You could do all the shit that chefs have to do these days – talking to customers, flattering reviewers, dealing with Dr Ferrara and so on – while I get on with the part I really enjoy.'

Twelve

Tommaso and Bruno made a trip to inspect the restaurant in which Carlotta's father was proposing to invest. As might be expected, since the existing owner was nearing retirement, it was a run-down trattoria with no airs or graces and an all-pervading air of neglect.

Christophe showed them around with an air of apologetic resignation. 'We have our regulars,' he confided in the two young men. 'But there are too many restaurants round here, and people don't eat out as much as they used to.'

'Hear that, Bruno?' Tommaso said meaningfully. 'People aren't eating out.'

'The best restaurant in Rome will always be full,' Bruno said loftily.

'It's a struggle to pay my staff,' Christophe continued. 'Sometimes we lose money, even in the good years.'

'How many people do you employ?' Tommaso asked.

'Two. Johann helps me in the kitchen, and Marie is our waitress.' He lowered his voice. 'Between you and me, she's the reason most of the regulars stay regular.' He called to a young woman who was sorting cutlery on the other side of the room, 'Marie, come and say hello.'

The young woman turned round. Marie was raven-haired, dark-skinned, full-mouthed and full-breasted; and as her curvaceous body squeezed between the tightly packed tables and chairs, Tommaso muttered '*Fosse a' Madonna!*' under his breath. Automatically he broke into his most winning smile. She scowled back at him, but he didn't take any notice. For a girl like her, a little scowling was only to be expected.

'Pleased to meet you,' Bruno said, shaking her hand. 'Tell me, Christophe, how often do you have the ovens serviced?'

'Every six months.' It was Marie who answered, not Christophe. 'At least, since I've been here. Before that,' she shrugged, 'who knows? The paperwork was a bit of a mess.'

'Marie helps with some of the administration, too,' Christophe explained.

'Sweet-talking creditors, mostly,' Marie said.

'I'm sure you're very good at it,' Tommaso said knowingly. Marie ignored him. 'Of course, we very much hope you'll stay on,' Tommaso continued.

'I may do,' she shrugged. 'It'll depend on what plans you have. If I like them, I'll stay for a bit, see how things work out.'

'Our plan is simple,' Bruno said. 'We're going to serve the finest food in Rome. Proper Roman food, the same dishes your grandmother made, but brought up to date; a bit simpler, a little lighter, and given a small twist here and there so that you look at everything afresh and don't take it for granted.'

'Hmm,' Marie said suspiciously. 'I suppose you'll change the décor?'

'I love it just the way it is,' Tommaso assured her.

Bruno reached up to where a string of garlic cloves hung from a dark beam. He squeezed it in his fist and watched it crumble to dust. 'Well, maybe it needs just a little updating here and there,' Tommaso acknowledged. 'But you know, this seventies look is very popular right now.'

'It's a shithole,' Marie said firmly. 'It needs to be changed

143

enough so that it brings in a younger crowd, but not so much that it frightens off the regulars. Some decent lighting would help, but you'll need to budget at least a thousand euros for rewiring.'

'She's nice,' Tommaso said casually as Bruno and he took a coffee together after their visit.

'Who?'

'The waitress.'

'She seems very organised. Which, to be honest, could be a godsend, since neither of us are.' He looked his friend in the eye. 'So. Are we going to do this or not?'

'Absolutely,' Tommaso said, his earlier misgivings apparently forgotten.

'Good. We'll need to call it something different, so people know it's under new management.'

Tommaso thought for a moment. 'What about Il Cuoco?' he suggested.

'"The Cook". Hmm. Meaning you, or me?'

'A bit of both.'

'Il Cuoco it is then.' Bruno raised his espresso cup. 'To the best restaurant in Rome.'.

It was one thing to create a few meals. To create a whole menu, Bruno soon discovered, was another thing altogether, and required much more work. But his inspiration remained the same: Laura.

From the little kitchen in their apartment emerged dish after dish. Bruno was trying to recreate the traditional dishes of Rome, but he was also trying to impose a little of his own personality on them, and to bring to them some of the quality he loved in Laura – the same mixture of complexity and simplicity, freshness and acidity, innocence and experience. In some way, every dish he created had to taste of her.

He hummed as he worked, and lost himself in a blizzard of

144

flavours and combinations. Later, when he looked back, he was to think of this as one of the happiest times of his life, when anything was still possible, and his heart was not broken, only fractured.

Laura had decided to show Tommaso some of her favourite paintings.

'Caravaggio was famously excitable,' she told him as they stood in front of the *Boy Bitten by a Lizard*. 'He once pulled a dagger on another artist during an argument about a painting. Oh, and he loved his food. He once asked a waiter which artichokes were cooked in butter and which in oil. The waiter told him that if he couldn't tell by smelling them, he certainly wouldn't be able to taste the difference when he ate them. So Caravaggio hit him.'

Tommaso nodded unenthusiastically. 'It's tough, being a waiter.'

'His big obsession was realism,' she continued. 'He wanted his paintings to show ordinary Romans, not idealised figures from the Bible.'

But Tommaso had already moved on. His idea of a tour round a gallery was a brisk stroll, glancing at whatever took his fancy, but certainly never stopping, the sooner to reach the exit.

Eventually Laura gave up. What did it matter if Tommaso didn't share her appreciation of art? He clearly had a lot on his mind at the moment.

Something *was* troubling Tommaso, in fact, and that was the refurbishment of Il Cuoco. Various things were conspiring to take them over budget. Dr Ferrara had acquired some new partners, about whom he was somewhat vague, but the amount of money he had to spend was finite and never seemed to be enough. First, there was the redecoration, which was proving incredibly expensive. Then there was old Christophe's wine cellar – Marie was insisting that the price paid for the restaurant include a fair allowance for all the wine he would be leaving. But the worst

145

thing was that Bruno was hiring staff and ordering state-of-the-art kitchen equipment with no regard to compromise or cost. When Tommaso asked his friend if a twenty-speed mixer or a wood-fired oven was really necessary, Bruno simply gave him a puzzled look.

There was only one thing for it, Tommaso decided: Bruno would have the equipment he wanted, but the rest of what was needed they would obtain in the same way Tommaso had stocked his larder when he was an impoverished waiter, just starting out. Night after night, therefore, Tommaso and Bruno left Templi with their pockets full of silver cutlery. Clanking audibly, they trudged back down the hill, before finally emptying their haul into a box at the apartment.

'At this rate it'll take us a year to get enough,' Tommaso said, inspecting the contents of the box one night. 'I'm going to put the word out.'

From then on, petty theft at Templi escalated to epidemic proportions. Franciscus would pull open the silverware drawer to discover that there were no teaspoons left at all, while bowls, platters, side plates and even lead crystal glasses seemed to vanish as surely as if there was a poltergeist in the building.

'It's the mafia,' Franciscus said despairingly to Alain. 'Once those thieving bastards have their eye on you, there's nothing you can do.'

Alain had no wish to see Teodoro and his pasta-eating companions again. 'We'll just have to live with it then. Order some replacements, and put the prices up by another ten per cent.'

Word of what was happening circulated quickly among their friends. Vincent, Sisto and various other colleagues past and present came by regularly to lend a hand or to drop off some booty. Il Cuoco's wine coolers bore the crests of the Hilton and the Intercontinental, and the kitchen was filled with bits and pieces smuggled out of the Radisson and the Marriott. Sisto even turned up on his scooter carrying an entire sink unit under one arm,

146

balanced only by the weight of the electric juicer he had jammed into his opposite pocket.

There was no money to employ decorators, so the two of them did most of it themselves before they went to work. They were painting the walls one day when they heard an unfamiliar sound coming from under the dustsheets. It turned out to be an ancient telephone, its bell so loose and pitted with rust that it could now manage only a wheezy rattle.

'*Pronto*,' Tommaso said into the receiver.

'Is that Il Cuoco?'

'*Si*, but we're not open yet.'

'Well, when will you be?' the voice said impatiently.

Tommaso plucked a date from the air. 'Two weeks on Saturday.'

'Good. I want to make a reservation.'

'Our first customer,' Tommaso said wonderingly as he replaced the receiver. 'It looks as if this is really going to happen.'

Laura decided to wear a pair of white linen shorts she hadn't worn for a while. When she came to do them up, however, she discovered they no longer fitted. She tried on another pair of trousers instead and found that they, too, were a little tight.

She had never needed to worry about her weight before. But now, as she inspected herself in the tiny mirror in her apartment, she had to admit that her figure had undoubtedly expanded.

'Never mind,' Judith said. 'I've got plenty of looser stuff you can borrow. And it's got to be worth it for all that fantastic sex, right?'

Laura hesitated. She hadn't yet told her friend that sex with Tommaso actually wasn't that fantastic. Oh, he was beautiful, for sure, and the food he cooked made all her senses tingle in anticipation, but when it came to the act itself she was slowly coming to the conclusion that Tommaso was just a bit too – well, straightforward. Not to mention perfunctory. In fact, you couldn't have cooked a Roman pizza in the time that it sometimes took Tommaso to make love to her. Slow and painstaking in his cooking, it seemed as if in bed he sometimes reverted to that other Tommaso, the impatient, exuberant Italian who drove at ninety miles an hour, swallowed espressos in a single gulp and toured art galleries at breakneck speed. But when everything else was so perfect, it seemed a small price to have to pay.

When Bruno finally plucked up the courage to tell Alain he was leaving, the *chef de cuisine* took him to one side.

'And where are you going?' he asked calmly.

'I'm going to open my own place.'

'In Rome?'

'*Si*, in Rome.'

Alain sighed. 'Listen,' he said kindly, 'you're a good chef. If I'm hard on you sometimes, it's only because I can see that you're like me; you understand food, you have potential. But can you honestly tell me that you know everything?'

'Of course I don't. No one does.'

'Then why are you in such a hurry to stop learning? If you really want to leave here, let me make some calls for you. I can get you a job with someone good, someone who'll teach you properly. Don't you want to work with the best? I can call Bras, Martin, Ducasse . . . even Adrià, if you fancy going to Spain. We all talk to each other, you know. A word from me and any one of them would create a job for you, just as I made room for Hugo. You're simply too inexperienced to start your own place. Wait a few years, learn a little more, and then, when you're ready, we'll help to set you up in a real restaurant, one where you can earn your own stars. Believe me, there's no point in doing these things by halves.'

Bruno hesitated. The names Alain was dangling in front of him were the names of his heroes. A few months ago he would have given his right arm to be told that he was good enough to work with Guy Martin or Michel Bras.

148

But a few months ago, many things had been different. In some way, his feelings for Laura had also changed the way he felt about food, and the dishes he had been cooking for her had been part of a voyage of discovery for him, too; one from which there was no turning back.

'It's kind of you, chef, and I will always be grateful,' he said. 'But my mind's made up.'

'Wily old bastard,' Tommaso commented when he heard what Alain had said. 'The only reason he wants you out of Rome is because he doesn't want Il Cuoco stealing his customers.'

Thirteen

'Tell me honestly, Tommaso,' Laura said as she got dressed one morning, 'am I getting fat?'

'Of course not,' he said; which was true, because although Laura had certainly put on weight, she was also a long way from being fat. Tommaso sighed. Laura's need for reassurance, not to mention the fact that she had a very slow fuse in bed, was making him a little weary.

There is not a great abundance of gyms in Rome. The average Italian male, when faced with the evidence of his increasing stomach in the mirror, will tend either to invest in a more generously cut pair of trousers or to buy a new mirror, while his female counterpart seems to be genetically programmed to slenderness, at least until her wedding day. It was perhaps not surprising, therefore, that when Laura went along for her first session at the grandly named Gymnasia de San Giovanni, she found several other Americans of her acquaintance among the clientele, including Kim Fellowes. Dressed in faded sweats emblazoned with the logo of his East Coast alma mater, he was pulling a steady stroke rate of twenty-eight on the ergometer.

'Hi, Dr Fellowes,' she called as she mounted a treadmill.

'Good morning,' he called back. He was nearing the end of his daily thousand metres but he was only a little out of breath. 'I haven't seen you here before.'

'I just joined today,' she explained.

He watched Laura as she began to run. Her skin was soon flushed with perspiration, and a sweet, almost imperceptible odour began to suffuse the air around her. It was the smell of summer herbs, and honey, and olive oil, and salt – the tastes of Bruno's cooking, released into the air for a second time, mingled now with the delicate scent of her skin.

According to the rowing machine's readout, Kim had reached the thousand-metre mark, but he kept on rowing for the pleasure of watching Laura. She had tied her hair back in a ponytail and the fine hairs on the back of her neck were now beaded with sweat, like the beads of moisture on a glass of cold white wine. There was something undeniably fine about her, he thought to himself. Usually the students were little better than brats, the indulged offspring of rich parents. Laura was different. In his art history classes she seemed to devour knowledge like someone who had been starved of it all her life, eagerly replacing the spoon-fed pap of her school classes with the real thing.

One could almost fall in love with a girl like that. Of course, relationships between staff and faculty were, strictly speaking, against the rules, but they were in Italy, and rules were a little more flexible here. And the age difference was only a few years – less than between Dante and Beatrice, for example, or Petrarch and his Laura.

After Laura had showered, she came out of the changing room to find Dr Fellowes waiting by the notice board, a sweater draped elegantly over his shoulders. 'I thought you might like to come with me on a little tour,' he said diffidently.

151

'What sort of tour?'

'A tour of my own personal Rome. There are some wonderful collections that aren't open to the public. And after that –' he shrugged – 'perhaps we could have a little lunch somewhere?'

'That sounds wonderful,' she said.

He took her to places she didn't even know existed – to tiny *palazzi*, where archivists and curators unlocked dark rooms containing priceless masterpieces. He ushered her past the security guards into the Farnese palace, now the French embassy, its fabulous Carracci ceilings long since closed to the vulgar hordes. At the Palazzo Doria-Pamphili he took her into the family's private apartments, where they chatted with someone who bore the same features as the Titian portraits on the walls. They visited tiny, jewel-like chapels, grand salons with majestic ceilings, dimly lit churches where at the flick of a switch vast frescoes of unimaginable beauty leaped out of the darkness.

'Enough,' he said at last. 'We mustn't cram you too full of art on an empty stomach.' He escorted her to a restaurant in a little square where the owner greeted him by name. A bottle of cold Orvieto and some long, irregular *grissini* arrived on the table a few moments after they sat down.

'I'm afraid my diet doesn't allow me much in the way of carbohydrate,' he said apologetically. 'I'm just going to have a salad. But please, order anything you want.'

'I'll have a salad too,' she said. 'I've been eating way too much, and I don't want to undo all that running at the gym.'

'Is Laura coming to the opening night?' Bruno asked Tommaso.

Tommaso screwed up his face. 'To be honest, I hadn't thought about it.'

'She should,' Bruno said emphatically. 'I'm planning something special for her. An authentic Renaissance menu, in honour of her studies.'

'You don't have to do that,' Tommaso said. 'Let's face it, on the opening night the place will be full of important customers – maybe even some reviewers. We should be concentrating on them, not Laura. Why create more dishes just for her?'

For a moment Bruno felt a terrible compulsion to tell Tommaso everything. *Because to me she's the only person who matters*, he wanted to say. *Because I'd swop all the good reviews in the world for a smile from her. Because I love her in a way that I don't think you, Tommaso, fine and noble friend that you are, are actually capable of.*

But he swallowed those words before he spoke them. He said, 'But think how it will look to the reviewers and all those important people to know that certain dishes have been created in honour of one particular woman. People will talk about it, and perhaps they'll bring their own girlfriends and wives to try it out.'

'Hmm,' Tommaso said. 'Yes, I like that. The grand passion of the chef, reflected in his creation of a dish of love. That's a great idea. I wish I'd thought of it myself.'

For inspiration, Bruno went to art galleries and studied the paintings, making sketches of the meals they showed. There were many paintings of fruit, of course, and pictures of Bacchus surrounded by grapes, but he was more interested in discovering what ordinary people would have eaten in the restaurants and taverns of the day. Luckily there were plenty of portraits that showed people eating. Even more useful were the studies of the Last Supper, for which the artists had clearly used as models the food that they themselves were served.

He was in the Galleria Borghese one afternoon, studying the paintings, when he suddenly heard a familiar voice calling his name. He turned around. It was Laura.

'Hello,' she said, clearly surprised to see him. 'What brings you here, Bruno?'

Putting away his notebook, he mumbled something about looking at a new display.

'Well, since you're here, let me show you my favourite painter,' she said, slipping an arm through his and guiding him towards the next room.

'Caravaggio, you mean?'

'How did you know that?' she said.

He shrugged. 'Tommaso must have told me.'

They stopped in front of Caravaggio's *Boy with a Basket of Fruit*.

'You like the light,' Bruno said. 'The way it falls from one side, putting half the face in shadow.'

'That's right. I *do* like that.'

'Whereas Tommaso,' he gestured at the paintings, 'sees all of these in terms of food.'

'He does?'

'Oh yes. He told me so. He told me that you could see what each painter ate, by the way he painted. So Michelangelo there –' he nodded – 'could only have been a Florentine. He would have liked simple grills, the plainer the better.' He pointed across the room. 'Raffaelo, on the other hand – he's all grace and lightness, like the cooking of his native Urbino. But Caravaggio was a Roman, with a Roman's hearty appetite. When he paints a Last Supper, it's simply that – a painting of a proper Roman dinner, with a real roast bird just out of the oven and a plate of *contorni* beside it, just as he himself would have been served at the *osteria* he was lodging at.'

'Tommaso said all that?'

He glanced at her, wondering if she was teasing him, but she seemed entirely serious.

'Actually, I think he may be right,' she said, slipping her arm through his as they continued through the gallery. 'Raphael fell in love with a baker's daughter, and started putting little pastries into his paintings in her honour. And Caravaggio was broke most of the time, so he was probably thinking about his next meal while he painted. I'll have to tell my teacher what Tommaso said. I think he'll be really interested.'

That afternoon, Bruno paid a fortune for an old cookery book in the Porta Portese flea market and started trying out ideas. Eventually he decided on a recipe for roast chicken stuffed with peppers that in turn were stuffed with figs, and set about fine-tuning it so that it would be a creation worthy of its intended recipient.

Laura lies in Tommaso's bed and stretches luxuriously. Tommaso himself has already left to supervise last-minute preparations at Il Cuoco. Today, finally, is the grand opening, and there are a million and one things he still hasn't done.

She gets out of bed and starts to dress. Last night they ate baby artichokes, flattened into stars and deep-fried in oil, and she sees to her consternation that there's a streak of olive oil on her shirt. She opens Tommaso's cupboard to find a clean one, and takes a step back.

The inside of the cupboard is covered with photographs. Photographs of girls. There are brunettes, redheads, a few black-haired Italians, but overwhelmingly the cupboard is filled with blondes. There's a picture of herself, and she remembers now the occasion when Tommaso took it, in this very room, right after they had slept together for the first time.

Oh, she says out loud, as the implications of that sink in.

She looks again at the other girls. There are dozens of them. Now that she examines them more closely, she sees that most of the photos were also taken here, just as hers was.

At the thought of all those women sharing a bed with Tommaso – the same bed that she now shares – the tears spring to her eyes.

'*Fuck*,' she says, like someone who has cut themselves and who sees the blood a second or so before they feel the pain.

And then she does feel it.

As the restaurant filled up with customers, Bruno kept a careful eye on the table in the corner that had been reserved for Laura and her roommate. But it stayed empty.

155

By one-thirty the orders were coming in thick and fast. They had done well to attract so many people to their opening. Carlotta's contacts in the magazine world had helped: the little dining room was full of people who would certainly never have visited the restaurant under its previous ownership. This included the mysterious business contacts of Dr Ferrara's, a group of rough-looking men in very expensive suits whom the other customers treated with careful deference.

For Bruno it was a new experience to be running an entire kitchen, and he had his work cut out making sure all the food was absolutely perfect. Eventually, though, during a brief lull, he had time to pause. Tommaso was looking as miserable as a dog that had lost its bone.

'Where's Laura?' Bruno asked, suddenly fearful.

'Not coming,' his friend said tersely. 'We had a row.'

Bruno stopped in the middle of taking a pan out of the oven. 'What about?'

'Nothing. Well, something, obviously. But nothing I could make any sense of. What do women ever pick fights about?'

Tommaso looked so crestfallen that Bruno put his arm around him. 'Tommaso, I'm so sorry. I can guess how you must feel.'

'It's just a row,' Tommaso muttered.

'I can tell how upset you are,' Bruno said gently.

'What are you talking about? Laura will be fine. I'm upset because I'm stuck in *here*,' he indicated the kitchen, 'while it's all happening out *there*.' As he spoke, Marie whirled in with another fistful of orders, slapped them into Bruno's hands and picked up half a dozen plates from the pass before rushing out again. 'I can feel it! It's alive out there. Whereas in here –' he looked around and shrugged – 'you're just cooking.'

'This is the bit that really matters,' Bruno pointed out gently.

'But it's *your* bit. I'm just hanging about. Can't you give me something to do?'

'Sure. We need some fish filleted for table four.'

'Great. And where's the fun in filleting a fish if there's no one to see you do it?' Tommaso demanded miserably as he moved off. Bruno had no answer. It occurred to him that if this venture was going to be a success, he'd need to find Tommaso some proper work to do.

He got back to his cooking, but a part of his mind was still coming to terms with the fact that Laura wouldn't be eating his creations. Suddenly, dishes that had flown from his fingers like sparks just a few minutes before seemed impossible. Marie came in with another fistful of orders, and he was distracted further by trying to call them to his sous chefs, as well as cooking other dishes himself. Within moments the smooth production line was backing up. People were colliding with each other, boiling water was being slopped from pans on to bare skin, orders were being double-cooked or missed altogether.

'What are you doing?' Tommaso hissed as he brought back the filleted fish.

'I've got in a muddle,' Bruno said tersely.

'You can say that again. You'd better unmuddle yourself pretty fast. That's the order for table six you've just fucked up, and there's a reviewer from *Trova Roma* there.'

'Oh shit,' Bruno said as he prepared to redo the order in its entirety.

Marie came in with yet more orders. 'Guess who's just walked in and asked for a table?'

'The prime minister?'

'Worse. Alain Dufrais. He's got a young chef with him as well.'

'That'll be Hugo Kass,' Bruno muttered.

'Let's hope he doesn't recognise the glasses,' Tommaso said. 'Put him on the next table to the *mafiosi*. That'll stop him looking around too much.'

Eventually everyone had eaten their fill, and the roar of noise from the dining room lessened to a contented hum.

Tommaso was outside, talking to a pleased Dr Ferrara. Bruno was alone in the kitchen. He saw Tommaso's phone lying on a counter, and then he saw that Tommaso had been composing a text message to Laura.

He picked it up and read it. It said: *Hi Laura. Sorry about all that. CU tomorrow? Regards, Tommaso.*

It hadn't been sent yet. Bruno picked it up and, with one eye on the door in case Tommaso came back, began to change it.

By the time he had finished it read:

There was something I wanted to cook tonight –

The recipe of love

Take 1 American girl with honey-coloured skin & freckles like orange-red flakes of chilli on her shoulders.

Fill her with flavours, with basil and tomatoes and pine nuts and parsley.

Warm her gently with your hands for several hours, turning occasionally, and serve with wine and laughter, straight from the dish.

– but sadly 1 of the ingredients was missing. Maybe tomorrow?

He pressed send, and waited for a long, agonising minute before the phone beeped with a reply.

That's lovely. Why wait till tomorrow? I'll come round later. Hope it went well, love L x.

When Tommaso returned, he picked up the phone and said 'Oh'.

'What is it?

'I must have sent my text without meaning to. Still, it looks like Laura's forgiven me.'

'That's good,' Bruno said, his face buried in the pan that he was cleaning.

◎◎

'*Pronto?*'

'Carlotta, it's me.'

'Hey, Laura. What's up?'

'I'm on my way to Tommaso's.'

'You two made up, then?'

'No, but we're just about to.'

'That was quick.'

Laura smiled. 'Let me read you this text he just sent me.'

When she finished Carlotta said, 'Oh Laura, that's wonderful.'

'Isn't it? That's one I'm definitely keeping.'

'This is getting pretty serious, isn't it?' Carlotta said softly. 'It sounds like you two really like each other.'

'Maybe. You know, I didn't really think about it too hard at first. But then, when I saw those photographs and I thought that one day someone else's picture could get pinned over mine – I couldn't bear it. Did I tell you he changes my ringtone every time I stay over?'

'Sweet. What is it at the moment?'

'"Stairway to Heaven."'

'Appropriate. If a little uncool.' Carlotta was silent a little while. 'Do you remember? At the beginning, all you were looking for was a man with dextrous hands. And now here you are, falling in love.'

'Do you know what's ironic? He actually isn't that dextrous.'

'He isn't?' Carlotta sounded surprised.

'When I first met him, it was definitely a physical thing. I mean, he's gorgeous, right? But what I love about him is that he really believes in something. He's got passion, and a sense of purpose. He knows he's got a gift and he'll do anything, anything at all, to use it. So I know I come second to cooking sometimes, but I don't really mind that, because what comes first is something so fundamentally generous.'

'Wow. You *are* in love.'

'I guess,' Laura admitted.

159

'What will you do? When you have to leave Italy, I mean?'

'I don't know. I've already told my parents I may stay until the very end of the summer. But after that – I don't even want to think about it.' She had reached the street where Tommaso's apartment was. She could see the boys in Gennaro's, sharing a jug of *grappa*. 'I'm here. I'd better go.'

'Have a good night, *cara*.'

'I will.'

Fourteen

From *Stozzi* magazine:

Cucina Romana becomes Cucina Romantica

Six weeks ago I ate one of the best meals I have ever had. The location was Rome, in the apartment of my parents, where a talented young chef, Tommaso Massi, had volunteered to cook us some of the dishes of our native city. The menu was a simple one, such as might be found in any one of the hundreds of *ristoranti* that crowd the city centre: *pinzimonio*; fresh *tortellini al pomodoro*; *saltimbocca*; a chocolate *tartufo* for dessert. What elevated this meal to the level of high art was, first, the quality of the ingredients and, second, the skill of the chef, whose passion is to recreate such traditional dishes and reveal them in their true glory. Just as the Sistine Chapel or the Stanze Raphael, expertly scrubbed clean of centuries of accumulated grime and soot, reveal unexpectedly glowing and vibrant colours which surpass anything that our imaginations could have devised, so these simple dishes were restored by this young magician to unimaginable freshness and splendour.

What was most remarkable about this meal, however, was the effect it had on me – and I do not just mean my palate. How can I put this? As the meal was consumed, I too found myself being consumed by passion of a different kind. Massi's intense, sensual flavours and deft handiwork in the kitchen seemed to have awoken appetites that could only be fully satisfied in the bedroom.

Massi is perfect casting for a god of love, being both handsome and charming. He is also winningly modest. When asked about any of his recipes, he struggles to explain what makes them work. 'It's just food,' he shrugs. 'You buy it, you cook it, you serve it. At the end of the day, the cook is no more important than the waiter. A really good waiter, now, has a skill that is often underestimated.'

The good news is that this remarkable chef is now cooking in his own establishment, Il Cuoco in Viale Ostenze. I was fortunate enough to eat there soon after the opening, and was delighted to find that his talents have survived the transition to a bigger stage intact. The women of Rome are in for a treat – and so are their boyfriends.

From *Wanted In Rome*:

The 'romantic restaurant' is not common in this city. The ordinary Roman would rather eat under floodlights than by candlelight, the better to inspect what he is putting in his mouth. The candles at Il Cuoco, in Viale Ostenze, however, do not conceal anything except perhaps the beauty of the food – and that would be clear even to a person wearing a blindfold. This is traditional cooking, creatively reinvented, and to judge from the blissful expressions on the faces of the other diners, they were as smitten as we were. Highly recommended.

From *Time Out Roma*:

Fellini meets foodie in hip young *überchef* Tommaso Massi's take on the traditional Roman trat. The crowd is young, the ambience dark, the music fashionably retro and the word-of-mouth impressive, but the food lives up to expectations. The buzz is that this is a chef who understands women; when Massi came out of his kitchen to tour the tables the reaction was more like that afforded to a rock star than a restaurateur. Book ahead – you'll need to.

From RomeBuddyBoard.com:

Posted by Alessandro Bonaguidi:

> Have you heard the rumour about Il Cuoco? Apparently women go wild for the food there.

Posted by Miko Trenti:

> Yeah, I went there with my girlfriend. It worked for us. Your mileage may vary.

From *Il Messaggero:*

The tradition and inspiration of the cultural imperative that is Rome can nevertheless be explored gastronomically through the fantasy of a chef. At Ristorante Il Cuoco, greedy pilgrims may entrust Tommaso Massi with the creation of an *abbachio cacciatore* or a *coda alla vaccinara*, as well as more mythical dishes according to his alimentary philosophy. Roman tradition is a reference point. Flavours are in harmony with the past and the present also, and thus the expression of a civilisation which is rigorously passionate and creatively orientated. Approximately €80 for two, with wine.

Posted anonymously on www.e-pinions.it/rome:

God, it's true! All of it! Take us to Il Cuoco, guys – there'll be much more than dinner on the menu!

From *The Pocket Guide*:

♉ ✔ ❗ ☼ 🚍 () 📖 📖 ➲ ☹ ☺ ☺ ♊ ♋ 🌀 🦎 ♦ ♦

From *The London Review*:

Readers of this column will already know that I was fortunate enough to be present at the last dinner given by President François Mitterrand of France, when he was already aware that his death from cancer was imminent. On that memorable occasion he served no cheese or dessert. The last dish the President wished to taste on this earth was the ortolan, a tiny songbird that is, ridiculously, protected by law in every country in Europe. Mitterrand ate his in the traditional way, with a cloth covering his head, the better to appreciate the intense flavour of this ornithological morsel. I did the same, popping it whole into my mouth, then biting off the head and spitting it into a bowl. All around me the only sound was the mutual gasp as my fellow diners inhaled the fatty juices that flowed out of the birds' tiny throats and into ours.

Once caught, the ortolan must be kept in a box and fed on figs for a month before being drowned in brandy and roasted for just a few minutes, whole, in a very hot oven. It is the traditional food of lovers. In Colette's novel *Gigi*, for example, when the eponymous heroine becomes a whore, she is said to be 'learning how to eat ortolan'.

I was reminded of this historical curiosity when I dragged my jaded palate, along with Fiona, my jaded trophy girlfriend, to the distinctly degenerate environs of Il Cuoco in Rome. If you like restaurants – and I detest them – then this may well be the sort of place you like. It has the usual complement of tables, chairs, attractive waitresses and so on, though the presence of so many other human beings had the usual depressing effect on my mood. The food, however, was not bad, although regrettably there was no ortolan on the menu. I forget what we ordered. It certainly seemed to have a stirring effect on Fiona, who later that evening informed me that she was leaving me. Frankly, this was something of a relief, as her sexual demands thus far had left me feeling rather enervated. Anyone wishing to replace her should write to me at the usual address, enclosing a photo and a stamped self-addressed envelope.

From *Roma'ce*:

Some of the best food this reviewer has ever had. Each dish tasted distinctly of its ingredients, which were of the highest possible quality. Simple, precise, imaginative reinterpretations of the classics. Chef Tommaso Massi is a wonder. Reservations essential.

Fifteen

It was full. Not just at weekends, either: every evening, and every lunchtime, too, the little dining room was packed to capacity. Two by two they came, for the reputation of Il Cuoco, as Dr Ferrara had predicted, rested partly on the wonderful flavours of the food and partly on the wonderful effect that eating the food had on the female libido. Husbands discovered that their wives forgave them their domestic shortcomings; young men on a first date found that picking up the bill at Il Cuoco was more persuasive than any number of whispered compliments; and lazy boyfriends realised that the subtle seductions of a five-course dinner were a congenial alternative to foreplay.

They had taken on a couple of extra *commis* to help with the prepping, but even so Bruno was busier than he had ever been in his life. His day started soon after dawn, when he arrived at the restaurant to check the deliveries. By ten he was making desserts, and by eleven he was preparing lunch. This being Italy, lunch started late. It was not unusual to have people turn up at three, and – this being Italy – these same diners, who had been tearing about and cursing each other and generally rushing around all day, suddenly lost any desire to hurry the moment they sat down at the table, and would be mortally offended if, say, their *secondo* arrived less than half an hour after the end of their *primo*. Thus the last lunchers would still be finishing their *distillati* at five or even six o'clock, barely two hours before the first evening customers were due. Bruno would be lucky to leave the restaurant by midnight to catch a few hours' sleep before it all began again.

But he was cooking, and that was all that mattered. For the first time in his life it was *his* signature on the plates that were going out of the little kitchen. The dishes were an exact expression of his personality, his influences: Roman, just as he was Roman; virtuoso, just as he was a virtuoso; sensual, passionate and physical, because that was part of his nature too. And if his own yearnings were unfulfilled, if his love for Laura was unreciprocated and uncon-summated, perhaps that only gave his dishes an extra piquancy; a tantalising sense of urgency mixed with regret. 'Eat me now,' they seemed to whisper; 'seize me quickly. For the fruit is only ripe for a day, the meat only tender for a moment. All things must pass; take your pleasures while you can.'

Tommaso had taught Marie everything he knew about waiting tables: how to balance trays piled high with hot dishes on one hand; how to pour wine; how to stage-manage the theatre of serving each table so that the customers knew, even before they tasted it, that this was serious food, worthy of respect. Her uni-form, though, had been her own idea: a tight black blouse tucked into a long white bistro apron, so that from the front she looked as if she was wearing traditional waiters' garb; not until she turned around did you catch a glimpse of the extremely short skirt under-neath. Inevitably, this only added to the heady atmosphere of Il Cuoco. The nature of Bruno's cooking meant that by the third or fourth course diners often found themselves experiencing sharp pangs of another appetite. Customers who were unaccompanied by loved ones – and even some of those who were – sometimes found their gaze wandering towards the beautiful raven-haired Roman girl with the flashing eyes, and more than once she had to discourage the attentions of some lovestruck admirer. Being a Roman girl, however, this was second nature to her, and anyone who overstepped the mark soon retreated, his cheeks and ears burning from a volley of abuse.

Tommaso, meanwhile, still had very little to do. Marie, although rushed off her feet, was so competent that front-of-house ran perfectly. In the kitchen he could help Bruno a little, but once service got under way his friend functioned on some kind of mystical autopilot, intuitively juggling a dozen different orders at once, and he didn't really want any assistance from an amateur. The highlight of Tommaso's evening, therefore, was his nightly tour of the customers' tables. The adulation he received on these occasions was like rain to a thirsty plant, and he needed little encouragement to pull up a chair and share a *distillato* or a glass of wine with his adoring public.

It was on one such tour that the Incident Of The Cigar occurred. Tommaso had accepted a *sambuca* – an anise-flavoured liqueur, traditionally ignited before being drunk – from two young women, who were telling him in some detail how brilliant he was, when the smoke from a neighbouring diner's cigar began drifting in their direction.

Tommaso wafted it away. Then he glanced over at the smoker and saw that his companion was still eating. He leaned over and said, quite mildly, 'I think perhaps your friend would be able to appreciate my chestnut mousse better if it didn't taste of your cigar smoke.'

The man regarded Tommaso with a weary sneer. '*Che cazzo stai dicendo?* What's this crap you're talking?'

'I'm talking, sir, about your cigar, which would perhaps be more appropriate when the other diners have finished their meals.'

A young woman at another table said, 'He's been smoking those things all evening.'

A pained expression crossed Tommaso's face. 'That's a little inconsiderate of you, my friend.'

'*Vaffanculo a lei, e a sua soreta*,' the smoker said, gesturing at Marie, who was walking past.

Tommaso calmly took the cigar and doused it in the man's wine glass. 'She's not my sister,' he said. 'And she doesn't.'

The smoker stared at Tommaso for a moment, his eyes bulging. Tommaso picked up his *sambuca*. As the man angrily pushed back his chair, his fist raised, Tommaso poured the burning liquid down his trousers.

'Marie, a glass of water for the gentleman,' he said. 'He appears to have set himself alight.'

The applause around the room was deafening.

That afternoon, Bruno and Tommaso and Marie had a visitor. He was polite and businesslike, and said that he was calling to inspect the restaurant on behalf of some interested investors. Marie, who had been expecting such a visit, made the polite gentleman an espresso and offered to show him the accounts, an offer the gentleman declined with a slight smile. He would, he said, much rather see the reservations book. Accounts, he explained, particularly accounts prepared for the authorities, could sometimes be overly pessimistic. In his experience, a reservations book was a rather better guide to the health or otherwise of a restaurant.

He glanced through the book, nodding approvingly. 'So,' he said at length, 'you are taking—' And he named a figure that to Marie's amazement was accurate to within a few euros.

'Which, after costs, is leaving you with a net margin of—' he added, almost as an afterthought. Again, Marie was amazed at his accuracy.

'We will take four per cent,' he said thoughtfully. 'Of the gross, that is. We'll charge it as a mark-up on costs, though, so it's effectively tax-deductible. You'll barely notice it on the bottom line. Now, is there anything you need?'

Marie thought about it. 'We could do with a permit to put tables outside, on the pavement, in summer,' she said. 'We've applied, but nothing's happened.'

'Consider it done. Is that all?'

'One of the neighbours has been complaining about the refuse out the back.'

'I'll get it collected twice a week then. Nothing else?'

'And the chef has been having difficulty tracking down wild seabass.'

'I'll tell my friend at the wholesalers to put you down for some.' The polite gentleman drained his espresso, stood up and offered Marie his hand. 'A pleasure doing business with you. I shall come to eat here myself, one day very soon. And if you need anything, anything at all, just speak to Franco, the one who brings your vegetables. He knows how to reach us.' He tapped his nose. 'But no need to mention this arrangement to Dr Ferrara, you understand?'

It was, they all agreed later, a remarkably good service for the price, certainly much better than anything they got in return for their income tax.

'*Uno ristretto, Gennaro, per favore*,' Tommaso said wearily next morning. 'No, better make that two.'

'Two?' Gennaro shook his head. 'Nobody drinks two *ristretti*.'

'Believe me, I can drink two.' Tommaso went and sat down, leaning his head on his hands. 'And even then I may go back to sleep.'

'You want them there, at the table?' Gennaro said eagerly, dollar signs appearing in his eyes.

'Give him a break, Gennaro.' Bruno sat down next to his friend. 'What's up, Tommaso?'

'It's Laura. She's wearing me out.'

Bruno flinched. If Laura was his girlfriend he wouldn't want to sleep much either. Tommaso, not noticing, continued in a low voice, 'She's just a bit – well, strange.'

'In what way?'

'She's obsessed with food.'

Bruno knew he ought not to have this conversation, but he couldn't help himself. 'Well – so am I, for that matter.'

'Yes, but this is in a weird way.' A noise like pistons hammering on a steel plate came from Gennaro's Gaggia as the vast industrial pump he had fitted to it pounded water into a space many times smaller than nature had ever intended. It sounded rather like a very old steam train going up a steep hill, and like an old steam train there was a ghastly moment when one thought it might not make it after all. The hammering got slower and slower, and more and more laboured, until at last, with a shrill protesting shriek of escaping pressure, water blasted into the packed coffee grounds. When this cacophony of groans, gusts, wheezing pipes and juddering joints finally subsided, Gennaro carried two tiny thimbles of *ristretti* over to the table.

'Tell you what – drink them both and I'll give you your next one on the house,' he joked.

Tommaso drained one thimble in a single gulp, and paused only briefly before following it with the second. 'As soon as you like, Gennaro.'

'Are you kidding? It'll kill you. I meant, next time you're in.'

'Now is good.'

Shaking his head at the folly of the young, Gennaro retreated behind his counter.

'Weird how?' Bruno wanted to know.

Tommaso leaned across the table and lowered his voice. 'Well, last night she wanted me to baste her with olive oil and rosemary and then turn her slowly on my spit.'

Bruno made a face. 'Rosemary?'

'I told you she was odd.'

'Very. Marjoram would be much better.'

'What?'

'Never mind. So the problem is what, exactly?'

'Now she wants me to think up some other recipe ideas, as she

171

calls it.' He lowered his voice even further. 'Between you and me, she's hard work sometimes.'

Bruno barely heard the last part. His imagination was racing. 'I would cover her with currants and dust her with icing sugar.' He blushed. Had he said that out loud? He was thinking of that damned wedding cake again. 'I mean, that's one suggestion. Or you could—'

'Hang on, let me write some of these down,' Tommaso said, pulling out a pen.

Gennaro brought over a third thimble. 'It's the strongest yet,' he warned. 'I just increased the pressure.' Tommaso tossed it down his throat with barely a glance.

By the time they got to the restaurant Tommaso, his brain sizzling, was bug-eyed and jumping around as if on springs. When the phone rang he snatched it up and yelled '*Pronto*' into the receiver like a madman. 'You want a what? A reservation? Why? Who are you?' There was a pause while he listened. 'What's wrong with your voice?' he demanded. 'A speech impediment? Well, we don't want anyone with a speech impediment eating here. Dentures? You have *dentures*? I am Tommaso Massi. How can you possibly appreciate my cooking with dentures? Yes, go to hell.' He slammed down the handset and said cheerfully, 'From now on, Marie, no smokers and no dentures. What?'

Bruno and Marie were staring at him open-mouthed.

'For a moment there,' Bruno said gently, 'you sounded just like Alain Dufrais.'

'Oh.' Tommaso looked crestfallen. 'Of course. Sorry. I must have drunk too much of that damn coffee.'

Tommaso liked to watch Marie working. He liked the way she had to go up on tiptoe to squeeze her ample bottom through the gaps between chairs; the fluidity of her bosom when she leaned down to clear a table. Occasionally he tried to flirt with her, but even though he employed all his considerable charm, she maintained a professional detachment. Tommaso wasn't used to this. He found himself thinking about her wistfully. Somehow he knew that Marie wouldn't be into having pitted olives skewered on her nipples, or playing strange games with meringue mixture.

Marie kept him in order, too. When, on a sudden whim, Tommaso announced that from now on the dining room was going to be kept completely dark, so that everyone could concentrate better on what was going into their mouths, it was Marie who took him aside and said, firstly, if you do that how am I supposed to see who I'm serving? And secondly, if you don't stop behaving like an arrogant prick I'm going to put this fork up your nose in front of the whole restaurant.

They were clearing up one evening, after all the customers had gone, when Marie said suddenly, 'I think you'd better tell me what the deal is here.'

'Deal?' Tommaso said innocently.

'You're supposed to be the chef, but *he* does all the cooking.' She pointed at Bruno. 'And don't tell me you came up with the recipes and he's just doing what you've shown him, because I know that isn't true.'

'Ah,' Tommaso said. He paused. 'You see, there was a girl, and she wanted to go out with someone who could cook, and I wanted to go out with *her*, so I told her I could. Cook, that is. And I couldn't. But Bruno could, and – and – it just all started from there,' he said helplessly.

'So you've started a restaurant because you didn't want to tell a girl you can't cook?' Marie said in disbelief.

'Um, yes, I suppose so.' Hearing it put like that, Tommaso experienced a feeling he got more and more these days – a feeling that he couldn't quite work out how or why things had got as complicated as they had. 'You see, if she thinks I'm only a waiter, she'll probably dump me.'

'And what's wrong with being a waiter?' Marie wanted to know, tapping her foot dangerously.

'Oh, nothing,' he assured her. There was something about Marie that made him not want to argue with her.

'That's the stupidest story I ever heard,' Marie decided.

'It's pretty stupid, yes,' Tommaso agreed.

'So when are you going to tell her the truth?'

'Soon,' he said. A thought was forming in his mind. If Laura found out the truth, she would dump him. Life would go back to the way it had been before, and actually Tommaso wasn't averse to that at all.

Sixteen

Ever since Bruno had started creating the menu for Il Cuoco, he had been struggling with the impossibility of creating the dish he had spoken of to Tommaso that first night, walking back from Templi, when the two of them had discussed the difference between aphrodisiacs and the food of love itself.

Bruno remembered very well what he had said on that occasion: 'If you want someone to fall in love with you, you cook them something that shows you understand their very soul.'

'Such as?' his friend had asked.

And Bruno remembered, too, every word of the answer he had given: 'You'd have to really know the person concerned: their history; their background; whether they are raw or refined, dry or oily. You would have to have tasted them, to know whether their own flesh is sweet or savoury, salty or bland. In short, you would have to love them, and even then you might not truly know them well enough to cook a dish that would capture their heart.'

But even though he knew he loved Laura, he found it far, far harder than he had expected to create a recipe that would do justice to her. He knew that it would have to be something sweet, and so insubstantial that it was barely more than a morsel, leaving the palate gasping for more. But it would also have to be perfect, and perfection remained elusive. Like an alchemist desperately pursuing the formula that will transmute base metals to gold, Bruno tried everything. Again and again he tried, always hopeful of success but never quite attaining it. There was something missing, some ingredient that he couldn't name or describe, even by its absence.

And then, one afternoon, Laura herself came round to Il Cuoco. She was looking for Tommaso, who wasn't in, and she came into the little kitchen before Bruno was aware of her presence. He was muttering to himself as he spun barefoot from stove to fridge to prep surface, trying different combinations of tastes and textures, half demented with his lack of success. He was close, he knew he was close, but something wasn't quite there . . . His face glistened with sweat from the heat of the oven, his hair was streaked with flour and oil and his hands were crusted with splashes of burnt sugar that he had barely noticed, much less stopped to wash off.

Laura had been drawn into the kitchen by the most extraordinary smell. She had expected to find Tommaso in there, and her surprise at discovering Bruno was matched only by her shock at the intensity of the aroma.

It smelled of baking cakes, which took her back to the kitchen of her childhood, coming home from school to find her mother making her cookies . . . but it also smelled medicinal, and that made her think of being ill and being looked after when she was tucked up in bed. Then there were spices, and a faint hint of Christmas: nutmeg, perhaps, and cloves . . . But underneath all of those was something else, something insidiously smooth and emollient, like vanilla or eucalyptus. She had a sudden memory of touching her father's cheek as he gave her a kiss goodnight – the rasp of his eight o'clock shadow, and that smell . . . she had it now: it was the smell of his cologne, the smell of his business suits, the smell of her parents' bedroom and the big double bed and the terrifying dark thought of what went on there. But after another moment she relaxed: there were comforting aromas in there too: apples, brandy, crisp butter pastry and cinnamon.

'What *is* that?' she breathed.

Bruno spun around and stared at her like a madman. 'I'm making apple pie,' he said.

Apple pie . . . Laura hadn't had apple pie for years. Suddenly she felt thousands of miles from home, and a tear welled into her eye. 'I'm sorry,' she gasped.

'Here. It's ready.' Without bothering to use gloves, Bruno pulled open the oven door and brought the pie dish out. She noticed that it was extraordinarily tiny, like something made for a doll. He put it on the counter. She buried her face in the steam and inhaled deeply.

'Can I have some?'

'Of course,' he said. 'I made it for you. It just needs a little cream . . . here.' He took out a spoon and thrust it into the pie, releasing more vapour. The whole creation was barely more than a single spoonful big. He poured a little cream on top and held it up to her lips. 'Don't worry. It's not too hot.'

She opened her mouth and he slid the morsel inside. She couldn't help gasping. She closed her eyes and chewed ecstatically, unwilling even to swallow lest she make the experience a moment shorter than it had to be.

'Bruno,' she said at last when she was capable of speaking, 'it's fantastic.'

He kissed her.

Shocked, she pulled away.

Bruno was looking at her with an expression of such intensity that she was almost frightened. Laura remembered all the situations she'd got into with other Italian men, the ones who'd groped her and stroked her and tried to sneak her into dark doorways. Surely not – not Bruno, who was her friend. Who was, even more importantly, Tommaso's friend. What was going on?

'I'm sorry,' he said quickly. 'It's an Italian thing. We – we kiss each other all the time. It really doesn't mean anything.'

'No, of course,' she said, recovering. 'I know it doesn't. I was just a bit surprised. Americans don't do that, you see.'

'No.'

'And I don't think we should mention it to Tommaso.' She looked him in the eye. 'I think he would misunderstand too.'

'Of course,' he said. 'And I promise you, it won't happen again.'

As she hurried back to her own apartment Laura found herself shaking. *Bruno, of all people. I mean, I like Bruno. I certainly don't want to lose him as a friend. He's funny and nice and thoughtful. How could he do a thing like that?*

But then, she was in a foreign country, and Italian men *were* impetuous compared to Americans. Maybe she was overreacting. Maybe it was the kind of thing an Italian would have taken in her stride.

So long as Tommaso never found out, no harm had been done.

Tommaso, returning from a pleasant morning arguing with friends over a coffee or two, was surprised to see Laura's textbooks on the kitchen counter.

'Laura's here?' he asked Bruno, who was busy washing up.

'She was, earlier.' Bruno kept his eyes on the sink, afraid that he wouldn't be able to meet his friend's gaze.

Tommaso put his finger in the little pie dish, licked it and made a face. 'Actually, I'm glad she's not around. I want to talk to you about her.'

'You do?'

'*Sì*. I think this thing I've been having with her has run its course. It's been fantastic and everything, but the truth is – well,

178

I'm getting itchy feet. Actually,' he added, for he was always honest with Bruno, 'maybe it's not my feet, you know?'

'You're going to dump her?' he said, stunned.

'Yes, but that's the problem. This is sort of new territory for me. I've never been in a proper relationship before, so I really don't know how it's done.'

'I'm probably not the right person to ask,' Bruno said. 'Since I've never been in a proper relationship either.'

'But you know things, like how to let her down gently.' An idea occurred to him. 'Maybe you could say something to her for me. Kind of preparing the way.'

'I really don't think that's a good idea,' Bruno muttered. 'This is something that's got to come from you.'

'But you could help soften the blow. You know – explain what an idiot I am, how I'm always messing around with other women . . .'

'Tommaso, there's something I've got to tell you.'

'Yes? What?'

Bruno kept his eyes on the sink. 'I'm fond of Laura.'

'Ah.' Tommaso nodded. 'You don't want to see her hurt.'

'No – not that. I'm not making myself clear.' Bruno struggled to find the words. 'I think I'm in love with her.'

'Oh,' Tommaso said. He thought for a moment. 'When you say "in love", you don't actually mean—'

'I mean I think about her every single moment of every single day. I think about her when I sleep, when I wake up, when I'm doing other things. I even think about her when I cook – especially when I cook. I think about her smile, about her frown, about her mouth, about the little orange-brown freckles on her shoulders. I have imaginary conversations with her. I dream of catching a glimpse of her. Then, when she turns up, I can barely look at her.'

'Oh. Ah. I see.'

'Are you angry with me?'

'Of course not. I mean, it's not your fault. You've done nothing wrong.'

'That's not—' Bruno had been about to say, 'That's not quite true', but then he realised that he couldn't. He had promised Laura that the kiss would remain a secret.

'Listen, it happens.' Tommaso slapped Bruno on the back. 'I'll tell you something I've never told anyone else. I fancy Lucia, Vincent's girlfriend. See?'

'But you're not in love with Lucia.'

'True,' Tommaso conceded. He began to pack coffee grounds into an espresso pot. 'That's weird, isn't it? All the time I've been going out with Laura, you're the one who's in love with her.'

'Yes. It's weird all right.'

'So after I finish with her, are you going to ask her out?'

'I can't.'

'Of course you can.'

'Trust me, Tommaso, I can't. She'd never have me.'

Laura's six-month residency permit was about to expire. Being a law-abiding sort of person she therefore presented herself at the appropriate office of the appropriate authority to get it stamped with an *estensione*.

When she finally made it to the head of the queue, however, the polite young man behind the counter informed her that there was a difficulty. Well, not so much a difficulty, perhaps, as a discrepancy. Her *residenza*, while appearing to be correct, had been stamped not with the *stampa di notifica* but the altogether different *stampa d' identità*, and was thus technically invalid. And since it would be altogether wrong of him – indeed, impossible – to extend a document that was invalid, Laura would have to provide an acceptable *residenza* before he could proceed.

'But it's just a mistake, isn't it?' she said. 'The official must have used the wrong stamp.'

The young man conceded that an error was indeed the most

180

likely possibility. He indicated the device in front of him, a wire merry-go-round with as many tiers as a wedding cake, which held a dozen stamps of various shapes and sizes. He showed her the *stampa di notifica*. It was, she could see, not dissimilar to the *stampa d'identità*. In addition, the *identità* had once been acceptable on such documents, although not any more. He produced from a dusty file a piece of official paperwork, an internal memorandum several pages long which apparently explained the change from *identità* to *notifica*. He pointed to the date, several years ago, and shrugged.

'So what should I do?' Laura asked.

Well, that was self-evident. She must get herself a valid *residenza* and bring it back to him, at which point he would be delighted to extend it.

'Can't *you* give me a valid *residenza*?' Laura asked with what she hoped was a winning smile.

Alas, no, the young man decided, giving her an equally warm smile in return. He would love to, particularly for such a charming foreigner, but he himself only dealt with extensions. It would be necessary for Laura to go back to the office of the *residenza*.

It was past two o'clock and the office of the *residenza* was now closed for the day. Laura returned next morning and presented her papers to another elegantly dressed young man. He was sympathetic; even more sympathetic than the last young man had been. Yes, yes, there had clearly been a mistake. It was certainly usual in these cases to use the *stampa di notifica*, not the *stampa d'identità*. But in his opinion a *stampa d'identità* was also perfectly valid, so she should have no difficulty in getting her *residenza* extended.

'And how do I do that?' Laura asked.

The official frowned. He pulled at his cheek. He frowned some more. 'I will go and consult,' he decided. Twenty minutes later he returned, smelling strongly of cigarette smoke, and indicated that she should come with him.

181

She followed him down an endless corridor that smelled of mildewy air-conditioning. Eventually she was shown into a small office in which an older man, also elegantly dressed, was sitting behind a tiny wooden desk. On the desk he had Laura's *residenza*. Another man was sitting with one buttock resting on the edge of the desk.

The owner of the desk, who exuded competence and intelligence, explained to her what the problem was. He seemed to take an almost intellectual pleasure in summarising the situation concisely and, apparently, wittily, since his account brought wry smiles and even appreciative laughter from the other two. The problem, it transpired, was that their friends and colleagues in the office of the *estensione* were as stubborn as mules about certain changes in procedure that everybody else had chosen to ignore.

'So it's the other department's fault?' Laura asked, still hoping that all this was leading to some sort of conclusion.

The older man lifted a warning finger and his voice took on a certain gravity. No, no, one did not use words like fault when talking about government departments. It was simply a question of differing interpretations. Laura had a perfectly valid *residenza*, this was certain, but unfortunately his colleagues in the office of the *estensione* were correct as well. Laura's document was valid as a *residenza*, but not as a *residenza*-for-extension, since a *residenza* that required extension, as his colleagues in the office of the *estensione* had pointed out, should have been stamped at the time of issuing with a *stampa di notifica*. Since Laura had always intended to stay for more than six months, she had therefore acquired the wrong stamp, and was thus technically not in possession of a valid *residenza*, and was technically an illegal alien. She saw, he hoped, the distinction he was making. It was not the *residenza* itself that was invalid, but Laura's possession of it, and therefore the understandable mistake lay with her and not with either department.

He sat back, smiling the satisfied smile of a theologian who has succeeded in reconciling two apparently contradictory principles.

'But what shall I *do*?' Laura asked, not caring very much whose fault it was.

The question seemed to take the man by surprise, and prompted some further consultation with his colleagues. At last he declared that she must bring all her papers to him and he would see if he could sort something out.

It was at this point that Laura made a crucial error of judgement. Had she consulted any of her Italian friends, they would have told her precisely what to do, which was nothing at all, since there was absolutely no reason whatsoever why anyone should come knocking on her door to check that she had a permit. But Laura was a tidy-minded person, and she assumed, quite erroneously, that it would be a time-consuming but straightforward matter to get one. She therefore went straight back to her apartment, called the administrator of the college to organise a letter of authorisation, found the necessary papers and returned to the office of the *residenza* the very next day, thus establishing in the eyes of the officials that she undoubtedly had something to hide.

'I have all the papers,' she announced to the theologian and his two colleagues. She laid them on his desk with the confidence of a poker player laying out a winning hand.

The theologian picked up her letter of authorisation and read it. Yes, he agreed, these were undoubtedly the right papers. Unfortunately, while they were undoubtedly the right papers, they also showed that Laura, as an illegal alien, had also been engaged in studying, something that was not permitted. Only if she had been in possession of a valid *residenza* would it have been permissible for her to have been studying in this way.

Once again, she asked what she should do.

She was obliged to return to America and re-apply for permission to visit Italy, came the answer.

'*What?*'

The theologian gave an eloquent shrug, which expressed quite clearly the impression that while he himself, as a civilised person, would not require such a course of action, the logic of it was quite inescapable.

With a heavy heart Bruno prepared a very different meal to all the others he had cooked for Laura. A simple chicken stew, rich and hearty, to be eaten with chunks of dense Italian bread. Comfort food – all he could do to soften the heartache to come.

'It's ready,' he told his friend, 'I'm going out. Just take it off the stove when you want to serve it.'

It occurred to Bruno, as he went down the stairs, that this was probably the last meal he would ever cook for Laura. He hoped Tommaso would at least break the news to her gently.

Tommaso tried to steer the conversation round to the subject of breaking up, but Laura was preoccupied.

'Tommaso, I need to find a lawyer,' she said as they ate the stew.

'A lawyer?' Tommaso would have crossed himself if he hadn't remembered in time that he was an agnostic. 'What on earth do you want a lawyer for?'

Laura explained the predicament in which she found herself, and Tommaso laughed.

'So you've discovered the *muro di gomma**. Congratulations. It's one of our oldest and most treasured monuments.'

He explained that in Italy, the state traditionally curried favour with the electorate by providing a large number of jobs for life. This in turn meant that government ministries were staffed largely by *statale*; people who had turned doing nothing at all into an art form. Laura's problem would be now bounced backwards and forwards between departments for ever, or at least until someone did something to resolve the situation.

*Rubber wall.

'But they're talking about throwing me out!'

No, Tommaso assured her, she was perfectly safe. The officials simply required a *bustarella* – a little envelope.

'A *bustarella*?'

'*Sì*. A bribe.'

Laura was horrified. Surely that was illegal. What if he was wrong? Then she'd be arrested and deported for sure.

'Trust me, Laura. *Siamo in Italia*. It's the way things are done here.'

'How did it go with Laura?' Bruno asked when he returned.

'I haven't told her yet. It's hard, I'm picking my moment. And she's got some problems right now.'

'Well, there's plenty of stew left for tomorrow,' Bruno muttered.

Seventeen

The following day Laura returned to the office of the theologian and once again laid her papers on his desk. This time, however, she also produced an envelope containing three hundred euros, which she placed next to them.

The theologian did not so much as glance at the envelope. For one horrible moment Laura thought she had made a dreadful mistake. But when he picked up her letter of authorisation, it now seemed to be, magically, perfectly acceptable. A substitute *residenza* was quickly found, and just as speedily stamped. Throughout this procedure the *bustarella* lay on the desk, apparently unnoticed, and it still lay there when she was ushered to the door.

Laura found that she was strangely exhilarated. When she had finally taken the *bustarella* out, her heart had been thudding. When she had placed it on the desk, it had been like getting into bed with a new lover. She felt authentically Italian at last.

She rushed back to the Viale Glorioso.

'Ah, Laura,' Tommaso said when he saw her. 'I'm glad you're here. There's something I want to talk to you about.'

'Is Bruno here?' she asked him.

'No. Why?'

'Why do you think?' she whispered, gluing her lips against his and sliding her hands inside his shirt.

If there was one thing Tommaso was never averse to, it was quick, uncomplicated sex. 'Whoo,' he said thoughtfully. And, a few minutes later, 'Whoa.' And a few minutes after that, 'Whee.'

'So what did you want to talk about?' Laura asked later, when they were done and were lying on the bed among a mess of rumpled bedclothes and abandoned underwear.

Somehow Tommaso suspected that these conversations were better held before wild, panting, exuberant sex rather than after, but he decided he was honour-bound to seize the opportunity.

'The thing is,' he began, then stopped. How was he going to put this? 'The thing is, it's like a meal. When you've had beef every day for two months, you're ready for some lamb. Which is not to say,' he added hurriedly, 'that there was anything wrong with the beef. The beef was perfect. Unforgettable, in fact. But eventually the time for beef is over.'

'You mean, like the seasons?' Laura asked, not understanding.

'Exactly. Beef season is followed by lamb season. Well, actually there isn't a beef season, but there is a season for lamb and it's over, and soon it'll be time for something different. Game, for example.'

'So you'll take lamb off the menu, and put game on.'

'Exactly.'

'And how will you cook game at the restaurant?'

'Ah.' He saw the difficulty now. 'I'm not talking about the restaurant,' he said helpfully. 'I'm talking about us.'

'Us?'

'Yes.' He struggled again. 'Let me put it another way. Sometimes, when two people linger over a long meal, it takes them a while to realise they've reached the end. They have a *grappa*, perhaps some *biscotti*, then they order some coffee, but really it's time to call for the bill. To say goodnight, and goodbye, and of course to tip the waiter. But instead they linger until the last possible moment.'

'And when that happens, the staff can't go home. They have to wait.'

'Yes. Exactly.'

'I understand, Tommaso. Sometimes you have to stay late. It's not a problem.'

'It isn't?'

'No. It's your job, and I love the fact that you're a chef. Even if it does mean that you sometimes fall asleep during sex.'

'I do not!' he said, offended.

'Not asleep during your bit. Asleep during my bit,' she reminded him. 'Remember two nights ago, when—'

'OK, but that was an exception.'

'But it's all right,' she assured him. 'I don't want to change you. You've got your cooking, I've got art history. That's why we're great together. We've both got other interests.'

'Talking of other interests—'

'I love you,' Laura said happily. 'And I love it when we talk about food like this. What's on the menu at the restaurant tomorrow?'

'I *will* tell her, honestly,' Tommaso said to Bruno later. 'I've planted the seeds. It just takes a little time.'

'There's only a little stew left now. It'll keep until tomorrow, but no longer.'

'Yes, that was Laura. She's developing quite an appetite.'

'I had the strangest conversation with Tommaso last night,' Laura reported to Carlotta.

'What about?'

188

'That was the weird thing. He didn't seem to be able to say. He'd cooked this wonderful stew, and he kept saying there was something he wanted to tell me, but instead he started talking about what a shame it was he had to work so late at the restaurant.'

There was an intake of breath at the other end of the phone. 'Maybe he's trying to propose.'

'No!' Laura laughed. 'We've only known each other a few months.'

'But he's sleeping with you. If you were an Italian girl, that would mean you *are* practically engaged.'

'But he knows I have to go back to America this summer.'

'All the more reason to ask you to marry him now.'

'Carlotta, that's crazy.'

'Is it? You said yourself that he adores you.'

'Yes, but – my God,' Laura said. 'Engagement? Do you really think so?'

'Maybe. And if he does ask, what will you say?'

'I don't know,' Laura admitted. 'It's so complicated. I'll have to think about it.'

Tommaso walked to the restaurant with a heavy heart. He had tried to spell it out to Laura, but it was so hard to say the blunt words that would break her heart. Everyone was going to be cross with him. There was Laura, of course, but there was also Dr Ferrara, his main backer, who was the father of Laura's best friend. The atmosphere at Il Cuoco was difficult enough already. Ever since he had revealed that he wasn't actually a chef, Marie had begun treating him with apparent disdain, while deferring with exaggerated respect to Bruno. Bruno, meanwhile, had fallen into a huge, inexplicable depression and barely spoke. The only time he opened his mouth was to ask whether Tommaso had dumped Laura yet.

'*Scusi?*'

189

He looked up. It was a girl who had spoken to him. She was blonde and pretty, and she was wearing shorts. There was a rucksack on her back and she was holding a guidebook.

'*Si?*' he said.

'Can you tell me how to get to the Piazza Navona?'

A tourist. Tommaso had forgotten how much he liked tourists. 'Of course,' he said. 'In fact, I'm going that way myself. But I'm afraid,' he dropped his voice gravely, 'that there has to be a fee for guiding you there. It's a city regulation.'

'It is, is it?' the girl asked sceptically.

'Absolutely.'

'And how much is this fee?'

'The fee is that, when we get there, you have to allow me to buy you a *grappa*.'

The girl laughed. 'And if I don't want to pay that fee?'

'Then you have to give me a kiss.'

'I'll settle for the *grappa*. For the moment.'

'Excellent. What's your name?'

'Heidi. I'm from Munich,' she said, putting out her hand for him to shake.

'Hello, Heidi. My name is Tommaso and I'm—' He hesitated. He had almost said, 'I'm a chef,' but at the last moment he stopped. 'I'm a waiter.'

As he said it he felt a wonderful sense of liberation, as if a great weight was lifting from his shoulders.

Two hours and many drinks later, Heidi and Tommaso went back to the apartment. Bruno was at the restaurant, cooking; Laura was at classes. Tommaso told himself that he wasn't actually cheating on Laura, since in effect they had broken up already, even if he hadn't quite finished making that clear to her.

So many women, and only one Tommaso. As soon as they were inside, he started making up for lost time.

☙

Laura runs up the stairs to Tommaso's apartment. Her diet, and the exercise she's doing at the gym, are *definitely* starting to have an effect.

'Tommaso?' she calls. 'Bruno?'

There's no answer. But someone has been here recently. The CD player is playing one of Tommaso's favourite songs, 'The Boys of Summer'. Which means, she thinks, that Tommaso has been here very recently. Bruno tolerates his roommate's taste in music but he doesn't share it.

Then she hears the shower hissing. He must be in the bathroom. She smiles and goes through to his bedroom to wait.

The printer by Tommaso's computer is whirring. Idly she goes to see what he's printing. And watches, dumbstruck, as a picture of a pretty blonde girl, taken in this very room, scrolls out, line by line.

She hears footsteps on the stairs. The door of the apartment crashes open. '*Due cappuccini,*' Tommaso's voice calls triumphantly. 'Heidi, I even persuaded the crazy old barman to serve us cappuccino in the afternoon!'

The shower is turned off. The only noise now is the whirring of the printer and the pounding in Laura's own head. Tommaso comes into the bedroom and sees her there, and for a moment everything is suspended in time, like a film that has been frozen—

And then she pushes past him, desperate to get out of there before the bathroom door opens, before the other girl comes out. She spills the coffees and does not stop; runs down the stairs, out into the street, with Tommaso calling her name somewhere behind her.

He catches her up but she won't listen. He tries to talk to her as he walks alongside her, dodging cars and pedestrians while she pushes forward, refusing to give way for anyone or anything.

'Laura, listen, I didn't mean for it to be like this, I wanted to break it to you gently—'

'Get away from me,' she hisses. 'Leave me alone. Go back to your cappuccino-drinking Heidi.'

'It's been fantastic, I'll never forget you—'

She snorts. 'That's funny. Because I'm unlikely to forget this either, Tommaso. Strangely enough, this is something that is unlikely to slip my mind for a very long time.'

'I tried to tell you I was fed up,' he cries.

She searches for the most hurtful thing, the very worst thing she can say to him, and she finds it. 'You're as bad as Bruno, you know that?'

'What do you mean?'

'Your friend Bruno. Kissing me. Making me promise not to tell you. Staring at me all the time. Making my skin crawl. You're a pair of perverts, both of you.'

She breaks into a run again, and this time he doesn't try to follow her.

When Bruno got back from Il Cuoco it was after midnight. Tommaso was waiting in the apartment, his face dark.

'How'd it go?' Bruno said gently.

Tommaso shrugged.

'You seem pretty upset.'

'Yes.'

'I hadn't realised it was going to be so hard for you.'

'It wasn't.' Tommaso said curtly. 'Not that part, at any rate.'

Bruno realised that something was very wrong. 'Tommaso, what's up?'

'Laura told me you kissed her.'

Bruno froze. 'Ah.'

Tommaso got to his feet. 'How many times?' he said threateningly.

'Once,' Bruno said. 'Maybe twice. Three times. Tommaso, I'm sorry. I told you how I felt about her—'

'You said you'd done nothing wrong.'

192

'Well, no, actually. You said that.'

'You tried to steal her,' Tommaso snarled. 'You're my friend – *supposed* to be my friend – and you made a pass at my girl.'

'It was just a kiss.'

'Only because that's all she'd let you do. If she'd been willing, would you have stopped there?'

Bruno couldn't answer that.

'If it was anyone else, I'd beat you to a pulp,' Tommaso said. 'As it is . . .' He slammed his fist into his palm. 'We're not friends any more, Bruno.'

'What about the restaurant?' Bruno heard himself say.

'Oh yes. The restaurant. Another great way to make a fool of me. Well, I don't give a shit about the restaurant. It was a stupid idea in the first place.' He pointed to the door. 'Now get out of here.'

Bruno stumbled out of the apartment, followed by Tommaso's shouts. A final '*Vaffanculo*', accompanied by the ritual gesture of a clenched right fist, with the left hand simultaneously clapped to the right bicep, issued from the window above his head as he staggered blindly down the little street.

He wasn't surprised that Tommaso was angry. The knowledge that another man has made a pass at your girlfriend would still, in some parts of Italy, be considered grounds for pulling a knife. The fact that he had been on the verge of finishing with her was no excuse: if anything, it made it worse, since it could be construed as trying to take advantage of a vulnerable situation.

Bruno started running. He had to find Laura. Perhaps if he could just explain how it had happened, how he had only gone along with Tommaso's crazy scheme as a favour to his friend . . .

At last he reached the Residencia Magdalena. There was an entryphone, and he buzzed the bell marked Patterson until a voice answered.

'Judith?' he panted. 'I need to speak to Laura.'

'Who is this?'

'It's Bruno.'

'She doesn't want to talk to you. She won't talk to either of you. Just go away.'

'Please,' he begged. 'Just get her to come to the intercom.'

'She doesn't—'

Then Laura's voice, brittle and hoarse, interrupted her. 'What do you want, Bruno?'

'I can't let you walk out of my life without telling you how I feel about you,' he said.

'Oh, sure. You and Tommaso both. Why don't you—' Bruno had to stand back to let a group of people into the building, and by the time he got back to the speaker she was just finishing, '—thought you were my friends. I actually liked hanging out with you both. What an idiot you must have thought I was. When I was just another tourist to warm up your beds.'

'No,' he said quickly. 'Laura, listen to me. I love you. I love you more than I've ever loved anyone.'

There was a moment's silence from the entryphone, and just for a second he thought he might have got through to her, but her voice, when she answered, was thick with tears and disgust.

'Just get away from me, you creep. Don't you know how repulsive that is? Go away and leave me alone.'

When Gennaro came to open up the coffee bar the next morning, he found Bruno slumped in the doorway.

'I need a favour,' the young man said as he hauled himself to his feet.

'By the look of you, you need a coffee.'

'That too. Look, Gennaro, you know that van of yours?'

'You want to borrow that old rust bucket again? It's in pretty bad shape at the moment. I'm not sure how far you'll get in it.'

'I was wondering if you'd sell it to me.'

'Oh.' Gennaro thought for a moment. 'It's a fine vehicle, structurally. I mean, when I call it a rust bucket, that's just my

194

affectionate name for it – for her. Cosmetically she may not be much to look at, but her engine's as sound as a bell.'

'I don't have time for this,' Bruno said wearily. 'How much do you want for it?'

Gennaro gave it some more thought. 'Well,' he admitted, 'the truth is that she may need a few minor mechanical upgrades. I've been cannibalising her, you see, for the coffee pump.' He pointed proudly to where his Gaggia stood, now almost invisible inside an elaborate cage of auxiliary pipes, stopcocks, valves, conduits and fans. 'So I'll accept five hundred.'

'I have two hundred. But I'll throw in these.' Bruno pulled something out of his jacket, a rolled-up bundle of cloth that he proceeded to open on the table.

'*Uanema!*' Gennaro breathed. 'These are your cooking knives, aren't they?'

'They were. I don't need them any more. What do you say?'

'It's a deal,' Gennaro said, picking up one of the knives.

'Can I have the keys then?'

'No point,' Gennaro said cheerfully. He pointed to where the ignition lock of a Fiat van was now built into his Gaggia.

'So how do I start it?'

'Here.' Gennaro handed him a spoon. 'This should do it.'

'Great.'

'Don't worry,' the café owner said confidently. 'No one will steal that van. Not unless they're completely off their heads.'

Insalata

'L'insalata is served invariably after the second course to signal the approaching end of the meal. It releases the palate from the grip of the cook's fabrications, leading it to cool, fresh sensations . . .'

MARCELLA HAZAN, *The Essentials of Classic Italian Cooking*

Eighteen

The young woman seated across the room at table twelve is familiar to us. As the crowd of attentive waiters finally steps back, leaving the couple to enjoy their *persillades* of wreck-caught salmon, celeriac purée, jasmine sauce and roasted fennel, not to mention their glasses of chilled Puligny-Montrachet, we can see that she is indeed Laura, though a rather different Laura from the one we left three months ago in Trastevere. For one thing, she looks fantastic. Gone are the extra pounds she put on when she was gorging herself on Bruno's extravagant pasta and rich desserts. Her newly sleek and almost muscular torso is a testament to the many hours she has put in at the gym, as well as the four kilometres she has been running every day. Her hair is different, too: shorter and tied back in a fetching little ponytail. We cannot see her eyes, because they are hidden behind a pair of elegant dark glasses which reflect the image of her companion, who is equally smartly dressed; for this is a special occasion.

'Potatoes, madam?' the waiter enquires, his spoon hovering over the silver dish of vegetables.

'Not for me.'

'Sir?'

'Just one, please.' Kim Fellowes adds to Laura, as an aside: 'The great thing about this kind of food is that the portions aren't too big. I still have twenty grams of carbohydrate left.'

'You're going to stick to the diet today?'

'Of course. Especially today. It isn't a diet if you throw it out of the window every time you walk into a good restaurant. It's places like this that separate those with self-control from the rest.' He reaches for the wine, nestling in its silver cooler, and a waiter's hand immediately completes the action for him, filling their glasses to the exact halfway mark. 'A toast,' Kim says, raising his own glass to his lips. 'To us.'

Laura drinks. 'To us.' Dabbing her lips with a crisp white napkin, she adds, 'You know, I thought this place was going to be different.'

'Why so?'

'That guy I—' She pauses, as if there is something in her throat, then continues: 'That guy I went out with for a while worked here. I thought it would be – well, more like the stuff he cooked. You know, Italian food.'

'Aren't you glad it isn't?' He tastes his wreck-caught salmon, one of Templi's specialities. 'One gets a bit fed up with pasta, to tell the truth. How's your essay coming on?'

He is changing the subject, she notices; something he often does when she tries to talk about Tommaso. It is almost as if her time with him was in Kim's eyes a brief period of madness; a sort of going native, best now forgotten.

'Quite well, I think,' she says dutifully. 'I'm up to the Baroque.'

'Then you've started on Titian? That's good. He's one of the few real masters of colour, don't you think?'

In another restaurant, just a few miles down the road, Tommaso is cooking. The dish is a simple one but the presence of several cookery books, their pages liberally encrusted with scabs of dried

200

meat-juice and calcified egg yolk, would suggest that he is having trouble. As he refers to his books one more time, a pan catches fire on the burner behind him and he spins round with a curse to deal with it.

'Two *saltimbocche*, one *tagliatelle*, one *insalata*,' Marie says, coming into the kitchen with an order on her notepad.

Tommaso doesn't reply.

'Did you hear me? I said—'

'*Me ne sbatto il cazzo*,' Tommaso fumes. 'Can't you see I'm busy fucking up the orders I already have? Just leave it on the side, I'll fuck that one up in a minute. *Dio cane*!' He has pulled the burning pan off the stove as he speaks and in the process slops black oil all over the orders. 'Now see what you've done.'

Marie knows when to retreat. She goes back into the dining room, where only three tables are occupied. News of Il Cuoco's rapid departure from its previous form has spread quickly.

Bruno, meanwhile, is standing by the side of an empty road in Le Marche, coaxing the engine of his old van back to life. His face wears an expression of rapt concentration, not dissimilar to the one he once wore when he cooked. Although his hands are black with grease, rather than white with flour or slippery with raw egg, the process by which he intuits through his fingers what new malady ails the ancient, half-cannibalised engine is not so very different from the methods he once used to conjure new depths of flavour from his recipes, though not nearly so successful.

When he left Rome he simply drove north. Quickly growing tired of the *autostrada*, and unable in any case to tease more than sixty or seventy kilometres an hour out of the rickety vehicle, he had turned on to the smaller roads. Near Florence he camped for the night in a tiny olive grove, next to a five-hundred-year-old tree as fat and short as a Tuscan grandmother. The next morning he found a tiny stream, where he caught a small trout which he cooked over a fire of fragrant olive wood. The trout would have been delicious, he knew, but on this occasion it might as well have been made of cardboard. He had completely lost his sense of taste.

The next evening he pulled in beside a roadside stall where T-bone steaks were being cooked *alla brace*, over hot wood charcoal. Again, he could taste nothing. Even when the owner proudly anointed the steaks with a dribble of his own olive oil, so young and fresh it was still a vibrant green colour, Bruno could barely register it. He slathered his steak in salt, ate it quickly and got back in the van, mumbling his thanks to the affronted stall-holder.

More than once the van stopped, apparently exhausted by the endless succession of hills and valleys, and had to be patched and cajoled with spare parts from roadside garages. One such garage was selling *mandolini*, ewe's milk cheeses. Bruno bought several to keep in the van so that he didn't have to stop every time he was hungry. He guessed he probably stank of the stuff, but he didn't care.

From Tuscany he continued to head north, hugging the Ligurian coastline as far as Genoa. Here he ate *minestrone con pesto*, soup with fresh basil, and *farinata*, the staple street food of the seaport: a batter made with chickpea flour, mixed with extra-virgin olive oil, water and salt, spread out on a two-foot platter and cooked quickly in a wood-fired oven. It was properly *croccante sopra e morbida sotto* – crisp on the top, soft underneath – but it gave him no pleasure.

The way north left the coast for the very different landscape of Piedmont. Here long, straight roads built at the command of imperial Caesars ran across smooth plains filled with flooded rice paddies, for this part of Italy is the largest producer of rice in the Western world. Each night, when the sun sank beneath the surface of the flood plains, he parked the van and prepared to sleep, while thousands of mosquitoes scribbled dementedly all over the windows. When he ate it was usually a simple, soupy *risotto* from a roadside *osteria*, the same food that the rice workers themselves ate: rice cooked with chicken or the ubiquitous frogs' legs, flavoured with cinnamon and made liquid with the heavy wine of the region. Eventually, though, there was no more paddy plain left and the bristling foothills of the Alps rose up ahead of him. Now when he stopped the van the locals spoke a harsh dialect, their speech a strange intermingling of Italian, German and French, and the roadside cafés served boiled meats, *sauerkraut* and Austrian-style pastries. He knew the van would never survive up there, in the thin mountain air and the snow, so he reluctantly turned east towards the Adriatic coast. Here he picked up another Roman road, the Via Emilia, now known more prosaically as the N90 but still running straight and true for hundreds of miles across Emilia–Romagna to the sea.

This was the gastronomic heartland of Italy, where every inch of the fertile soil was cultivated. In Parma he visited shops festooned with hams, each one postmarked with the stamps of a dozen different inspectors – the regions of Italy are fiercely protective of their produce, and only a handful of towns between the Enza and the Stirone rivers are allowed to designate themselves as true producers of *prosciutto di Parma*. Because the huge lofts in which the hams are aged are always left open to the wind, the villages of the Enza valley seemed scented with the aromatic sweetness of the meat as he drove through them. In a valley to the north of Parma Bruno sampled *culatello di zibello*, perhaps the greatest of all Parma's pork products and for that reason almost never exported, even to other parts of Italy: a pig's rump marinated in salt and spices, then sewn inside a pig's bladder and aged for eighteen months in the humid air of the flat river basin. It is a process so delicate that almost half the hams are spoiled before they are ready, but those which survive are incomparably delicious. There had been a time when the almost creamy texture and sweet, intense flavour of the meat would have made Bruno laugh out loud for sheer joy. Now, although he still found it curious, he was like a man trying to taste from a photograph, or someone who eats with a bad cold. It was as if his palate, usually so exact, had become no more sensitive than that of any ordinary person.

He was interested, though, to see the process by which *aceto balsamico tradizionale* was made in Modena, just twenty miles to the south but as different again from Parma as vinegar is from meat. In a traditional *acetaia* he was allowed to peer briefly though the door of the attic, where a dozen barrels of different sizes dripped their precious contents with infinitesimal slowness into open buckets lined with brown paper. The air was heady with grape must, and even the songbirds that clustered at the open window seemed stunned into silence by the thick, viscous aroma. For an exorbitant fee Bruno was given a coffee-spoon-sized mouthful of the fifty-year-old vinegar to sip. As rich as old cognac, perfectly balanced between sweet and sour, the taste was so powerful that it seemed to flood through his chest like medicine. But it gave him no pleasure, and since even a tiny 100 ml bottle cost many hundreds of euros, he drove on without buying any.

In another village he stopped to buy cheese, and watched the two owners of the dairy as they whisked a huge tank containing hundreds of gallons of whey with a *spino*, a whisk as big as a broom. It was backbreaking work that at the end of the day would yield just two large cheeses, although it would be another three years before they would be ready to be sold. However, the same dairy also made *slattato*, a soft, fresh ewe's cheese, which he ate rolled up in a piece of *piadina* – a flat tortilla-like bread – for nourishment.

As Bruno neared the sea the little road became crowded with tourists spilling off the *autostrada*, heading for the fashionable resorts around Rimini. It was time to change direction again. This time Bruno set the van's nose south west, once more heading inland.

He had been driving for weeks, but he had never experienced such an empty, rural landscape as the one in which he now found himself. This was Le Marche: the Marches. There were few major towns here. For mile after mile the only signs of life were tiny hamlets and villages, dotted between the wild limestone gorges, where peasant farmers scratched a living much as they had always done, tending a few pigs, a few cows and a few sheep on a couple of steep fields. The roads tended to be winding, following the contours of the land and the serpentine rivers, and Bruno made slow progress. That suited him fine, though. It was becoming apparent that unless he stopped somewhere, and perhaps got himself a job as a labourer, he was eventually going to end up back in Rome again, where all roads led, and that was the last place he wanted to be. Almost as if it sensed its driver's mood, the van began to slow down, so that even when he did come across a stretch of straight road he was unable to travel at more than fifty kilometres an hour without gusts of black smoke belching from the old vehicle's patched-up guts.

Bruno picked up another Roman road, the Via Flaminia, which took him through the dramatic Furlo gorge. The road was squeezed alongside the river by towering cliffs, just as it had been ever since it was built in 220 BC, and even though the traffic was light he was soon holding up behind him a queue of impatient drivers. After the three-kilometre darkness of the Furlo tunnel, also built in Roman times, he pulled off at the first turning and drove upwards, into the hills. Here there was no traffic at all. Eagles spun lazily overhead, and once he thought he heard the distant howl of a wolf.

As he climbed higher above Acqualagna the van began first to breathe heavily and then to wheeze, all the time going more and more slowly; until finally, with a coughing fit worthy of a forty-a-day smoker, it came to a complete stop.

Bruno got out and contemplated the silent engine. He was about three hundred feet above the valley floor, somewhere between the little towns of Cagli and Città di Castello. He could not, however, see a single house or farm. It was deathly quiet. The sound of goat bells clattering in the distance as their owners methodically chewed at a meadow indicated, however, that there was some sort of settlement nearby. The fields, too, although tiny, were clearly well cared for. Underneath each tree was a tidy stack of firewood, piled up to dry for the winter, and the rows of vines in the pocket-sized vineyards were heavy with ripening fruit.

He tried in vain to coax the engine back to life. Once he thought he had it, but the van seemed to splutter apologetically and then lapse back into its coma. Sighing, Bruno pulled his back-pack from the passenger seat and prepared to walk. Since he knew there was nothing for miles the way he had come, he walked uphill, hoping that the woods which obscured his view were also concealing the presence, somewhere, of a village.

Tommaso's evening had been a disaster. By the time the last diners left, only partially mollified by several free *digestivi*, he was just about ready to collapse. But there were still the books to be done. Glumly he emptied a box of crumpled invoices on to one of the tables.

'The thing is,' Marie explained, 'we're still getting in food from our suppliers, who are still expecting to be paid, and on top of that there's the mafia's four per cent. But there's no money coming in. What's more, all those freebies we have to hand out are costing us a fortune. And because the waiters aren't getting any tips, they're skimming off the top. Every night we open for business simply adds to our debt. We need to shut down now, before we lose Dr Ferrara any more of his investment.'

Tommaso sighed. 'If the waiters are skimming us, let's get rid of the waiters. It's not as if there's anything for them to do anyway.'

'What about the *commis*?'

Tommaso hesitated. The two *commis* were youngsters, fresh out of catering school, but at least they had some idea of what they were doing, unlike himself. 'We'll keep one of them,' he suggested as a compromise.

Marie punched some buttons on her calculator. 'We'll still be losing money,' she said gloomily. 'We can't even pay Dr Ferrara his next instalment of the capital.'

'I'll pay him out of my savings.'

'Don't be stupid.'

'I don't want this place to close, Marie.'

'You're sentimental about it,' she commented. 'That's dangerous, for a business.'

'You don't have to stay yourself if you don't want to.'

'That's different,' she said gruffly.

After she had gone, Tommaso sat for a long time going through the bills, looking in vain for some way of cutting the operating costs and returning Il Cuoco to profit. Even he, though, could see that it was hopeless. They simply spent too much and made too little.

After Bruno had left Rome, Tommaso's anger had evaporated as quickly as it had come. In fact, he soon started to feel a little guilty. What he had said to Bruno was certainly true – Bruno *had* kissed his girl behind his back – but given that he himself had been unfaithful to the same girlfriend with a pretty blonde backpacker from Munich, he suspected that he was hardly entitled to claim the moral high ground. Besides, Tommaso loved Bruno, and the harsh words had been as much from his own sense of hurt that he hadn't been told the whole story as from any real injured pride.

As the realisation had slowly dawned that Bruno wasn't coming back, Tommaso had sunk into gloom, along with the fortunes of Il Cuoco. Had the restaurant not by now owed money to everyone from Dr Ferrara to the mafia, he might have tried to walk away from it. But gradually he realised that there was another reason why he couldn't leave. It was to do with the look on Marie's face when she'd discovered that he wasn't a real chef. He was determined to show her, and the rest of Rome as well, that he was just as capable of running a restaurant as Bruno had been. But the truth, at this moment, seemed to be that he wasn't.

೦೦

The nights had been the worst. That was when Laura had found herself thinking that she actually couldn't stand the pain; that she would do anything, anything at all, if only Tommaso would take her back; that she would even share him with all the tourists in Rome if it meant she could be with him again. On nights like those she would sit numbly on her bed, leaning against the wall, and wait for the morning, her cheeks burning with humiliation and her eyes stinging with wretchedness.

She had cried all the time. She had cried all over Judith, and on the phone to Carlotta. She had come within a whisker of abandoning her course and going back to America. She had cried over the student counsellor, who had arranged for her to see a doctor, who in turn had prescribed anti-depressants. She had cried over Kim Fellowes. He had been sympathetic, arranging to see her privately to help her catch up; at which kindness, of course, she had simply cried some more. He did not seem to be in the least repelled by her tears: if anything, the more she cried, the more attentive he became, and she soon got used to the familiar comforting smell of the cologne on his elegant linen handkerchiefs. Gradually the pain receded, and when, finally, he had escorted her to his bed, she realised how lucky she was to be loved at last by someone who genuinely cared for her.

Bruno walked uphill for over an hour. Although the sun was setting it was still hot, and only dogged determination, and the knowledge that if he didn't find somewhere to stay he was going to have to sleep out in the open, kept him going.

Eventually he saw houses in the distance. There was a plume of smoke beyond them, as straight and upright in the windless air as the cypress trees that dotted the hillside. As he climbed higher he saw that it was indeed a tiny village, consisting of no more than a dozen or so stone houses. On one of the buildings there was an ancient advertisement for Fernet Branca, painted directly on to the crumbling plaster. That was a good omen: it meant there was probably some kind of *osteria*.

As he walked into the village a couple of dogs on chains barked at him, but otherwise the place seemed deserted. But he could smell something coming from the direction of the smoke he'd seen from the road. He recognised the aromatic smell of burning beech wood immediately, but it was the scent of roasting pork that made his mouth water and his pace quicken. Someone was barbecuing a pig, and Bruno suddenly realised that he had not eaten for days.

He rounded the corner of the piazza – which was hardly a piazza at all, but an open space around which the houses and a church were grouped. Its surface was unpaved and it contained little apart from a few lime trees and a vast Fascist-era war memorial representing Victory as a naked woman being held aloft by half a dozen soldiers. It did, however, contain the source of that wonderful smell. Outside a tiny bar, someone had set up a makeshift spit over a fire. A few people were milling around it, tending to the golden-brown piglet that was slowly rotating above the hot embers. Chairs and tables had been dragged out into the evening sun, someone was fingering an accordion, and one or two elderly people were dancing. Half a dozen pairs of eyes turned to watch Bruno as he approached, although no one spoke to him.

Bruno hardly noticed. *I can smell it*, he thought. *Really, properly smell it.*

Once, as a child, he'd been swimming and had got some water stuck in his ear. For days every sound had been muffled, and no amount of banging and poking would shift it. Then, quite suddenly, a warm trickle in his eardrum had announced the return of his hearing – and, having almost got used to being without it, he'd found each sound new-minted and fresh. So it was now with his palate. Somehow, the smell of that *porchetta* had done what all of Emilia–Romagna's finest produce had failed to do. His extrasensory perceptions of taste and smell, which had all but disappeared, were flickering back into life. *Porchetta* . . . The piglet was a deep honey colour, its back blistered and split open where salt had been

209

rubbed into it for crackling, and the ears, nose and tail were covered with individual caps of tinfoil to prevent these delicacies from burning in the intense heat. Even now several people were fussing over it: one turning it, another basting it with a lump of lard on a skewer, while a slim figure in an apron and a headscarf was opening the meat up with a sharp knife to see if the middle was done.

Stuffed whole suckling pig is a feast-day speciality everywhere in Italy, although each region cooks it slightly differently. In Rome the piglet would be stuffed with its own fried organs; in Sardinia, with a mixture of lemons and minced meat. Here, evidently, the stuffing was made with breadcrumbs and herbs. He could make out each individual component of the mixture: *finocchio selvatico* – wild fennel – garlic, rosemary and olives, mingling with the smell of burning pork fat from the fire, which spat green flame briefly wherever the juices from the little pig, running down its trotters, dropped into it.

'Hello,' Bruno said politely to the person nearest to him. 'My van has broken down and I'm looking for somewhere to stay the night.'

The man scratched his ancient brown suit while he considered this. He pretended to wave a couple of flies away from his forehead with the back of his hand, although there were in fact no flies around. '*Ueh*, Gusta,' he called at last.

One of the people near the fire turned around. It was a woman, her face weatherbeaten and leathery from the sun. Bruno surmised that this was the owner of the bar and repeated his request.

The woman stared. 'We don't rent rooms, usually. You can use the telephone, if you like, to get someone out to your van. Where are you trying to get to?'

Where was he trying to get to? It was a good question, and one that Bruno had no answer for, having given up using a map several weeks before. He shrugged.

Another voice spoke from the group around the fire. It was the person who was squatting down, the one in the apron. Although

210

the speaker didn't turn around, Bruno heard a female voice, murmuring something.

Gusta shrugged. 'My daughter says it's too late to get anyone out from Acqualagna, and Hanni, who usually deals with the breakdowns, has gone to Belsaro to help his brother build a roof. We can make up a room, if you really have to stay, though as you can see, we're cooking *porchetta*, so don't expect any choice for dinner.'

Bruno assured her that he would be delighted to eat *porchetta*, and that he would try to be no trouble as he could see that they were busy. He sat down at one of the tables with his backpack at his feet and tried to make himself as inconspicuous as possible. The villagers, for their part, pretended to ignore him. The only one who looked directly at him was Gusta's daughter. She stood up and stepped back from the fire, wiping her hot forehead with her sleeve, and glanced at him for a moment with dark, unreadable eyes. Bruno smiled politely at her, but evidently he had been too familiar, because she scowled and looked away.

Someone put a glass of wine in front of him, and a plate containing a few squares of crispy pork skin. He ate them gratefully, by now very hungry indeed. Eventually, after much discussion, the *porchetta* was ready, and was lifted away from the heat to rest. But first, of course, there was pasta – great bowls of fresh green *tagliatelle*, made with spinach and just a hint of nutmeg, served with *fagiole* – fresh beans – and a little goose broth. No, not spinach after all, Bruno decided after a second taste: the green in the *tagliatelle* was actually from young stinging nettles. Rather to his surprise, it was excellent.

He was by now squashed between two large women, their accents so thick he could barely understand what they were saying. He asked what they were celebrating and they launched into a long explanation, the gist of which seemed to be that someone had borrowed a tractor from someone else, but the brakes didn't work properly, and then it had hit this poor three-legged piglet

211

and killed it, so of course it had to be eaten straight away. Had Bruno not noticed that the *porchetta* had only three legs? Bruno confessed he hadn't, a comment that prompted much hilarity from those around him. He was asked where he came from. Rome, he answered. His companions nodded thoughtfully, as if that explained everything. You couldn't expect a Roman to see what was under his nose. Trying to make a joke of it, Bruno remarked that in Rome all pigs had three legs, only for his comment to be passed up and down the table as seriously as if he had said that he was personally acquainted with the Pope. After that he tried to keep his mouth shut, except when he was eating.

This wasn't difficult, since the *porchetta* was delicious. It was handed round not on plates, but wrapped in myrtle leaves, so that the bitter flavour permeated the meat. Everyone else had fallen silent too, and the only sounds were the satisfied sighs of the diners and the crunch of bones being chewed. The only light came from a couple of tiny candles and the deep red embers of the fire. Finally the bones were removed, or thrown to the small army of waiting dogs, and bowls of fresh peaches were brought out, served sliced and covered in sweet wine. Then the accordion struck up again. The large lady on Bruno's left, who must have consumed at least a dozen glasses of wine during the meal, immediately asked him to dance, much to the amusement of their neighbours; and feeling that part of his payment for their hospitality was to provide them with entertainment, Bruno agreed. He happily made a fool of himself for a few minutes before excusing himself and sitting down again.

Someone sat down in the large lady's place, and he turned to find that it was Gusta's daughter. She had changed out of her cooking clothes immediately before dinner was served and was now wearing a long, dark dress; a patchwork of silks and other shimmering materials. There was something almost Romany about it, and now that he thought of it he could see that there was a similar look to the clothes of some of the other women, too. He

212

remembered reading that some of these remote villages were descended from gypsies who had settled and turned to farming, hundreds of years ago. Her hair was dark; as dark as the night behind it.

'I've made up your room,' she told him. 'When you get tired, just tell mother or me and we'll show you where it is. Though I'm afraid you may not sleep very well. Once this lot get started, they'll be drinking and dancing all night.' There was an affection in her voice, he noticed, which belied the curtness of her words.

'Thank you. But I'm enjoying myself, really. And that was a remarkable meal.'

She shrugged. 'Just a pig. It doesn't take much to cook a pig.'

'That pasta, too,' he said gently. 'The nettles and the nutmeg – fantastic. Who made that?'

'My mother,' she said. She looked up. A huge young man with sandy blond hair and the broadest shoulders Bruno had ever seen was standing on the other side of the table.

'Time to dance, *bella di casa*,' he said. Though he spoke to the girl, his eyes were on Bruno. He leaned across the table and placed a large, muscular hand in Bruno's. 'I'm Javier,' he said. 'Pleased to meet you . . .'

'Bruno,' Bruno said. He felt his hand being crushed for a moment, then released. 'My van broke down.'

'Yes, I know.' Javier turned back to the girl. 'Come on then.'

She got up, her dress shimmering. She said to Bruno, 'But I added the nettles. And the nutmeg. It makes people . . . happy.'

He watched her dancing, his eyes straining in the dark for the shimmer of her dress as she spun. Then he realised what he was doing. Yes, Laura was right. I'm a *guardone*, he thought wearily. A pervert; always watching, never doing. He got to his feet and went to find Gusta and directions to his room.

Nineteen

When Bruno got up the next morning, the little piazza was deserted. He assumed they were all sleeping off their hangovers – the music had gone on late into the night, just as Gusta's daughter had predicted. Then the doors of the church opened and a stream of villagers poured straight down the steps and across to the bar, where Gusta, still in her church clothes, immediately got to work dispensing *distillati* from unmarked bottles while her daughter took round a tray of pastries. Bruno accepted both. The drink was a fiery peach alcohol, not unlike schnapps, while the pastries were soft and sweet, dusted with almond flour.

He was introduced to Giorgio, a dishevelled-looking young man who was happily having third helpings of the liqueur. Giorgio, he was told, had brought his tractor to church and would soon take Bruno to pick up his van. 'Soon' turned out to be a relative concept. It was another hour, and several more schnapps, before Giorgio finally took Bruno behind the piazza, where the tiniest tractor Bruno had ever seen was parked. Giorgio shooed a mongrel off the seat and settled himself at the controls. There was barely room on the machine for his body: if he lowered his feet from the pedals they would drag along the ground, like an adult riding a child's pony. He pressed a button and the engine belched black smoke. An elderly man, walking in the opposite direction, laughed and shouted something over the noise of the engine. It sounded like 'Nice pig, Giorgio'. Giorgio scowled and didn't reply. It occurred to Bruno that this must be the tractor responsible for running down last night's meal. It seemed unlikely: surely even a three-legged piglet could outrun this relic.

Bruno and the dog walked behind as the tractor putted slowly down the road. Rather to Bruno's surprise, however, the dwarf tractor turned out to be easily capable of towing the defunct van up to the village, and his vehicle was eventually uncoupled and pushed into a small barn which contained a reassuring number of wrecked, half-cannibalised cars, all awaiting the return of Hanni the mechanic from his brother's roof.

'Hanni has a piece of everything here,' Giorgio commented, rolling himself a cigarette now that work was over. 'He'll sort you out. Mind you,' he added thoughtfully, 'it's been three months since he said he'd find me some brake discs, and I'm still waiting. That'll be fifteen euros, please.'

There was nothing to do now but wait. Bruno went back to the piazza, where the smells of lunch were already wafting out of Gusta's kitchen. Plates of *antipasti* were placed on the tables in the square, which magically filled with people – whole families, still in their church suits, and the priest himself with a paper towel tucked into his cassock. Bruno took a piece of chicory and dipped it into a saucer containing oil and vinegar – a tiny black yolk of *aceto balsamico* floating in the middle of the golden oil. He was amazed to find that both the olive oil and vinegar were among the very best he had ever tasted. The village might look poor to the casual eye but the villagers certainly knew how to eat. Italians called it *il culto de benessere*: keeping the very best produce for themselves, being self-sufficient but living well, combining the strong stomach of a peasant with the refined palate of a cardinal.

The pasta was *taglierini*, thinner and longer than *tagliatelle*, sparsely flavoured with garlic and *porcini* mushrooms. Again, Bruno was surprised: the season for *funghi* was many months off. But these were undoubtedly fresh. He commented on this to the family whose table he was sharing, and they nodded.

'It's all a matter of knowing where to look,' the man told him. 'And there's not much the Galtenesi don't know about *funghi*.'

The Galtenesi, it turned out, was the collective name for those who lived in these hills.

'You see those two?' the man continued, nodding at a mongrel scratching itself in the dust, not far from where a weatherbeaten old man with a long stick was methodically polishing off an enormous bowl of *taglierini*. 'That's Alberto, and his dog Pippino. He's one of the best *trifolai* in all Italy.'

Bruno looked at the old man with new respect. If there were truffles here, that explained why the locals ate so well and seemed so contented with their simple lifestyle. A good *trifolau*, or truffle hunter, could make a fortune during the winter season. Then, for the rest of the year, he could relax and tend his small-holding.

'But don't the best truffles come from Piemonte?' he remarked. This caused a gale of laughter from his eating companions, and more laughter as his comment was repeated up and down the long table.

The villager shook his head. 'The Piemontese have the best markets,' he confided, leaning forward conspiratorially, 'and of course they like to pretend that what you buy in the markets comes from the hills in their own region. But if it wasn't for Le Marche, the market at Alba would be empty most of the season. As for us, we're happy to sell them up north. Here there are so many truffles that we wouldn't get anything like the same price.'

This conversation was interrupted by a sudden shout from the direction of the bar. A little terrier was scurrying from the door, carrying off a huge joint of meat in its jaws, hotly pursued by a red-faced Gusta, yelling profanities. The chuckles of the villagers rapidly turned to alarm when it became clear that the animal had just made off with the *capretto*, the joint of kid that had been going to be the *secondo*.

There was a long wait, punctuated by occasional bursts of shouting from inside the house. Tensions in the kitchen were clearly running high. Then there was a double burst of shouting, followed by a loud crash, and silence.

Bruno got to his feet. 'Excuse me,' he said politely to his companions, 'I think I should go and offer to help.'

The man looked at him in alarm. 'Are you crazy? There are knives in there. And believe me, the women in that family have a temper; they're famous for it.'

Bruno shrugged. 'Still, I'd better see what I can do.'

He made his way into the tiny bar, and from there to the kitchen behind it. It wasn't much bigger than the bar and it contained both Gusta and her daughter, who were staring fiercely at each other across the kitchen table. Evidently he had walked in to the middle of a row.

'Excuse me,' Bruno said mildly, 'I came to see if you would like some help.'

'Everything's fine,' yelled Gusta, flapping her apron at him. 'Go and sit outside.' She glared at her daughter. 'And take Benedetta with you.'

'For example,' Bruno continued, 'I thought perhaps I could turn the leftover *porchetta* from last night into meatballs, while your daughter makes a tomato and olive sauce, and you, signora, prepare some *finocchio fritto*.'

There was a brief silence while the two women thought about this.

'For that matter,' Benedetta said at last, 'we have some sheets

217

of pasta left over from making the *taglierini*. We could make a sort of *vincisgrassi**.'

'We don't have a food processor,' Gusta said dismissively. 'If we have to dice all that *porchetta* by hand, we still won't have fed everyone by the time evening Mass starts.'

'With respect, signora, I am a very fast worker,' Bruno said.

'You're a man,' Gusta said with an air of finality, as if it were self-evident that this ruled out both the possibility of Bruno being a cook and of him being a fast worker. Bruno found himself wondering whether there had ever been a signor Gusta.

'True, but—'

'*Porco Dio!*' yelled Benedetta. 'Can we stop talking and start cooking?'

Bruno reached for a knife, a chopping board and, since no one stopped him, opened the meat safe to remove the platter that held the remains of the *porchetta*. There was rather less than he had remembered: even if he flayed every ounce of meat from the bones, it was going to be hard to make it stretch to feeding the twenty or thirty hungry villagers who were waiting outside.

'We'll need some stale bread,' he decided. 'We can soak it in oil and use it for bulk. And some herbs, of course. What do you have in your garden, signora?'

'Sage, thyme, marjoram, oregano, bay, basil—'

'And what vegetables?'

'Celery, courgettes, peas, tomatoes—'

'Bring in as much as you've got,' Bruno said, 'particularly the celery and the *zucchini*.' As he spoke, his knife, almost without his thinking about it, was dancing over the carcass of the pig,

---

*Lasagne of the Le Marche region, named after an Austrian general, Prince Windisch-Graetz, who fought against Napoleon. The authoritative *vincisgrassi* is made with Béchamel sauce and a meat base comprising lamb testicles, liver, cockerel giblets and no tomatoes but, like pizza, there are many variations possible on the basic theme.

stripping it of meat. He saw Benedetta glance down at his hands, her eyes widening a little, although she said nothing. She reached for a length of tomatoes, still attached to their vine, and with her own knife began to chop them without even bothering to strip them from the stem.

Bruno started to dice the strips of pork into tiny pieces. Not needing to look at what his own hands were doing, he looked instead at Benedetta's. She was good, he thought: she must have been cooking for years. Her knife was a blur as she worked her way along a celery stalk. He realised that Benedetta, too, wasn't looking at her own hands but at his. Then, at the same moment, they both looked up at each other's face and their eyes met.

Bruno's knife didn't miss a beat, but he felt a shock of recognition. It was like looking in a mirror.

'You're left-handed,' he said, noticing.

'And you're a chef,' she said drily.

'Yes.'

'So what are you doing in Galtena?'

'Just passing through.'

'Really? The road up here doesn't go anywhere else.'

He opened his mouth, and a moment later felt a sharp pain on his knuckle as the knife sliced deep into the skin. 'Shit!'

'There are plasters by the sink,' Benedetta said, sounding amused.

He rinsed the cut and wrapped the plaster around it before picking up the knife again. 'I'm a little out of practice,' he muttered.

'So I see. Never mind, we need all the meat we can get, even if it comes from your fingers.'

Angry with himself for making such an elementary mistake, Bruno chopped even faster, as Gusta returned with the vegetables.

In half an hour the three of them prepared a meal that would normally have taken four or five hours. It was not the best dish he had ever cooked, Bruno admitted to himself as he sent the first plates out of the door, but it was one he would always remember. In particular, he would remember the way that he and Benedetta had worked together, in silence but in perfect accord.

Finally there were just three plates left, and the small child who had been roped into service as a waiter reported that everyone outside was eating.

'These are for us,' Gusta said, taking off her apron. 'Let's go outside.'

If the customers had minded the wait, they didn't show it. The accordions were out again and the children were being allowed to run around, teasing the dogs and each other into a frenzy of excitement. There were places left at the main table, but Javier was sitting there, his food untouched, waiting for Benedetta with a scowl on his face. Bruno thought it was probably tactful to go back to the table he'd been sitting at before.

'Did you make this?' the man he'd been talking to earlier wanted to know.

Bruno shrugged. 'Well, I helped.'

'It's not bad,' the man commented, 'though there's a touch too much marjoram for my taste.'

Damn, Bruno thought as he ate his own plateful, *he's probably right at that.* These country people had more sophisticated palates than any he'd come across at Templi. To change the subject, he said, 'What happened to signor Gusta?'

'Ah. He ran away. Years ago, when Bene was just a little girl. People say that's why his daughter learned to cook so well, because she had to help her mother instead of going to school. Now,' he sighed, 'we're going to lose her anyway.'

'Oh? Why's that?'

'Are you crazy? She's twenty-one, she's beautiful and she cooks like an angel. Every young man in the Galteni wants to come home to her, temper or no temper. Sooner or later she'll be cooking for her own husband in his kitchen, and none of the rest of us will get a look in. What's more, her mother won't be able to manage all by herself so the bar will probably have to close too. All in all, it's a disaster.'

Bruno looked across to where Benedetta was sitting next to Javier. 'So is Javier the one she'll marry?'

The man shrugged. 'Who knows? It's the dog who howls at the moon, but the fox who eats the chicken. Just because he's following her round like an idiot doesn't mean that he's getting anywhere. In fact, he's probably doing it as much to impress his rivals as anything.'

Looking at Javier's vast frame as he silently shovelled food into his mouth, Bruno could see how that would work. But it was nothing to do with him. He was just passing through.

Back in Rome, Tommaso was looking at the empty walls of his apartment. He had already sold all of Bruno's kitchen appliances, his own watch and his digital camera. The restaurant had been picked clean of its wine: he was down to a skeleton stock of just half a dozen bottles and there was barely a corkscrew left to open them with. Yet still the bills kept coming. Now there was nothing left but to sell his prized CD collection, and when the money from that was gone, he would have to fire Marie.

Sighing, he packed the CDs into boxes and lugged them downstairs to where the vast Porta Portese street market stretched from the Tiber right up to the Viale Glorioso. There was a record dealer just across the street. Tommaso put the box down on his stall.

'How much for all of them?'

The stallholder flicked through the collection, which was full of Japanese imports and rare bootlegs. 'Five hundred,' he said at last. It was worth double, but he recognised a fire sale when he saw one.

'Done,' Tommaso said wearily. The stallholder pushed some notes into his hand quickly, as if afraid Tommaso might change his mind.

As he was going back to his door, Tommaso heard a voice

whispering from one of the doorways: 'Grass, speed, pills, coke . . .' It came from an ageing Scottish hippy who hung around the markets, doing a little dealing to fund his own prodigious habit. Tommaso stopped. A desperate idea had just begun to form in his mind.

That evening, the menu at Il Cuoco was reduced to a choice of just one pasta, followed by a single *secondo*.

Unknown to the four couples who comprised the restaurant's only customers, their *spaghetti carbonara* had been dusted not with *pecorino romano* but with a highly idiosyncratic and frankly unpredictable mixture of cheese and ecstasy. What Bruno had achieved with his culinary skills, Tommaso was hoping to replicate with simple pharmacology.

Bruno, meanwhile, had finally made the acquaintance of Hanni the mechanic, who was examining his old van with a portable lantern and an expression of dismay.

'You're looking at about four weeks,' Hanni informed him. 'More if I can't get a gearbox.'

'Four weeks? But that's impossible. Nothing takes four weeks.'

'The problem is, they don't make these any more.' Hanni shrugged. 'It's like waiting for a heart transplant. Some other vehicle has to die and give up its parts before yours can be repaired.'

With a sense of dread Bruno asked, 'And how much will it cost?'

Hanni shrugged again. 'Who knows? Could be a hundred, could be five hundred. We'll just have to see what's available.'

The results of his experiment exceeded Tommaso's expectations. Once again the air at Il Cuoco was filled with passion. True, it was a little more anarchic than before. Of the four couples, one was trying to kill each other, and a woman was dancing very slowly on

222

the bar, half naked, while her partner was nowhere to be seen. But everyone was having a good time, that was undeniable.

'This is how we cook rabbit in Rome,' Bruno said. 'A little sage, a little rosemary, then we leave it to simmer in the wine.'

'Interesting,' Benedetta said. 'But incorrect. In Le Marche we stuff the rabbit with peppers, *pancetta* and liver before cooking. And when we simmer it we leave the lid off, like *this*.' She reached out and pushed the lid of Bruno's pan askew. 'That way it reduces while it cooks.' She glared at him.

Bruno sighed. His plan to ask Gusta for a job in exchange for board while he waited for Hanni to get the spare parts he needed was proving trickier than he'd expected. Gusta had insisted on giving him a trial run, and Benedetta in turn had demanded that he use it to demonstrate that he could cook the local dishes in the local way – which, of course, meant *her* way.

'Well,' he suggested, 'we could be a little creative.'

'What do you mean, creative?' Benedetta asked suspiciously.

'Instead of stuffing the rabbit with the peppers, we could stuff the peppers with the rabbit.'

Gusta laughed. 'Are you joking? Our customers would riot if you tried to pull a crazy trick like that.'

Bruno said nothing. He was looking at Benedetta.

'It's an interesting idea,' she said slowly. 'You could grill the peppers first, and then you could put some lemon zest in with the rabbit—'

Gusta looked horrified. 'Now why in God's name would you want to do that?'

'To balance the sweetness of the roasted peppers,' Bruno explained. 'And I see that you have *serpillo** growing wild around here. You could put some of that in as well.'

---

*A bitter wild herb, particularly used to flavour cheese.

'Oh, you young people cook what you like,' Gusta said impatiently, throwing up her hands. 'I've got customers to attend to.'

While Bruno cooked the stuffed peppers, Benedetta made pasta. But they were both watching each other surreptitiously.

'Do you have some cloves?' Bruno asked politely.

'Yes. In the cupboard. But don't use them.'

'I thought just a couple—'

'—would kill the delicate taste of the *serpillo*.' She glared at him.

'Or complement it.'

'Uh-uh. Too many flavours,' Benedetta said firmly.

Bruno sighed. 'May I be permitted some nutmeg, then?'

There was a pause. 'A pinch, no more.'

She watched suspiciously as he grated a little nutmeg over the rabbit meat. The message was clear: this was her kitchen and she was in charge of it. Bruno sighed again. Not since he'd worked for Alain Dufrais had he encountered anyone quite so opinionated about cooking.

'When you said that nutmeg makes people happy, why was that?' he asked, hoping some conversation would break the ice.

'Because it does,' she said tersely. 'Just as fennel relaxes people, and cardamom is good for the digestion, nutmeg makes people dance.'

It sounded like one of the crazy superstitions country grandmothers clung to. 'I've never heard that before,' he muttered.

'Oh well, in that case it can't be true, can it?' she said icily. She pounded the pasta dough with her fists, a quick one-two that left deep depressions in the mixture. It occurred to Bruno that, skinny as she was, it wouldn't do to get on the wrong side of Benedetta. He got on with his cooking in silence.

He had to admit, though, that he had never seen anyone make pasta as well as this. When she rolled out the *sfoglia*, the sheet of fresh dough, she barely glanced at it, but it was so thin and so even that he could see the grain of the wooden table through it.

He couldn't help himself. 'How do you get it so thin?' he asked.

'Practice.' Then, relenting, she added, 'And I have the right hands.'

'What sort of hands would that be?'

'Here.' She held out her hands to him. They were warm, almost hot. 'You can't make good pasta with cold hands,' she explained. 'That's the secret. So I eat a lot of *peperoncino*. It keeps my hands warm.'

Bruno opened his mouth to point out that this was unlikely to be the cause of her warm hands, but closed it again. They were just about talking to each other, and there was no point in starting another fight.

Benedetta was looking pointedly at her hands. With a start Bruno realised that he was still holding them. Abruptly, he let go.

Benedetta turned back to her pasta. But just for a moment, a ghost of a smile flitted across her face.

When she had finished making the pasta, Benedetta cut it roughly into *maltagliati*, random shapes that were traditionally made from leftover scraps. Then she pressed each piece against a strange implement with long, stiff wires, like a comb.

'What's that?' Bruno asked.

'That's the *pettine*.'

'What's it for?'

'Don't you have these in Rome?' she said, surprised. 'I don't know. I suppose it gives the pasta more grip.'

He nodded. He could see how that would work: the grooves left by the comb would give the thin pasta more surface area, which would hold a creamy sauce better.

'Do they use them in Romagna and Abruzzo as well?' he asked.

'I don't know.'

'When you go to other regions, don't you eat?'

She didn't answer.

'You've never been outside Le Marche, have you?' he guessed.

'Why would I want to?'

It was a good question. Changing the subject, he asked, 'What sort of pasta are you making?'

'*Pasta con funghi*.'

He watched as she took a bowl of strange, round, reddish-brown mushrooms out of the larder. The air was immediately filled with their rich, earthy scent. Ripe as a well-cellared cheese, but tinged with the odours of leaf-mould and decay, it reminded Bruno a little of the smell of offal in his native Roman dishes. 'How many kinds of *funghi* do you cook with?' he asked.

'Oh – hundreds. It just depends on what I find in the woods.'

'You pick these yourself?'

'Of course.'

As the smell of *funghi* combined with the scent of hot butter and garlic in the frying pan, Bruno felt his nostrils flare. And not just his nostrils. The aroma was stirring up his blood, awakening sensation in a part of him that had been quiescent for a long time.

'They say these are an aphrodisiac,' Benedetta said, as if reading his thoughts. 'Of course, it's just a kind of superstition that the old grandmothers like to talk about.'

'Of course,' he said stiffly.

Was it his imagination, or was the look she gave him almost one of pity?

Two could play at that game, though. Bruno's retaliation was to make a *dolce*.

For sheer showmanship, it is hard to beat the creation of a really flashy dessert. Without asking Benedetta's permission, Bruno assembled his ingredients. Eggs. Sugar. Cream. Pastry. A large dish of blackcurrants and other fruits from the garden.

First he spun sugar into delicate lattice bowls of crisp brown caramel. Then he made meringues, inside which he placed individual baked peaches. Where the peach stone had been he inserted a berry *gelato*, made with pieces of solid fruit. It was pure Alain Dufrais – virtuoso, exuberant, and completely over the top.

'Careful,' was all Benedetta said when he had finished. 'We don't want our customers to think we've gone completely poncy.'

'They won't think that when they taste it.'

'People round here,' she said firmly, 'have pretty high expectations.'

'They won't have eaten anything like this, I can assure you.'

'Hmm.' She squeezed past him to get a whisk. 'Excuse me.' Their eyes met. Just for a moment, Bruno was confused by what he saw there. *Are we fighting?* he wondered. *Or flirting?*

He decided on the direct approach. 'How long have you been going out with Javier?' he asked casually as he wiped down his prep surface.

But Benedetta, now carefully slicing *salume* for *antipasto*, would not be drawn so easily. 'Who told you I was going out with Javier?'

'One of the villagers.'

'People here do love to gossip.'

'Actually, I don't think my informant was too keen on the idea. He said you'd soon be cooking for a husband rather than the whole village.'

'People here like to think about their own stomachs, too.' She stretched across him for a pan. He felt her softness press briefly against his shoulder. Flushing, he pushed himself back as far as he could. Luckily, Benedetta didn't seem to notice.

This is a tiny kitchen, he told himself firmly. *If you are going to work here – and let's face it you have to work here, since your tractor-driving skills are non-existent – you will simply have to learn to be professional about your co-worker.*

☙

227

Laura, in Rome, does not spend the nights crying any more. She attends concerts with Kim; small gatherings for a select few, held in the salons of baroque palaces. But sometimes, in the intervals, she surreptitiously takes out her mobile phone – the mobile phone that no longer plays Rod Stewart or Eric Clapton when it rings, but Vivaldi – and scrolls through the text messages until she finds one that she rereads for the hundredth time:

> There was something I wanted to cook tonight –
>
> The recipe of love
>
> Take 1 American girl with honey-coloured skin & freckles like orange-red flakes of chilli on her shoulders.
>
> Fill her with flavours, with basil and tomatoes and pine nuts and parsley.
>
> Warm her gently with your hands for several hours, turning occasionally, and serve with wine and laughter, straight from the dish.
>
> – but sadly 1 of the ingredients was missing. Maybe tomorrow?

Then she allows a tear to roll silently down her cheek until it reaches the corner of her lip, where she licks it off absent-mindedly, salty and insubstantial and tasteless on her tongue.

Twenty

Rather to Gusta's surprise, the new menu at her little *osteria* was a great success. Since there was almost no choice of dishes, the customers were forced to try what they might otherwise have spurned; and having tried it, they decided that they liked it. What was more, they talked about it to their friends. Within a few days Gusta was having to put out extra tables.

'It's just a novelty,' Benedetta told her, shrugging. 'It'll settle down in a week or so.'

It seemed as if each lunchtime they fed the whole village. Labourers in vests and blue serge trousers sat alongside the priest and the doctor. Children, released from school for lunch, ate with their parents before sliding from their chairs to run riot in the square while the grown-ups chatted in the shade before their siesta. People were even starting to come by car and scooter from villages further down the valley.

One person who was always there, usually eating with his friends, was Javier. Bruno noticed now that, although Benedetta was friendly towards Javier, and would sometimes sit with him while he had an *amaro* after his meal, she never kissed him or sat

229

on his knee as the other courting couples did. He wondered about their relationship, but thought it best not to enquire further.

Giorgio, the owner of the miniature tractor, was often there too. One day Bruno overheard him talking about the new disc brakes Hanni had finally fitted to his tractor, and decided that it was time to pay the mechanic a visit himself.

He found his van propped up on bricks, which seemed to indicate that Hanni had started work; but the mechanic was apologetic.

'I've phoned round all my contacts but none of them have the necessary parts,' he explained. 'They will come, eventually, but we just have to be patient.'

'No problem,' Bruno said. Now that he'd found work, a couple of weeks' wait wasn't the end of the world. Besides, the villagers were talking about this weather turning into a heatwave, so maybe staying up here in the relative cool of the hills for a while wasn't such a bad idea.

Abruptly, summer had come to the Marches. Bruno was used to the city, and to the scorching temperatures of restaurant kitchens. But the fierce humidity that enveloped them now was another matter. Tendrils of heat reached from the plain right up as far as the village, and only at night did a breath of cooler air press down from the hills above them. Lunch was served early, and dinner late. In the kitchen, Benedetta had taken to working in shorts and a T-shirt. The insidious smell of her skin mingled with the cooking smells, distracting Bruno. He gritted his teeth and did his best to ignore it.

The heatwave lasted only a few days, a brief harbinger of the furnace to come. One morning Bruno woke up with a start, certain he had heard Benedetta's voice. He listened. It was still dark. He must have dreamed it.

'Bruno?'

It *was* her. She was standing in the doorway of his little room. Just for a moment a crazy notion popped into his mind.

'Do you want to come and pick *funghi*?' she whispered.

So that was why she was here. He pushed the crazy notion away. 'Sure.'

'Come on then. I'll see you downstairs in ten minutes.'

A little while later they set off uphill in the darkness, both carrying the shallow wicker baskets in which they would bring home their haul. 'Are you sure there'll be any? At this time of year, I mean?' Bruno asked.

'Of course. Perhaps not so many now as autumn. But there'll be *coprini*, and *orecchietti*, and *piopparelli*, and *pleurate*, and *cepatelli* if we're lucky—'

'OK,' he said hastily, 'I get the idea. And none of these are poisonous?'

'Some of them are very similar to poisonous mushrooms, yes. But don't worry. I know what we're looking for.'

By the time they reached the woods it was starting to get light. She led Bruno to where, in the long, lush grass at the edge of the trees, a darker green circle twenty feet across stained the paler green of the pasture.

'*Gambe secche*. A fairy ring. This one is quite old – it gets a little bigger each year as the mycelium spreads out.'

'It's edible?'

'No, but once the fairy ring's established, the *prugnolo* comes and shares the circle.' As she spoke she was rummaging in the wet grass, pushing it apart gently with her fingers. 'See? This is the *prugnolo* – what the people here call San Giorgio.'

'Why's that?'

'Because it first appears on the feast of San Giorgio, of course.' She twisted the mushroom deftly from its stalk and put it into her basket. 'There'll be more, if you take a look.'

When they had harvested a dozen mushrooms from the fairy ring they went into the woods, each plucking a hazel stick on the way to push aside the undergrowth. After a few minutes Benedetta stopped and sniffed the air. 'Can you smell it?'

231

Bruno sniffed too, but all he could smell was the dank, mouldy scent of the woods.

'Over here.' She pushed a little way off the path and there, like a tiny neolithic henge in the forest floor, stood a cluster of squat mushrooms. 'These are good,' Benedetta confirmed. 'Make sure you snap them off without pulling them or you'll damage the roots.'

'What are they?'

'*Ceppatelli*. Like *porcini*, but they fruit earlier in the year.'

Bruno plucked one. It was lighter than the chocolate-brown *porcini* he was used to in Rome, but it had the same heady, pungent smell.

'And tap the spores on to the ground,' Benedetta added. 'That way you'll make sure it grows again.'

After the *ceppatelli* they followed a tiny trail left by a deer, pushing deeper and deeper into the woods.

'There's one,' Bruno said, pointing with his stick to where a tall, pale mushroom with a spotted cap stood at the base of a beech tree. It seemed to glow faintly with phosphorescence in the dim light.

'Now that *is* poisonous. It's an *Amanita phalloides*. You can guess why it's called that from the shape.' She had crouched down beside the mushroom and was plucking it carefully, her hand wrapped in a tissue to avoid touching the mushroom's flesh.

'Why are you taking it?'

'Oh, poisonous ones are useful too. We use these to kill mice. And there are others we put into remedies.'

Nearby was a tree stump covered in undulating black rills of fungus. They looked deeply unappetising, and Bruno was surprised when Benedetta said they were edible.

'And here, look,' she called, moving on to a neighbouring beech tree, 'this is what we call an *apartamento* – an apartment block. There are *gelone* at the bottom, and then a layer of *pioparelli*, and then *pleurate*, oyster mushrooms, all the way up. If we don't pick them they'll destroy the tree.'

By mid-morning it was hot. Both baskets were full, though

Bruno was frustrated to find that he was still unable to follow the scent trails Benedetta was tracking so easily.

'We may as well give up now,' she said at last, sitting down in a little clearing on a bank of moss and thyme. 'The smell of the *funghi* isn't so strong any more.'

Bruno sat down next to her. Below them, the village basked in the sun. Trails of smoke and the distant sound of chainsaws reached them. Benedetta stretched and lay back.

'It's so quiet up here,' he said.

'Yes. No one from the village ever comes up this high.'

The weight of their bodies was crushing the thyme, releasing wafts of warm scent that mingled with the dank smell of the *funghi* in their baskets. Benedetta began unbuttoning her shirt. His surprise must have shown on his face, because she added, 'I'm going to sunbathe.'

'Oh. Right. Go ahead, I won't look,' he said, averting his gaze. Out of the corner of his eye he could still see her, though; a flesh-coloured shape lying back on the warm moss. Was he blushing? And if so, how could he have so much blood in him, that it was rushing to his cheeks and his groin at the same time? He lay back and closed his eyes.

There was the rustle of cloth on skin. A few moments later, Benedetta rolled over and slipped her hand under his T-shirt.

'Oh,' Bruno said, his eyes opening again. There was a pert nipple dangling inches from his face, as ripe as a fruit, and that warm pasta-making hand was stroking his stomach in slow, circular movements. 'Benedetta,' he said. His voice came out hoarse. 'You should know – I'm just – just—'

'Passing through? Of course. That's why I can sleep with you.'

'What do you mean?' He gasped as her fingers slid under the waistband of his jeans.

'Isn't it obvious? If I sleep with Javier, I'll have to marry him. If I sleep with one of the other men from the village, they'll tell each other and I'll be labelled a *puttana* and a witch. Whereas

233

you –' she stood up and pulled off the remainder of her clothes, before lying down again and easing herself against him, skin against skin – 'aren't going to tell a soul.'

'How do you know?' he asked, as she undid his jeans and freed his cock with both hands.

'Because you never tried to grab me in the kitchen. Not even after I started putting the special herbs in your food.'

'You've been putting what . . . ?'

She laughed softly. 'Couldn't you tell? And you such a great chef.' One long leg lifted itself over his hips, and then she was straddling him. He felt wetness on his stomach, and realised that it must be hers. Reaching out, she plucked a sprig of thyme and crushed it between her lips, then bent forward to kiss him. As the flavour flooded his mouth like wine his hips bucked impatiently, but he was securely held captive under her and she had no intention of allowing him to hurry.

'When did you—?' he whispered.

'The first night. When you smelled the nutmeg.' She pushed his arms over his head and pinned them to the forest floor with one hand, leaning forward over him so that her breasts brushed his mouth. He found a nipple and bit it gently. It was hard, and salty as a pistachio with her sweat. He groaned. 'Please—'

She rose up and positioned herself. 'Like this?' she said softly. And, still teasing him, 'Or like *this*?'

And then everything was cinnamon and cream, fennel and strawberry, the scent of crushed thyme and sweat and sweet honey, and he was amazed at how ridiculously easy it was.

They walked back down the hill in a companionable silence. That afternoon, as well as *pasta con funghi*, Benedetta cooked *salame da sugo*, the traditional wedding meat of Ferrara: ground pork, liver and tongues, enriched with spices and wine, said to maintain a bridegroom's potency.

∾

The next day they went to pick *fragole di bosco*, wild strawberries, and made love in a deserted old barn above the pastures, their lips still smeared with the pulp of the fruit. The next day it was *misticanza*, wild leaves for salad. Benedetta was scrupulous that they must always pick first. If anyone saw them walking home with empty baskets, she warned, tongues would start wagging instantly. So they filled their baskets with rocket, wild fennel, dandelion and lamb's lettuce before temptation overcame them and they collapsed into a quiet corner of a field, hidden only by the tall fronds of the *finocchio* stalks. Bruno made her close her eyes, teasing her naked body with a spray of fennel: when he kissed her between her legs the aniseed mingled with the faint, faraway taste of the sea. *We were all fish once*, he thought, *and this is the proof of it, this whisper of oceans in the deepest recesses of the body*.

The day after that it was wild currants, and the day after that they took a gun with them and shot hares. Their lovemaking was different after that hunt, fast and furious and urgent, while the dead animals with their bloody noses watched them from the baskets.

The next morning she woke him very early again, while it was still dark, and took him to a dense wood they had never visited before. She wouldn't tell him what they were after, but when they were deep inside the trees she told him to smell the air. He sniffed obediently.

'Can you smell it?' she whispered.

'No. Can you?'

'Yes. Over here.'

He followed her into the dense undergrowth. She was turning her head this way and that, sniffing like a dog. He understood that whatever scent she had caught, it was elusive and precious, so he kept quiet, not wanting to disturb her concentration.

'Now,' she whispered. 'Smell again.'

This time, just for a moment, he thought he caught it – a faint, feral reek, almost sexual.

'Wild boar?' he whispered back. But Benedetta shook her head.

She tracked backwards and forwards between the trees, her nose close to the ground. Abruptly she stopped, and began to lever up the earth carefully with the end of her stick. The smell was stronger now, heady in the cold clear air of the dawn. Then, suddenly, Benedetta was pulling a knobbly object like a tiny misshapen potato from the roots of the tree – a *tartufo*, quite small, still caked with earth, its reek filling the air.

'Alberto would kill us if he knew,' she whispered. 'We shouldn't really pick them at this time of the year.'

She broke the truffle open and pressed it to his nose. The scent was almost overpowering: sex and old socks and musk. He felt himself becoming aroused, and saw by her eyes that she was too. He reached for her, pulling her towards him.

Afterwards, she took some of his seed on her hand and wiped it on the tree roots, to encourage the precious fungus to spore again in the same place.

Tiny as it was, the truffle lent its intoxicating flavour to enough dishes to feed the whole village. *Taglierini*, sautéed in a frying pan with lesser *funghi* such as *cardoncelli* and *orecchietti*, had some truffle shaved over them before they were served. Then a leg of kid was served from a giant casserole into which the rest of the truffle had been diced, along with tomatoes, marjoram and rosemary. There was a noticeable air of excitement in the little piazza that evening during dinner. Laughter was louder, flirting more obvious, more wine was consumed, and afterwards the accordions came out. Bruno had no idea how much Gusta charged for the food – there was nothing so straightforward as a price list, let alone a menu, and the electronic cash register, as required by the tax authorities for every retail business, sat untouched in a corner, gathering dust. However, he saw her folding up a great wad of banknotes and tucking it away carefully in a pocket, so presumably she was doing quite well out of the truffle too.

236

Javier was sitting with a group of his friends. They were drinking beer rather than wine, and vast quantities of it at that. Benedetta and Bruno helped Gusta wait tables by carrying plates outside when the food was ready, and Bruno noticed that there was much ribald laughter and joshing between Javier and his friends whenever Benedetta went out.

Suddenly he heard a yelp. He looked up. It was instantly clear what had happened. The young farmer had just grabbed Benedetta's behind. The two of them were frozen in a tableau: she had jumped away from him, her eyes blazing, and he was laughing at her. Bruno took a step towards them, his fists clenched. Benedetta's eyes swivelled towards Bruno and saw what he was about to do. Instantly she took the plate she was holding and smashed it down over Javier's head, breaking it in two. There was a moment of stunned silence, then his friends started applauding and whistling. Bruno stepped back, his fists unclenching.

At first Javier sheepishly joined in the applause. Then his eyes followed Benedetta's own gaze, over to where Bruno was standing, and his face darkened.

She came to his room after Gusta was asleep and slipped into bed beside him. 'That was quick thinking earlier,' he whispered.

'I only did it because I thought you were going to hit him.'

'I probably would have done,' he admitted.

'But you mustn't. Promise me, Bruno. As soon as you do something like that, he'll think he has to fight you. And let's face it, he'd beat you to a pulp.'

'Don't you think he's guessed anyway?'

'He may suspect. But so long as it isn't obvious – so long as there's nothing public – he'll tell himself that it's just gossip.'

'People are gossiping?'

'Of course. We work together in the kitchen all day – people would talk even if we were a nun and a priest. But that's to our advantage. Because everyone here gossips all the time, and most of the time it turns out to be nonsense, no one quite believes anything they hear. As long as they can tell themselves it isn't true when they need to, they'll even believe two different things at once.'

'Like the councillors coming to the restaurant on Fridays, but eating *fagiolini*?'

'Exactly.' The local council was staunchly communist, like most of the rural councils in this region. However, there wasn't a communist in the area who would eat meat on Fridays, and every Friday the *osteria* kitchen was kept busy shelling a vast pile of *borlotti* beans, fresh from the garden, for vegetarian stews and pasta dishes.

'But if Javier knew, it might stop him making a nuisance of himself.'

'No, it wouldn't,' she said firmly. 'I've known him all my life. Besides, I don't think I want Javier to lose any sleep over you. I may want to marry him one day.'

'What! Are you serious?'

'Of course.' She put her hand on his chest. 'You won't be here for ever, and I don't intend to be an old maid. Javier is a good man. Any woman would be lucky to have him.'

'I—' Bruno felt awkward. He knew he ought to tell her that he loved her, that he wanted to stay here with her for ever. But he couldn't, because it wasn't true. He thought she was the warmest, most generous person he had ever met; he adored her; she was beautiful and sexy, and she was a soulmate and a friend. But his heart had already been given to someone else. So he said instead, 'You're wonderful, Benedetta.'

'I know.' She wriggled on top of him and opened his lips with her tongue, the way a fisherman opens an oyster with a knife. 'So let's enjoy it while we can.'

He had thought they were being discreet, but the next afternoon he had a strange conversation with her mother.

It was the quiet part of the day, the siesta between lunch and starting to prep dinner. Bruno was reading. He had asked Benedetta if there were any local recipes written down and she had shown him where the family notebooks were kept – ancient, handwritten cookbooks, row upon row of them, going right back to pre-unification days, the oldest on yellowing paper as fragile as tissue. The combinations of local ingredients were still relevant today, however, even if some of the raw materials – such as *creste di gallo*, cock's combs, or *camoscio*, wild goat – would be hard to come by now.

Just as practised musicians can read an orchestral score and hear the music in their heads, Bruno could read a recipe and taste the result in his mind. He was turning the pages slowly, garnering ideas, when Gusta came into the room. She was holding a tiny jug.

'Ah, there you are,' she said. 'Benedetta said you were going through the old books. Where have you got to?'

'Goose stewed in red wine.'

'Oh yes. *Oca in potacchio* – my grandmother's recipe. You cut the goose into pieces and stew it in *peperoncini* and wine, very slowly. Then, just before you serve it, you add a little vinegar to offset the richness of the goose fat.' She hesitated. 'Actually, that reminds me. Have you got a moment? There's something I've been meaning to show you, upstairs in the attics.'

Intrigued, he followed her. He suspected that this had something to do with Benedetta, but although Gusta paused outside his room, and seemed to glance meaningfully at the tousled bed, she said nothing.

She led him up the stairs to the very top of the house. Producing an old key the size of a spoon from her pocket, she unlocked a dark wooden door and ushered him through.

The moment he smelled the air he knew what the attic contained. The sight of a dozen or more wooden barrels, all of different sizes, confirmed it. It was smaller than the *acetaia* he had visited in Modena, but the smell of balsamic vinegar was just as overwhelming.

'Here.' Gusta had crossed to the largest barrel and put down her jug. 'Look at this.' She pointed to a date carved roughly into the wood.

Bruno crouched down next to her. 'My God,' he breathed. '1903.'

She nodded. 'And it still isn't empty. It was my great-grand-mother's dowry, the same one who wrote that recipe for goose. This barrel was started by my great-great-grandfather when she was just a baby.' She tapped each of the barrels in turn with her fingers. 'This one's oak, but this small one is beech . . . and that's juniper . . . and chestnut . . . and cherry. After the vinegar drips out of one barrel, it gets put into the next, and then the next, getting a little thicker every time, taking a little of the flavour of each different wood. Then some of it goes back into the first barrel, along with a little new wine to keep it going.'

Around the bung there was a tiny ooze, as thick as toffee, straining to fall into the bucket beneath. As Bruno watched, it fell, making hardly a ripple in the viscous liquid.

Gusta said softly, 'When I married, this was my dowry too. And when Benedetta marries, it will go with her.' She was not looking at him, her eyes carefully fastened on the barrel, but he felt her hand reaching for his, lifting it, pressing his finger into the thick, sticky liquid. 'Go on, try it.'

He put his finger to his lips and felt his mouth flooded with the taste of it – old wine, and honey, and wood sap, and the almost citrus sharpness of the vinegar itself, flowing like warmth through his stomach and chest. He gasped.

'It's good, isn't it?' she said.

Unable to speak, Bruno nodded.

'Do you know why they call it *balsamico*? They used to believe it was a balm that was able to cure anything. Any illness you had.' She reached to the smallest barrel and carefully opened the tap, allowing a tiny amount into the little jug. 'Even a broken heart.'

240

Twenty-one

Bruno didn't tell Benedetta what her mother had said. Evidently Gusta had a similar conversation with her daughter, though, because Benedetta no longer confined their lovemaking to the outdoors. Most nights she slept in his room now, and although they never referred to it in her mother's presence, it became, like so many things in Italian life, *pubbliche bugie e verità private**; something that was accepted but never spoken of.

Even between the two of them they did not actually discuss the implication behind Gusta's tacit acceptance of the situation: that she approved of him as a prospective son-in-law. Perhaps if Bruno had been absolutely certain that he did not want to marry Benedetta he would have said something. But the truth was that he wasn't so sure any more. *I could be happy here*, he found himself thinking as he trailed through the fields behind her, finding mushrooms or salad leaves or fruit for the table, or watched her rolling pasta shapes with those deft fingers on the kitchen table.

*'A public lie and a private truth.'

241

I've never found anyone before who shares my gift, let alone a woman. I'd be crazy not to marry her. Together we'd build up the osteria into a famous restaurant, one that people would come to from right across Italy, and we'd make love every day and have babies and do all the things that happy people do.

If only it was Laura.

If only it was Laura who was sharing her bed with him, who was cooking with him, who was his friend and his lover and, yes, whose family owned a beautiful little restaurant in the middle of nowhere. Because no matter how wonderful a time he shared with Benedetta, the truth was that his heart had already been given to a girl with orange-red freckles on her shoulders. There was simply nothing he could do about it.

Then he'd sigh, and try to stop scratching the itch in his mind.

He went to see Hanni the mechanic to find out how the van was coming on. The answer was that it wasn't. It was still up on blocks, and Bruno was rather surprised to see that the wheels had disappeared.

'That's just because I was taking a look at the brake discs, and it was easier to get the wheels out of the way,' Hanni explained. 'Don't worry, they're around here somewhere.'

Bruno looked rather doubtfully at the heaps of rusting spare parts that slopped up against the walls of Hanni's barn like tidal debris on a beach. 'They are?'

'Of course. And look, don't worry. I had some news of a possible set of spares the other day. I'm just waiting to hear.'

Bruno thanked him for being so persistent and made his way back to the restaurant. On his way he passed a tractor which was sporting a windscreen and a pair of windscreen wipers that looked remarkably like those on his van. He stopped. Now that he thought about it, had there been any glass in his van? In the gloom of the barn, it had been hard to tell. He turned around and went back to check, but Hanni had already disappeared and the barn was now securely padlocked. It suddenly occurred to him to wonder why Hanni had been fiddling with the brake discs at all, since as far as Bruno knew the brakes were one of the few parts of his van that worked reasonably well. Presumably the mechanic had his reasons, but Bruno couldn't imagine what they were.

Tommaso's restaurant was full again, though the clientele had changed somewhat. The food might have the desired effect but it tasted awful, and now the couples chewing their way with grim determination through his *saltimbocca* or *padellata di pollo* were the desperate or those who simply didn't care – jaded Eurotrash businessmen, dripping with jewellery and chest hair, lunching their perma-tanned young mistresses, or groups of drunk students looking for the quickest route to another high. Even foreigners had started turning up – a sure sign that Il Cuoco had dropped off the culinary map.

What was more, he had failed to stem the financial haemorrhage. The restaurant might be booked out, but he had been forced to buy huge amounts of drugs through the restaurant mafia contact, Franco, and although the deliveries were as regular as clockwork, the costs were ruinous.

'I can't believe we're losing so much money,' Dr Ferrara shouted at him when he saw the monthly audit.

'Neither can I. Look, we've turned the corner,' Tommaso said desperately. 'Just stick with it for a few more weeks. There'll be more tourists then.'

'I'll have to go to the bank and arrange a bigger overdraft. This is my pension on the line, you know.'

Tommaso paused. The last thing he wanted was to leave Dr Ferrara penniless, but there was nothing else he could do. 'It'll be all right,' he promised. 'Just a few more weeks.'

❀

Here is Laura, wandering contentedly around the picture gallery of the staggeringly beautiful Palazzo Doria-Pamphili, hand-in-hand with her handsome lover. They are both listening to audio guides, and though the guides are just a little out of sync they turn and nod to each other as each useful nugget of information about the treasures on display is revealed into their ears. They spend a long time in front of Caravaggio's *Repentant Magdalene*, for Laura is now writing her final essay of the year, a thesis-length dissertation on themes of redemption in the Roman Renaissance, and this strangely tragic painting is one of her subjects. They note the tiny tear, all but invisible in reproductions, glistening on the side of the Magdalene's nose, and the wine at which she seems to cast a longing glance, but which remains untouched, as if she must fast in perpetual atonement.

Here is Laura with her boyfriend in Castroni's, the food store. Her days of buying Skippy and Folger's are long gone, for she is acclimatised now, and culinary homesickness is not among her vices. She comes here just once a week to buy low-fat margarine and skimmed milk, since these are never available in the street markets where, at Kim's insistence, they do most of their shopping.

'Just look at them,' Kim murmurs, casting a dark glance at a gaggle of tourists. 'Don't they realise that the real Italy is outside?' He speaks in Italian, something he often does with her now, although Laura has noticed that he is more likely to do it when there are other Americans around.

Here is Laura with her boyfriend in bed. The city is swelteringly hot but the apartment is air-conditioned, and their bodies move together with practised precision. There is just a tiny glitch when Kim's headphones get caught in Laura's hair; for her lover likes to listen to Puccini when making love, while Laura prefers silence. But the entanglement is quickly resolved and they see-saw smoothly on.

She does not speak to Carlotta so much now, what with being so busy, but when she does her friend is surprised to note that

Laura sounds happy. She has lost some of her gauche otherworld-liness and embraced something of the Italian notion of *bella figura* – the art of looking elegant in public, of cultivating a sophisticated detachment from the frustrations of daily life.

There was no option but to sack Marie. Tommaso was dreading it, but he couldn't think of an alternative.

She seemed to take it quite well, he thought. She listened to him in silence, nodding occasionally as he explained that there was simply no other way for Il Cuoco to survive. Only a foot, tapping dangerously, gave a hint of her feelings.

'So what you're saying is, there's no money to pay me,' she said when he had finished.

'That's it, in a nutshell.'

'And you're not paying yourself?'

'No. I haven't been for months.'

Marie seemed to make a decision. 'Right then. I'll work for nothing too.'

'You mean that?' He stared at her.

'I said so, didn't I? But there are two conditions.'

'What are they?'

'First, I want a share of the profits when we do make money. And second, I want to go through the books to see why we're losing so much. I may want to make some changes. If I could keep this place going for all those years before you came, I can certainly keep it going now.'

August came to Le Marche like the opening of an oven door. It had been hot before, but now people felt as though they were being cooked. For a month no one walked fast, or ventured out in the afternoons; and the houses in the village closed up their shut-ters as if against a storm, conserving what little coolness lingered inside their thick stone walls, until evening brought with it a wel-come trickle of colder air.

The Galtenesi, always great meat-eaters, stopped eating lamb, kid and pork and started eating the inferior summer meats – *asino* – donkey – and *carne di cavallo* – horsemeat. There was nothing much you could do with it – the donkey's meat was sometimes cured, as *coglioni di asino*, and the horsemeat was stewed with juniper berries and other flavourings to tenderise it. Bruno did his best, but one just had to accept that this was not the time of year for great meat dishes. Instead Bruno concentrated on introducing the villagers to the richly concentrated ice creams of his native Rome, and to *granite*, the flavoured ices from further south. There was some grumbling at first when he served as a dessert a simple paper cup of crushed ice into which a shot of *mocha* had been poured, or a scoop of ice cream made from the peaches that now hung ripe in every garden, but the locals soon discovered how refreshing they were and devoured them eagerly.

There were tourists in Le Marche now – not many, by comparison with other parts of Italy, most of them just passing through en route for the cooler seaside resorts of Ancona and Rimini. *Ferragosto*, August the fifteenth, when Rome closed down for its annual holiday, came and went without Bruno noticing. Only when the heat began to wane and the woods began to fill with skylarks and thrushes, migrating gradually southwards along with the warm weather, did he stop and think that by now Laura, too, would have gone back to America, her studies in Italy over.

And then, suddenly, August was gone and he was busy again. There were myrtle berries to pick and then to serve gratinated with a topping of mascarpone. There were blackberries to gather, to make into pastries and sorbets. Chestnuts and walnuts added their sweet richness to pasta sauces and stews. The walnut trees were surrounded with bibs of white netting to catch any prematurely falling fruit. Whole families climbed the trees to pick them, or walked down the rows of grapes in the vineyards with panniers on their backs, filling them with the fruit that would become the local wine.

And there was Benedetta. Each new harvest was an excuse to take to the fields above the village and, as soon as their baskets were full, to make love. And each night, too, when the dishes were finally washed and put back in their racks above the range to dry, there was the darkness of his bedroom, and her warm body slipping quietly into his bed while her mother snored softly in the room below.

The woods were dense with *funghi* now. Shaggy ink caps grew along the verges of the lanes, with chanterelles and *spugnoli* just a few yards further in. *Porcini*, king of mushrooms, dotted the gaps between beech trees, and the even more splendid Caesar's mushroom, the *ovolo*, clustered under the gnarled roots of oaks in twos and threes like eggs in a nest. As if from nowhere, truffle-hunters appeared in the village, taciturn individuals who downed a solitary *distillato* in the bar before heading off to the woods with their dogs and an air of feigned nonchalance, careful not to let anyone know exactly where they would be looking. Benedetta and Bruno paid them little heed. They had their own secret places.

Her ability to smell out truffles without the aid of a dog amazed him. His own palate, so highly attuned to scents and tastes in the kitchen, was thoroughly outclassed. She was determined to teach him, however, and little by little he too began to be able to discern the faint feral perfume they trailed on the still night air.

These truffles were a different thing altogether from the summer truffle he and Benedetta had found earlier in the year. Pale in colour, and as large as potatoes, they were both awesomely pungent and deeply intoxicating. Gusta and Benedetta threw them into every dish as casually as if they were throwing in parsley, and after a while Bruno did the same. He would never forget the first time they cooked a wild boar with celery and truffles: the dark, almost rank meat and the sulphuric reek of the tuber combined to form a taste that made him shiver.

He was aware that Benedetta was deliberately cooking dishes

designed to bind him to her. As well as the truffles there was *robiola di bec*, a cheese made from the milk of a pregnant ewe, rich in pheromones. There were fiery little *diavolesi*: strong chilli peppers that had been left to dry in the sun. Plates of fried *funghi* included morsels of *amanita*, the ambrosia of the gods, said to be a natural narcotic. He didn't mind. He was doing the same to her: offering her unusual *gelati* flavoured with saffron, the delicate stigmas of the crocus flower; elaborate tarts of myrtle and chocolate; salads made with lichens and even acorns from her beloved woods. It was a game they played, based on their intimate appreciation of the taste of each other's body, so that the food and the sex became one harmonious whole, and it became impossible to say where eating ended and lovemaking began. He no longer went to enquire about his van. Its red bonnet had appeared on one of the olive lorries, and he thought he recognised its headlights on somebody else's scooter. He noticed, too, that when Hanni the mechanic sat down to eat at the *osteria*, he got up again without paying, which made Bruno laugh. Never mind: the body of the dead van had been recycled into the life of the village, like a fallen log in the woods sprouting *orecchietti*, or *trombette di morte* growing on the rich earth of a grave.

A different kind of tourist came to the restaurant now from as far away as Urbino and Pesaro. These were people who were serious about their food. In particular they came to eat the seasonal truffles, and Bruno served plate after plate of *carne al albese* – slices of raw beef covered with celery, parmesan, truffle shavings and olive oil – and salads of caesar mushrooms, truffles and potatoes. These dishes were simple to prepare but, with truffles selling for over two thousand euros a kilo, ridiculously profitable. Occasionally Gusta pressed huge piles of banknotes on Bruno, which he accepted without counting.

Twenty-two

The car that made its way up the winding road from the valley was hired, and its occupants clearly tourists: they stopped several times to admire the views, and when they finally parked in the piazza and folded up their touring map they first of all went off to take a look round the church, the war memorial and the rest of the sights. But even the most determined sightseer could not find much to detain them in Galteni, and it was inevitable that, come lunchtime, they would settle themselves at a table for two and wait contentedly for Gusta to come and tell them what was on offer that day.

Gusta's face, when she came into the kitchen with their order, bore the studiously blank expression she put on whenever she was confronted by the oddness of strangers.

'One truffle salad, *to share*,' she said pointedly.

'And?' Benedetta asked, not looking up from the stove.

'And nothing. No pasta. No *secondo*. A *glass* of wine each. And they want to know what kinds of mineral water we have.' She shrugged. 'They're foreigners, of course.'

Since Gusta used the word foreigners to describe anyone from beyond the valley, Bruno didn't pay much attention. 'I'll make the salad a large one then. No point in sending them away hungry.' He began to arrange the ingredients in a dish.

Then he heard her voice.

The small kitchen window overlooked the square where the tables were and conversation often drifted in – so much so that Benedetta and Gusta would sometimes join in, shouting their contributions over the crash of pans. Benedetta was searing meat now, and the hiss made it hard for him to hear. Bruno put a hand on her arm to stop her and listened.

'Probably about another hour or two from here to Urbino,' a man's voice was saying, in American.

'So there'll be plenty of time to go right up to the top,' his companion agreed. The hairs on the back of Bruno's neck tingled, and his heart stood still.

Benedetta looked at his face. 'What's wrong?'

'Nothing. I thought – nothing.'

Through the window, they heard the voices again.

'. . . can't believe how much cooler it is up here than Rome,' the man was saying.

'And so beautiful. And that food smells *fantastic*.'

When he heard her say that, Bruno was sure. He put down his knife and went through to the tiny bar, from where he could see all the tables.

She was thinner than when he'd last seen her, and she was wearing sunglasses, but there was no mistaking the sweep of her neck or the way she sat with her long legs spread out over the chair next to her. He felt dizzy.

'It's her, isn't it?' Benedetta said softly beside him. He nodded, unable to speak.

'Do you want to speak to her?'

He shook his head and made his way back to the kitchen. There was a dish of snails to prepare, ordered by the Luchetta family, and he tried to force his mind to concentrate as he cleaned them. But his hands were shaking and the slippery shells clattered all over the floor.

Benedetta grabbed a board and began chopping livers in silence. *Thwick – thwick – thwick* went the knife through the soft flesh, just a little harder than was necessary.

'I'm sorry,' Bruno said at last.

'For what?' Benedetta's reply was even sharper than the knife.

'For being upset, I suppose.'

Benedetta tipped the chopping board against the pan and scraped the livers into the bubbling oil. 'You can't help the way you feel.'

And nor can you, Bruno thought, looking at the angry flush on the back of Benedetta's neck.

'I did think I was over her,' he said apologetically.

'And I always knew you weren't.'

He opened his mouth to protest, then closed it again.

'She's pretty,' Benedetta said, taking an onion and slicing it in a dozen deft movements before reaching for another.

'Yes.'

'Prettier than me.'

'No,' he protested. 'Just – different.'

'And you love her.'

It wasn't said as a question, but it was a question nevertheless, and Bruno knew he had to try to answer it. 'Well,' he began, 'it's complicated. I fell in love with her but she didn't love me back, and I'm not sure whether – I mean, they say you can't really be in love with someone unless they love you too, don't they?'

'That's what they say.'

He looked at her but she was concentrating on what she was doing. Her voice was a little thick, but that might just have been the onions.

'So you told her that you loved her, and she told you she wasn't interested,' Benedetta went on. 'What happened next?'

'It was a bit more complicated than that,' Bruno confessed.

'She was in love with my best friend, and – well, it all sort of spiralled from there.'

Benedetta wiped her hands and poured two glasses of wine from the bottle that stood open by the stove.

'I think you'd better tell me exactly what happened,' she said gently.

So Bruno talked, and Benedetta listened and nodded, cooking while she did so, and Gusta, coming in and out of the kitchen with empty plates, pretended she wasn't eavesdropping.

'And that's why I don't want to go and speak to her,' Bruno said finally. 'She thinks I'm a complete pervert and I don't blame her.'

'Nor do I.'

'Thanks,' he said wearily. 'Anyway, it's best she just has her lunch and leaves.'

'Perhaps.'

At that moment there was the sound of shouting from outside, followed shortly afterwards by the unmistakable sound of someone retching. Bruno heard Laura's voice in the bar. She sounded panicked. '*Scusi*, signora, is there a doctor? My friend has been taken ill.'

Bruno glanced at Benedetta but her face betrayed nothing. They heard Gusta's voice saying that she would call for the doctor straight away. In the meantime, they would make her friend comfortable on a bed. Benedetta went to see if she could help.

'What's all that about?' Bruno asked when all was quiet and Benedetta was back in the kitchen.

'It must have been the *funghi*.'

'In what way?'

'Some people have an allergic reaction to *coprini**. Particularly

*Shaggy inkcaps.

252

if they mix them with alcohol. He must be one of those.' She gave him a blank look. 'He'll be laid up for at least two hours. There's nothing the doctor can do, but he'll have to wait for him anyway, and my mother will give him some *aceto balsamico* to settle his stomach.'

'Benedetta, we don't have any *coprini*.'

'No, but that's because I used them all.'

He gave up. It seemed to him more likely that Laura's companion was suffering from a small amount of one of those poisonous mushrooms that Benedetta insisted on collecting during their forays into the woods. But the important thing now was what he was going to do about Laura.

'I can't talk to her,' he decided. 'She thinks we've given her boyfriend food-poisoning, for God's sake. I can't go out there and start talking to her as if nothing's happened.'

'No,' Benedetta agreed. 'But my mother's already told her about the effects of *coprini*, and of course we're not going to charge her for her meal, so . . .'

'. . . so I could cook her a *dolce* on the house, by way of apology.'

'Brilliant. What about the tart with the myrtle berries?'

He shook his head. 'Too sweet.'

'Then baked figs?'

'Too straightforward.'

'*Zuppa inglese*?'

'Too heavy.'

She threw up her hands. 'Your turn, then, maestro. What are you going to cook her?'

'I don't know,' he said slowly. As he spoke his hands were already reaching for ingredients. Figs, yes, and cream, and nuts. Some sort of cake? 'But whatever it is, I don't think there's a recipe for it.'

He was not thinking now, but improvising. No: even improvising wasn't the right word for what he was doing, Benedetta thought as she watched him juggle candied fruits and pastry cream, and pound hazelnuts into a creamy paste. Bruno was composing. Occasionally she made a comment, or a quiet suggestion, but he could barely hear her, so focused was he on the feel and taste of what was in his hands.

Eventually it was done. He blinked, and there in front of him was a kind of trifle cake, a many-layered mousse that was sweet and bitter, smooth and sharp, cold on the outside and warm underneath: a dessert, he thought, that was as rich and as simple as life itself.

'Well done,' Benedetta commented. 'Although it has to be said, it might be better prepared in advance next time.'

He stared at her. How long had he been cooking? He had no idea. Then he heard the church bells striking four. Four o'clock! He had been making this dessert for over an hour.

'I'll take it to her,' Benedetta said beside him.

'Are you sure?'

'I said so, didn't I? She should taste it first, before she knows who it's from.'

He knew what an extraordinary thing it was that she was offering to do. He watched as Benedetta picked up the little plate. She touched her finger to the side of the cake, picked up a crumb and tasted it. For a moment her eyes met his, and there was something in them he didn't quite understand. Then she took his *dolce* outside.

Laura had been terrified when Kim started having convulsions at the table, but now the doctor had confirmed that it was just an allergic reaction to a particular type of mushroom, and that he would be right as rain within a few hours if he was left to sleep quietly. The other customers and the lady who ran the place were sympathetic and helpful, and now, with the sun filtering through the trees and the amazing view beyond the war memorial to entertain her, and a bottle of the restaurant's best wine open in front of her, she was feeling quite mellow. She helped herself to another glass, a little guiltily. Poor Kim. On the other hand, if he were here he would almost certainly be reminding her of the one-glass-a-day rule, and it was really rather nice to be able to indulge herself a little.

Heavens. Here was one of the kitchen staff coming towards her, a strikingly pretty girl in a white jacket, her black hair cascading over her shoulders in defiance of all normal kitchen regulations. She was bearing a plate on which a dessert sat, an island in a little lake of sauce. The girl put it down in front of her and said, 'Here. This is for you. Cooked specially by our chef, with his compliments.'

Was it her imagination, Laura wondered, or did the other girl's eyes search her face with a quizzical look while she spoke, as if she was subjecting Laura to some kind of scrutiny?

'Oh, thank you,' Laura began. 'But I couldn't. You see, I don't eat desserts.'

'And a *vin santo*,' the girl said, ignoring her and placing a glass of golden liquid on the table.

'No, really,' Laura said firmly. 'Please take it away.' But the girl had already gone.

Laura told herself she didn't want to appear rude. She would have a couple of mouthfuls, and she could always slip the rest to the dogs that lay panting in the shade of the church wall. She pushed the teaspoon into the top of the pudding, through the layer of sauce, and tried a little.

The sauce. Memories flooded into her brain. It was *zabaione*. She had a sudden vision of herself, that first night in Tommaso's apartment, licking sauce from her fingers.

Coffee. The next taste was coffee. Memories of Gennaro's espressos, and mornings in bed with a cup of cappuccino . . . but what was this? Bread soaked in sweet wine. And nuts – a thin layer of hazelnut paste – and then fresh white peaches, sweet as sex itself, and then a layer of black chocolate so strong and bitter she almost stopped dead. There was more sweetness beyond it, though: a layer of pastry flavoured with blackberries; and, right at the centre, a single tiny fig.

She put down the spoon, amazed. It was all gone. She had eaten it without being aware of eating, her mind in a reverie.

'Did you like it?'

She looked up. Somehow, she wasn't surprised. 'What was it?' she asked.

'It doesn't have a name,' Bruno said. 'It's just – it's just the food of love.'

'How do you make it, if it doesn't have a name?'

'Well, there's a sort of recipe.'

She was silent, remembering the apology that Tommaso had texted her once, still stored on her phone. It seemed so long ago.

As if reading her thoughts, Bruno said: 'Take one American girl . . .'

She looked at him, surprised.

'With honey-coloured skin,' Bruno continued softly, 'and freckles like orange-red flakes of chilli on her shoulders. Fill her with flavours, with basil and tomatoes and pine nuts and parsley. Warm her gently between your hands—'

'It was *you*,' she said, realising at last.

'Yes,' he agreed. 'It was always me.'

'You're the cook. And Tommaso . . .'

'Tommaso is a fine person in many ways. But not a chef.'

She closed her eyes. 'Why?'

'As a favour to Tommaso, originally. And then – I really did love you, and I loved to see you eat. And it all got horribly complicated, but I was too stupid to see that it would end the way it did, and before I knew it everyone was shouting at everyone else.'

'There *was* a lot of shouting, wasn't there?' she agreed with the faintest of smiles.

There was a sudden commotion at the door of the *osteria*. Gusta's voice could be heard, and it was clear that she was arguing with someone. A moment later Kim appeared, looking pale and angry, with Gusta and Benedetta just behind him.

'Sweetheart,' he said icily, stopping at Laura's table. 'When we ordered, do you recall seeing anything like a menu?' There was a note of petulance in his voice Laura hadn't heard before.

'I guess not,' she said.

'And do you remember reading, on this non-existent menu, a non-existent warning to the effect that dangerous mushrooms were being served at this restaurant which might precipitate an allergic reaction?'

He waited. Laura was clearly meant to play her part in his tirade. With an apologetic glance at Bruno, she muttered, 'No.'

'Was there any verbal warning, explanation or other rider to the effect that this meal was actually life-threatening?'

'Not that I heard,' she said, looking at the ground.

'Not that you heard.' He turned to Gusta, who was standing with her arms folded and a face like a dog that has just swallowed a wasp. 'And *that*'s why I want the name of your lawyer. So that I can sue your fat ass into the ground.'

Laura flinched visibly, though Gusta herself didn't blink.

'It might have been the wine,' Benedetta said. She shrugged. 'Everybody knows that you have to be careful if you drink white wine with mushrooms.'

'Everybody except *me*,' Kim said firmly. 'And who served me this wine?' He pointed at Gusta. 'She did. Did she tell me to be careful? No, she did not.'

Bruno stood up. 'I prepared the food,' he said calmly. 'If anyone's going to be sued, it's me. I'll happily give you my name and address, though I'm afraid I don't have a lawyer.'

There was a brief silence as the two men stared at each other; Kim still flushed with rage, Bruno apparently unconcerned. 'Oh, forget it,' Kim snapped at last. 'Come on, Laura. We're going.' He stalked off to where their car was parked next to the church, leaving Laura to follow.

257

'I'm so sorry,' she said awkwardly to Gusta. 'He doesn't like being made to look stupid, that's all. It was,' she hesitated, 'it was really good to see you, Bruno.'

'When do you go back?'

'To Rome? Right away.'

'I meant to America.'

'Next week. I've left it as late as I can, but I have to get back for college.'

He nodded. She was flying away, like the skylarks. He watched the two of them buckle themselves into the car, and then the car itself move off rapidly down the hill, towards the *autostrada*, and Rome.

They went back into the kitchen to finish clearing up. For a long time nobody spoke. After a while Benedetta announced that she was going up to her room to rest. Bruno tried her door later, but it was locked.

He had to wait until much later, when the evening service was over and the house was quiet, before he was able to speak to her. There was no answer when he knocked, but this time when he tried the door it opened.

She was sitting at her dressing table, brushing her long black hair. 'Go away,' she said without turning around.

He sat down on the end of the bed. 'I wanted to say thank you,' he began. 'What you did earlier – that was unbelievably generous.'

'Too generous.'

'What do you mean?'

'If I really cared that much about you, I wouldn't have helped you go after someone else.'

'You cared as my friend,' he said gently. 'That means a lot to me, Benedetta.'

'That's what we are, is it – friends who have sex?'

'You're my mirror image, Benedetta. We understand each

258

other. We even have the same gift. If I'd never met Laura I'd want to be with you, but I did meet her.'

'So why didn't you go after her today?'

He shrugged. 'I did my best.'

'Oh, sure. You offered to let her boyfriend sue you. Nice work.'

'What was I meant to do?'

'You were meant to hit him. Wasn't it obvious?' She stamped her foot. 'I went to a lot of time and trouble to arrange things so that you and he were out there, with everyone shouting, and you didn't even hit him! What sort of an Italian are you?'

'Not a very good one, evidently,' he muttered.

'I should have realised you were spineless when you first arrived, and you never tried to grab my ass when we were together in the kitchen.'

He opened his mouth, then closed it again. Benedetta was just getting warmed up and was brooking no interruptions.

'You know your problem, Bruno? *Menefreghismo**. You don't really give a shit about anything or anyone apart from your cooking. Not her, and certainly not me.'

'That's not true,' he protested.

'Isn't it? Did you even *ask* Laura to choose you over that idiot today?'

'No,' he admitted.

'And why not?'

'Because she would have chosen him.'

'How would you know, if you haven't asked her?'

'Look at me,' he said hopelessly.

'What do you mean?'

'Just – look at me.' He gestured at his own face in the mirror. 'That guy she was with – he's good-looking. Tommaso – he's

*An expression that combines '*Me ne frego*' – 'I don't give a damn' – and '*machismo*': in other words a cultivated attitude of not bothering.

good-looking. Laura's beautiful. Why should she choose a guy like me when she can have a guy like that?'

There was a brief pause, during which Benedetta regarded him with narrowed eyes. 'You're beautiful, too, of course,' he added belatedly.

'Thank you. So why did *I* sleep with you?'

'I've absolutely no idea,' he confessed. 'I'm very glad you did, but it's a complete mystery to me.'

'*Santa Cielo!*' she cried in exasperation. She dragged his face closer to the mirror. 'Tell me, Quasimodo,' she commanded, 'which part of you exactly is so ugly?'

'Well . . .' He made a vague gesture. 'All of me.'

'Specifics, please.'

'My nose,' he muttered.

'Your palate, you mean? The secret of your success?'

'When I was little, other kids used to say things.'

'Such as?'

'"Can I plug you into the TV so we can pick up the football in Tokyo?"'

'Is that all?'

'"Your nose is so long your ID card won't fold."'

'Ha! Very good.'

'"Your nose is so long that if you shake your head you'll hit the person next to you . . . Your nose is so long that if you sneeze we'll hear an echo . . . Your nose is so long that if you were a sheep you'd starve to death—"'

'Enough about the nose,' Benedetta snapped, putting up her hands. 'Bruno, you have a perfectly normal Roman nose. What else?'

'I'm overweight.'

'No, you're not.'

It was true: hard work, vigorous lovemaking and the healthy diet of Le Marche had trimmed the extra pounds from his frame. He shrugged. 'I'm just not good-looking enough. Not for a woman like Laura.'

'Then I have a question for you.'

'Go ahead.'

'This friend of yours, Tommaso. He's nice to look at, you say?'

'Undoubtedly. Women throw themselves at him.'

'But he can't cook?'

'Good God, no.'

Benedetta held up a comb from her table. 'This is a magic wand. Now pay attention, because I am going to offer you the chance to make one wish. Understand?'

'I think so.'

'If you want, you can wish that you become as good-looking as Tommaso – but at the same time, you will become like Tommaso in every other way as well, with Tommaso's talent for cooking.'

He saw what she was getting at, and the realisation took his breath away.

'So. Just say the word and you will become handsome and talentless, just like Tommaso. That's what you want, isn't it?' She raised the comb expectantly.

'No!' He stared at her. 'If it meant I couldn't cook, I wouldn't want to be like anyone else. Cooking is who I am.'

'Exactly,' Benedetta said quietly. 'That's who you are. So stop regretting that God has made you exactly the way you actually want to be.' She tossed the comb back on to the dressing table. 'And if you want to be with Laura, go to Rome and tell her so. Tell her so, and keep telling her until she understands.'

He kissed her, wrapping his arms round her and hugging her until she gasped. 'Thank you,' he whispered. 'Thank you for everything.'

'Now get out. Go on. And take your hands off my tits. They're not yours any more.'

The next morning he was up early, battering at the door of Hanni's barn and shouting that he needed his van back.

'Come in,' Hanni said, opening the barn door. 'And don't worry. I got the message yesterday.'

Bruno had no time to wonder exactly what he meant. 'It's mended? You've finally got the parts?'

'More or less. Of course, I had to improvise a little.' He led the way to where, in the middle of the barn, a strange vehicle now stood. It had the body of Bruno's van, the front wheels of a tractor, and the pop-up headlamps of a very old Alfa Romeo. Inside, Bruno could see that where the steering wheel had once been there was now a pair of scooter handlebars. 'It may not look much,' Hanni added unnecessarily, 'but I reckon it'll get you as far as Rome. After all, it's downhill most of the way, isn't it?'

Dolci

'In the relationship of its parts, the pattern of a complete Italian meal is very like that of a civilised life. No dish overwhelms another, either in quantity or in flavour, each leaves room for new appeals to the eye and palate; each fresh sensation of taste, colour and texture interlaces with a lingering recollection of the last. To make time to eat as Italians still do is to share in their inexhaustible gift for making art out of life.'

MARCELLA HAZAN, *The Essentials of Classic Italian Cooking*

Twenty-three

Laura had arranged to meet Judith for lunch at one of her favourite restaurants, Cecchino's. It was not, Judith thought as she entered the long, low, tunnel-like room, the sort of place she would have chosen herself. For one thing, it was distinctly lacking in what the guidebooks would call 'ambience'. The tables were plain and functional; the lights, which hung directly overhead, were relentlessly bright; and the waiters, who all seemed to be at least sixty, could barely manage a token smile, even for beautiful young women dining without male company. But the food, Laura had assured her, would more than make up for these short-comings.

Judith paused by the door. On a trolley, displayed as proudly as any array of desserts, were the specialities of the day: a dozen or so calves' feet, neatly laid out in rows, along with several mounds of a white, gristle-like substance whose function in the body Judith could only guess at. She made a face. Then because, after all, this was a girl who for the past year had happily worn a phial of blood around her neck, she shrugged and looked around for her friend.

Laura had been seated right at the back, a bottle of wine already open on the table. Her lunches with Judith were a chance to abandon Kim's dietary strictures and restricted intake of alcohol, and Laura had already made inroads into her first glass of Sangiovese.

'Hey, girl,' Judith said, kissing her friend before taking the other seat. 'How was your trip?'

'Great. But, ah, a bit shorter than we planned.'

Judith raised an eyebrow.

'Kim got sick. A touch of mushroom poisoning.'

Judith sensed there was something she wasn't being told. But the waiter had arrived at their table, flipping open his order pad with a bored expression that suggested he knew already what they were going to eat.

He had clearly not expected to be interrogated fiercely, in Italian, about the day's specials. The cart by the door was wheeled over and a long discussion ensued, during which the waiter began to look at Laura in a different light. To discuss gristle with knowledge and passion in Cecchino's is to command instant respect, no matter what your appearance or country of origin.

Eventually the girls ordered – *rigatoni con la pagliata* and *zampetti* for Laura, *bucatini all' amatriciana* and *scottadito* for Judith – and Judith was able to tease some of the details of Kim's misadventure out of her friend. Eventually Laura got to the part where she had met Bruno unexpectedly in Le Marche. Judith gasped and prepared to dispense sympathy. Knowing how much Laura hated even to hear Bruno or Tommaso's name, she could see how meeting him by chance must have been an unsettling experience. As yet more details tumbled out of Laura's mouth, Judith became increasingly horrified.

'So they were lying to you? All that *time*? That's—' She wanted to say 'humiliating', but she settled for the milder 'weird'.

'Yes,' Laura said. 'All the time I thought it was Tommaso doing the cooking, it was actually Bruno.'

'But why?'

266

Laura shrugged. 'I suppose—' She stopped. 'I suppose because he was in love with me.'

'Tommaso?'

'No. I think Tommaso – well, if it hadn't been for the food it would only ever have been a quick fling. Of course, I thought that because he was cooking for me like that, it must be something more he wanted. Whereas Bruno . . .' She hesitated. 'Bruno was probably someone I'd never have looked at twice, to be honest. And I think he knew that. So he went on cooking for me because it was all he could do.'

'You're well shot of both of them,' Judith said. 'And all's well that ends well – if it hadn't been for Bruno and Tommaso, you'd never have got together with Kim.'

'Absolutely,' Laura said. But there was a note of doubt in her voice which her friend immediately picked up on.

'Things *are* all right with Kim?'

'Oh, of course,' Laura assured her. 'Things with Kim are great.' Because although she knew Judith very well by now, there were some things – some niggling doubts – that you couldn't say even to your best friends without seeming – well, a bit disloyal.

Hanni had been partly right: the way to Rome lay downhill as far as the valley and the long road-tunnel of the Furlo gorge, but after that there were more mountains to cross – the fearsomely high Sibylline peaks, capped with snow even at this time of year. The van gasped for breath, and Bruno gasped with cold, since a heating system was not one of the luxuries Hanni had thought worth installing. His maximum speed was barely more than a tractor's, thanks to the various modifications, and it was an exhausting day and a half's drive before signs to familiar towns such as Frascati, Nemi and Marino came into view. He stopped as infrequently as he could. Before leaving, Gusta had given him a basket of food: some *piadina* and *salume* to eat on the way, and other culinary treasures for the task ahead: two large white truffles, the finest they had, prised from the roots of a nut tree and now wrapped separately in foil to preserve their aroma; a sheep's cheese matured in the cool limestone caves beneath the village; and a tiny flagon of the family's precious *aceto balsamico*. At the very bottom of the basket, wrapped in a piece of old brown canvas, he found four chef's knives, their blades ancient and discoloured but their cutting edges gleaming and newly honed.

When he finally entered Rome, Bruno's first task, however, was not to find Laura but to repair another fractured relationship. He drove slowly through the outskirts, oblivious to the whistles and honks of his fellow motorists, and finally drew up outside the little building that had once housed Il Cuoco. With a heavy heart he pushed open the door.

He stopped, amazed. It was full. More than full: there were people waiting patiently at the bar for tables. The long cellar where once bottles of wine had gathered dust had been opened up to make more space; the wall between the kitchen and the main dining room knocked through; and there was Tommaso, cheerfully cooking away to the accompaniment of deafening rock music—

Pizza. At every table, Bruno now saw, they were eating pizza. He laughed out loud. Of course! As he watched, his old friend flung a huge ball of dough into the air, spinning it nonchalantly above his head to aerate it before slamming it down on to the counter again and grabbing a pair of rolling pins to bang it flat in a blur of movement, like a drummer. There was a burst of whistling and applause from the waiting customers, which Tommaso acknowledged with a huge grin and a roll of his shoulders, before flicking the pizza across the kitchen into the wood-fired oven as casually as if it were a Frisbee. Now that Bruno looked more carefully, he realised that many of the adoring customers were young women, and that they were not so much hanging round the bar as hanging round the kitchen, moving their bodies in time to the music.

Another familiar figure rushed past. It was Marie. If Tommaso was drawing plenty of female admiration, Marie was getting the same from the men in the room. Her top was the shortest Bruno had ever seen, exposing a swathe of brown midriff, and instead of an order pad she had been writing orders directly on to her arms, legs and even her stomach, which were covered in scribbles of different colours. Together with her newly pierced eyebrow, low-slung hipster jeans and cowboy boots, she looked more like a rock chick than a waitress. He noticed, too, that the normal rules of restaurant service seemed to have broken down: when you saw a pizza going past, you grabbed a slice, before passing the plate on to your neighbour.

He made his way over to the kitchen, squeezing through the crowd. There was a pizza on the counter in front of him and he broke off a tiny piece to try it. It was really very good – a thin Roman crust, a slather of fresh tomato pulp, some chunks of creamy buffalo mozzarella, sea salt and two fresh basil leaves, nothing else. As he watched, Tommaso added a looping signature of olive oil to the one he was making. The oil, Bruno was pleased to note, was from the same estate he had used himself when cooking here – though he had never been able to pour it from over his head, like a bartender making a cocktail, the way Tommaso was doing now.

'Tommaso,' he yelled over the din.

Tommaso saw him and froze for a moment. Then he wiped his hands on his apron and clapped Bruno on the shoulder. 'How are you? I didn't expect to see you here, old friend.'

'Neither did I. Tommaso, I'm sorry I went off like that.'

'My fault. I overreacted about that girl. What do you think of the place now?' He spread his hands proudly.

'Well, it's the first time I've ever seen a restaurant with a mosh pit.'

'Isn't it great?' A worried look crossed Tommaso's face. 'I suppose you want your job back. But I should warn you, our new clientele doesn't go a bundle on calves' intestines and all that shit.'

'It's all right, I don't want a job,' Bruno assured him. 'I've come to look for Laura.' He noted the way Tommaso was able to keep track of half a dozen pizzas even while they were talking: pounding the dough on one, dragging another out of the oven, sliding a third down the counter for collection by a waitress, and still finding time to play air-guitar on his rolling pin to Status Quo's 'Caroline'.

'Is this music ironic?' he shouted.

'Ironic? Never heard of them. This is the Quo.'

Bruno gave up. 'Listen, I'll see you later. Oh, and this is for you.' He took one of the foil packages from out of his pocket.

'We don't do that stuff any more,' Tommaso yelled.

'It's a truffle. Just grate it on the pizzas.' He gestured at the crowds. 'It'll be the best pizza they've ever had.'

He drove to the Residencia Magdalena. But Laura's name was not on any of the doorbells. Eventually he stopped someone coming out and asked if they knew which apartment was hers.

'I don't think she's here,' the man explained. 'This is a summer school course on Etruscan history. I guess the regular students had to leave.'

'Do you know where she's gone?'

'Sorry.' The man shrugged. 'You could try the university office. They may have an address for her.'

He drove around the streets of Trastevere, searching for her. He knew it was hopeless but he couldn't bear to do nothing. Eventually, well after midnight, he went back to the little side street that snaked down the hill from the Viale Glorioso. It occurred to him that he hadn't actually asked Tommaso if he would mind him sleeping there: it was perfectly possible his friend had a new roommate now.

He climbed the stairs to the top floor and let himself in. It was

270

quiet and dark. Then, from the direction of Tommaso's room, he heard a familiar sound.

'Oh – ah – oh – oh—'

Laura.

He heard another female gasp, and Tommaso laughing throatily in response. His blood boiled. Kicking open the bedroom door, he flicked the lights on.

'*Scusi,*' he said apologetically as Tommaso and Marie stopped what they were doing and stared at him. 'I thought – ah, that is – I'll just go now.'

'Nice to have you back,' Tommaso called as Bruno beat a hasty retreat.

Gennaro was so delighted to see his van again, he offered to take it back for what Bruno had paid for it, plus free espresso and *cornetti*, a deal that Bruno thought remarkably generous.

'I'm impressed by these modifications you've added,' Gennaro explained. 'Not to mention the old girl's homing instinct, of course.'

If only I had a homing instinct for Laura, Bruno thought gloomily. He had already phoned the university office and got a recorded announcement saying it was shut until term started the following week.

'But a week's not long to wait, is it?' Marie asked, her arm looped casually through Tommaso's as they drank their coffees.

'No, but in a week's time, give or take a few days, Laura's next term will start too – in the US. If I leave it until then it'll be too late. She'll have gone back home.' He sighed, then a thought occurred to him. 'Tommaso – her mobile phone number. It's programmed into your phone!'

'Ah. It was, yes. But Marie has wiped all my old numbers from my card.'

'An accident,' Marie shrugged.

'Damn. So what do I do?'

A girl roared past them on a scooter, helmetless, her dark hair flowing out in her own slipstream like a cape. Automatically, Tommaso turned his head to look. When his gaze returned to the others, Marie slapped his face, once, very hard. Tommaso continued, as if this were barely worth remarking on, 'I guess Carlotta could tell you her number.'

'It's like training a dog,' Marie explained under her breath to Bruno, seeing his puzzled expression. 'Carrot and stick. That's the stick.'

'What's the carrot?'

She smiled and patted her breasts.

'I see,' Bruno said. 'Tell me, do you know about the cupboard?'

'I'm the only girl in the cupboard now.'

'Nice work, Marie,' he said, impressed. 'And the accident with the phone numbers . . . ?'

Marie shrugged enigmatically.

'Will you two listen to me?' Tommaso complained. 'It's a good idea. We phone Carlotta, she tells us where Laura is.'

'Except we don't have Carlotta's number.'

'Maybe not, but we know a man who does.'

Bruno looked at him quizzically. 'Dr Ferrara,' Tommaso explained. 'Remember? My backer, who just happens to think the sun shines out of my *culo*.'

But when they called Dr Ferrara, they discovered he was out of town.

'We'll just have to look for her ourselves,' Marie decided. 'Where does she like to hang out, Bruno?'

He shrugged. 'Art galleries, mostly.'

'Then that's where we'll look.'

'Art galleries?' Tommaso looked pained. Marie poked him in the ribs.

'Yes, art galleries. And don't think you're not helping, because you are.'

∽

272

There are over five hundred art galleries in Rome. By the end of the day the three of them had succeeded in visiting twenty-five.

'This is hopeless,' Tommaso groaned. 'I have to work this evening and I'm already exhausted.'

'I'll come and help in the restaurant,' Bruno offered. 'It's the least I can do.'

Tommaso looked stern. 'OK – but remember, my customers have come for pizza, not fancy cooking.'

Bruno would have laughed if he hadn't been so worried about finding Laura. 'So what are you telling me? That I mustn't get too creative?'

'Exactly. We do Margherita, Marinara, Romana and Funghi. Our motto is: you want anything else, you eat somewhere else.'

'That's fine by me. I'll just do what you tell me,' Bruno promised.

While Tommaso delighted his female fans by kneading the dough in swooping, flamboyant gestures, spinning it like a lasso or tossing it from hand to hand, Bruno concentrated on quietly adding the toppings. It was undemanding work and he was able to let his mind return to the problem of finding Laura. He knew she went to a gym but he couldn't remember which one, and in any case he guessed that you couldn't hang around gyms all day watching the customers. What was left? Bars, he supposed. He realised he had absolutely no idea where Americans hung out in Rome. He lifted his head, thinking that there were bound to be some Americans in the crowd waiting for pizza. He would ask them where he should search.

He looked up, straight into Laura's eyes.

There was a group drinking beers near the entrance. Laura was standing with a bottle in her hand, blowing across the top of it absent-mindedly as she listened to something one of her companions was saying. Then she looked up, saw Bruno staring at her, with Tommaso standing next to him, and her face darkened. She said something to the person next to her and turned towards the door.

She's going, Bruno thought. *She's going and I'll never see her again*.

He leaped on to the counter. The crowd, thinking this was part of the show, roared their approval. Bruno jumped down the other side and tried to force his way through. It was impossible. They were packed too closely and, because anyone in a white jacket could be distributing pizza, they were trying to get closer to him, not give him space. He pushed and shoved but it was like trying to swim through treacle, and he made no headway.

He had an idea. Turning back to the bar, he got up on the counter again. This time when the crowd roared he simply fell forwards on to their hands as if he were stage-diving.

For one awful moment he thought they were going to let him fall, then he felt himself bouncing back up again, carried aloft towards the back of the room on a moving conveyor belt of hands. Of Laura, though, he could see no sign.

Running out into the street, he thought he saw a figure hurrying round the corner. He ran after it. Yes, it was her: she was walking fast, her head down. He shouted but she didn't hear him. Then a taxi with its light on came towards her and slowed as she waved at it, and she was climbing into it, and though he sprinted after her as fast as he could, he was just one more yelling Italian in the driver's rear-view mirror.

He had lost her.

Wearily he trudged back to Il Cuoco. *My one chance*, he thought, *and I blew it*. And even worse than that thought was the knowledge that she had seen him and turned away. She hadn't even wanted to talk to him.

'Bruno?'

He looked up. 'Oh. Judith.'

'It *is* you. I thought it must be.'

'When you saw Laura run away, you mean?' he muttered. 'Yes, I think I'm the only person who has that sort of effect on her.'

She was silent for a moment, then she said, 'I wouldn't be too sure.'

'You mean there are others? That's some consolation.'

'I probably shouldn't say this,' Judith said slowly, 'but she's been talking about you a lot since they came back from their trip.'

'Saying what?'

'Nothing in particular. Just talking. But a bit too much, if you know what I mean. I think that's why she doesn't want to see you, Bruno. Because it's too late to turn the clock back. Why make everyone miserable by talking about how much better things could have been if you hadn't been such a dickhead?'

'I've got to find her, Judith, please. You've got to tell me where she is.'

'I don't know where she is right now. But I know where she'll be tomorrow. There's a restaurant called Templi—'

'I know it.'

'There's a big dinner there tomorrow night. Everyone who's still here from the course is going, and all the faculty as well. To celebrate our last night in Italy.'

The next morning Bruno made his way to the restaurant at the top of Montespaccato and asked to see Alain Dufrais. When he was taken to the great chef's office, he asked for his old job back.

Alain smirked. 'I knew you'd be back. Your own establishment is making pizza now, I hear.'

'Yes,' Bruno said meekly. He didn't tell Alain that he hadn't been working there for some time.

'Well, I'll think about it. Come back in a week or so.'

'I need the job immediately.'

Alain raised an eyebrow. 'You haven't got any more reasonable while you've been away, have you? I can't just take on another chef at the drop of a hat.'

Instead of replying, Bruno reached into his pocket and took out a little flask and a small package wrapped in foil. He unstoppered the flask. Silently he held it towards the other chef's nose.

Alain's nostrils flared. He took the tiny container, dabbed a few drops of the hundred-year-old *aceto balsamico* on to the end of his finger and touched it to his tongue. His eyes closed, and for a few moments he seemed incapable of speech. Then he said, 'Remarkable.'

Bruno unwrapped the one remaining white truffle. There was no need for Alain to hold it to his nose. The smell gushed into the little office, flooding every corner and cranny, saturating both men's brains with pleasure, like bread soaking up oil.

'How much do you want for it?' Alain said hoarsely.

'Nothing — so long as I can cook with it, here, this evening.'

'Done,' Alain agreed, quickly resealing the truffle in its foil to preserve the precious aroma. 'But you can't be a *chef de partie* – I already have every station covered. You'll come back as a junior, or not at all.'

Like Alain, the other chefs assumed that Bruno had returned to Templi with his tail between his legs. Hugo Kass, in particular, lost no time in putting him in his place.

'Go and chop those chillis, chef.'

'Yes, chef.'

'Now dice those onions.'

'Yes, chef.'

Somebody laughed. They understood what Hugo was doing: if Bruno wiped his eyes while he was chopping the onions, the chilli would get in them.

Bruno chopped the chillis and the onions, then washed his hands and walked over to where Hugo was preparing a ferociously complicated *gratin* of crabmeat and pink grapefruit. Without a word, Bruno picked up a crab and began to copy the other chef's movements.

'What are you doing?' Hugo Kass enquired icily. Bruno didn't answer. He simply worked faster. By the time Hugo had finished his first crab, Bruno had already moved on to his second. Hugo snarled and concentrated on what he was doing. But Bruno had already finished his second crab and was reaching for a third. Unlike the duel the two of them had fought the last time Bruno had worked here, this was a hopelessly uneven contest. Beads of sweat popped from Hugo's forehead as the heat of the burners combined with the humiliation of being shown up. With an oath he reached for a sharper knife, and in doing so dropped his crab on the floor.

There was silence in the kitchen. Bruno calmly walked away from the counter and made himself a space to work between two of the other chefs. He knew that Hugo would not be troubling him again. But Bruno had more important things to think about now, such as what he was going to cook Laura.

Meanwhile, outside a little bar off the Viale Glorioso, Gennaro the *barista* was humming happily as he dismantled the engine of his van. Bruno appeared to have fixed it up with tractor parts, and Gennaro was keen to see whether any of them could be fitted to his Gaggia to help in his quest for ever-increasing amounts of pressure. Some of them, he thought, looked very promising indeed.

Like Bruno, Kim Fellowes and Laura were getting ready for their big meal at Templi. But while Bruno was chopping, dicing, peeling and sifting, Kim and Laura were washing and dressing.

It was a particular ritual of Kim's that he liked to dress Laura himself. She stood naked in his apartment in front of the mirror as he pulled a red chenille dress over her head, then slowly brushed her hair so that it fell against the collar.

'This dress is kind of heavy,' she murmured, half hoping to persuade him to change it for a lighter one.

'But it makes you look like a Botticelli *princessa*,' Kim said, standing beside her. He put his hand on her stomach, feeling the gym-toned hardness of it through the cloth. 'And it's not as if you have to wear anything underneath.'

She smiled at the reflection of his own smile.

'Besides,' he murmured. 'This evening is going to be special. You'll want to have looked your best.'

'I know. I've been looking forward to it.'

'That's not what I mean, Laura.'

'And of course, it's the last night. Last time either of us will see all the guys.' For Kim was leaving Rome, too, off to take up a plum appointment at his old college.

'I didn't mean that either.'

She shot him a puzzled glance. He closed his eyes for a moment, as if wondering how much he should tell her, then said, 'In my pocket is a ring.' He touched the side of his dinner jacket. 'An exact copy of the one in Michelangelo di Merisi's portrait of Mary Magdalene. I had it made up specially by the head jeweller at Bulgari. I thought you'd like to know now, so that when I say something later you'll be prepared. I know you'd hate to be so overcome by surprise that you'd spoil the perfection of the moment. And believe me, I've arranged everything so that it *will* be perfect.'

'Kim, what are you saying?'

'I simply want you to be prepared for something special to happen tonight, Laura. But when I do say a few words, later, will you do me a favour? I'll speak in Italian, and I'd appreciate it if you'd do the same. It will sound so much better, and I want everything, every tiny detail, to be just right.' The doorbell buzzed. 'There. That'll be our transport.'

'You ordered a taxi?'

'Not exactly. Like I said, everything about tonight is going to be special.'

☙

He had booked a horse and carriage; and waiting in the back of the carriage was a bucket of ice and a half-bottle of champagne. As he helped her on to the seat, it was all still sinking in: her last night in Italy, in Rome, was also going to be the night that Kim proposed to her. It was so unexpected that she felt completely stunned.

As the sunset turned the church towers orange, a flock of doves wheeled over Santa Maria de Trastevere. 'Next week it'll be back to stressed-out Americans, psychotic panhandlers and Don't Walk signs,' Laura said.

'How ghastly. Let's not think about it.' Ghastly: that was a word he was using a lot these days.

Suddenly the cart lurched and came to a stop. A tiny Fiat van had reversed into the road without looking and was now blocking the street as it tried to straighten out. The driver of the cart shouted something: the Fiat's window was wound down and the young man at the wheel retorted that he would only be a moment, and in any case the cart-driver might like to use the time to make love to the horse, who was probably also his mother. Laura laughed. Kim took her hand. 'Thank you for not minding,' he said quietly.

'Mind? Why should I mind? It's—' She had been about to say, 'It's the best bit,' but thought better of it. 'It's just one of those things,' she said tactfully.

The cart-driver had obviously come up with a suitably inventive response, because the Fiat-driver had abandoned any attempt to unblock the road and was now telling the cart-driver what he had previously done to the cart-driver's sister, who was apparently famous throughout Rome for the enthusiasm with which she gave blow-jobs to complete strangers. In case the cart-driver was not familiar with his sister's technique, the Fiat-driver helpfully mimed it.

'You know what?' Laura said. 'This might take a while.' Others were being drawn into the discussion. The man whose courtyard the Fiat had been reversing out of had appeared, and was now proposing to make the cart-driver back up a few feet so that the Fiat would have room to turn. The cart-driver was refusing to budge. From a window above their heads a woman was complaining about the noise, at full volume. The Fiat-driver's response was to drown out her words with his horn. The horse, far from being startled, appeared to be asleep. Then it suddenly opened its eyes and, ducking its head, ate one of the potted geraniums that lined either side of the doorway, causing further protest from Fiat-driver's Friend.

'Ghastly,' Kim said again. 'Rome's wasted on these people.'

'Let's walk to the end, then get a taxi,' Laura suggested.

Twenty-four

Kim's mood was quickly restored when the taxi deposited them at the door of Templi. Alain's establishment had lost none of its graciousness, and from the moment the man whose sole job it was to open the door to them opened the door to them, Kim was in heaven. Nor was the cosseting provided by Templi the only soothing influence. Kim had pulled out all the stops. As they greeted their friends in the bar, a barbershop quartet dressed in dinner jackets sung Puccini arias, their mellifluous voices mingling with the quiet hum of conversation.

Laura suddenly had the sensation that she was waking from a dream. The dream had been quite pleasant, but like a sleepwalker who suddenly wakes up and knows where they are but not how they got there, it was a complete mystery to her how her life had come to this point.

'Kim,' Laura said carefully. 'There's something I've got to tell you.'

'What is it, *cara*?'

'What you're going to ask me later – if it's what I think you're going to ask – I'm so flattered and pleased, and you really are

281

special to me, but – well, I just need much more time before I'm ready for something like that . . .'

Kim's eyes flashed, but he said mildly, 'I've told you before, Laura: you've got to learn to be more spontaneous. Don't be so American. Just go with your heart.'

'Yes, but—'

'It's your last night in the Eternal City. What better place to pledge eternal love? Ah, here are the flowers I ordered.'

A waiter was bringing over the largest bunch of roses Laura had ever seen. They were, she noted, the exact same shade as her dress. The other diners, having realised by now that something special was happening this evening, started nudging each other and looking expectant. Laura, who had gone as red as the roses, tried to accept the flowers in a way that looked grateful but not engaged. Definitely not engaged.

It is hard to carry a bunch of thirty-six long-stemmed red roses and maintain a conversation at the same time. By the time the students and staff moved to their table, Laura felt like the statue of Daphne in the Villa Borghese, caught at the very moment she turned into a tree. Finally, she managed to persuade a friendly waiter to take the flowers away on the pretext of putting them in some water. By this time Kim and some of the others were having earnest discussions about which wine to choose, and she was able to look around.

'I guess tonight's a big night for you,' said the man on her right conspiratorially. 'Kim's a lucky guy.'

It dawned on Laura that Kim had already told some of his colleagues what he was intending to do. He must have been planning it for days, weeks even, without saying anything to her. If she turned him down in front of all these people his vanity – never inconsiderable – was going to be horribly punctured. He would, in fact, be totally humiliated. Did she really want to do that to him? Or was there some third option, such as saying she'd think about it, or saying yes but then changing her mind a few days further down the line?

She sat there, sick with nerves, trying to think of a way out of this. As a result, she was the only one of the party not to eat any of the *amuse-gueules* that were being passed around the table and loudly exclaimed over.

In the kitchen, a second plate of *amuse-gueules* was waiting at the pass when Alain suddenly strode over to take a closer look.

'What are these?' he demanded. No one answered him.

Bending down, he tasted one. For a long moment, as he ate it, his face took on the distant look of a man who has seen beyond the mortal world and witnessed seraphim. He turned towards Bruno. There was no need for either of them to say anything. There was only one person in the kitchen who could have been responsible for what was on that plate.

Alain stared at Bruno. Then he took the plate and tipped it into the bin. 'Do these again,' he said quietly. 'No, not you,' he added quickly as Bruno reached for his pastry knife. 'You.' He nodded at Hugo, who shrugged and prepared to do as he had been told.

'Orders for table twelve,' Karl called. 'One salmon . . .'

Table twelve. That was the Americans' table. '. . . one scallops, one velouté, one caviar—'

'*Oui*, chef, *oui*, chef, *oui*, chef,' Bruno was calling as he scrambled to claim all the orders for himself.

With two long strides Alain was standing in front of him. 'What in God's name are you doing now?' he snapped.

'Cooking,' said Bruno, to whom the answer was obvious.

'Not in my kitchen, you're not. Get out.'

'But you said—'

'—nothing at all about you coming in here and destroying the discipline of my brigade. Get out, before I have someone throw you out.'

Stunned, Bruno picked up his knives and went. He couldn't

believe it. Just when he'd got everything organised at last, it had all gone horribly wrong.

He blundered out the back door and straight into a waiter. '*Scusi*,' he mumbled, his head still down.

'What's up, Bruno?'

He looked back. It was Tommaso, dressed in his old Templi uniform. 'See? Still fits,' his friend said, pulling at the sleeves of his jacket. 'Though not as well as hers.' He pointed to where Marie was emerging from the changing room, trying to make the uniform she was squeezed into look like it belonged to her instead of to a short Italian man several sizes smaller.

'What are you two doing here?' Bruno said.

'We brought you a pizza. Thought you might be hungry.' Then, when he saw Bruno was in no state for jokes, Tommaso added, 'That is, we thought you might need some help.'

Bruno sighed. 'Thanks, but it's no use. I've been thrown out of the kitchen.' He explained briefly what had happened with Alain.

'And where is the head prick now?'

'In the kitchen, supervising the service.'

'Any way we can get him out of there?'

'Absolutely not. He never leaves the kitchen during service. Not for anything.' A thought occurred to Bruno. 'Apart from when he throws people out, that is.'

'Excellent.' Tommaso delved into the pocket of his waiter's jacket and came up with an order pad. He scribbled something on it. 'You two wait here, and get ready to lock him in the coat cupboard as soon as he comes out.'

Tommaso walked up to the pass and handed the slip to Karl, who glanced at it and froze.

'What is it?' Alain snapped.

'Table twelve. One of the Americans has asked for,' Karl lowered his voice, 'steak with ketchup.'

284

'Has he indeed?' Alain said icily. 'Hugo, come with me. The rest of you, get on with your work. This won't take a minute. And cancel all the orders for table twelve,' he called over his shoulder as he walked towards the doors.

Seconds later, Alain and Hugo were safely incarcerated in the coat cupboard. 'Now what?' Tommaso asked.

'Now I have to talk to the others.' Bruno walked back into the kitchen. 'Listen to me, everyone,' he called.

Instantly he had the attention of the room. But now that all their eyes were on him, he wasn't sure what to say.

'It's like this,' he began. 'There's a girl here tonight, on table twelve, and I want to cook her the best meal she's ever had. It means changing the menu, because I know this girl, and the kind of food she really loves isn't Alain's food, good though that is. It's Roman food, the kind of food *I* like to cook. But I can't do it on my own, not at this level. We'll have to prep an entire menu from scratch, right now, and that means I need all of you to say you'll help.'

There was a long pause. Then Karl said, 'Where's chef?'

'Locked in the coat cupboard.'

There was another long pause. 'He'll fire us,' someone said nervously.

Bruno shook his head. 'No, he won't. If you *all* agree to help, how can he pick on any one of you? And if he fires all of you, he wouldn't be able to open tomorrow, any more than I can cook tonight without your help. The truth is, he needs you more than you need him.'

Karl said, 'I liked that Roman dish you showed me how to cook when the mafia turned up. And I've been calling out that idiot's orders long enough anyway. It's time we had some fun. I'll help you.'

'What about the rest of you?' Bruno said, looking around.

One by one, with various degrees of enthusiasm or reluctance, the kitchen brigade nodded.

'Right,' Bruno said. 'Let's get to work. You,' he pointed at the *sous* nearest to him, 'get me some whites.'

'Yes, chef.'

'The rest of you, listen carefully.'

'Hi,' Marie said brightly to table twelve. 'Has anyone told you guys the specials?'

'We've already ordered,' someone pointed out.

'I'm afraid what you ordered is off.'

'All of it?'

'Pretty much. But we do have, uh, *carpaccio* of pan-fried *capretto* with a sleepy margherita jus and line-caught *radicchio*,' she said, rattling off the ingredients very fast since she actually had no idea at all what Bruno planned to cook.

'Sounds good to me,' said the young man nearest to Marie's breasts.

'Me too,' said the girl next to him, who couldn't remember what she'd ordered in the first place.

'Good. Chef's specials all round. And let me get you some more of that wine,' Marie said quickly, bending low over the table to pour the last of the bottle into Kim Fellowes' glass.

'Does the chef's special have carbohydrate in it?' he asked suspiciously.

'Absolutely not,' she assured him. 'It's one hundred per cent organic.' She was gone before he could ask her to explain. At the next table, Tommaso was also busy explaining that the menu had been unavoidably changed at short notice.

The kitchen staff at Templi had never worked so hard under Alain's dictatorial rule as they did now for Bruno. Dishes that should have taken hours to prepare were being turned out in a matter of minutes.

'It's going great,' Tommaso confirmed when he came back for more plates. 'Just keep the food coming.'

'I'm doing my best,' Bruno muttered.

'I need your best, but faster. There are people in there who'll start to get hungry in about ten minutes.'

Bruno cooked faster. Soon a stream of dishes was being carried out to the dining room, but he had no time to rest. He immediately got the kitchen to work on the *secondi*.

Something strange was happening in the dining room. The kitchen staff became aware of an unfamiliar hum, like the buzzing of a swarm of bees, coming from beyond the swing doors. One or two of them, who had been present during the night of the eels, looked up apprehensively. Then a waiter pushed through the doors and the sound, previously muffled, suddenly came into focus. It was the hum of animated conversation. And not just conversation. Mingled with it was the sound of laughter, laughter of every sort – amused, bawdy, raucous, jovial, and even that of one unfortunate lady whose laugh sounded like the honk of a goose.

At table twelve, only two people remained immune to the changing mood. Laura, sick with nerves, wasn't eating a thing. And Kim, rigidly adhering to his diet, was looking increasingly puzzled as all around him his fellow diners became more and more animated.

Kim's barbershop quartet filled the interval between courses with their own mellifluous arrangement of a theme from Rossini. But Tommaso was having none of that. From his pocket he took a CD, and a moment later the opening chords of 'Rocking All Over The World' swept through the dining room. The singers soon gave up in disgust.

Looking around, Tommaso saw that there were still too many people without any food in front of them. Everything was fine for the moment, but sooner or later they were going to wonder where their next course was.

෨෧

287

'Someone should check on Alain,' Bruno muttered to Tommaso. 'Make sure he hasn't had a heart attack.'

'Don't you worry about him. I'll give him some more of your *amuse-gueules*,' Tommaso said.

Going to the coat cupboard, he unlocked it and eased the door open so that he could peek inside. Alain's chef's hat had fallen off, and he was pressing his lips passionately against those of Hugo Kass.

Tommaso smiled to himself as he quietly shut the door again and locked it.

At last the *secondi* were organised and Tommaso, supervising the flow of food between kitchen and dining room, began to relax.

'You can concentrate on cooking for Laura now,' he informed Bruno.

Sweeping the dish he was working on to one side, Bruno reached for another set of ingredients.

All around him, Kim's fellow diners appeared to be intoxicated. They weren't even staying in their seats, he saw to his horror: people were walking around, chatting to complete strangers, laughing and joking. He made a decision. Better to do this now, before these noisy Italians ruined the perfect atmosphere he had worked so hard to engineer.

'Turn that music off, please,' he told a harassed-looking waiter. Eventually, the Quo fell silent. Kim stood up. One by one the other diners stopped whatever they were doing and turned to see what was going on. Kim nodded to his barbershop quartet, who began to sing. The hum of laughter died, replaced by the quiet, solemn harmonies of Allegri's *Miserere*.

'Laura, my darling,' Kim began in Italian. 'It was in this very city that Petrarch wrote some of his most beautiful poems about a girl called Laura. Now, five centuries later, I too have fallen in love with her . . .'

It's happening, Laura thought as forty-eight pairs of eyes swivelled to look at her. *What on earth am I going to do?*

'It's a disaster,' Tommaso shouted to Bruno as he rushed into the kitchen. 'The American's proposing to her.'

'*What?*'

'*Si.* You'd better come quickly.'

Bruno looked at the mess of ingredients on his board. 'But it's not ready.'

'Too bad. By the time you *are* ready, it'll be too late.'

Kim was reaching the end of his speech. It was fine and noble and deeply moving: men as well as women were openly brushing away tears as Kim finally went down on one knee, pulled out a small box and flipped it open. There was a collective gasp as the ring flashed in the evening sunlight.

'Laura – *bellissima* – will you be my wife?' he said, just as the singers drew to a close.

All around the room, people lifted their hands expectantly, ready to clap. There was just the little matter of Laura's response – which would undoubtedly be equally as beautiful and equally as moving – and then they could all go wild.

Laura took a deep breath.

'Kim, you've asked me this question in front of all these people, so it's in front of all these people that I have to respond. You're a wonderful, intelligent, sensitive person, and I've really enjoyed our time together. But the answer's no. You can ask me to explain now, or I can explain later, but I'm sorry, my mind's made up.'

You could have cut the silence with a knife. Kim said quickly, 'Laura, it's a lot to take in. Yes, let's talk about it. Of course we must talk about it. You've drunk a little wine, you've eaten well – you know how stupefied carbohydrate makes you feel – so I'll take that as a maybe, and you can have all the time you need—'

'You're not listening,' she interrupted. 'No isn't a negotiating position, Kim. You've taught me a lot, but you were only ever my rebound from – from something before that went horribly wrong. I don't want to spend the rest of my life being told what to do by you, and I don't want to be told that I have to marry you.'

At the back of the room, Tommaso pushed Bruno forward. 'It's now or never, my friend,' he whispered.

Bruno was holding a plate on which there were some pieces of pear and a small amount of *zabaione* sauce – all he had had time to prepare. As he walked towards Laura the other diners, suddenly sensing that the entertainment wasn't over yet, swivelled to watch him. Somebody sniggered. Bruno felt his cheeks go red.

At last he was standing in front of her. In her eyes there was nothing he could read, no expression from which he could take either comfort or despair.

'This is for you,' he began, putting the plate in front of her.

Laura looked at the pear in its little island of *zabaione*. Suddenly Bruno knew that it wasn't enough. There was a long, terrible silence.

'I was going to tell you that it expresses what I feel better than I ever could,' he said helplessly. 'But that isn't true, is it? It doesn't express anything. Sometimes food is just – food.' He glanced at Kim, who was staring at him with an expression of fierce disdain. 'At least *he* had the guts to tell you what he wanted. Whereas I always thought that my silence, and my cooking, would somehow be enough.'

Laura nodded slowly.

'When I think back to all the meals I made for you,' he said, 'I remember meals that were meant to impress you, meals that were meant to dazzle you, to excite you, to comfort you, even to seduce you. But there was never a single dish or recipe that was designed to tell you the simple truth.'

She said nothing.

'The truth is,' he began. He stopped, aware that every single person in the room was staring at him, their expressions varying from amusement to incomprehension. The silence stretched on for ever. He could taste it. It was filling his mouth like uncooked dough, sticky and cloying, making speech impossible—

'The truth is that I love you,' he said softly. 'I've always loved you. I always will love you. And what I want, more than anything else in the world, is to go on loving you.'

'I'm going home tomorrow,' Laura said.

'I know,' he said simply. 'But we've got tonight.'

As she stood up, she took one of the pieces of pear and slid it into his mouth.

'In that case,' she said, 'let's not spend it here.'

In a little bar in a side street off the Viale Glorioso, Gennaro had finally finished the modifications to his Gaggia. There was a rudimentary turbo-charger, created from the tractor parts he had found on his van, and an auxiliary pressure pump adapted from the engine cooler, as well as various other improvements he felt sure would make a difference. Having packed the barrels with coffee grounds, he turned on the ignition and stood back.

For a moment nothing happened. Then, with a great clanking throb, the vast engine caught and began to build the pressure.

Across the street, on the top floor, Bruno and Laura did not hear the chugging of Gennaro's coffee machine. Finally, they were oblivious to everything except the sweet, long-awaited taste of each other's body.

As the needle on the pressure gauge climbed towards the maximum, Gennaro exhaled a sigh of satisfaction. It was working. He had achieved his life's ambition – the perfect cup of coffee. He reached for the valve that would release the pent-up water into the coffee grounds. But he reached for it a moment too late.

There was an explosion that was heard on the other side of the Tiber, and the sky above Trastevere lit up briefly.

'What was that?' Bruno said, pausing for a moment. Then, because Laura didn't answer, he went back to what he had been doing before.

Ricette

'The taste [these recipes] have been devised to achieve wants not to astonish but to reassure. It issues from the cultural memory, the enduring world of Italian cooks, each generation setting a place at table where the next one will feel at ease and at home.'

MARCELLA HAZAN, *The Essentials of Classic Italian Cooking*

Twenty-five

To: Bruno
From: Laura
Re: Well, here I am.

And there you are. A long way away. This place seems very big and stressed-out after Rome. College, though, is exactly the same. Weird, when I've done so much, to come back and find the same people doing exactly the same stuff as before I went away.

In ten weeks it'll be the holidays, and then I'll be straight back to see you (thank God for cheap flights). In the meantime . . . this afternoon I went down to Little Italy and found a deli. OK, it isn't Gigliemi, but it's got lots of stuff you'd recognise. And guess what? There's a cooking class here I can sign up for. You'd better watch your laurels, boy.

love,

L.

PS Where should I start?

To: Laura
From: Bruno
Re: re: Well, here I am.

Spaghetti ajo e ojo.

This is about as simple as it gets . . .

Actually, spaghettini – the thin stuff – probably holds the oil better than spaghetti. If you can't get that, try linguine or even vermicelli.

Slice a clove of garlic as thinly as you can and fry it in some good oil until it goes soft (not brown). Add some dried chilli flakes. Remove the garlic. Meanwhile, boil the pasta in salted water, drain, and tip it into the frying pan to fry for a minute. Serve with salt, pepper and a lot of grated pecorino romano.

Alternatively:

Tagliatelle con ragù bolognese

The Bolognese are famously undiscerning about what they put in their mouths, which is why 'Bolognese' also means a blow-job. But the classic ragù isn't too bad.

Fry some chopped vegetables – onion, carrot, celery, maybe a couple of mushrooms. You'll need about 115g of pancetta or chopped bacon for 325g of minced meat. (Pork is best.) Fry until the meat goes grey, then add a little wine: wait till it evaporates, then add four tablespoons of tomato paste and season. A dash of chilli helps too. Gradually add the rest of the bottle and half a pint of stock. Traditionally you should cook this 'from sunrise to sunset', but actually a couple of hours will do. Then stir in some cream and cook, uncovered, until it goes thick and sticky.

Or, if you're feeling a little braver:

Pappardelle con sugo de lepre

Fry some chopped bacon or pancetta, add your hare in (fairly small) pieces & brown it all over, remove and keep warm. Fry a chopped onion and some garlic gently until soft but definitely not brown. Stir in a handful of flour (gradually), then add three-quarters of a bottle of wine. Drink the rest. Put the hare back in, season, add a clove and plenty of thyme (not the stalks) and a dash of pepper sauce. Simmer for two hours, then strip the meat off the bones and shred it before returning it to the sauce. Turn the heat up to reduce it further. (If you have the hare's liver, fry it and blend it with the sauce to thicken it.)

Serve with pappardelle and grated parmesan.

Did I tell you I love you?

B

To: Bruno
From: Laura
Re:re:re: Well, here I am.

Yes, several times.

Tried the ragù last night on my new roommate, Lucy. Which led, of course, to the whole story coming out, bit by bit, over dinner . . . She actually cried. So, to make a long story short, she's appointed herself your official representative, keeping me from temptation, singles bars and middle-aged lecturers. I think I may be able to give her the slip, though. (Joke.)

Tomorrow I have my first cooking lesson. Apparently we will be learning how to chop. Ha! I shall soon be a mean hand with a sharp knife, so don't mess with me, lover boy. I know what you Italians are like, remember.

Laura

PS If you really think we can get hares over here . . .

To: Bruno
From: Laura
Re:re:re: Well, here I am.

Thanks for the hare. You're very sweet. The man from FedEx looked a bit puzzled, though.

According to Martha, my cooking teacher, I have nimble fingers!

To: Laura
From: Bruno
Re:re:re:re: Well, here I am.

Actually, I remember those nimble fingers very well . . .

To: Bruno
From: Laura
Re:re:re:re:re: Well, here I am.

Speaking of which . . . phone sex, tonight, about ten p.m. my time?

To: Laura
From: Bruno
Re:re:re:re:re:re: Well, here I am.

Mmmmmm. That was nice. Sleep well.

To: Bruno
From: Laura
Re:re:re:re:re:re:re: Well, here I am.

Wasn't it? & I will.

What's for breakfast?

To: Laura
From: Bruno
Re:re:re:re:re:re:re:re:re: Well, here I am.

<u>Zabaglione</u>

– eaten as a breakfast dish in the countryside here, I'll have you know.

Beat 6 fresh egg yolks with 3 tablespoons caster sugar until pale, then stir in a glass of dry white wine. Pour into a bowl which you have placed in a saucepan of gently simmering water, and whisk. It will swell to a thick foam. Lovely.

Serve with asparagus, toast, muffins, desserts, breasts . . .

To: Bruno
From: Laura
Re:re:re:re:re:re:re:re:re: Well, here I am.

That zabaglione . . . pure heaven. Lucy says: if I am ever unfaithful, can she have you please?

In the meantime, what about dinner?

To: Laura
From: Bruno
Re:re:re:re:re:re:re:re:re:re: Well, here I am.

<u>Saltimbocca</u>

Now this is a proper Roman dish.

For 2, you need four slices of veal. Wrap them in greaseproof paper and beat them very thin with a rolling pin. Place a slice of prosciutto on top of each one, then a couple of fresh sage leaves. Traditionally you should hold this together with a cocktail stick, but I find it's easier to just fold the veal over and bang it all into place with that same rolling pin. Dip them in a mixture of flour, salt, pepper and maybe a few chilli flakes. Then you just fry them for a minute or so each side. Remove & keep warm. Pour a glass of white wine or marsala into the juices and reduce quickly. Add some butter and a squeeze of lemon before pouring over the meat.

To: Bruno
From: Laura
Re:re:re:re:re:re:re:re:re:re:re:re: Well, here I am.

I can now make Béchamel sauce! Martha says I have a knack . . .

Shall we have dinner together tomorrow?

To: Laura
From: Bruno
Re:re:re:re:re:re:re:re:re:re:re:re: Well, here I am.

Let's. Same time, different continents, same meal.

This next one takes a little longer but believe me, it's well worth it.

Coda alla vaccinara

You'll need an oxtail, about 1.8kg, washed and chopped across the joints. Boil for ten minutes and remove any scum. Add one carrot, one leek, one celery stalk & some parsley or thyme. Simmer for about three hours. If you can get ox or pork cheek, put that in too. Keep the liquid.

Next, in a different saucepan heat some lard or oil and gently fry a chopped onion, chopped carrot, the chopped pork cheek (or some bacon if you couldn't get pork cheek) and a chopped garlic clove. Add

300

some chopped parsley, and the oxtail. Pour in half a bottle of dry white wine and allow some to evaporate. Then add half a dozen chopped tomatoes (i.e. about a tin and a half) and a big spoon of tomato paste. Nutmeg and cinnamon could also make an appearance. Simmer for two hours, adding a little of the stock from the other pan whenever it gets dry.

You could also add some boiled, sliced celery hearts, raisins, pine nuts, or even some bitter cocoa powder. If so, add at the end and cook for ten minutes extra.

B

To: Bruno
From: Laura
Re:re:re:re:re:re:re:re:re:re:re:re:re: Well, here I am.

'Remove any scum', eh? Story of my life. I managed to track down some oxtail – it took forever, and the butcher I eventually got it from asked me if it was for my dog! However, it's cooking now. I'll go and check it for moistness in a minute.

Here's a milestone: at class we were told to buy our first Italian cookery book, a massive tome written I'm sure by a real *nonnina* – for example, this is what she says about making pasta:

'Do not be tempted by one of those awful devices that masticate eggs and flour at one end and extrude a choice of pasta shapes through another end. What emerges is a mucilaginous and totally contemptible product and, moreover, the contraption is an infuriating nuisance to clean.'

I thought at first 'mucilaginous' must be an Italian word, but according to my dictionary it means 'having the properties of a thick, viscous animal secretion'. The lady certainly has a way with words.

301

Did I tell you that I am determined to learn to make you pasta by hand? Then I'll be a real Italian housewife.

Call tonight when supper's ready. I'll be eating it in bed.

L

To: Laura
From: Bruno
Re: last night

I know I've said this before, but I thought you might like to have it in writing: I love you.

B

To: Bruno
From: Laura
Re:re: last night

Me too. In fact, I keep getting all mucilaginous at the most inappropriate moments.

Lx

To: Bruno
From: Laura
Re:re:re: last night

. . . like today when we were doing vegetables and I found a zucchini that looked just like you. I gave it a little kiss when no one was looking.

To: Laura
From: Bruno
Re:re:re:re: last night

Lucky zucchini.

This is a nice recipe for an antipasto:

<u>Fried zucchini flowers</u>

Make sure you get the male flowers (from the stem) and not the female ones (from the fruit) – the males stay crisper. They must be fresh and firm. In Rome they sometimes stuff the flowers with a little mozzarella and anchovy before frying.

Make a batter from 135g flour, salt, pepper, nutmeg, two tablespoons of oil and two egg yolks (keep the whites). Gradually beat in 6 tablespoons white wine and 6 tablespoons water, maybe a little more – just enough to make the batter creamy. Rest for 30 minutes. Then beat the egg whites until stiff and fold in. Remove the stamens, dip the flowers in batter, then deep-fry quickly in a pan of very hot oil. Toss on to kitchen paper, season, and serve at once. Goes well with:

<u>Peppers stuffed with rabbit</u>

– a recipe from the countryside.

Cut the tops off four peppers and keep. Scrape out the insides. Bake at Gas mark 4 (350°C) for 20 minutes, no more. Meanwhile, fry your rabbit, cut into small pieces, in some butter. Add a double handful of sliced mushrooms and a glass of dry white wine; allow to evaporate slowly. Add the same amount of chicken stock and a little tomato paste. Cook gently for another 10 minutes, then spoon into the peppers. Replace the lids and bake for 15 minutes.

B

To: Bruno
From: Laura
Re:re:re:re:re: last night

Now this is just getting fancy. How about some simple ones? Desserts, for example?

(From my cookery class textbook: 'The juices of those two quintessentially Mediterranean fruits, the olive and the lemon, have a beguilingly fragrant effect on poached brains . . .' – *now* I understand what happened to me in Italy. My brain got poached in the heat and then I was beguiled. Not to mention fragranced. And it's all your fault.)

To: Laura
From: Bruno
Re:re:re:re:re:re: last night

Two desserts coming up. Make these and take them and the phone to bed with you. I'll call about eleven your time . . .

Tiramisu

Beat 5 egg yolks with 180g (about 3/4 of a cup) sugar until the latter has dissolved and the mixture is light and fluffy. (It should leave a ribbon trail when it drops from the whisk.) Add 250g mascarpone and beat until smooth. Whisk the egg whites in a separate glass bowl until peaks form. Fold into the mascarpone mixture.

Pour 250ml of very strong ristretto and 3 tablespoons of brandy/Marsala into a wide dish. Soak about 40 sponge fingers in this mixture, but don't let them fall apart. Pack about half of them into the base of a serving dish. Then add a layer of the mascarpone mixture, then a layer of biscuits, then more mascarpone. Refrigerate for at least two hours. Dust with grated chocolate before serving.

There's a favourite Roman dessert that's even easier –

Peaches in red wine.

Just pour boiling water over the peaches to help you skin them, slice them into bowls, sprinkle them with sugar and pour red wine over them. They're ready to eat after about 1 hour in the fridge.

Talk to you later in bed. Oh – you won't need a spoon.

B.

To: Bruno
From: Laura
Re:re:re:re:re:re:re: last night

Messy . . .!

love L xxx :)

PS What are you going to cook me the first night I come back to Rome?

To:Laura
From: Bruno
Re: coming back?

Now that is a tricky one.

Perhaps we could cook it together?

B

To: Bruno
From: Laura
Re:re: coming back?

Oh no, maestro – don't forget, I've only been doing this stuff for about two minutes. And I know what you chefs are like. You'll shout at me if I get it wrong, won't you? You'll probably make me cry.

L

To: Laura
From: Bruno
Re:re:re: coming back?

Shout at you? I'd rather cut out my own heart and fry it. And sharing a kitchen with you would be just the most wonderful thing I could imagine . . . which reminds me, there was something – someone – before we got together that I probably need to tell you about. Call me later – but not before you've closed your eyes and thought about:

<u>Abbacchio alla cacciatiore</u>

Remember this?

A dish that's best left until the first suckling lambs are available.

You need about a kilo or more of shoulder and loin, cut with a meat cleaver into bite-sized pieces. Brown it thoroughly, preferably in lard. Add salt, pepper, chopped garlic, a big handful of torn-up sage and some rosemary. Cook for 1 minute, stirring, then dust the lamb with flour through a fine sieve. Turn the pieces once, then add 8 tablespoons of good wine-vinegar. After half a minute reduce the heat to a simmer and put in a few splashes of water. Cover the pot, with the lid slightly askew, adding more water if it dries out. It's done when the lamb starts to fall off the bone – maybe an hour or so.

Just before serving, mash 4 anchovies with some of the lamb juices and a little water. Add this to the lamb and stir.

Or:

Porchetta

You can get suckling pig any time of year. (Well, maybe not where you are.)

There are so many ways of doing this. I had some once that was stuffed with sage and wild fennel, which was amazing. But I prefer this recipe, which is more Roman:

Take the pig's offal – heart, lungs, liver etc – slice finely and sauté in lard or oil. Add a large amount of rosemary, garlic and sage. Bone the pig and stuff with the mixture before sewing it together again, scoring the skin, and roasting for five hours over a wood fire. If no wood fire is available, a wood-fired pizza oven would do.

Let's talk later,

B

To: Bruno
From: Laura
Re: that conversation last night

Well, I suppose I should thank her. She obviously taught you a lot. (I'm talking about cooking here, of course.)

To: Laura
From: Bruno
Re:re: that conversation last night

Of course.

Winter's almost here now. I only noticed it at first because there were chestnuts in the market, and in the restaurants they've put Monte Bianco on the menu . . .

<u>Monte Bianco</u>

A seasonal dessert from the north. Before you start, put a mixing bowl in the freezer.

Soak 500g fresh chestnuts in water, then cut around the shells to loosen them – your cookery book will show you how to do this. Boil for 25 minutes and peel while warm.

Put in a pan and cover with milk. Simmer. After about 15 minutes the milk will have been absorbed. Reduce to a purée with a food processor. Add 200g chocolate, melted in a double boiler, and a little rum. Cover with cling film and refrigerate for one hour. Use a food mill or a pierced piping bag to turn the mixture into little worm-sized pieces, like mince. Pile up on a plate. Mix 300ml cold whipping cream with a teaspoon of caster sugar, whisk until it stiffens and pour it over the dessert so that it looks like Mont Blanc – which we call Monte Bianco – covered in snow.

Now that it's getting cold my bed seems very empty.

B

To: Bruno
From: Laura
Re: cold

Cold? In Rome? You must be joking. It's –10 degrees here.

How's the new season's oil? According to my Italian lady's cookbook: 'On those brisk days that bridge the passage from autumn to winter and signal the release of this year's freshly pressed olive oil, toasting bread over a smoky fire and soaking it with spicy, laser-green newly minted oil is a practice probably as old as Rome itself . . .'

**To: Laura
From: Bruno
Re:re: cold**

Yes – she's describing bruschetta. Just grill some good Italian bread, preferably on a flame (a naked gas flame would do). Rub it with a mashed garlic clove and pour on a thin stream of the new season's olive oil your faraway lover has just sent you by FedEx. Sprinkle with salt. For a more filling antipasto, top with diced tomatoes and fresh basil.

love you,

B

**To: Bruno
From: Laura
Re: that recipe for bruschetta**

Thing is, I just don't seem to be able to get that one right. It's simple but difficult, as Tommaso would probably have said. Every time I try to do it, something goes wrong. Tell you what – I think I need someone to show me how to do it . . .

**From: Bruno
To: Laura
Re:re: that recipe for bruschetta**

?????????

I'm not with you.

To: Bruno
From: Laura
Re:re:re: that recipe for bruschetta

Aha! No, you're not. And that's my whole point.

To: Laura
from: Bruno
Re:re:re:re: that recipe for bruschetta

I mean, I don't understand. How can you not be able to cook bruschetta, when you can do all those other things? And what do you mean about needing somebody to show you?

B

To: Bruno
From: Laura
Re:re:re:re:re: that recipe for bruschetta

Well, it's like this . . .

I was talking to my cooking teacher the other day. She says she knows of at least a dozen Italian restaurants over here where someone who's cooked at Templi could get a job . . .

What do you think?

To: Laura
From: Bruno
Re:re:re:re:re:re: that recipe for bruschetta

I think I'm on my way.

Want to send me a shopping list?

The End

'. . . it is a pattern of cooking that can accommodate improvisation and fresh intuitions each time it is taken in hand, as long as it continues to be a pattern we can recognise; as long as its evolving forms comfort us with that essential attribute of the civilised life, familiarity.'

MARCELLA HAZAN, *The Essentials of Classic Italian Cooking*

www.thefoodoflove.com

Acknowledgements

I'd like to thank Nick Harris at A.P. Watt for putting the pot on the stove; Caradoc King and Linda Shaughnessy for giving it a stir; Bobby Thomson for tasting it; Peter Begg for showing me how a real chef would do it; Alessandra Lusardi for adding some Italian flavours; Ursula Mackenzie and Clare Ferraro for ordering it; Tara Lawrence and Carole DeSanti for sending it back to the kitchen; and of course my family, for a much-needed pinch of salt.

This book is dedicated to the memory of Nunc Willcox, a good man and a good friend.

THE WEDDING OFFICER
Anthony Capella

A sumptuous tale of food to heal the deepest wounds, of the hungers of war and the bittersweet nature of love.

Naïve but already war-weary, twenty-four-year-old James Gould arrives in Naples in 1944 as part of the Allied administration. What he doesn't anticipate is that this involves eating a limited menu of fried Spam fritters and dissuading beautiful Italian girls from marrying British soldiers. James's chance at true heroism arrives when a German tank is sighted and he is caught in its path. However, the tank is being driven by a fiery Italian girl, Livia Pertini, who is trying to get her home-made mozzarella to market.

The disaffected girls of Naples, sensing their chance, secretly arrange for Livia to become James's cook, believing that a man who has eaten well must surely be more amenable to the idea of matrimony. Gradually, James falls in love – not only with Livia, but with the language, tastes and zest for life of Italy itself. But then the eruption of Vesuvius triggers a chain of explosive events that will force the two to flee behind enemy lines and will alter their lives immeasurably.